Also by Sallie Bissell
available from Random House Large Print

In The Forest of Harm

A DARKER JUSTICE

Sallie Bissell

RANDOM HOUSE
LARGE PRINT

*The Library of Congress has established a
Cataloging-in-Publication record for this title*

0-375-43251-5

www.randomlargeprint.com

FIRST LARGE PRINT EDITION

10   9   8   7   6   5   4   3   2   1

This Large Print edition published in accord
with the standards of the N.A.V.H.

For
Lolita Bissell
With love and gratitude

My thanks to:

The Nashville Writers Alliance for years of friendship, support, and encouragement.

Marc Archambeault, Geneve Bacon, Bill Bissell, Rochelle Groom, Toby Heaton, Heather Newton, Sharon Oxendine, Cynthia Perkins, Michael Sims, and Diana Stoll for first readings and technical advice.

Madeena Spray Nolan and Alana White for endless patience and enthusiasm.

And to Kate Miciak, for once again making me go deeper.

Jesus, Jesus, rest your head
You have got a manger bed
All the evil folk on earth
Sleep in feathers at their birth

—TRADITIONAL APPALACHIAN CHRISTMAS CAROL

PROLOGUE

SIXTH U.S. CIRCUIT COURT
Cincinnati, Ohio
November 21

Squeeaak.

The first time, it came so softly into her awareness that she thought she'd imagined it. She squeezed her eyes shut, then opened them wide, trying to concentrate on the pages in front of her. Then she heard it again. *Squeeaak.* A cry of sorts, but soft, like the complaint of an un-oiled hinge or the cracked leather heel of a shoe. *Squeeaak.*

"Carmen? Is that you?" Judge Rosemary Klinefelter looked up from the small puddle of golden light that the lamp cast upon her desk, puzzled by the sound that seemed to come from her empty courtroom. The clock had struck nine as she'd begun reading this page, and she would have sworn that her secretary Carmen had left hours ago with the rest of the judicial staff workers. Judge Klinefelter cocked her head to listen again, but the squeaking stopped. Only the distant rumble of an airplane overhead disturbed the silence of the room.

She shook her head and returned her attention to the opinion she was proofing. She was working late tonight, adding her signature to the documents of her last case, trying hard to clear her desk. Tomorrow would be Thanksgiving, and she and her husband Rich were flying to Miami to board a ship that would ultimately deposit them on one of St. Bart's sandy beaches. Smiling, she glanced up at the three framed photographs clustered beneath her lamp—her daughter Emily unpacking at Penn, her son Mark in his Navy uniform, and Rich, grinning from beneath a hard hat as they broke ground for one of the skyscrapers he'd designed. She rubbed a smudge from his picture and sighed. How wonderful it would be to get away, just she and Rich, with nothing facing them but sapphire blue sky and an aquamarine sea.

Suddenly she jumped. She heard another noise. Not a squeak this time, but a single *thump,* like a book dropped on a carpeted floor. She frowned. Carmen wouldn't stay past five-thirty unless asked, and asked nicely. Could it be one of her clerks, coming back in for something and trying not to disturb her?

No, she decided, dismissing the chill that crept

up her spine. It was probably just the cleaning crew, trying to finish early because of the holiday. Decisively she pushed away from her desk and rose from her chair. She crossed her red-carpeted office in three strides and turned her dead bolt into place, then she tried the heavy brass doorknob, just to make certain her door was locked. It did not budge. Now safe from all disruptions, she could get her own work done.

"You're getting dotty, kiddo," she murmured, suddenly aware of the joggity rhythm of her heart as she brushed a speck of lint off the black judicial gown that hung on the back of the door. "You're way past due for a stretch on the beach."

She recrossed the room and settled back in her chair, wondering if she were being visited by the ghost that reputedly walked this courthouse at night. Boots, they called him. Supposedly the spirit of some maligned bootlegger seeking exoneration for an erroneous murder conviction.

She tried to refocus on her work, but she felt edgy, inadvertently tensed for Boots's next manifestation. The words that she'd written this morning seemed to squirm like small black bugs on the pages, not forming clauses or sentences or anything that made sense.

"Come on, Your Honor," she scolded herself formally, trying to pump herself up. "Just two more pages to proof, then you're out of here.

Let the ghost or the cleaning people have the damn courtroom. Beginning tomorrow you can make love all night and have a massage every morning."

This time the letters formed words that made dull but legal sense—her learned opinion about whether a bank could cancel its own cashier's check. Searching for errors and typos, she scanned down the lines Carmen had typed from her own handwritten notes. Finding none, she turned the page and released the breath that she had been unconsciously holding. Three more paragraphs, then she could sign her name and get out of here. She started reading aloud, hurrying. Finally she came to the last line. She uncapped the heavy Mont Blanc fountain pen she always used to sign her opinions, then she heard the third noise. Not a squeak this time. Or even a thud. This time she heard a series of soft bumps moving from left to right across the courtroom, plaintiff to defendant side. Could they be footsteps, she wondered, staring at the doorknob, waiting for it to turn.

"Okay," she said aloud, suddenly irritated with both the noises and her own nervous Nellie reaction to them. "That's it. I'm calling security."

She picked up the phone and dialed the code that connected her with security. The phone rang four, five, six times, but no one answered.

"Probably outside smoking," she muttered as she hung up in disgust.

Annoyed, she picked up her pen and scrawled her name, Rosemary Rogers Klinefelter, with a flourish. The very act gave her courage. After all, she was a federal judge in the Sixth Circuit Court of Appeals, not some nitwit who spooked at ghosts.

She remembered a memo she'd seen on Carmen's desk. The courthouse had experienced a number of cases of vandalism lately. Obscenities spray-painted on the second-floor men's room, files in a clerk's office strewn all over the floor. Everyone assumed the vandals had sneaked in during the day and done their mischief while court was in session. But maybe they broke in at night and did their damage then. Maybe they were just outside the door now, quietly spraying "fuck" and "dickhead" on her hundred-year-old burled walnut paneling.

"Bastards," she cried, all at once furious at the idea of anyone desecrating her courtroom. She reached down and opened the bottom drawer of her desk, fumbling for her revolver. The short-barreled old Colt .32 had been her Aunt Esther's chicken coop gun, but within its limited range, it shot straight and true. She cocked the hammer, fuming. No pimple-faced punks were going to trash *her* courtroom.

She tiptoed to the door and pressed her ear against the crack. Now she heard nothing except the rapid beating of her own heart. For a moment she wondered if she wasn't just tired: if her imagination hadn't embellished the thousand tiny noises that empty buildings invariably make, but then she decided no, she wasn't. She'd definitely heard three separate, distinct noises that had no business coming from a locked courtroom. She reached for the wall switch and turned off the lights behind her. All she had to do now was open her door and flip the light switch on the other side of the wall. The whole courtroom would be illuminated instantly, and when she caught the little bastards who were spray-painting her walls, she'd train this gun on them until she could get security on the line.

Gripping the revolver tightly in her right hand, she turned the dead bolt. It made a soft click, the door shuddering slightly as the bolt slid out of the lock. Slowly she pulled the door open. The cooler air carried the familiar smell of her courtroom—a combination of lemon furniture polish and leather-upholstered chairs. Grasping the gun, she took a step forward, peering into the darkness. Moonlight from the tall windows on the left wall cast everything in deep shadow—the courtroom chairs looked like dark hulks on the other side of the bar. Keeping her eyes straight ahead, she groped for the light switch on the wall. Her left hand fumbled against the plaster. Where was that stupid thing? She'd turned it on and off a million times. The edge of her palm brushed against the fixture. There! She had it! Now she would see what was going on.

Suddenly, though, before she could reach any of the three switches that would set her courtroom ablaze with light, she felt someone grab her right arm, hard. Her attacker forced her wrist backward, almost to the point of snapping; then, with a single ruthless motion, he flicked the gun from her hand. The pistol clattered against the back of the witness stand, then fell somewhere on the dark floor.

"What?" was the only word she could utter before the same someone moved behind her, twisting her arm viciously against her spine. Something banged against the back of her knees, and before she could draw a breath she'd fallen to the carpet. Hands explored all of her now, racing up her fleshy thighs, plucking at her panty hose.

She realized, then, that this was far worse than vandals spraying curses on her walls. She curled her free hand into a claw and tried to swipe at her attacker's eyes, kicking and squirming with all her strength. But the dark figure was strong.

He sat down on top of her, pinning her legs beneath him, wrenching her hand so hard, it felt like it was caught in a vise.

"What do you want?" she managed to croak. Surely not her. She was sixty-two, soon to be a grandmother, of sexual interest to no one but her husband.

"To kill well," he whispered.

Judge Rosemary Rogers Klinefelter felt a tiny pinprick on the left side of her neck, then her limbs grew soft and heavy, like loaves of unleavened dough. She watched her attacker move the prosecutor's chair to the center of the room, realizing queasily that she could do nothing to stop whatever this man intended for her. With her body limp as a rag doll's, she felt him push her arms into her own black judicial robe and lift her to the chair.

She thought back to her children when they were young—her daughter's voice—musical as a little flute; the sweaty, sweet smell of Mark in her arms. Then she thought of Rich, his arms around her as they sailed on a boat bound west, skimming over the waves, into a luminous and fiery sea. She lingered there a moment, as if to bid farewell, then she began to scream in silence, watching as the young man smiled and unsheathed a long, dark sword that glittered like death in the moonlight.

CHAPTER 1

DECKARD HILLS COUNTRY CLUB
Atlanta, Georgia
December 23

"Come on, Mary. You haven't danced with me in years." With a broad grin, Wyatt Prentiss held out his hand. Behind him, the Darktown Strutters Jazz Machine launched into a sinuous version of "Brazil," a trio of trombones keeping the hot, pulsating rhythm at a slow boil.

Mary Crow smiled. How could she refuse? The Strutters were Atlanta's most seductive band—when they played, everyone not confined to a wheelchair jumped to their feet and moved to the beat. She grabbed Wyatt's hand and together they rode the music like a wave, gliding across the floor, holding each other tight.

"Who'd have thought anybody would get married the day before Christmas Eve?" Wyatt turned Mary in a tight, sexy circle that brought the bride and groom into her view. Mary's oldest and dearest friend, Alexandria McCrimmon, now Mrs. Charles Ensley Carter, was dancing with her new husband. Though the Latin music throbbed around them, they danced their own private sway in the middle of the room, laughing and kissing at the same time. Mary closed her eyes and offered a silent prayer of thanks. Just fourteen months earlier Alex had accompanied Mary on a camping trip in the Nantahalah Forest. The trip had turned bad when Alex had been abducted by a psychopathic trapper. Ultimately she'd been airlifted from the Appalachian forests, half-naked and nearly beaten to death. That Alex was functional at all was astounding. That just an hour ago she had married a man who had never once faltered in his love for her, Mary considered a true gift from God. She smiled at Wyatt. He had no idea what an utter miracle this wedding was.

"I think it's wonderful," she said, winking at Alex as she caught the bride's gaze. "Christmas will just start a day early this year."

"These Texas McCrimmons really know how to celebrate." Wyatt held her closer and danced her past the long table that stretched along one entire side of the country club ballroom. At one end of the table stood a huge wedding cake topped with flowers; at the other end a fountain bubbled with champagne. In between lay all manner of Christmas delicacies, from Georgia sugared pecans to great platters of Texas barbecue, interspersed with conveniently placed bottles of Jack Daniel's whiskey. A number of Stetson hats bobbed among the crowd of Atlantans, but nobody seemed to mind. The Texas McCrimmons and the Carters from Georgia got along well, finding—as all Southerners can—common ground in good food and strong whiskey.

The song ended. Wyatt escorted her off the dance floor, next to the only other woman dressed in a long, elegant green gown identical to Mary's.

Joan Marchetti grinned at Mary. "Some bash, huh?"

"I'll say. I nearly cried."

"Me, too," said Joan. "Particularly when that bagpiper cranked up and led them away from the altar. Jeez! They call that music?"

"I think it's some kind of tradition with them," Mary explained. "Means good luck or lots of children or something."

Joan rolled her eyes. Mary studied her in the diffused light. Joan, too, had been a victim of that camping trip from hell. She'd been raped and beaten—her nose broken so severely that even the simple act of breathing had been nearly impossible. Today the only evidence of her injuries was a tiny red scar curled alongside one nostril. Her Uncle Nick had gotten her the best plastic surgeon in Manhattan. The results were amazing. Her skin had regained its creamy luminosity; her dark Italian eyes again flashed with life.

"Alex makes a beautiful bride, doesn't she?"

Mary nodded, recalling the little stone church bedecked with emerald and scarlet-berried holly and white orchids and Joan's voice soaring high into the air, the notes floating so perfect and beautiful that everyone instinctively held their breath. "She looked gorgeous. And you sang like an angel."

"Thanks." Joan smiled, then leaned over to whisper in Mary's ear. "I was hoping Jonathan might be here . . ."

Mary hastily shook her head. "I haven't heard from Jonathan since my grandmother died. He sent me a card from Little Jump Off."

"You miss him a lot, don't you?" Joan asked softly.

Mary nodded. "I miss both of them a lot." An odd little bubble of sadness encompassed the two friends, then the band started up again. As Hugh Chandler, Joan's longtime boyfriend, appeared from the buffet table and swept Joan onto the dance floor, Mary again felt Wyatt's hand on her arm.

"May I have another dance, Ms. Crow?" he asked, courtly as ever.

"I'd love to, Wyatt." Mary winked at Joan as she and Hugh swirled into a sea of couples. "Dance on, girlfriend," Mary called. "We don't get the Strutters every day."

As Joan and Hugh whirled away, Wyatt began a languid two-step, perfect for the soft, soulful version of "Honeysuckle Rose" the Strutters were playing. He led her so perfectly to the music's rhythm that goose bumps ran down her spine.

"If I didn't know better, I'd say you'd taken dancing lessons."

"I spent one miserable year at Miss Forte's Ballroom Academy," Wyatt drawled. "I was thirteen and stood eyeball to collarbone with every girl in the class."

Mary laughed. "You must have learned something, though."

"Oh, I'm terrific when I have the right partner," he replied, swooping her in another quick, sexy circle.

He pulled her closer. She nestled her head on his shoulder and closed her eyes again. His cheek was smooth and soft, and he clasped her hand against his chest so tightly, she could feel the beating of his heart. She smiled ruefully. Every unmarried woman in Atlanta would give her eyeteeth to be dancing with Wyatt Prentiss, the youngest man ever to make partner at Dawson, Church & Gahagan, yet all she could do was compare him with Jonathan Walking-stick. How Wyatt's muscled shoulders were sculpted at the gym instead of earned in the forest; how the hair on the nape of his neck grew bristly instead of soft; how he smelled of expensive sandalwood cologne, rather than Jonathan's Ivory soap.

Stop it, she scolded herself. *You and Jonathan gave it a shot, but it didn't work out. Now let it go.*

"You okay?" Wyatt was looking down at her.

"Fine." Mary assured him. "Just trying to keep the beat."

Wyatt held her close as the sax player took a long, smoky solo, then the husky-voiced singer began again. Just as the singer started the last chorus, Wyatt began dancing her quickly over to the other side of the floor.

"Is something wrong?" Mary said, lifting her head at his abrupt movements.

"Unless I'm seriously double-parked, I think someone wants to talk to you," said Wyatt. "There's a big, mean-looking cop motioning me over."

Mary looked up, astonished. Wyatt hadn't been joking. On the far side of the room stood Martel Madison, former tackle for the Atlanta

Falcons, now a Deckard County sheriff's deputy assigned to the courthouse. Although Martel stood with his cap under his arm, trying to look inconspicuous in the frock-coated crowd, he was failing miserably. Three hundred and fifteen solid pounds of armed, deputized power were hard to miss.

"Martel?" Mary failed to keep the surprise out of her voice. "What are you doing here?"

"Mr. Falkner said to come get you. He needs to see you right now."

"What's the matter?" Mary had nothing on the docket; she wasn't scheduled to even show up in court until after New Year's.

"Don't know. Falkner's up in his office with Santa Claus pants on, talking to some dude from D.C." Martel shrugged. "I just got the call to come here and take you back to the courthouse, ASAP."

"Like this?" Mary gestured at the green silk maid-of-honor dress that wisped around her ankles. Surely Jim Falkner wouldn't actually call her away from Alex's wedding to come back to work.

Martel shrugged again. "I just do what they tell me, Ms. Crow."

Mary looked around. Already some of the wedding guests had begun to stare, curious about why an armed officer had intruded on the festivities. "Okay, Martel," she sighed. "Go wait in your squad. I'll be there in three minutes."

She watched as Martel disappeared through the doorway, then turned back to Wyatt, smiling apologetically.

"Looks like you'll have to finish this dance with someone else."

"Can't do without you, can they, Mary?"

"I guess not." Usually she didn't mind being called back to work. Tonight she did. Tonight was her best friend's wedding. Tonight was the most fun she'd had in a long, long time.

Wyatt squeezed her hand, which still rested in the crook of his arm. "I'm sorry you have to go. Any chance we could get together over the holidays? We could go to Mack Church's eggnog frolic. It's the day after Christmas."

"I don't know, Wyatt. Jim Falkner keeps me pretty busy."

"Well, don't say no yet. Call me if you get free. We'll just make an appearance, then go do something fun."

"Okay. I'll try." She pecked him on the cheek, then she began to move through the crowd toward Martel's squad car. She wished she could say good-bye to Alex before she left, but the bride and groom stood engulfed by a crowd of well-wishers. As Mary twisted through the crowd toward the doorway, she glanced back over her shoulder. Alex had seen her and was looking at her, her expression at once knowing and sad.

"I have to go!" Mary mouthed.

Alex nodded. Smiling, she gave Mary a thumbs-up sign, then blew her a kiss.

Mary stopped for a moment, wanting to freeze Alex's image like a photograph. A clear winter evening, the ballroom looking magical as a snowflake, Alex beautiful and happy and waving good-bye. From here on, their lives would go down different paths. Mary would still know her dearest friend, but never again in quite the same way as before. She swallowed as sudden tears stung her eyes, then she walked out of the ballroom and headed toward the squad car. Alex had a man to love. Mary probably had another one to hang.

CHAPTER 2

FAITHAMERICA PAC HEADQUARTERS
San Francisco, California
December 23

"Brothers and sisters, last night I had a dream. I dreamed that all of us rose up like a mighty army and got rid of the false idols around us. We got rid of the violence in our schools and the smut on our airways. We got rid of the poison in our water and the filth in our air. Then, when we got rid of all those things, we looked around for the ones who put them there. The ones who pretend to act for us, like wise old Solomon, but who are really selling us out, just like Judas. I'm telling you, brothers and sisters, someday soon these false Solomons will crumble. Then we'll be able to take America back!"

An endless loop of Reverend Gerald LeClaire's words echoed through the long hall. Escorted by a security guard, former Sergeant Robert Wurth heard LeClaire's famous "Solomon" speech over and over again, along with ten-second segments of cheers, whistles, and a thunderous chanting of "Take America back!" that separated the sound bites. In a way, the preacher's words reminded Wurth of Dr. Martin Luther King, Jr.'s soaring oratory. In another way, LeClaire brought back the memory of the carnies who rolled into his hometown every fall and inveigled little boys to part with their quarters for peeks at three-breasted women and grotesquely misshapen livestock.

"You ever get tired of hearing that?" Wurth asked the armed guard who walked at his side.

"Not when I'm listening to the next President of the United States." The guard glared self-righteously at Wurth, who gave up on any further conversation and followed him to the end of the hall, where the guard opened a door marked "Apostles."

"They're waiting for you in there," he said without smiling.

Wurth stepped into a large, low-ceilinged room, one entire wall of which was covered by a photograph of Gerald LeClaire, barefoot on the beach, gazing at the sun setting over the sea. In front of that photo-mural sat seven men at a long table, decidedly not smiling and not in any mood for a frolic on the beach.

"Sergeant Wurth." The man in the center of the table locked eyes with Wurth. "Just the man we've been waiting for."

Wurth strode toward them, his footsteps soundless on the thick carpeting, the collective gaze of the seven hard upon him. This was worse than he'd thought. He figured he'd have some explaining to do to Richard Dunbar. He had no idea all the FaithAmerica powers would be here. A foot from the center of the table, he stopped and struck the pose he always took at times like this—standing at ease, his legs slightly spread, his arms behind his back. His only concession to the room and the men was a quarter he rolled across his fingers, a feat of legerdemain he'd used for thirty years to keep his hands from trembling when he felt on edge.

"I've got just one question for you, Wurth," snarled Dunbar.

"Yes?"

"What the hell did your boy mean by this?" Dunbar held up a picture of Rosemary Klinefelter, or at least the body of Rosemary Klinefelter, sitting primly in her judicial robe, her own head nestled in her lap.

"I guess my boy got carried away," Wurth said, working the coin behind his back. "He was young. It happens, sometimes."

"He got carried away?" Dunbar repeated incredulously. "Wurth, next month I've got to deliver a fulfilled prophecy to ten thousand

FaithAmericans who are poised to begin the presidential campaign of Gerald LeClaire. Now is not the time for any of your people to get carried away!"

"I realize that." Wurth kept his voice soft.

"Then why the fuck did he cut off her head?" shrieked Dunbar, the large vein that bisected his forehead swelling with rage. "I thought I made it clear to you—these judges are supposed to be killed by the hand of God. Not some teenage ninja-in-training!"

Wurth kept his eyes straight ahead. "The Army doesn't consider an operative reliable until they've eliminated half a dozen targets. This was Forrester's third."

There was a tap on the door. All the men looked past Wurth as a young woman in a black uniform entered the room bearing a tray laden with coffee. Dunbar quickly swept the gruesome photograph into his lap as she put a steaming cup in front of every man seated at the table, along with a big basket of pastries. "Anything else, Mr. Dunbar?"

"Not right now, Judy." Chameleon-like, Dunbar beamed appreciatively, looking, in Wurth's estimation, exactly like the slimy huckster he was. Gold rings on his fingers, razor-cut hair moussed to perfection. And so much cologne

that Wurth knew none of the men seated at the table would taste their crullers at all. They would sit there and consume little morsels of Polo or whatever the hell Dunbar doused himself in.

Wurth knew he would have to play this carefully. He'd been summoned to FaithAmerica only once before, and never to the Apostle Room, the underground bunker where FaithAmerica political decisions were made. Yet here he stood, trying to explain his actions to Richard Dunbar and the six other men who were secretly engineering the presidential candidacy of Reverend Gerald LeClaire.

"Wurth, your boy's little spasm of extravagance may have cost us our election!" Dunbar resumed his tirade after Judy left the room. "After eleven months of everything going like clockwork! If *any* FaithAmericans ever catch wind of this, everything will go up in smoke!"

Wurth tried to judge the mood of the other men. Though they all looked just like Dunbar—white men in dark suits with elegant gold watches on their wrists—all did not share Dunbar's hustler background. Some were the well-educated black sheep of old-money families. Others had graduated from the college of the streets, climbing to the ranks of millionaire on schemes of their own devising. All were rich.

All were powerful. All were keenly attuned to any opportunity that might make them more so.

"Just explain this to us, Wurth," said a bald-headed man at one end of the table. "Explain how this could have happened."

Wurth turned to the man, a wealthy hardware magnate from Chicago. "David Forrester was the best student I ever had. He eliminated his first two targets perfectly, and I had every reason to think he would execute his third in the same way," he said. "Obviously, I was wrong."

"Where is this boy now?" asked a state senator from Texas who was seated on Dunbar's left. "Can we talk to him about this?"

"Not in person." Dunbar pulled another photograph from his jacket and tossed it on the table. Wurth stole a look at it. It was David Forrester as he'd found him two weeks ago, lying on the ground, his legs broken, his battered face gazing sightless into the sky. Wurth's coin bobbled as he clamped his jaws shut against a hot rage that began to simmer inside him. David Forrester, his only student to ever earn the Black Feather, hunted down and killed like an animal.

"You know that the Feds are on to us now, don't you?" asked a fretful little sausage of a man at the far end of the table. Conrad Driessen was the mayor of a fair-sized city in Ohio and heir to a deodorant fortune.

"I'm aware of that, Mr. Driessen," Wurth replied. "You can't decapitate a federal judge and go unnoticed."

"Washington's assigned bodyguards to every Federal court in the country," drawled an aristocratic-looking Virginian from the other end of the table. "There are more Feds in Richmond now than there were during Grant's occupation."

Dunbar shook his head. "The fact of it is, Wurth, my two boys obeyed my orders a lot better than David Forrester did yours."

"Your two goons beat Forrester to death." Wurth felt an angry heat flood his face. "Any thug could do that. Offing a federal judge takes considerably more skill."

"*Clandestinely* offing," Dunbar shot back. "I think that word might have had too many sylla-bles for your boy to understand."

"And I suppose your two grasp that concept?"

"They do. And they're in Charleston right now, just awaiting my word."

Wurth looked up at the photo of Gerald LeClaire gazing into the ocean. This Faith-America command was no better than Uncle Sam's. Get the grunt to do the dirty work, then if he fucks up, get rid of him. It made him want to puke.

Dunbar pointed his finger at him. "Wurth, the simple truth is that this headless judge picture proves you and yours aren't reliable anymore."

"But I didn't do it!" Wurth cried. "An eighteen-year-old boy did!"

"But he was *your* prize pupil. And he could well have cost us a presidential election!"

Wurth looked at Dunbar's hands. His nails gleamed with clear polish and grew well beyond the ends of his fingers. How had it come that a man with manicured nails could toy with his life like a cat with a piece of yarn?

"What if I do the last one myself?" Wurth asked suddenly, the coin flashing behind his back.

Dunbar shook his head. "I've already got my boys in place."

"Call them off. Let me prove that I'm not quite as unreliable as you think. I'll do that woman who lives near my camp. There are so few women in the federal judiciary. Getting rid of another one would make our point even better."

Dunbar's mouth fell open. "You want to kill a judge who virtually lives in your own backyard? Oh, that's smart, Wurth. That's real smart."

Wurth smiled. "I can get it done. Quickly. Quietly. You'll get your prophecy fulfilled in time and the Feds won't suspect a thing."

"Yeah, right," said Dunbar. "I can just imagine how that will go."

Wurth leaned forward and stared into Dunbar's eyes. "If you think I'm such a fuckup, then put it to a vote. These six men have as much riding on this as you do. See if they like your two goons in Charleston better than me."

Wurth looked up and down the table. The timber baron from Idaho and the city councilman from Arizona looked as if they'd just eaten something slightly spoiled. The man who was the shoo-in to be the next governor of Indiana pondered his reflection in the dull silver coffeepot. All knew that if Gerald LeClaire was elected president, they were assured cabinet seats. All knew equally that if any of this prophecy fulfillment scam was discovered, nothing could save them, either from Gerald LeClaire's faithful or the U.S. government.

"Well, gentlemen? Who will it be? You want to feed at that big hog trough in Washington, you've got to have D.C.–sized balls."

Silence hung over the table as Wurth looked at each man in turn. Finally Conrad Driessen's fat little arm lifted.

"I do," he said, sweat popping out on his forehead. "Wurth has always delivered before. I don't think this beheading thing was his fault."

Dunbar spoke to the six at the table. "Gentlemen, next month in Miami, ten thousand Faith-Americans will gather in our first convention. If we can prove that the false Solomon prophecy has been fulfilled, it will electrify them. They will rise and carry us all to the White House on their shoulders! Do any more of you share Dreissen's belief that Wurth's killing his next-door neighbor will get us to that point?"

The silence stretched even longer, then the Texan's arm came up, followed by the Virginian's. When the councilman from Arizona finally joined them, Wurth had Dunbar, four to three. Slowly, he began to breathe again. His years of hard work had earned him one more chance. "That's it, Dunbar," he said. "Call your boys in Charleston off."

"Do all of you realize what will happen if Wurth fails?" Dunbar's voice grew shrill.

"Wurth's the devil we know," said the Virginian. "And what he said about your boys made sense. Killing a federal judge requires more skill than taking a baseball bat to one of your old classmates."

"Okay." Dunbar held up his hands, as if to absolve himself of the consequences of this act. "Wurth, are you sure you want to go for the woman in your hometown?"

Wurth grinned at Dunbar. "Does the word 'undoubtedly' have too many syllables for you to understand?"

No one at the table spoke.

"Then I thank you for your confidence, gentlemen. I'll be in touch." Smiling, Wurth pocketed the quarter as he walked toward the door.

CHAPTER 3

DECKARD COUNTY COURTHOUSE
December 23

"Sorry I took so long," Mary gasped as she burst into the office. "Martel had to drive me all the way from the country club." She paused to catch her breath. "What's going on?"

"I'm sorry I had to interrupt the wedding, Mary. This is Daniel Safer, FBI." Deckard County DA Jim Falkner, the lower half of a bright red Santa Claus suit barely visible above his desk, jerked his head toward a man sitting on the other side of his office. "I'll let Dan here explain."

Sitting in front of Jim's desk was a man who looked more like a foreign diplomat than a federal agent. Around thirty-five, he had wiry dark hair that curled around his forehead and tumbled into a close-cropped beard the color of pitch. Though his blue silk tie accented an elegant Italian suit, his eyes were what caught

Mary's attention. Dark and deep-set, they seemed to open like the aperture of a camera, instantly taking in everything from the dark green pumps on her feet to the now slightly ridiculous flowers that she still wore in her hair.

"Hi." She extended her hand. "I'm Mary Crow."

"Daniel Safer." He stood and shook her hand. He was tall, with a commanding demeanor that with his beard reminded her of a Russian Cossack. He would look perfect in heavy black boots and a sable hat.

Mary smiled, but chose the chair farthest away from Agent Safer. The man had a kind of dark gravitational field that made her want to keep her distance.

"You want to fill us in on this now?" Jim Falkner said gruffly.

Without a further word of explanation, Safer clicked open a black leather briefcase. "Anybody here squeamish?" he asked as he withdrew a large manila envelope.

"We're prosecutors, Safer." Jim rolled his eyes at Mary. "We got over being squeamish years ago."

"Good." Safer opened a smaller red evidence file on the desk, revealing a photograph of a white-haired man. "This is the Honorable

Arthur Fitzgerald of New York, late of the Second Circuit Court of Appeals. On September 18, Judge Fitzgerald was killed by a single knife wound to the kidney just outside his home in Greenwich Village. He was walking his dog about ten o'clock in the evening. No one saw anyone, the police have no suspects."

"Okay." Jim flipped through the file, then passed it to Mary. "What's next?"

Safer opened a second red file. This time a chubby man lay sprawled out on an Oriental rug. "The Honorable Edward Hebert, late of the Fifth Circuit Court of Appeals in New Orleans. On Halloween night, a cleaning crew found Judge Hebert on the fifth floor of his office building, hanging from a staircase banister. The coroner ruled it a suicide. His widow vehemently denies this, insisting that the judge was a happy, satisfied man with no history of depression and no reason at all for taking his own life."

Jim grunted, passed the file to Mary, then Safer tossed out a third.

"Let me warn you, this one is not pleasant."

"I thought we handled the first two pretty well," snapped Jim, taking the third file from Safer's hand.

"That's the Honorable Rosemary Klinefelter, of the Sixth Circuit Court," explained Safer.

"She failed to come home the night before she and her husband were due to fly to the Caribbean for a Thanksgiving vacation. The husband drove down to her office and found her himself. The photo more or less says it all."

Jim scowled at the picture. The body of a woman sat in a tall leather chair, clad in a judicial gown. On her lap rested her severed head, a baffled expression of astonishment frozen on her lifeless features. "I read about this in the paper." Jim handed the picture to Mary. "Of course they didn't say she'd been beheaded. Who do you guys think did it?"

"Someone strong enough to administer a single blow to the back of the neck, with an extremely sharp sword approximately six millimeters thick, perhaps four feet long."

"But how did he get her to stand still long enough to chop off her head?" asked Jim.

"Poison," replied Safer. "Judge Klinefelter had been injected with some kind of hemlock derivative, laced with something we haven't identified yet. Depending on the dosage, hemlock's either instant death or a slow, fully conscious paralysis that ends in death. Our boy had some fun with Rosemary Klinefelter."

"Your *boy*?" Mary looked up from the last grisly file, hoping the wedding cake she'd consumed an hour ago would stay in her stomach. Judge Klinefelter's was the most sickening crime photo she'd ever seen.

"He, almost certainly. The amount of upper body strength needed to sever a head in one blow is enormous—beyond that of most females, even if they were pumped up and on steroids. The good Dr. Guillotin used gravity and a heavy blade in his machine for that very reason."

"Have you gotten any other physical evidence?" asked Jim.

"Just some partial prints off Klinefelter's desk and one of these." Safer tossed a plastic bag on the desk. Mary picked it up. Inside was a sleek ebony feather.

"Crow?" She lifted an eyebrow at Safer.

He shook his head. "A common starling. And the MO doesn't match anything on anybody's computer, either here or on Interpol."

"How do you like that," Jim muttered. "All those wonderful computers and they still can't tell you a damn thing." He sat back in his chair, studying Safer through narrow eyes. "Okay. Now tell me what all of this has to do with Deckard County, Georgia."

Safer fumbled in his briefcase again, then pulled out a single sheet of yellow paper. "I work in the Cincinnati office, so the Klinefelter case was assigned to me. I happened to be in New York at the time of Judge Fitzgerald's murder, so I remembered that case and did some digging on my own. I came up with this."

Safer put the paper down on the desk between Jim and Mary. "Statistically, the federal court system loses about 2.3 judges a year to death. Since most federal judges are white males over forty, most succumb to heart attacks. In each of the past eleven months, a federal judge has died unexpectedly. Five have had fatal accidents, two have had heart attacks. One's an apparent suicide. Three have been murdered quite obviously."

"Mmmm." Jim ran his finger down the list. "District Judge Bryan Woody thrown from his horse in Casper, Wyoming. District Judge Kendrick Eaton lost in a boating accident off the coast of California." He frowned over his glasses at Safer. "Have you guys gone back and done toxin screens on these victims?"

"We're in the process of doing that. Unfortunately, three were cremated and two drowning victims have not been recovered."

Jim grunted. "I still don't see what this has to do with us. We're in the Eleventh District. According to your chart, our judge died in a wreck in Decatur, Alabama, back in March."

"I don't think it has anything to do with the Eleventh District, Jim," said Mary. She looked at the agent. "It's about the Fourth District, isn't it?"

Safer nodded.

"You're thinking the next one could be Irene Hannah, aren't you?"

"You got it," he replied.

"Wait a minute." Jim sat up in his chair. "Who the hell's Irene Hannah?"

"Appellate judge, Fourth Circuit, Richmond," Mary explained. "I clerked for her in law school, when she sat on the Fourth District bench in Asheville. She's an old family friend." Mary thought how much more than an old friend Irene Hannah was. She had known her ever since she was eleven years old. It had been Irene who'd come roaring up in her brown Mercedes the afternoon her mother was murdered. She'd wrapped a blanket around Mary's trembling shoulders and driven her back to Upsy Daisy farm, holding her tight in her arms while Mary had wept that long, hellish night away.

Safer said, "If this rather loose pattern holds, some judge in the Fourth District should be killed sometime within the next eight days."

"And that judge will be injected with poison and have her head cut off?" Mary asked, her eyes on Safer's.

He nodded. "Possibly. Or her heart could simply stop, or she could have an automobile accident or someone could fake her suicide. All are lousy ways to die."

"But why?" asked Mary.

Safer shrugged. "That's what we're trying to figure out. The who and the why. Whether it's just one psycho birdwatcher with a grudge, or a conspiracy of freaks who hate federal judges. Obviously, we need to keep our judiciary safe until we can nail down a suspect."

"So why don't you just put guards on them?" Jim demanded. "Jesus, you guys are the FBI!"

"We have, Mr. Falkner," Safer replied, his tone sharpening for the first time. "We've alerted every federal judge in the country and put round-the-clock bodyguards on every Fourth District judge. All except Judge Hannah are extremely well taken care of."

"Then why the hell don't you guard her?" Jim groused.

Safer gave a bitter smile. "Because Judge Hannah refuses federal protection. She says that for a federal judge to require bodyguarding smacks of a regime rather than a republic, and she won't have any part of it."

Mary fought an urge to leap from her chair and have Martel speed her immediately to Hartsville, North Carolina, lights and sirens blaring. In the years since that long-ago April afternoon, Irene had stepped in and filled a void in Mary's life that no one else could fill. Irene knew her better than her grandmother Bennefield, in some ways better than even Alex McCrimmon. Though they now lived miles apart, Mary could not conceive of her life without Irene Hannah in it.

Jim was frowning. "You still haven't told me how you want my prosecutor to help you out, Agent Safer."

"If we can keep everything quiet for the next week, we'll have broken the pattern. We'd like Ms. Crow to go to Irene Hannah in person, and talk her into accepting FBI protection." Safer turned to Mary. "Since you're a friend of hers and an assistant DA, we thought you might have better luck convincing the judge that she could be in serious danger."

"What makes you think she'll listen to me?"

"She may not. She probably won't. All we can do is take you up there and hope you can talk her into it."

"Here." Jim turned the phone on his desk around. "Call her, on my dime. Save yourself a lot of time and gas."

Safer shook his head. "Judge Hannah disconnected her phone last week. At the moment she's incommunicado with the outside world."

"So where does she live?" asked Jim. "Timbuktu?"

Five miles away from Jonathan, Mary thought, her heart both leaping and aching at the same time. "She's got a thirty-acre farm near Hartsville. She raises Appalachian Single Foot horses."

Jim blinked. "The woman raises horses that only have one foot?"

"It's a special breed of mountain horse," Safer explained. "They have the normal number of feet." He turned to Mary. "Would you be willing to help us out?"

Mary grabbed her purse. "If I leave now I can be up there by midnight."

"Whoa," protested Jim. "Mary, you could be stepping into a real situation up there."

"My team has already formed a perimeter around Judge Hannah's farm. We'll keep Ms. Crow safe the entire time she's there." Safer looked at Mary. "Have you ever fired a gun?"

"I shoot a 9mm Beretta twice a week," she replied promptly. "I'm no sharpshooter, but I do okay."

"Then it might not be a bad idea if you brought the Beretta with you."

"Just a minute!" cried Jim. He turned to her, his thick gray brows drawn with concern.

"Look, Mary, I know how loyal you are to your old friends, but you've got no business in the middle of a federal operation like this."

Mary thought of her mother's death years ago, and her grandmother Bennefield's death in September. Jonathan had left her, and as of two hours ago, Alex was a married woman. She looked at her boss with somber eyes.

"Jim, Irene Hannah is the last shred of a family I've got left," she answered softly. "I would do anything to keep her alive."

Jim shook his head, knowing further protest would be a waste of breath. He knew all too well what Mary Crow was like when she dug her heels in. However much he might say, she would go off and try to talk this judge into being guarded by these idiots, everyone else be damned. He took off his glasses and rubbed his eyes, then he stabbed his finger at Daniel Safer.

"I can remember when the FBI would have been embarrassed to ask a female civilian to help with an investigation. . . ."

"This wasn't my idea, Mr. Falkner," Safer interrupted. "I have orders to follow, just like Ms. Crow."

"I don't give a damn what you've got," Jim thundered. "If this girl comes back here with as much as a broken fingernail, I'll personally hack off one of your most treasured parts. And I won't do it in a single blow, either! I don't care if you're J. Edgar Hoover reincarnated."

"That won't be a problem, Mr. Falkner." Safer snapped his briefcase shut, then turned his dark eyes on Mary. "Meet me here at the courthouse at seven tomorrow morning. Bring your weapon, Ms. Crow, and be ready to do some fast talking in North Carolina."

CHAPTER 4

Two hundred miles north of Atlanta, two boys were exploring the third floor of Camp Unakawaya's castle. The first two floors of the old place held little interest for these boys; they attended home school on the first floor and slept in a drafty dormitory on the second. But the third floor was something else. Long regarded as haunted, the third floor was an old, shadowy warren of hospital rooms that still held medical equipment from 1919. It was said that during thunderstorms you could still hear the screams of the mutilated ghost-soldiers as they revisited the trenches in their nightmares. It was, of course, here that the boys explored.

"Look!" Willett Pierson thrust one pudgy hand deep into an old chifforobe. "There's some cool stuff back here!"

Tommy Cabe watched as Willett pulled out a

small, suede-bound notebook and something that looked like a weird set of false teeth. Grinning, Willett handed the book to Cabe and immediately stuck the teeth in his mouth.

"*Cheeldren* of ze *night*," Willett moaned, imitating Bela Lugosi. "I *vant* to suck your *blood!*" Holding his hands out like claws, he began to creep toward Tommy. At just an inch over five feet, with hair the color of a carrot, Willett Pierson looked more like a North Pole elf than a Transylvanian vampire. Tommy Cabe laughed.

"Man, can you believe somebody actually wore these?" Willett spat the teeth from his mouth. They were the top front teeth only, constructed long ago, with thin, painful-looking wires to hold them in the wearer's mouth.

"I guess." Tommy Cabe examined the book Willett had handed him, squinting at the spidery old-fashioned script. "Somebody wrote this diary. Captain Nigel Dempsey of the Eleventh Fusiliers."

"I bet he was one of the patients here," cried Willett. "This must be all his old shit. I told you there's tons of cool stuff in here!"

"Probably." Tommy leaned over to peer into the old chifforobe. On the top shelf lay a round hat box; next to that an old photograph of a soldier in puttees with a young woman wearing a long dress. He'd just started to reach for the photograph when a bell rang. Both he and Willett jumped as if they'd been stuck with pins.

"Awww, fuck!" Willett looked at Tommy. "Anthropology class."

"We can come back later." Tommy stashed the diary back in the chifforobe and gathered his books from the cot. "Let's go. I still don't have any demerits this week."

Willett hid the teeth behind the diary and closed the chifforobe. "Man, are you still having your phone-call fantasy?"

"David Forrester swore you get one phone call for every week you have no demerits. He's my senior proctor."

"He *was* your senior proctor," Willett reminded him. "Nobody's seen Forrester's sorry ass in over a month."

"Maybe he ran away," Tommy suggested, always buoyed by the idea that somebody might have said to hell with Camp Unakawaya and taken off for parts unknown.

"You can't get away from here, man. Wurth probably sent him on some kind of secret mission and got him killed."

Tommy shook his head. "You're crazy, Willett. Wurth can barely stand to put Forrester on guard detail, much less send him on a secret mission."

"Maybe. But I still think when pigs have

wings is when they'll let *you* make a phone call." Willett scooped up his books from the cot and pulled a Chicago Bulls baseball cap down backward on his head.

Tommy's eyes grew large. "Are you gonna wear that cap?" Two days ago Sergeant Wurth told Willett that if he ever caught him wearing any more nigger sports gear he'd put him in Attitude Realignment for six months.

"I am." Willett grinned at him, cocky as ever. "The operative word is 'catch,' Tommy-boy. Wurth ain't gonna catch me. Wurth couldn't catch cold, even if he tried."

"Come on, Willett. Let's just get down to class so I can finish this week without any demerits."

"Suit yourself, sucker," Willett shot back. "Don't say I didn't warn you!"

They closed the door to the old bedroom and raced down the hall. Though nobody ever came up to the third floor, they still made their way cautiously to the stairs. Spies lurked everywhere in this old castle, and you never knew when they might be watching.

The staircase, however, was safe. With their legs pumping, they flew down the flights like firemen on their way to a three-alarm blaze. As Cabe watched Willett's Chicago Bulls cap bounce down the stairs ahead of him, he kept thinking that in just eighteen more demerit-free hours he would get his phone call. How wonderful it would be to hear his grandfather's voice. He could finally tell him where he was, let him know at least he was still alive.

With a final leap he reached the first floor and followed Willett down the hall. He wished he'd run this fast into the woods behind the shopping center that night when his mom didn't show up. He'd told the sheriff that she'd probably just gotten drunk somewhere and passed out. It was okay, he assured the cop. He was used to it, no big deal. But the sheriff had slapped him in the back of that cruiser, and called some stupid social worker, and before Tommy knew it he was standing in front of Sergeant Wurth at this shithole they called Camp Unakawaya. *Pisgah County wants me to make a man out of you, boy,* Sergeant Wurth had said, grinning at him and standing so close that Tommy could count the hairs sprouting from his wide nostrils. *Someday you'll make your mother sorry she was such a sot.* But Tommy didn't want to make his mother feel that way, and he wasn't at all sure he wanted to become the kind of man Wurth had in mind. Neither did Willett Pierson. Thank God they'd become friends. Tommy didn't like to consider what Camp Unakawaya would be like without Willett.

"Take your cap off, Willett," Cabe whispered

as they neared their classroom. "They'll bust both our asses."

With a quick swoop of his hand, Willett tore the Bulls cap from his head and stuffed it under his T-shirt. Cabe skidded up behind him as he opened the classroom door. Although the other boys had taken their seats, Sergeant Wurth was not yet standing behind the podium. Keeping their eyes on the floor, Tommy and Willett scurried to their respective desks, fourth from the front in the second and third rows, plopping into their chairs a nanosecond before the bell sounded for the second time. *Just in time,* Tommy thought, his forehead damp with sweat. *Still no demerits for me.*

"You were almost late, C-C-Cabe!" Wayne Tallent, one of Wurth's Troopers, taunted from the seat behind him. Tommy knew that since the other three old faculty geezers had gone home for Christmas, Tallent would regard him as fair game until Wurth arrived to teach the class. He hunched his shoulders forward, hoping that Wurth would come before Tallent had time to get started.

"What have you and your girlfriend Wilma been d-d-doing?" Tallent gave Tommy's ear a hard twist. "Spanking your little monkeys? Or popping those big old pimples on your chin?"

Tommy Cabe stared at the empty podium, his tweaked ear burning, while Tallent and his buddy Grice laughed. Willett turned around and poked up his middle finger.

Grice reached over from the fourth aisle and thumped Willett viciously between his shoulder blades. "Put that finger down, Pierson," he growled. "Somebody's gonna think it's your dick."

"Hey, Cabe." Tallent thrust his long, black-booted feet around Tommy's desk. "Upchurch told me you was smart. Is that true?"

Searching for the right response, Cabe stared at the flag that was draped above the blackboard. It looked like a regular American flag, except in place of the stars was an eagle lifting a cross in its talons. He always hoped that bird would give him the answers to Tallent's questions, but all it seemed to do was make his stutter ten times worse. He was just beginning to formulate a reply when Tallent struck him between his shoulders, whooshing the air from his lungs with a loud slap.

"I asked if you was smart, boy. You answer me!"

Slowly Tommy Cabe turned sideways. He sighed, resigned to the inevitable wrongness of his reply. Blinking through thick glasses that had already been broken and mended twice, he was about to choke out an answer when Willett piped up.

"Cabe's not nearly as smart as I am, Tallent. What do you want to know? What two plus two makes? Or maybe we should take it slow for you, and start out with one plus one."

Instantly Grice's fist shot out, slamming into Willett's ear. "You shut up, you little ridge runner! Tallent was asking Cabe a question."

"Hey, C–C–Cabe, since this is anthropology, answer me this. Who do you figure would be hardest to kill—a nigger, a woman, or a Jew?"

With his back still burning, Cabe stared at the floor, trying to figure out which answer would earn him the least grief. Finally he gave up, re-alizing there was no best answer; Tallent would beat him whatever he said. Reluctantly he raised his eyes and spoke. "A J–Jew, I think. They al-ways put up a good fight."

Tallent snorted. "Those little long-nosed nig-ger lovers? The ones who faked the Holocaust?"

"They d–d–didn't fake it, Tallent," Cabe said wearily, knowing he would regret it.

"Sure they did!" Tallent said, indignant. "They filmed the whole thing in Hollywood, at MGM. They got people from TB hospitals to play the parts!"

Willett started to laugh. "God, Tallent, you'd

have to double your IQ to reach moron. In 1939 the Germans had a standing army of a hundred and six combat divisions. The Jews didn't even have the right to vote."

"Bullshit!" screeched Tallent, his face growing red. "That's not what it says in our history book."

"Tallent, our history book says the moon landing took place in Winslow, Arizona, and Jimmy Carter's real mother was black." Willett cackled. "Cabe's right. You go one-on-one with a Jew, he'd give you a hell of a fight."

"He wouldn't give me a hell of a fight," muttered Tallent.

Willett leaned across the aisle. "Tallent, my old stove-up grandma'd give *you* a hell of a fight."

"Fuck you, you little nigger-lover!" Tallent lunged forward, ready to pummel Willett. Cabe reached out to grab him; just then the door opened. All twenty boys in the room shot to their feet and snapped to attention as Frank Upchurch, a senior Trooper from Texas, strode in. He wore Wurth's full uniform, khaki trousers stuffed into black combat boots and a khaki blouse with red stripes on the sleeves. A red beret peeked from under his arm.

Upchurch gave the class a brisk salute as he walked over to the podium. As he watched the students sit back down, his gaze skittered along each row of upturned faces, then his badly hair-lipped mouth spasmed in a grin.

"Sergeant Wurth just called and said he wouldn't be here tonight," Upchurch reported. "His orders are for everyone to get to the gym and load up the FaithAmerica Christmas boxes. We'll start delivering them at oh eight hundred tomorrow morning."

"So who's in charge, Up-chuck?" called Tallent. "You?"

"That's right, Tallent, me. You got a problem with it?" Upchurch's eyes narrowed into beads of an indeterminate color.

"Naw, Up-chuck," Tallent snickered. "I guess even a monkey can get a truck loaded."

"Okay, then. Let's go." Upchurch scowled at the group, waiting to see if they would accept his authority. For a moment nobody moved; then, slowly, the Troopers began to rise from their seats. Upchurch looked relieved.

"I'm not forgetting about you, Wilma," snarled Tallent, wrenching Willett's ear brutally as he walked by. "Watch your back, boy. I'll see *you* later tonight."

Tommy Cabe kept his eyes lowered as Tallent and Grice strode past him. After they left the room, Willett again lifted his middle finger at them.

"They're going to get you sent to AR," said Cabe.

"They're going to try," Willett replied.

"What are you going to do?"

"I don't know." Willett tugged his cap from under his T-shirt and pulled it back on his head. "I'll come up with something, though. AR is the last place I'm gonna spend Christmas."

★   ★   ★

A few miles away from Tommy Cabe and Willett Pierson, in an old barn built before the doughboys sailed to France, a chestnut mare stood in a foaling stall. Although her belly was swollen and her front legs splayed, she ate her hay placidly, returning the gaze of her owner with kind brown eyes.

"Lady Jane ain't ready yet, darlin'."

"Are you sure? After supper she looked like she was going to go at any minute."

Hugh Kavanagh leaned over the stall and rubbed the horse's nose. He'd seen a hundred mares foal during his lifetime, first in County Wexford, Ireland, then in North Carolina, and not one birth had been exactly like another. Some mares went about their task serenely, as if it were just another hedge to jump, while others grew peevish weeks beforehand, whisking their tails around and snapping at their handlers.

He smiled over at his silver-haired neighbor and shook his head. "She ain't doing it tonight. I'd say Christmas Day, at the earliest."

Irene Hannah looked at the horse and frowned. "Darn. I was so sure it would be this week, I canceled my dental appointment."

Hugh chuckled. "Next time, get your choppers fixed. It's great good luck to be born on Christmas Day, anyway. Means whatever it is will be fey." He put an arm around Irene's shoulders. "Have you decided on a name for this one?"

"Cushla McCree, if it's a filly."

"Cushla McCree?" He frowned. "For a horse?"

Nodding, Irene laughed at Hugh's pronunciation of "horse," which sounded to her American ears like "harse."

"What if she throws a colt?" Hugh asked.

"Aloysius. Or Patrick."

"As in Ireland's famous saint?"

"Yep. Then he can drive all the snakes out of the upper pasture."

Hugh Kavanagh shook his head. "Irene, you're the only woman I know who can see an unborn colt clearin' snakes from a pasture."

"I've spent forty years in the courtroom," Irene Hannah said. "I can imagine most anything." She put an arm around Hugh's waist.

"Come on inside. I'll fix us a drink and something to eat. I owe you one for dragging you out here on a false alarm."

"Let me freshen Lady Jane's straw a bit, then," Hugh replied, wiping his hands on a towel. "She'll sleep better on something soft."

Irene turned to go, then stopped and studied the mare. "You're sure she'll be all right?"

Hugh nodded. "This makes six for Lady Jane. I'd say she knows what she's doing."

Turning, Irene walked out of the barn and back up to her old farmhouse. The light she'd left on in the kitchen glowed like a solitary square of gold in a field of dark blue. It was almost midnight, and a breeze blew from the north, carrying the cold scents of frosty pine and cedar. She'd always had mixed feelings about the last week of December. Sometimes the anticipatory hum in the air could make her giddy as a girl awaiting a visit from Santa Claus. Other times, she remembered a Christmas three decades past, when she and her husband had sat up all night trying to assemble a bicycle for Phoebe. It had been comical, with Will frantically trying to decipher the bicycle instructions while she had run back and forth from the living room to Phoebe's bedroom, making sure their daughter was fast asleep and not tiptoeing down the hall to see what Santa Claus had left her. Two days later both Will and Phoebe lay dead, victims of a drunk driver.

Irene looked up at Venus, glimmering like a pale ruby in the sky. For years after that night she despised Christmas—hated the tinsel and the carols and the bright presents that would never again hold what she truly wanted. Slowly, though, time made good on its promise. Her heart scarred over, walling Phoebe and Will up in a little chamber all by themselves, safe from tears, safe from pain, safe from her endless recriminations. Finally, one Christmas morning years later, she woke up and gazed at their pictures beside her bed and she smiled—grateful for having known them, feeling that in some way they were with her still. She had not wept for them since.

"Merry Christmas, you two," she whispered, knowing her words went nowhere but up into the cold air, yet somehow certain that Will and Phoebe could hear them. A sharp whinny came from the barn. "Come on, you silly old woman," she chastised herself as she hurried to her back door. "Go get warm inside your kitchen and leave Christmas past alone."

She poked at the log burning slowly in her fireplace, then pulled a bottle of brandy from a cupboard. After arranging it with two glasses in the middle of the kitchen table, she turned on the burner underneath her iron skillet. She looked in her refrigerator. A big bowl of pale beige eggs that she'd gathered just that morning sat there. Earlier today she'd almost beaten them into a coconut cake; now she was glad she'd saved them for a greater purpose. Humming a bouncy version of "Good King Wenceslaus," she plucked them from the refrigerator, along with a slab of bacon. By the time she had break-fast almost ready, she heard Hugh's footsteps coming up the stairs.

"If it's a filly I think you ought to call her Noël or Holly or something," he told her, stepping out of his boots before he entered the kitchen.

"Noël?" Irene cringed as she poured brandy into a snifter. "What's wrong with Cushla McCree?"

"Can you say 'This is my horse Cushla McCree' without laughing?"

"Better than I can say 'Noël,' " Irene replied. "This is my horse Cushla McCree, who just won the Kentucky Derby. This is my horse Cushla McCree, who just swept the Irish sweepstakes. This is my horse Cushla McCree, who was born on the luckiest day of the year."

"Okay," Hugh laughed. "I give up." His eyes twinkling, he took the brandy. "Shall we take our first sip in honor of little Cushla, who's not yet born?"

"Absolutely." Irene grinned as she raised her glass.

"To little Cushla or Aloysius Hannah of Upsy Daisy Farm, soon to be the newest, most wonderful horse in all of North Carolina."

"To Cushla," Irene repeated, holding the brandy up to glow amber in the firelight. She took a swallow, enjoying the savage warmth as it traveled down her throat and into her stomach. She put the glass down and looked at Hugh. Suddenly she saw not a seventy-three-year-old retiree with sun-wrinkled skin and a drooping mustache, but a deeply tanned man with laughing blue eyes who could teach her about horses and farming and sex. All at once she felt a fierce longing for everything just as it was—the two of them standing close together in her kitchen, awaiting the birth of a tiny new bit of creation. "Oh, Hugh," she whispered softly, her eyes brimming with unexpected tears. "Hold me."

Hugh grabbed her as if she were ill, but then relaxed when she nestled against his neck and held him close against her. "Are you all right, girl?" His brogue sounded soft in her ear.

She could only nod. "I just wish we could stay like this forever."

"We can't," he said gently. "But we can have a bloody good go of it for a while."

Suddenly she started to laugh, and the feeling

that it was all going too quickly away left her as she sensed his attention shift. "You're looking at those eggs, aren't you?"

"Well, 'tis a shame to burn good eggs," he admitted, moving the skillet off the burner.

She gave him a final squeeze. "How about we eat some breakfast. And then we can go check on Lady Jane again."

"Or we could go upstairs," Hugh suggested with a wink. "Lady Jane won't be doing a thing till tomorrow morning, at least."

"You think you can last till tomorrow morning, Hugh?" Irene asked, her eyes sparkling.

"Any man from County Wexford who can't last the night in bed when a good horse is about to be born is a shame to his country!" Hugh thumped his chest like a gorilla. "Let's eat some breakfast, girl. Then we'll go upstairs, and I'll prove it!"

CHAPTER 5

Wurth drove to the airport, trying to control his fury, his fists strangling the steering wheel of his rental car. People were turning his sweat and effort to shit again, just like those assholes in the Army. From that stupid Vietnamese cunt Minh to that bitch Lieutenant, somebody always shafted him, usually for doing nothing more than carrying out a direct command. Now it was Richard Dunbar, the ex–advertising man who pouffed up his hair and worked the strings of Gerald LeClaire.

"Idiot," he muttered. "Chickenshit fool."

So he'd sent the wrong boy. So David had lost control. So what? Dunbar and his men hadn't spent ten minutes in the service, much less nineteen years. They'd never savored the stink of fear; never felt what it was like to dangle someone's death right in front of them. They'd all been sitting at their big mahogany desks in Maine and Arizona while he and his boys had been doing their dirty work. Didn't he deserve some consideration for that?

Where is this boy now? The question rang again in his head. This boy was now dead. Dunbar had sent two older boys down from Virginia to take care of David, and indeed they had. They'd ambushed him at the edge of camp and pummeled him to death with baseball bats. His one young Feather Man hadn't had a prayer.

"Goddamn traitors," muttered Wurth. Dunbar was no better than any of the other wonks he'd known in the Army—all desk jockeys who couldn't fight their way to the bathroom, but who loved to pile on when you fucked up. Pussies, the lot of them. He could strangle every one and not even work up a sweat.

Still, Dunbar's words rang in his head. *You aren't reliable anymore.*

"I'll show you how re-fucking-liable I am," Wurth muttered aloud. He'd already been cut loose from one army. He'd be damned if he let Dunbar cut him out of another.

With his fingers still clenching the steering wheel he drove toward the airport. Once he got back to the mountains he would be okay. He had his camp and his boys there. He had his own friends in high places.

"Control," he whispered as he pressed down harder on the accelerator. "You've got to remember control."

He exited the highway to top off his tank, pulling up behind a white minivan with a rainbow bumper sticker that advised everyone to celebrate diversity. Shoving his gearshift into park, he remembered the first time he'd met Dunbar. He'd called him from California ten years ago, saying he'd gotten Wurth's name from an old Army buddy. *Would he be willing to come out and discuss the possibility of some employment?* Sure, Wurth had said. He'd be glad to come. He was a washed-up lifer selling cigarettes at a convenience market. Why wouldn't he jump on a free first-class ticket to California?

How it had impressed him then. The old hotel high on a hill, the Pacific Ocean crashing like spilled beer on the coast below. They'd treated him like somebody special—putting him up in a suite that had an icebox full of booze and a thick terrycloth robe hanging in the bathroom. Then, at dinner that night, over steaks that oozed pale, pearlescent blood, Richard Dunbar explained why he'd sent for him.

"Have you ever heard of Gerald LeClaire?"

"The preacher on TV?"

Dunbar nodded.

"Sure, I've heard of him," Wurth said agreeably, not wanting to admit that his only glimpses of Gerald LeClaire had been while flipping over to the Sunday pregame football show. "Why?"

"The employment opportunity that I mentioned concerns Reverend LeClaire."

"You're kidding." Wurth stopped chewing. What skills did he have that would interest Gerald LeClaire?

Putting his knife and fork aside, Dunbar leaned forward and began to speak as if they were sitting in church.

"Sergeant Wurth, I don't know how much you know about Gerald LeClaire, but to put it mildly, he's an extremely charismatic man. In the two years since he took his television show national, membership in his FaithAmerica organization has quadrupled. Do you know how many people we're talking here?"

Wurth shook his head.

"Half a million," Dunbar practically whispered, as if the words had a holiness all their own. "Do you know what that means?"

Wurth struggled, hating it when people asked rhetorical questions. "Uh, lots of prayer cards sold?"

"Yes, but more than that, it means five hundred thousand people out there who will do pretty much what Reverend Gerry says. Like what he approves of. Hate what he despises."

Dunbar leaned closer, his voice now a whisper. "Believe the way he tells them to."

Wurth stared, still not catching on. He was an Army lifer who'd blown his career and now sold beer to teenagers. What did any of this have to do with him?

"Sergeant, many of our FaithAmerica members feel that the government has abandoned the principles that made this country great. They believe that Reverend LeClaire can restore the values of our forefathers."

"I see." Wurth nodded.

"To that end, FaithAmericans all across the country have begun small political action committees. They want Reverend LeClaire to run for President and turn us back to the Lord."

Wurth's heart sank as he watched two gulls skimming the surf beyond the windows. He'd come out here hoping for some kind of job, not for a political chat with a religious lunatic.

Dunbar sat back and wiped his mouth with his napkin. "As you know, incumbents in this country have a huge, unfair advantage. It's virtually impossible for little guys with little money to be heard, and I'm sure you're aware of how the liberal media feels about anyone affiliated with a religious group."

"I sure do," Wurth chummed Dunbar along, wishing he were down in the bar or even out on the beach with the sea gulls. Anywhere but here with this loony tune.

Dunbar continued. "A few of us think that if we take certain steps now, LeClaire's support will grow. Eventually, a great groundswell of people will anoint him their leader and carry him all the way to the highest office in the land. That's where you come in."

Wurth sat up straighter. Apparently this conversation did have a point. "How do you mean?"

"We want you to level the playing field."

"Level the playing field?" Wurth watched as a grin spread across Dunbar's narrow face.

Dunbar nodded. "We're very impressed with your history, Sergeant. We know the name the Vietnamese gave you."

Wurth blinked, surprised. No one had mentioned that name in years.

"Danh tu," Dunbar whispered as he lifted one eyebrow. "Feather Man. The one who leaves no trace."

Wurth gazed at the white tablecloth that stretched between them. Once the Army had spent a lot of time and money turning him into Danh Tu, a Feather Man, a silent deliverer of death. He had performed admirably, but that war ended and no new war took its place. The Army had no use for Danh Tu then. In fact, the

Army seemed embarrassed that Danh Tu had ever existed. "And how would I be leveling this field?" Wurth asked.

"By doing just what the government has trained you to do. Eliminating certain candidates in certain races. Our organization has grown so solid that we can win any race we choose, as long as the candidates with the party machines behind them are out of the way."

"And this will get Gerald LeClaire elected President?" Wurth asked.

"Not right away," replied Dunbar, showing his rat terrier teeth. "You'll start out on small races in key states. We figure by 2000, we'll have a number of governors and senators. Then they, along with our people in the smaller offices, will work as the present parties do now. With your help, the 2004 presidential election will be a silent, nearly bloodless coup of historic proportions."

"But LeClaire's supposedly a man of God. This doesn't square with any of the gospels I grew up with."

"That's the beauty of it." Dunbar smiled. "Gerald LeClaire doesn't know about any of this."

"He doesn't know people are clamoring to elect him President?"

"Of course he knows that. And he knows I'm helping FaithAmericans become politically active." Dunbar winked. "He's just unaware of some of the methods I'm employing."

"And you don't think he'll find out?"

Dunbar shook his head. "Gerald LeClaire is a good man who believes that anyone sent to FaithAmerica is sent by God Himself. He has complete faith in the Book of Revelations, and the goodness of those God sends him."

"I see." Wurth shifted in his chair. This man was more clever than he'd first thought.

Dunbar picked up a dinner roll and swiped it in the pink blood that remained on his plate. "Sergeant Wurth, all your life you've either fought or trained others to fight honorably for the principles of democracy. We think you deserve far better than the treatment you received from this country. We would consider it an honor to have a man of your caliber join our FaithAmerica team."

Wurth listened, amazed. Though he knew he was being conned as profoundly as poor blind Gerald LeClaire, he enjoyed hearing Dunbar's words. For once somebody was seeing his situation as he did. For once somebody was taking his side.

"Does it pay anything?" he asked, wondering if Dunbar had any cold hard cash to back up his hot air.

Smiling, Dunbar handed Wurth the small

leather legal case he'd been carrying since they first met. Wurth glanced at him, then unzipped it. For an instant he thought his heart would stop. Inside was the deed to a property he knew well—an old abandoned sanitarium not far from where he grew up. Beneath that lay a thick, bank-bound stack of thousand-dollar bills. Both the deed and the paper band around the money had his name on them. This Richard Dunbar had just given him ninety-seven acres of pristine mountain property and a hundred thousand dollars in cash!

"We'll give you the money to turn this old sanitarium into a private training facility for the boys we send you," said Dunbar. "As a cover, you'll run a legitimate recreational camp in the summer, but the rest of the year you'll be training operatives for us. We've already got the faculty lined up. You'll have no more than two dozen boys, from age fourteen to eighteen. By the time they finish your curriculum, they should be well versed in the same skills Uncle Sam taught you."

"Is this for real?" Wurth flipped through the bills, listening to the soft *thrish* of the money. No more worrying about his lost pension now.

"Absolutely, Sergeant Wurth," said Dunbar. "Every July you'll get at least this much money from us, in cash. There are only two things you have to remember."

"What?"

"First, that not a wisp of this must ever, ever touch Gerald LeClaire. He must never suspect a thing."

"I understand."

"Second, don't ever forget that I'm the one in charge. You take orders from me, and me alone."

Wurth looked back out over the ocean, where two surfers bobbed beyond the break line, their skin tawny in the setting sun. Right now, at this table, his life had just been resuscitated. Where the Army had tried to drown him like an unwanted cat, this Dunbar had pulled him back up into the bright, life-giving air.

"Not a problem, Mr. Dunbar." Wurth looked back at the strange little man and smiled. "As far as I'm concerned, you're the number one guy."

A horn blasted behind him. Wurth blinked, jarred back to the present. The diversity-celebrating minivan had pulled away, leaving the gas pump free. Inching up, he got out of his car and lifted the nozzle from the pump, glaring at the old man who'd honked so loudly behind him.

You're not reliable anymore. Again Dunbar's words echoed as gas fumes shimmered up into his face. *Fuck that,* thought Wurth. He'd show them precisely how reliable he was. Reliable like they'd never dreamed of.

The old man behind him revved his engine as the gas bubbled up in the neck of the tank. Wurth topped it off, then glared at the guy as he walked into the gas station to pay. Inside, a tall Latino boy stood behind the cash register. He looked about eighteen. His dark hair curled around his face like David's. Wurth handed the boy a twenty-dollar bill and again felt the rage rise inside him. *He would teach them. He would show Dunbar that it was never wise to fuck with a Feather Man.*

The Latino boy gave him two dollars and three cents back. He crammed the bills in his wallet and left the three pennies on the counter. As he walked back to his car, he noticed the geezer hadn't moved to another pump, but still waited behind him, his mud-covered Ford grinding like a barrel full of bolts.

"Get a move on, mister," the old man brayed out the window. "Some of us got jobs to get to."

Indeed we do, you old bastard, Wurth thought. *I've got a real fine job to get to.* He looked at the man and smiled. "Sorry to keep you waiting, buddy. I'm leaving right now."

He hopped in the car, started the motor. Grinning at the old man's agitated expression in the rearview mirror, he pulled the gearshift into reverse, then floored the accelerator. As his Chevy's bumper crashed into the rusted Ford, he watched the old man's face bounce against the steering wheel. He repeated the procedure once, then twice, then he put the car in park and sauntered back to the old man.

"Sorry about that, buddy. I was in such a hurry to get out of your way that I just lost control."

The old man sat, slack-jawed, his glasses shattered. Blood streamed from his nose.

"Here." Wurth grabbed a blue paper towel from the dispenser. "Let me help you out. You're bleeding like a stuck pig." He rubbed the rough towel all over the old fart's face, smearing blood up into his eyebrows and hair.

"Awrrrr," the old man groaned, woozy in the seat.

"You take it easy there, old-timer." Wurth wadded up the paper towel and threw it on the passenger seat. "I hear there's a lot of road rage out here in California."

With that, he got back in his car and turned toward the airport. He would have to show the rental agent what happened, but he didn't care. The car had been charged to the FaithAmerica account; Dunbar could get it fixed. After all, what's a busted bumper when you were out to rearrange the entire United States?

CHAPTER 6

"Good morning and Merry Christmas, Atlanta! We're gonna start off this hour with a real blast from the past, Roy Orbison and 'Sweet Dream Baby'!"

Mary smiled at the disk jockey's choice of tunes. According to her mother, "Dream Baby" was the first song her father ever sang to her. "He just got out his guitar," Martha had told her daughter one evening long ago. "And suddenly Roy was right there in the store. Singing 'Dream Baby,' just to me."

"Could he really play the guitar?" Mary had asked, impressed that anyone related to her could play anything beyond the radio.

"Oh, yes." Martha smiled. "He was wonderful. He could play the Beatles, Jimi Hendrix. Everybody."

Mary listened until Roy finished, then she

switched off the radio. On workdays, the oldies station helped her wake up as she inched along in her tedious, bumper-to-bumper commute. But today, this early on Christmas Eve, the streets were empty. Downtown Atlanta looked like a ghost town.

Impatiently, she drummed her fingers on the steering wheel as two joggers wearing red elf hats loped across the street in front of her. *Seven days.* Surely she could talk Irene into being guarded by the FBI for that long. *Irene.* Where would she be without Irene, the infinitely kind, wise woman who'd taken Mary home with her the afternoon they'd loaded her mother up in the back of an ambulance, a black body bag zipped over her head. She'd taken her to Upsy Daisy and fed her soup with crusty bread. Then Irene had made a pallet on the leather couch in front of the big kitchen fireplace and held her while she'd cried from a well of tears that seemingly had no end. Two years later, when every picture Mary had painted in her art classes gave her nightmares, Irene had driven down to Emory and taken her to lunch, suggesting that perhaps art was not the course of study she should follow. *Why not try the law?* she'd said that day, gently squeezing Mary's arm. *Let the seeking of justice retool the workings of your heart.*

"That's exactly what I'm trying to do," Mary murmured, trying to shake away the image of Rosemary Klinefelter holding her own head.

She turned her car into the courthouse parking lot, coming to a stop in space number twenty-nine. The lot was empty, except for a black Dodge pickup with a camper top, around which paced Agent Daniel Safer. Though he'd changed from his sleek Italian suit into worn jeans and a red flannel shirt, she could tell by the urgency of his stride that Safer was a city boy; concrete probably did feel better under his feet. She waved at him as she parked her car. He glared back.

"Well, screw you," Mary said as she shoved her car into park. Angrily she grabbed her backpack and walked toward the truck. If this Agent Safer was going to pout about being saddled with a "female civilian" all the way to Hartsville, North Carolina, she would just drive up there by herself.

"Morning," she called, her footsteps brisk on the damp pavement.

"Morning." Safer took her measure with his dark eyes, which were just as intense as they had been yesterday. "Glad to see you're on time."

"Actually, I'm fifteen minutes early." Mary dropped her backpack an inch away from Safer's toe.

He glanced at his watch. "So you are." He looked at her single small bag. "What are you taking with you?"

"A sketch pad. A paperback. A Christmas present for Irene."

"Didn't forget your gun, did you?"

Glaring at him, Mary allowed her down jacket to flop open. His eyes made a brief appraisal of her breasts before they noted the Beretta nestled in her shoulder holster. "Good," he said. "Let's get going."

He opened the back of the truck. Mary shoved her pack in beside Safer's black briefcase, a battered camera bag, and two impressive-looking tripods.

"You a photographer?" She couldn't imagine Safer needing a camera to snap anything. His eyes alone seemed to etch everything permanently on his brain.

"No." He moved the tripods to one side. "These make a good cover up there."

"So what's the plan?" she asked, stepping back as he slammed the tailgate shut.

"I'll drive you to Judge Hannah's farm. If you can talk her into accepting our protection, I'll work as a liaison between her and the rest of the team."

"And if I can't talk her into it?"

"Then we'll do the best we can by ourselves.

Either way, we'll fly you back here." He gave her a tight smile. "You'll be home in time for Christmas."

Mary buckled herself into the front seat. Safer kept a cell phone on the console, nestled beside a paperback *Guide to the Eastern Night Sky*. A glow-in-the-dark bookmark in the shape of an alien protruded from the pages of the book. Mary repressed a groan. Surely this guy wasn't of the Mulder and Scully persuasion.

"You into spacemen?" Mary gave Safer a dubious eye as he jammed his key into the ignition.

"No." He looked at her challengingly, not embarrassed to be caught with a luminous alien bookmark. "I like astronomy. My daughter gave me that bookmark."

"Oh." For some reason, Mary could peg Safer as an obsessed astronomer far more readily than a contented family man. "You have children?"

"Just one daughter." He adjusted the rearview mirror. "Leah. She's four. She lives with her mother in Montreal."

"That's pretty far away."

"Yep." He put the truck into gear. "My ex-wife made sure of that."

Mary heard the acid in Safer's voice. The rest of the story was so common, she knew it without asking—a woman marries a cop, then she grows tired of the hours and the brutality and the alcoholism or any of the other thousand things that eat cops alive. So she leaves, and puts as much distance between them as she can. It was sad, but it was a fact of life, and everybody who went into law enforcement ought to be forewarned—*abandon normalcy, all ye who enter here.* Quickly she changed the subject.

"Do you know the way to Hartsville?"

"Like the back of my hand," Safer replied, his dark brows drawing together so sternly that he reminded her of a Byzantine icon she'd seen once at the High Museum. "I've put in some hours up here before."

"Work the Eric Rudolph case?" The man who'd five years ago allegedly bombed a gay nightclub in Atlanta and a Planned Parenthood clinic in Birmingham had been spotted in the southern Appalachians. Battalions of federal agents had given furious chase, but ultimately came up empty-handed and humiliated.

Safer nodded.

"Too bad you couldn't catch him. He would have landed on my docket."

Safer shrugged as they pulled out of the parking lot. "A couple of times we were five minutes behind him. Then the mountains just swallowed him up."

She thought of her own mother's murder,

years before. That killer had vanished into the mountains just like Rudolph. "Yeah," she agreed quietly. "The mountains can do that."

They drove north in silence. Even though traffic was light, Safer tailgated the cars ahead of them as if they were intentionally impeding his progress to North Carolina. Mary pulled her seat belt tighter, grateful that they weren't driving in the everyday lethal, take-no-prisoners Atlanta traffic.

Before they crossed into North Carolina, they stopped at a service station to get the less expensive Georgia gas. As Safer filled up his tank, Mary went into the little convenience store and bought black coffee and two peach fried pies, hopeful that sugar and caffeine might turn him into a less dour traveling companion.

"Here." She gave him a bright smile as she set the coffee and pastries on the hood of the truck. "Have some Appalachian cop food."

He looked at her strangely, as if nobody had ever given him anything before. Opening one end of the fried pie wrapper, he scrutinized the small, oblong tart, then folded the wrapper back up and returned the pie to Mary. "Thanks. But I don't normally eat dessert for breakfast."

"Neither do I," replied Mary. "But neither do I normally pack my gun to spend Christmas Eve twisting an old friend's arm into being guarded by the FBI."

Safer just shrugged, so she ate both fried pies while he paid for the gas. By the time he'd climbed back in the truck, she'd pulled out the sketch pad she'd packed and was drawing large circles with a pastel pencil.

"You an artist?" Safer glanced at her lap.

"I'm a hobbyist," Mary replied. "My mother was an artist."

"I understand she was quite gifted."

Mary looked over at him. "How would you know?"

Amazingly, he blushed. Mary watched as his cheeks blossomed like crabapples above his dark beard. "They tell us these things when we enlist civilian aid," he finally stammered.

"You've read my jacket," Mary snapped, suddenly sorry that she'd bought him anything to eat. "What else do you know about me, Agent Safer?"

His look darkened. "That you're half Cherokee. That you grew up here, in the Nantahala. That your artist mother was murdered when you were eighteen," he said. "Then you went south, where your paternal grandmother enrolled you in Emory University. There you studied law and became a crackerjack DA. That you're excellent in the woods and you're like a daughter to Irene Hannah."

Mary stared at him, realizing that he must also have read that the last time she was up here she succeeded in killing one man and tried very hard to kill another. *He knows all of that,* she thought, her anger shrinking into a cold little knot of discomfort.

"You got it." At least he had the decency not to mention everything. "I'm a real whizbang in the forest."

"That's what I understand," Safer said, for once his voice soft with apology. "And that's why I'm glad you're here."

She turned back to her drawing. They rode in silence as the road curved up into foothills that were warm brown in the winter.

"So what about you?" She looked at him.

"What about me?"

"What's your story? You know an awful lot about me. Seems hardly fair for me to be riding up here with a total stranger. How long have you been with the Bureau?"

"Not that long, actually. Seven years ago I was teaching Russian at the University of Memphis." Safer smiled as if recalling a pleasant vacation.

"You speak Russian?"

He nodded. "I'm a Russian Jew. My great-grandfather emigrated from Kiev just after the First World War."

Mary blinked. No wonder the guy had the air of a Cossack. "Okay," she said. "So why did the Bureau drag you out of your classroom and give you a gun?"

"Actually, they dragged me out to transcribe some wiretaps. The Russian Mafia was infiltrating businesses along the Mississippi River, and using a dialect from the Ukraine."

"The Russian Mafia?" Mary laughed, picturing Josef Stalin knocking back vodka on the *Robert E. Lee.*

"They are dangerous men," Safer replied without smiling. He spat out some word in Russian. "Beasts, all of them."

"So did you help the FBI crack the case?"

"I did. And by the time we'd nailed them, I was hooked. Gave the university my resignation and applied to the Bureau."

"Dr. Safer became Agent Safer. What did your family think?"

"They thought and still think I'm crazy." He chuckled. "How about you? What does your family think of your being a prosecutor?"

She remembered her grandmother's funeral, three months ago. "Actually, I don't have enough family left to think much of anything."

They rode on, passing through green pastureland grown gold, letting the Dodge's heater warm the sudden coldness that filled the truck. After a time, Safer spoke again.

"So did you give any thought to these judges last night?"

Mary tried to sort through her jumbled memories of the day before. Everything seemed chaotic—first she'd been dancing to the Strutters, then she'd raced downtown in a police car, then she'd seen the picture of that poor woman with no head. When she'd finally gotten home, she'd pulled off her silky green gown and fixed her special martini—three fingers of frozen Sapphire gin, not shaken, not stirred, not altered at all except for being sloshed in a glass. After that she remembered packing, then dozing, then waking from a terrifying dream where Irene Hannah was being loaded into a cattle truck and driven away.

"Some," she lied, quickly starting her prosecutorial wheels turning. "I wondered if there was any commonality between the victims."

Safer raised one eyebrow. "Opinion-wise, they were all middle-of-the-road jurists. Five had been appointed by Democratic presidents, six by Republicans. Most had supported fourth amendment rights and ruled against hate crimes. Klinefelter had just signed an opinion involving interstate banking."

"That's not exactly a hot-button issue." Mary frowned. "How about personal? Anybody divorced? Gay? Minority?"

"The Alabama judge was African-American. The guy in Wyoming was Latino. The rest were white. All were married to people of the opposite sex. Six were Protestant, two were Roman Catholic, the other three had no religious affiliation."

"No religious axe-grinding there," Mary said.

"How about Irene Hannah?" asked Safer.

"She's a white Democrat, sixty-two, and widowed," replied Mary. "I don't know her judicial record chapter and verse, but politically she's pro-choice, anti–hate crime, and thinks DUI ought to be a capital offense."

"I read that she spent a lot of time in Japan," said Safer.

Mary nodded. "After the war. Her father was in the diplomatic corps. She's fluent in Japanese, speaks good Cherokee, and doesn't suffer fools lightly."

"Well." Safer gave an ironic smile as he zoomed past a Greyhound bus. "Then I'm doubly glad you're here."

★   ★   ★

They drove on, considering the possible connections between the eleven dead judges. As the highway began to twist through the old familiar territory of the mountains, Mary started sketching again. In the winter, the fiery red and orange leaves of autumn were gone, replaced by skeletal maple and oak branches that waved thin fingers at a stark gray sky. The mountains themselves stood like sheep after a shearing. The great humps of iron-brown earth looked strangely humbled, shrouded with fog at the lower elevations, dusted with snow at their peaks. *How different it is this time,* she thought, abruptly remembering Jonathan's hands and mouth and eyes so fiercely that the breath seemed to catch in her throat. *How very different from before.*

She looked up from her sketch pad.

"Would you turn there?" She pointed at a road that veered off into the mountains to the west. "There's a little store I'd like to visit before we go to Irene's."

Safer frowned. "We don't have a lot of time—"

"I won't be long," Mary promised. "I just want to stop in and see if an old friend of mine is there. He hunts a lot. He might know if anything weird's going on up here."

"Old boyfriend?" Safer looked at her with a sly smile.

Mary thought of Jonathan, how they'd re-

united after so many years, only to find themselves different, changed. They'd tried to make it
work—for six months he'd lived with her in
Atlanta. She'd been happy, but he'd always felt
edgy in the city, looking beyond the high-rises
into a horizon that held something only he could
see. Finally she'd come home one night to find
him gone, and a note that said, "I love you, Mary,
but I can't live here anymore. Come home when
you're ready. I'll be waiting."

"Not a boyfriend," Mary shot back. "Just
someone I used to know."

Safer turned the wheel, and they twisted
around the base of a mountain, following the
curve of a river that spewed white foam over
rocks the size of small cars. When Mary began
to feel nauseous from all the twisting turns, the
Little Jump Off store came into view. It looked
as it always had, an ancient, ramshackle log
cabin that sold everything from slop jars to zip
drives.

"Turn here," Mary said, searching the porch
for the long lengths of wood that would indicate
the presence of a bowyer. Strangely, they were
gone. In their place stood a towering collection
of cardboard boxes.

Safer pulled the truck into the parking lot.
"We haven't got much time, so no tearful re-
unions, okay?"

Mary jerked open the door without replying. She had intended to ask Safer inside, but now he could sit in the Dodge and rot, for all she cared. What an asshole this man was. She leaned in the window. "Stay out here and go over your evidence files, Agent Safer. I might be a while."

"Five minutes, Ms. Crow," Safer replied. "We've got a lot of ground to cover today. This isn't old home week."

CHAPTER 7

Up yours, Mary fumed. Though she wanted to storm away from Safer and his stupid truck, she walked calmly up the steps to Little Jump Off. Her years in the courtroom had taught her the value of a poker face; she was not going to allow Agent Safer to know that he'd rattled her. God, what a jerk. How glad she would be when she could hand him over to Irene.

She paused when she reached the top of the steps. Although an angular pile of computer boxes had replaced Jonathan's usual stock of hickory, the old porch otherwise looked the same. In the thirteen years since her mother's death, she had not trod upon it without a shudder. Whoever had murdered her mother had escaped along these old heart-of-pine boards, and the sound of those footsteps still echoed in her heart. Even now it was difficult to think about, and she crossed the planks quickly, with downcast eyes, hurriedly pulling open the door.

She sensed something different the instant she stepped inside. Although the old stone fireplace was bedecked with blinking lights, and Little Jump Off's traditional cedar Christmas tree listed in one corner, something beyond the holiday trappings was different. The air smelled charged—tinged with a sweet, dry aroma that reminded her of Alex's home in Texas.

"Can I help you?" A soft, female voice floated across the store.

Startled, Mary turned. Behind the counter stood a woman who looked surprisingly like—her. Dressed in a faded denim shirt and jeans, she had blunt-cut dark hair, high cheekbones, and cinnamon skin. She looked about thirty and wore the trappings of the West—turquoise studs in her ears, a silver ring on her right finger, long agate beads dangling between ample breasts. Her dark eyes sparkled with intelligence and curiosity. For a moment, Mary didn't know what to say.

"Uh, does Jonathan Walkingstick still work here?" She felt as if she had blundered into the middle of a play with no idea of her lines.

The woman studied Mary, then broke into a broad smile. "You're Mary Crow, aren't you?"

Mary nodded, puzzled. "Do we know each other?"

"No." The woman shook her head. "I'm Ruth Moon, from Tahlequah, Oklahoma." She stepped from behind the counter and stuck out her hand. "Jonathan has told me all about you, Mary."

"He has?" Mary grasped the woman's hand. It was strong, like a tough little prairie bird. "Is he here?"

"He drove over to Cherokee," Ruth Moon explained. "He volunteered to deliver some computers for me, just in time for Christmas."

"Computers?" Mary felt like some idiotic parrot, repeating whatever came out of this Ruth Moon's mouth.

Ruth nodded. "Two," she said proudly. "One for the library, another for the day care center at the Methodist Church."

Mary was speechless. When she last saw Jonathan, he'd just carved an inlaid bow of hickory and poplar for a turkey hunter in New Hampshire. Now he was delivering computers to the children of the Quallah Boundary?

"I guess you two haven't talked in a while, huh?" Ruth Moon called over her shoulder as she turned and walked back behind the counter.

"No." The last night she and Jonathan talked

was the last night they'd made love, moving together fluidly as silk, fitting each other like fingers slipping into soft kid gloves.

"We came back here four months ago, from
Oklahoma. We met out there—I'm a Legend
Teller and had been planning to come east to
collect some more stories, so I asked him if I
could tag along."

Mary tried to clear the sudden frog in her
throat. "And Jonathan said yes?"

Ruth nodded. "He's helped me gather half a
dozen more stories, I helped him reorganize his
bookkeeping. We do the computers together."

Immediately Mary caught the *we:* apparently
Jonathan and this Ruth Moon came as a set.
Again, all she could do was parrot Ruth Moon's
last phrase. "The computers?"

"We refurbish old ones. You'd be amazed at
how many businesses just throw them in the
garbage. I clean them up, put in bigger hard
drives, faster modems. Jonathan picks them up
and delivers them."

"To whom?"

"Mostly to Cherokee families. Native Americans have been grossly underserved by the computer revolution." Ruth hopped up on the stool
behind the old cash register. For the first time
Mary noticed that on the wall, taking the place
of Jonathan's *Farmer's Almanac* calendar, hung an

enormous poster of the U.S. Capitol made up of white, black, and brown dots. The caption beneath read *"When Will Congress See Red?"*

Ruth Moon smiled as Mary tried to decipher the poster. "You haven't heard of REPIC, have you?"

Before she could answer, Ruth handed her a brochure. Printed on bright yellow paper, it cited statistics about the demographic makeup of Congress, then asked the blunt question, "Why are WE not represented in Washington?"

The brochure went on to describe REPIC, a grassroots movement started by several Spokane Indians living in Seattle. REPIC wanted to amend the Constitution, giving each of the identified tribes in the United States a seat in the House of Representatives. According to the pamphlet, the idea had spread like wildfire, consuming Cherokees in Oklahoma, Seminoles in Florida, Iroquois in upstate New York.

Mary looked up at Ruth Moon, wanting to laugh and cry at the same time. Did these Indians not know how the government worked? Rich people sent other rich people to Congress to protect their interests, and everybody else— black, white, yellow or red—could go to hell. She handed the brochure back to Ruth.

"Is Jonathan working for REPIC?" she asked, unable to imagine her tall ex-lover jousting at this kind of windmill. Acid rain, perhaps, or too much CO_2 in the air, but not Indians in Congress. It sounded like something from her mother's generation, a hopeless cause espoused by hippies unaware of the political realities of life.

"Not really. He's just letting me use the store as my home base. The Cherokee REPICs in Oklahoma are hoping I can enroll a lot of our Eastern brothers and sisters." She picked up a mayonnaise jar. "Would you like to sign a list and make a donation?"

"I'll make a donation," Mary replied. "But I'd prefer not to sign anything."

"So what brings you up here on Christmas Eve?" Ruth Moon smiled. Her teeth were so straight, Mary wondered if she'd grown up with braces. "Visiting someone for the holidays?"

"Actually, I'm visiting a friend."

"Anybody we know?"

Something about this woman confused Mary, kept her off balance. How could Ruth Moon know the same people Mary knew? She'd only lived here four months. How could she get Jonathan to go out and deliver computers? Mary had practically had to wage war to get him to put on a tie. She dug through her wallet, pulling out old grocery receipts and ATM slips. Finally she extracted a ten-dollar bill and stuffed it in the jar.

"No," she answered Ruth's question slowly. "I don't think you'd know them." She glanced once at the front corner of the store, where she'd found her mother on the floor, strangled to death.

"I know about your mother." Ruth lowered her voice respectfully. "And I'm awfully sorry. It must have been terrible to lose someone like that."

"Yes." Mary's face grew clammy and hot. Had Jonathan told this woman everything about her? Everything about them? "It was."

She dropped her wallet back in her purse. Ruth Moon looked at her from behind the counter, as if waiting to see what she might do next.

"Well," Mary said. "If Jonathan's gone to Cherokee, I guess I'll be going."

Ruth smiled. "I'll tell him you came by. He'll be disappointed he missed you, but I'm so glad to have gotten to meet you. He talks about you all the time. Any message you want me to give him?"

Mary met Ruth Moon's gaze with a look of her own. "Tell him I said hello."

"Are you sure I can't talk you into joining us?"

Ruth again held out her REPIC brochure. "We could use someone like you, someone who really knows the system from the inside."

Mary tried to focus on the brochure. From what she'd seen of the federal government, she wanted as little to do with it as possible. "The system I know is judicial, at the local level. What you're seeking to change is the legislative branch, at the national level. It's like apples and oranges."

"But you're used to dealing with white people," Ruth Moon said excitedly. "You know how they think. You'd be such an asset."

"I'm used to prosecuting criminals," Mary replied. "And they think pretty much alike, whatever color their skin."

"But . . ."

For a *Tsalagi* woman, this Ruth Moon was insistent to the point of rudeness.

"You have a happy holiday." Mary smiled wistfully at the Christmas tree, strung with popcorn and cranberries, a few brightly wrapped packages peeking from underneath the branches.

"You, too," said Ruth, at last giving up on enrolling Mary in REPIC. "If you're here for a few days, come and have dinner with us some night. I know Jonathan would love to see you again."

"Thanks," said Mary. With a single final glance at the front corner of the store, she walked out the door and back to the truck, hoping with all her heart that Safer was reading his damn evidence files and not seeing the sorrow that was etched across her face.

CHAPTER 8

Sergeant Wurth frowned as he twisted in his seat, trying to get comfortable. Where ten years ago Richard Dunbar had treated him to his one-and-only first-class ticket, today he was stuffed in between a tiny window and an overweight woman who had dark sweat rings beneath the armpits of her Christmas red blazer. A bald-headed man reclined in front of him while to the rear, a tow-headed brat kicked his seat, whining to his apparently deaf mother about wanting a cherry Coke. Though the plane was crammed with cranky passengers, he had not seen a flight attendant since they left San Francisco.

Disgusted, he turned to the window. From thirty thousand feet, the mountains and ridges of Nevada looked like ironed-in wrinkles in a buff-colored quilt. Somewhere down there Las Vegas glittered like a jewel in the desert; somewhere else the Hoover Dam provided the power to make her slot machines jingle. Wurth could not see either from up here. All he saw was a crackled, sun-baked expanse of brown rock that might as well have been Mars.

As he stared out the window with a headache stabbing into his left temple, he considered his fourteen-year association with FaithAmerica. Much to his surprise, Dunbar had made good on his promises. Though he'd easily held up his end of the deal—training the boys they sent him and eliminating the soft, unwary incumbents Dunbar wanted out—what had amazed him was the way FaithAmerica had grown as a political player. Never had the FaithAmericans wobbled in their conviction that Gerald LeClaire was the one man who could lead America back into the ways of the righteous. Touchingly loyal, they toiled like ants building a grassroots organization for LeClaire. At last count, FaithAmerica numbered two governors, eleven congressmen, and one senator among its faithful. Not bad for Dunbar, a man who had once made his living selling twenty-second spots on an all-talk radio station.

Though Dunbar had been tempted to push LeClaire forward in 2000, he held back, sensing, somehow, that the momentum was not yet there. "Our people are all in place, but we need something to really set us off!" Dunbar had railed at him during one of his rare visits to the camp. "Some huge, irrefutable sign from God."

Six weeks later, it came. Wurth opened a letter sent to every FaithAmerica patriot from Gerald LeClaire himself. It delineated his hopes and wishes for "his new America" and ended with his false Solomons dream. Though LeClaire had signed the letter, Wurth knew it was Dunbar's handiwork. This Solomon shit was the huge and irrefutable sign he'd been searching for. Wurth just wondered who the twelve Solomons were.

The next day he found out. He was called to a secret meeting in St. Louis, where Dunbar told him that federal judges would serve as the false Solomons, and had given him a list of every judge in each of America's twelve federal districts. His only instructions to Wurth were to make the eliminations look accidental and execute them one per month in no discernible geographic pattern. Beyond that, it was Wurth's choice. By December 31, the twelve Solomons would need to have all passed away. Then Dunbar could present evidence of the fulfilled prophecy in Miami and the awed believers would sweep Gerald LeClaire into the highest office in the land.

Now, Wurth thought, everything depends on me. If he didn't eliminate this last judge in the next week, the twelve false Solomons would become just another entry in the great book of prophecies that had come to naught, and the folks who were now convinced that LeClaire was God's own chosen might reconsider. He squinted down at a particularly dismal-looking part of Nevada and again thought of David Forrester. Right now he didn't care if Gerald LeClaire got elected dogcatcher. Right now he just wanted to teach Richard Dunbar that he couldn't butcher his boys when they made a mistake. Particularly not his boys who'd become Feather Men. They were simply too precious a commodity.

The kid behind him kicked his seat again, jolting the migraine knife deeper into his temple. He could, he supposed, go back to his camp, pack his gear, and just forget about the twelfth judge. That would leave Dunbar with an unfulfilled prophecy and a fair amount of egg on his face. But that would demean him more than Dunbar. His honor as a soldier was in question here. Never once had he failed to carry out an order. He would do the twelfth judge as planned. Then he would take the black briefcase that held all his numbered bank accounts and quietly slip away. He would be a dead man then, anyway. Feather Men were always expendable when their usefulness was over.

He plugged in his earphones. Bouncy Christmas music assaulted his eardrums as he gazed out the window again. As the plane's wing sliced through a wispy cloud bank he saw Dunbar's picture of headless Judge Klinefelter and felt a warm glow of pride. Even though David had gone overboard in his killing of the judge, he'd done it perfectly. One clean, beautiful blow between the fifth and sixth vertebrae. The woman probably hadn't felt a thing.

The brat behind him started another tap dance on the back of his seat, sending tendrils of pain deeper into his brain. He squeezed his eyes shut, mentally raising the great *hara zukuri*. He would grasp the great sword with both hands, steady himself, then choose his spot. When the tip of the blade hung like a raindrop, he would swing. With a silent chuckle he pictured himself rising from the airplane seat, turning, and with a single fluid motion lopping off that whiny brat's head. His little noggin would hit the floor with a thud, but after that, there would be blessed silence. The kid's kicking would cease. His incessant mewling for a cherry Coke would stop. His mother probably wouldn't even look up from her magazine.

Wurth opened his eyes to find his sweaty seat-mate staring at him, her bright red bosom heaving. With a contrite smile, he removed his earphones and looked out the window, refocusing on the matter at hand.

He would, of course, do the last judge as David should have done the other woman. Quietly, with stealth. To accomplish that within the next week, he would have to work fast.

He would start as soon as he got back to camp. Then, after he had taken care of this last judge, he would turn his attention to Dunbar.

"Sir?"

Someone touched his arm. He looked over. A harried blonde flight attendant was pushing a cart of drinks. "Would you like Coke, Sprite, or mineral water?"

"Coke," he replied, wishing she were peddling aspirin or Percodan. That would make his headache go away.

"Peanuts, pretzels, or trail mix?"

"Peanuts."

The flight attendant poured him a small plastic glassful of Coke, tossed him a minuscule bag of nuts, then moved back toward the brat.

"It isn't like the old days, when you used to get real food, is it?" asked his seatmate, tearing open her bag of trail mix with her teeth.

"No," he said, suddenly feeling nauseous as the woman poured an array of M&M's, nuts, and Rice Chex into her sweaty-looking palm. He sipped his Coke as the plane adjusted its course for Dallas–Fort Worth. "But when you think about it, not much is."

CHAPTER 9

Mary yanked open the truck's door and sat down hard in the front seat. Safer must have eaten a mint, for the cab smelled vaguely of wintergreen. She squeezed her eyes shut and breathed deeply, thinking how much better even a lousy Life Saver smelled than the western sage aroma with which Ruth Moon had perfumed Little Jump Off.

"What'd you find out?" Safer asked.

"Nothing," Mary lied. "My friend wasn't there. I had a chat with his girlfriend."

"You didn't tell her where you were going, did you?"

"I told her I was visiting an old friend," said Mary, turning her face away as he started the Dodge. "I didn't tell her who."

Whatever else Daniel Safer had learned in his months of searching for Eric Rudolph, he had gotten to know the roads of Pisgah County well. Without asking Mary for directions, he pointed the truck toward Hartsville and navigated the curving mountain roads like a native. As he drove she stared out the window, replaying her conversation with Ruth Moon. That Jonathan would find another woman, she could understand. But why some New Age activist? Jonathan was the most apolitical person Mary knew. What did he see in a Legend Teller whose burning desire was to send Indians to Congress?

"Do you speak Cherokee?"

"Hunh?" Safer's question pierced her gray cloud of doom.

"I said, do you speak Cherokee?"

She sighed. It was among the standard set of queries everyone asked when they found out her heritage—did she speak Cherokee, did she know lots of wood lore, had she lived in a teepee.

"I know enough to chitchat. I couldn't discuss economic theory or cancer research."

Safer snorted. "Could you do that in English?"

She raised one eyebrow. "Depends on who I'm talking with."

"Oh." Safer coughed. "I guess it would."

Smiling at his discomfort, she changed the subject, resisting the urge to phrase her next question in Cherokee. "So who do you think might be killing these judges?"

"Well, decapitation is an unusual MO, which indicates an individual, perhaps one with a Middle Eastern background."

"You're thinking maybe a terrorist?"

"Possibly. Several Islamic countries have been known to administer justice in this fashion. What I can't figure out is why they would so carefully assassinate the first ten and then whack off the eleventh one's head. Like I told your boss, decapitation gets everyone's attention."

"Maybe somebody screwed up. If he'd already injected her with poison, maybe he just got cocky and decided to go for a big finish."

"But why the eleventh judge? You'd save your big finish for the last—particularly if you wanted to send some kind of message."

Mary clutched the armrest as Safer careened down the twisting road. "Who's on your short list of suspects?"

"Given the random order of the murders and the physical distance between them, the Bureau likes a conspiracy better than a single individual with a hard-on for federal judges. The State Department's already got the willies about it being some international Islamic fundamentalist faction."

"Okay. What domestic groups make the chart?"

Safer shrugged. "Take your pick. It could be anybody from pro-lifers to pro-choicers to people who are still pissed about Ruby Ridge. Everybody in America's got some kind of grudge against the judiciary."

She gave a grim smile as a bright red cardinal flitted through green pines. "It's just a big bad country out there, isn't it?"

"That it is, Ms. Crow," he replied, shifting the truck into fourth gear. "That it is."

They drove on, finally twisting down into the little town of Hartsville. When Mary had left thirteen years earlier, everyone had been atwitter about McDonald's coming to town. Now Hartsvillians could choose between Taco Bell, BoJangle's Chicken, Arby's, and the Pizza Hut. As they stopped at the first of the town's three tinsel-laced traffic signals, the sun broke through the clouds, bathing the street in soft gold light. Like Atlanta, the little town looked both festive and deserted at the same time. Most mountain people spent this day at home, either cooking monumental Christmas dinners or wrapping packages for relatives who would show up on their doorstep, ruddy-faced with egg nog and good cheer. The usual group of curmudgeons, however, were still gathered in front of Comer's

Drugstore, where old Doc Comer provided them with free coffee and enough rocking chairs so they could play their banjos and gossip. Mary smiled as she watched the old men frailing away, playing the tunes their ancestors had brought from Scotland two centuries ago. Hartsville's fast-food options may have expanded, but Christmas Eve still looked exactly as it had when she was five.

Her smile faded, however, as Safer drove through the intersection, then nosed the big Dodge into a parking space in front of the sheriff's office.

"Why are we stopping here?" she asked, opening her door to a tinny version of "Silent Night" that issued from a speaker above the sheriff's office door. "Don't we need to get on to Irene's?"

"We do. But we're checking in with the sheriff first."

"But . . ."

"Let's just say the Rudolph case taught us a lot about the way things work up here." Safer's voice took on a Southern edge. "These good ol' mountain boys don't take kindly to Yankee G-men sniffing around their territory."

Though Safer's drawl was laughable, Mary had to admit he'd gotten the accent perfectly. She almost expected to see a brown bullet of tobacco juice come flying from his mouth as she followed him into the sheriff's office.

The jail had been built around the turn of the century. High-ceilinged with thick stone walls, it was tiny by Atlanta standards, heated by a woodstove that burned short lengths of hard seasoned oak. Although much of the building looked so old as to be picturesque, an elaborate communications center spread over one corner, a significant arsenal of rifles stood locked in a case along one wall, and the cells themselves looked every bit as substantial as any she'd seen on the tenth floor of the Deckard County Courthouse. As quaint as Hartsville law might look, it obviously still meant business.

A waist-high railing separated the small waiting area of the jail from the office part, where half a dozen desks stood in two rows. A female dispatcher sat at one of them, staring at a television tuned to the FaithAmerica Christmas extravaganza. The woman turned when Mary and Safer walked in.

"Merry Christmas," she called, a sequined holly wreath pin sparkling above her badge. "Can I help you?"

"Sheriff Logan, please," said Safer.

"Is it an emergency?" The woman's voice rose in concern.

"It's official." Safer flashed his badge to let the woman know he wasn't kidding. Leaving her television, she got up and hurried over to a door in the corner. "Just a minute," she called over her shoulder. "I'll tell him you're here."

Mary and Safer waited while a huge Faith-America choir sang an upbeat rendition of "Joy to the World." Moments later the dispatcher reopened the door. Behind the desk in the room beyond sat a man Mary recognized immediately. Except for a slightly pudgier jaw and a good bit less hair, he had not changed since the day she'd first met him, that April afternoon in 1988, when her mother lay dead at her feet. He wore the same khaki uniform with the same gold badge pinned to the left breast pocket. In his other pocket he would have chewing tobacco and a small spiral notebook. Though his trademark white cowboy hat sat on the credenza behind him, she knew that if he stood up she would see tooled leather cowboy boots on his feet and a .357 just beneath his right arm. Stump Logan had always been a curious combination of Roy Rogers and Dirty Harry.

"Mary Crow?" He called, squinting at her. "Is that you?"

"Hi, Sheriff Logan." Stepping ahead of Safer, she pushed through the little gate in the railing and entered Logan's office. The sheriff grinned broadly, as if she were some local hero come home.

"Mary Crow! I can't believe you're here. We haven't seen you in a coon's age." He stood and pumped her hand heartily, his paw engulfing hers like a catcher's mitt.

"No, I guess you haven't." Not since I brought Alex and Joan camping, Mary thought, hoping Stump would not choose to stroll down that particular block of memory lane.

"Are you spending Christmas with Walking-stick?" Logan widened his smile and winked conspiratorially.

"Why don't I let him explain." Mary turned to Safer, who stood behind her. "You want to tell the sheriff why we're here?"

Safer shot her a dark look, but again pulled out his ID. "I'm Agent Daniel Safer," he said as Logan scanned his badge.

"Have a seat." Logan motioned to the chairs stationed at the corners of his desk. "Make yourself at home."

As Mary sat down, she practiced an old trick Jim Falkner had taught her. She pulled her chair closer to the desk and studied the photographs on Logan's credenza. She saw a sweet-looking woman she decided was his wife, three blond little boys who looked like grandchildren, and an older, black-and-white photograph of a teenaged Logan dressed in a Hartsville Rebels football uniform. The wall behind the desk was decorated with plaques from the Lions Club, twenty years of citations from the Department of Human Services, and an old photo of four rail-thin young men in jungle fatigues, grinning amiably with a long rock python draped over their shoulders. She knew immediately that Logan was a family man, a veteran, and had carved himself a niche in his community. Once again Jim's theory had held true—people revealed themselves best by the images they treasured.

"FBI, huh?" Logan raised his eyebrows at Mary, as he closed the door and sat behind his desk. "You working for the Feds now?"

"No, I'm just along for the ride." She looked over at Safer, cuing him into explaining their mission.

"Sheriff, we have an unusual situation on our hands. We suspect that federal judge Irene Hannah could be the target of an assassination plot. Ms. Crow is assisting me in trying to protect her."

"Judge Irene Hannah?" Logan's slate-gray eyes narrowed. "Here in Pisgah County?"

"Either here or at her home in Richmond," replied Safer.

"Could I ask what kind of plot you suspect?" Logan lowered his voice.

"We're not sure. We're guessing either an individual or a fringe political group acting against the judiciary."

Logan whistled through his lower teeth. "I'll be damned."

Safer pressed on. "Have you heard of any outsider groups around here who might have a grudge against federal judges?"

Logan pulled his long left earlobe and scowled at the calendar on his desk. "Let's see. Midget Smith still flies the Confederate flag every Sunday. And two years ago somebody burned a cross in front of Rafe Gardner's tobacco barn, but it was Halloween night and the boys that did it were dressed up like vampires." He frowned a moment longer, then shook his head. "That's honestly all I can come up with. People aren't much concerned with federal judges up here. Asheville's where all the political activists live."

"I see." Safer's smile was tight. "Well, before we met with Judge Hannah I wanted to check in with you and let you know that we'll be maintaining a presence in Pisgah County until Judge Hannah returns to Richmond." He pulled a business card from his wallet. "If you happen to think of anybody who might be hostile

toward either Judge Hannah or the federal government, could you give me a call at that
number?"

"Absolutely," Logan said. "Are you gonna
need any backup from me? We aren't as fancy as
you Feds, but I've got three deputies who are
dead-on with a varmint gun."

"I might take you up on that, Sheriff," said
Safer grimly. "I'll know more after we talk to
Judge Hannah."

Logan leaned back, squeaking his chair. "I
don't mean to tell you your business, son, but
did you happen to work the Eric Rudolph case
up here?"

Safer nodded. "I did."

"You know I think you boys made a big mistake by runnin' after that turkey. You coulda
caught him easy if you'd just set a trap and laid
low." Logan winked at Mary. "Don't you think
it's amazin' what can wind up in a trap if you
just set it in the right place?"

"I'm amazed by that every day, Sheriff."

Safer smiled. "That's good advice, Sheriff. I'll
keep it in mind."

"Well, it's good to see the both of you," Sheriff
Logan said as they both stood to leave. "Mary,
you've turned out to be as pretty as your mama.
I'm glad to see you brought a man up here with
you this time."

Mary tried not to laugh. "Oh, I always try to be prepared, Sheriff."

"That's good." Logan nodded vigorously. " 'Specially up in this neck of the woods. And I'll be waiting to hear from you, son," he added to Safer. "You can count on me, twenty-four seven."

Safer nodded. "Thanks, Sheriff. It's good to know the local law's behind you."

★   ★   ★

They drove on, heading northwest out of Hartsville. A few miles down the road Safer pulled something from his shirt pocket. "Here's that cell phone I told you about. If you key in your mother's birthday, you'll get me."

"My mother's birthday?" Mary frowned. "June eighteenth, 1948?"

"Oh-six, oh-one-eight, forty-eight. It's a number we figured you'd never forget."

Mary shrugged. He was right about that. "And I'm to call you when?"

"When you talk the judge into letting us on her property." Safer looked at her. "Or when she gives you a final and definitive no."

As they sped deeper into the mountains, rural mailboxes decorated with bright red bows dotted the side of the road, far from the homes for which they collected mail. Finally, as the road forked at the bottom of a creek bed, Safer pulled off the asphalt and stopped.

"Okay," he said. "Here we are."

"Can't you turn up the driveway?" Mary peered up into the trees. The only thing that revealed the location of Upsy Daisy Farm was a small mailbox that had been nailed to a fence post.

"One of Judge Hannah's cronies on the bench issued an order. We've been forbidden access to her property."

"I see." They both got out of the truck. Mary watched as Safer pulled out her backpack, feeling as if she were some homely blind date being dumped early back at home.

"I wish I could take you to the front door," he said as he plunked the little bag at her feet. "But we have to obey the law, too."

"Don't worry about it." Mary shouldered her belongings. "The walk will do me good."

"Stay in touch!" Safer called sternly. "You've got your cell phone . . ."

"Right." Mary watched as Safer got back into the truck, then she started up the drive, wondering what Irene would say when she found out what Santa Claus had in store for her this year.

CHAPTER 10

The remnants of a light snow still dusted Irene Hannah's farm. Though most of it had melted, some lay thick along the edge of the slick clay driveway, making the footing treacherous. Mary slipped and slid up the drive, alternately crunching through the icy snow or sliding along the slimy clay soil. With her backpack on her shoulder, she clambered between two rolling pastures of vibrant orange grass. Unlike most mountain farms, Irene's land lay soft, her acres rolling out almost flat in a little cove tucked between two ridges.

Mary remembered the day she and her mother first visited Upsy Daisy. Irene had been riding in her front fields and had galloped up to the driveway to greet them.

"Hi, Mary!" she'd called, grinning down into the car. "You ever ride a horse before?"

"No," Mary answered, embarrassed. She and her mother lived in the woods. She'd never even seen a real horse before.

Irene laughed. "Want to learn how?"

Mary glanced at her mother for permission, then nodded.

"Come on, then," said Irene. "I'll make you a deal. I'll teach you how to ride if you'll teach me how to speak Cherokee."

"Okay." Mary got out of the car. Irene told her to stand on the hood and she'd pick her up. Mary climbed up on the fender and in an instant Irene had pulled her up on the back of the horse. "Are you okay?" Irene asked as Mary clung to her, terrified to be sitting on such a powerful animal so high off the ground.

"I think so."

"Good. We'll go slow this time. But pretty soon, I bet you'll be beating me out to the mailbox."

And so Mary had, over that and succeeding summers, learned to ride as Irene had learned *Kituwah*. Now she smiled as she saw two of the small, elegant Appalachian Single Foot horses nuzzling in the tall grass, looking for the tender buds of clover that lurked close to the ground. What fun she and Irene and her mother had that day. How she treasured the memory of that afternoon!

She trudged on. The driveway ended at a narrow suspension bridge that spanned a broad, shallow creek. Across the stream sat Irene's bungalow, looking like an illustration on a calendar. Cheery and well kept, it had white clapboards that sparkled in the sun while brightly colored winter pansies poked their fierce little faces up from two long boxes that edged the porch. Smoke curled from the chimney, a big wreath of holly graced the front door, and a substantial brood of small chickens scratched in the grass.

It looked just as it had when she'd come as a kid to ride; just as it had that awful afternoon when she was eighteen. In all the world it was the one single physical place she allowed herself to rely upon. Whatever might befall her beyond these thirty acres, she knew she could always walk up this drive and over this bridge and return to this safe harbor.

Mary smiled as the chill fear in her stomach that had been there since Safer entered her life warmed. By all indications, Upsy Daisy Farm looked fine. Now she had to cross the bridge and find out if Irene Hannah was equally well.

"Okay," she said aloud. "Here goes nothing." Switching her backpack to her left shoulder, she grasped the thick wire railing of the bridge and took a deep breath. She didn't mind heights, but this suspension bridge had always presented a challenge. Not only did it sway, but whenever she walked it, she started a syncopated jounce that made it increasingly hard to navigate. Unless she waded the creek, though, there was no other way to get to Irene's house. Stepping as gently as she could, Mary put one foot forward and started across. The rushing water tumbled over the creek rocks below, and chilly, coppery-smelling spray dampened the hem of her jeans. She had gotten just three steps along when the bridge began its dance. Last time she'd been here she'd figured out to step forward only on the rising motion, but after eighteen months, she was out of practice. As she walked along, the bucking grew worse, and soon she had to clutch the rail and bend her knees to keep from falling. She tried going faster, then slower, but nothing helped. The bridge rumbled on, sounding like fifty men stomping across it all at once.

The guineas, alarmed by any commotion, flapped their stubby wings and started to squawk. Holding tightly to the railing, Mary had to laugh. Between the shrieking chickens and the bouncing bridge, Irene might be better guarded than Agent Safer could have dreamed.

Finally she reached the other side of the creek, and the tumult ended. She paused, fully expecting Irene to burst out onto the porch to see who was making such a racket, but nobody beyond the guineas seemed to take note of her arrival. Walking up on the porch, she knocked once, then pressed her face to the window and looked inside. Irene's living room looked just as always. A gleaming grand piano commanded most of it, surrounded by floor-to-ceiling bookcases crammed to overflowing. The portrait of Phoebe, Irene's long-dead daughter, still hung over the fireplace, and in one corner stood a Christmas tree, covered with tiny, dazzling lights. Mary smiled. She loved this farmhouse better than her grandmother's mansion, better even than her mother's old cabin on Otter Creek. Every time she came here, she felt as if she'd come home.

She knocked again on the door, but still no one answered. She had just lifted her hand to knock a third time when a loud *hoonnkk* came from behind her.

She turned. Not a foot away from her stood a huge white goose.

"Hoonnkk!" The bird eyed Mary with a bright, malicious gaze. *"Hoonnkk!"*

"Hi, there, fella." Mary gave a nervous grin. Except for its bright orange beak and steel-blue eyes, the bird looked as if it had been carved from snow. It kept its neck stuck out and its beak parted, revealing the tiny, ratchet-like teeth. Though she had no memory of Irene ever owning anything like a goose, this creature acted as if it belonged here.

"Do you know where Irene is?" Mary adopted her grandmother Bennefield's habit of talking to who- or whatever was available. "Is she out feeding the horses?"

Though the goose kept its beady blue gaze on her, it did not move to attack. Mary decided to leave her pack on the porch and tiptoe around to the back of the house. The goose sentry notwithstanding, a silence had suddenly fallen on Upsy Daisy. Mary shivered. Surely she hadn't gotten here too late.

With the goose waddling behind her, she circled the house, hoping to see some kind of activity. A new brick patio spread out from the rear of the house; more winter pansies bloomed in flower boxes along one end. Just beneath the back door, a big German shepherd lay dozing in the sun. The dog leaped to its feet, lips curling in a growl as Mary approached, but when it caught sight of the goose, it hunkered back down and peered up meekly with worried brown eyes.

"Hi, boy," Mary said, again taken aback. When she'd been here two summers ago, Irene had nothing but her horses, the guineas, and a tiny, nearly toothless Chihuahua named Chico that someone had dumped outside her office in

Richmond. Now she had an attack goose and a German shepherd who had a full set of fangs and was ten times the size of Chico. Again it occurred to Mary that Irene might have no need of the FBI.

Moving cautiously toward the dog, she crossed the patio and peered through the glass-paned door. She could see one large room—a kitchen at one end, the other end a den dominated by a fieldstone hearth, where a small, banked fire flickered. Irene had lit a fire, Mary thought. But where had she gone? Once more she lifted her hand and was just about to knock when she became aware of motion in the room. On the floor, in front of the fireplace, two blanket-clad figures were moving close together, in tandem. The figure on top had short, steely gray hair, and was thrusting back and forth over a tangled mass of longer hair the color of a cloud. Mary's heart started to hammer as she peered hard through the thick glass, terrified she'd stumbled upon the very attack the FBI feared. Then she realized what she was seeing.

Mortified, she pivoted and turned her back instantly to the door. Judge Irene Hannah, one of the most prominent jurists in the nation, was boffing someone in front of her fireplace. No wonder the place had been quiet! She smoth-

ered the laugh that bubbled up as she wondered
what she should do next. She couldn't knock on
the door now and pretend she hadn't seen anything; neither could she just casually sit there
with the dog and the goose and wait for the
couple inside to finish. Quickly, with both animals trotting behind her, she tiptoed off the patio and back to the porch. She would pretend to
have seen nothing and just start all over again.
This time she would bang on the front door as
hard as she could. Maybe the dog would bark.
Maybe the goose would honk louder. Surely
between them and the guineas, she could rouse
someone's attention.

She sat down on the front steps. The dog and
goose watched her quizzically, as if intrigued to
see what this strange human would do next. She
waited there a few moments, giving the embarrassment time to drain from her face, then she
got up and knocked on the door again. This
time she pounded hard, like cops on a drug bust.
A cacophony erupted in the front yard. The dog
barked, the guineas shrieked, and the goose
made a noise that sounded like a broken saxo-
phone. She waited, without peeking in the windows, a full minute, then pounded again.
Suddenly the lock turned, the knob twisted, and
the door opened with a jerk. A broad-

shouldered man with tousled gray hair stood there bare-chested, red suspenders holding up a pair of canvas work pants.

"Aye?" he demanded gruffly, his blue eyes blazing.

Mary met his withering gaze evenly. "I'd like to see Judge Hannah, please."

"Is it business you've got with her on Christmas Eve?" He scowled. His speech sounded musical and strange.

"My name is Mary Crow. I'm an old friend of hers."

The man peered at her, his expression softening only slightly. "Hang on, then."

He closed the door, but did not relock it. Mary heard his footsteps echoing through the house, then in a moment, other, swifter footsteps approached.

"Mary?" This time Irene appeared, fully dressed in a white blouse and faded jeans. Her silver hair floated like an aura around her head, and she looked radiant, with high color on both cheeks, her brown eyes sparkling like sherry.

"I can't believe this!" she cried as she swung open the door, her still-rosy lips breaking into a smile. "You are the last person in the world I expected to see!"

"No kidding." Mary chuckled as she stepped into Irene's warm embrace. The women hugged for a long moment while the goose flapped around them, honking like something gone mad. Finally Irene stepped back and studied her.

"I figured you'd bug out of Atlanta for the holidays. I was picturing you sunning on some beach in the Caribbean."

"Surprise!" said Mary. "This year I decided to drop in on you."

"But how did you get here?" Irene's shrewd gaze darted to the backpack at Mary's feet, then to the goose, who stood eyeing them both. "How did you get past Lucy?"

"It wasn't easy," admitted Mary, laughing at the creature, who was now rubbing her feathered head up and down Irene's leg.

Irene held the door open wide. "This is wonderful!" She pointed to the back of the house, toward the kitchen. "You're just in time for Christmas dinner!"

"Thanks." With a final triumphant glance at Lucy, Mary picked up her pack and walked into Irene Hannah's home.

CHAPTER 11

"Don't get your hopes up, Cabe. It ain't gonna happen!"

Tommy Cabe glanced over at Willett, who stood in line next to him. Though Willett was speaking through the badly split lip that Tallent had gifted him with, his words were clear. He still did not believe that Sergeant Wurth would award Cabe a phone call for a week of no demerits.

"I'm still gonna ask," whispered Cabe.

"You'd better watch out, Tommy-boy," Willett warned. "He's been in a piss-poor mood ever since he got back from wherever he went!"

Tommy Cabe held his breath as Sergeant Wurth made his way down the inspection line. The boys stood lined up in front of the castle, the Troopers toasty warm in leather flight jackets while the Grunts shivered in whatever clothes FaithAmerica had donated. For half an hour Wurth delivered some Christmas harangue about how richly blessed they were to have a roof over their heads and food on their table. Now, with his clipboard out in front of him, he worked his way down the line, reading each boy's report.

They always held this formation on Sunday. Everyone called it "Judgment Day" because various forms of "corrections" were doled out to the boys, depending on the number and nature of demerits they'd collected during the week. The Troopers always got off light. The Grunts soon learned that their Sundays were expendable: an untucked shirttail might condemn a boy to spend a sunny afternoon in the dark library, copying Bible verses; an unmade bed could send him high up in the hills to chop kudzu. Insubordination garnered the worst correction. For that, Wurth sent them to the basement of the old castle for "Attitude Realignment." In six months, Tommy had chopped a mountain of kudzu and copied Ecclesiastes three times over, but his attitude had never once had to be realigned. He'd heard from Willett what went on down in the basement.

Today, though, was different. For the first time since he'd come here, Tommy Cabe was about to stand before Sergeant Wurth demerit-free.

He gave his shoes a final swipe against his pants legs as Wurth drew near. If David Forrester had told him the truth, Tommy would soon be talking to his grandfather. Maybe together they could figure out a way to get him out of here. Maybe they could even figure out a way to get Willett out, too.

"Mr. Cabe!"

Tommy jumped as Wurth towered in front of him. Despite all his efforts to "stand like a man," his knees began to quiver.

"Sir?"

"This says you've not had one demerit all week." From over his clipboard, Wurth eyed Tommy suspiciously. "How can that be, Mr. Cabe?"

"I j-j-just tried real hard, sir." Someone down the line snickered. Only Willett never laughed when Tommy talked.

Wurth made a mark beside his name. "Well, Mr. Cabe. That's good news. Maybe you should try-try-try real hard more often."

Tommy nodded, his cheeks on fire.

"Congratulations, son," Wurth told him. "You're finally beginning to catch on."

With a gulp, Tommy waited for Wurth to award him his phone call, but instead the sergeant moved on down the line, questioning

Willett about his split lip. Why hadn't Wurth said anything? Surely he hadn't forgotten.

"Uh, sir?" Tommy asked, sweat beginning to trickle down his armpits, despite the freezing temperature.

Wurth glared at him as the hiss of twenty-six breaths being simultaneously held rose from the line. No one had ever called Sergeant Wurth back to stand in front of them a second time. "Mr. Cabe?"

Tommy swallowed hard. "C-c-can I make my phone call now?"

"Your phone call?" Wurth frowned.

Out of the corner of his eye Tommy saw Tallent and Grice growing red-faced as they struggled to suppress their laughter.

"What phone call would that be, Cabe?"

He realized then that it had been a lie. David Forrester had been no better than the others, setting him up for the unlikely day when he stood here, demerit-free. But there was nothing he could do now. He could not call back his request for a phone call; the whole camp was waiting to hear what he was going to say. He heard Willett groan beside him.

"I thought that if you had a perfect week on Judgment Day you got to m-make a phone call, sir."

Wurth took a step back; his bulging eyes narrowed. "Just who is it that you want to call, Mr. Cabe?"

"My grandfather, sir," explained Tommy over the tittering line. "He lives in Kentucky. He doesn't know where I am."

"Is this your mother's father, Mr. Cabe?"

"Yessir." Tommy's voice cracked.

"Is this the father of the woman who's currently in jail for robbery and prostitution? The woman who spends every dime she makes on whiskey? The woman who cared so little about you that she dumped you at a skating rink so she could flee prosecution for passing bad checks?"

His cheeks blazing as more giggles broke from the line, Tommy shook his head. "It wasn't like that, sir. She didn't—"

"Yes, she did, Cabe. I've seen your mother's criminal record. This grandfather of yours raised a whore and a thief."

"He did not!" Tommy cried. "She's not like—"

Suddenly Wurth stepped forward, and pushed his face into Tommy's. "I'm not sure where you got the idea that you could make a telephone call, Cabe, but you are sadly mistaken. I am working very hard to see that you grow up to be a decent human being. To communicate with an old man who raised some whiskey-besotted sow would run exactly counter to that purpose. Do you understand, Cabe?"

Fighting hard to keep the tears from spilling down his cheeks, Tommy shook his head in protest. He moved his mouth, but his words balked, now worse than ever. "She's n-n-not—!"

"N-n-not what, Cabe?"

"N-n-not—"

"What, Cabe?"

"N-n-n—"

"He's telling you she's not like that!" came a small, angry bellow. Tommy glanced to the left. Willett stood glaring up at Wurth, his face white with rage.

A silence akin to death fell over the line of boys. No one had ever spoken in such a way to Sergeant Wurth. Willett's words seemed to burn and crackle down the line, like a live wire twisting among them. Wurth lowered his head and looked at both boys, his eyes dark angry holes in his head.

"I don't know what in the hell you two are talking about." Wurth's voice quivered with fury. "But there won't be any phone calls for you, Mr. Cabe, until you're eighteen years old. And for this little request, you just earned yourself five hundred demerits. Do you understand me?"

Trying with all his might to keep from weeping aloud, Tommy Cabe nodded. Five hundred demerits was easily a whole year of hard work.

Wurth moved on to Willett. "As for you, Pierson, I would put you in Attitude Realignment ASAP, except the proctors who run AR don't deserve to spend their Christmas with scum like you!" Wurth stepped forward and pressed his forefinger into Willett's trachea. Involuntarily, the boy began to cough. "But at oh eight hundred hours on December twenty-six, Pierson, you will report to me in my office, where I will personally escort you down to AR. Do I make myself clear?"

"Sir, yes, sir!" Now Willett answered like a boot-camp Marine, throwing in a snappy salute for good measure. "How long can I expect to stay, sir?"

For a moment Wurth looked as if he might incinerate Willett with his gaze alone. He stretched his lips back to speak; then, abruptly, his expression changed. The anger drained from his face, and his eyes took on a resolved look, as if he'd just settled some irksome quarrel within himself.

"Indefinitely," he answered, his voice soft as a feather.

★   ★   ★

Cabe didn't remember the rest of the inspection. A hot, impotent rage surged through him, and it seemed that all the poisonous words Sergeant Wurth let loose about his mother had floated up into the sky like ugly black balloons. Everyone had heard them. Everyone had laughed. And now Willett had waded into it, too.

When Sergeant Wurth finished with the last boy, he strode back up to the front of the line and addressed them all. Usually he dismissed them for their corrections, but today he stood and looked at them.

"Gentlemen, we have a big week ahead of us. Beginning the day after Christmas, we at Camp Unakawaya will be undertaking an important mission. Troopers and Grunts alike will be asked to cooperate, doing jobs you may not necessarily understand. I know, though, that you will all make me and your country proud. We'll be running on a tight schedule here, and slackers will not be tolerated. Do I make myself clear?"

"Yes, sir!" shouted everyone but Willett and Cabe.

"So in view of the extremely hard work that I'm expecting from you later, and of course the fact that tomorrow is Christmas, everyone is hereby granted liberty until oh eight hundred hours on December twenty-six." Wurth smiled up and down his line of boys. When his gaze fell on Willett and Cabe, his smile grew strangely broader. "Merry Christmas, gentlemen! For the next day and a half, have fun. Then be prepared to work as never before."

The Grunts waited for Wurth and his Troopers to march away, then they broke ranks and ran—some thundering up the steps into the old mansion, others streaking across the stiff dead grass to the gym. As they jostled past, Tommy Cabe and Willett Pierson stood side by side, alone.

"Oh, man," Willett finally said when they were the only two left standing. "What an asshole."

Cabe turned to his friend. For the first time in the six months he'd known him, Willett Pierson looked scared. "You didn't have to say anything, Willett. I would have gotten the words out."

"I know." Willett looked up at him, his skin still pale beneath his freckles. "He just pissed me off. So you wanted to make a fucking phone call. Hell, so would I—if I had anybody to call."

Cabe looked at the ground. Most of the Grunts at Camp Unakawaya were outcast mountain boys, what city people called trailer trash. Willett was the son of a homeless girl from Charlotte. Together they'd bounced around the North Carolina welfare system until she died of an overdose. When he came to Camp

Unakawaya two years ago, he'd come as a true orphan of the streets, preferring Eminem to 'N Sync, Michael Jordan to Mark McGwire.

"I'm sorry, Willett," Tommy said miserably. "I didn't mean for you to wind up in AR."

"I know." Willett wiped his nose with the sleeve of his jacket. "I just wish he'd told me how long I was going to have to stay."

Tommy tried to put a good face on it. "You'll be out before I work off my demerits."

"Tommy-boy, I'll be *dead* before you work off your demerits."

The boys gazed at the lake that sparkled dark blue in the wintry sunlight, then Willett put his Bulls cap back on and said, "Come on. I want to show you something. We've got a day and a half of liberty. We may as well make the most of it."

With that, Willett turned and ran to the back of the castle. Cabe loped behind him, following as he scampered past the cottages that ringed the back of the huge old building and up into the ridge beyond. They climbed high, through frozen gorse and scrub cedar, scrambling through the weeds like a coon chased by hounds. Halfway up the ridge Willett stopped. When Cabe huffed up to stand beside him, the castle lay far below. Other than a few Grunts tossing a football in the side yard, the grounds

were empty. The house had turned in on itself;
no one was watching them at all. Grinning at
Cabe, Willett scrambled higher, cresting the
mountain with his cheeks ablaze from the cold.
When he reached the top he thrust his short
arms up in triumph, then he ran across a flat
quarter-acre of ground overgrown with tall yellow weeds. Cabe watched, astonished, as Willett
dashed over to the foot of the mountain. Passing
a weatherbeaten sign that said "Welcome to
Russell Cave! It's Cooooool Inside!" he turned,
waved, then abruptly disappeared.

"Willett?" Tommy called, amazed and a little
frightened by his friend's vanishing act. "Willett?
Where did you go?"

"Come on," came the distant muffled reply.
"It's cooooool inside!"

Tommy ran over. Willett stood on the other
side of some rusty iron bars that barricaded the
mouth of the cave. He grinned from the
penumbra of light, his face luminous as a ghost's.

"Step right up, my boy." Willett beckoned.
"Come see the mysteries of Willett's Den. You
can shimmy, you can shake, and you can go flying inside your own head. And for you,
Tommy-boy, today only I'll reveal the secret
weapon that will destroy Sergeant Wurth!"

"I don't know, Willett." Tommy wrinkled his

nose as the cave's breath wafted toward him. "I think the only thing in here that could destroy Sergeant Wurth is the smell."

"I've got something better than that," Willett replied, his voice suddenly serious. "Come on. I'll show you."

Tommy wiggled through the bars while Willett walked over to the side of the cave and reached behind a rock, pulling out one of the long flashlights Wurth assigned to his Troopers.

"Where'd you get that?" Cabe cried. "Grunts aren't supposed to have those."

"You ever hear of the old five-finger discount?"

Cabe nodded, not wanting to seem stupid. He guessed Willett meant that he'd stolen it.

Willett switched the flashlight on. Though the beam was not enormous, it gave enough light so Tommy could see they were standing in a chamber the size of a large living room. The cave walls were amber-colored and smooth, and towered up to a ceiling that was shrouded in shadow.

"Come on," said Willett. "Follow me."

He walked through a gap in the boulders and down a hall-like passageway. After a moment, Tommy followed. Water seeped along the right wall, making the surface glow pearlescent in

Willett's light. Though the air was no less smelly, the cave itself was beautiful; it reminded Tommy of those caverns in France with the Stone Age horses drawn on the walls.

"In here." Willett made a sharp turn to the right, then he dropped to his knees and began to crawl through a short tunnel. Tommy did the same, not wanting to be left in the utter darkness of the flashlight's wake. They entered a small chamber that water had probably carved from the mountain millennia ago. Dusty orange, it was veined with streaks of purple and speckled with glittering quartz. Along one side was a shelf-like formation upon which Willett kept an airplane magazine, a Polaroid of Tarheel, a dog he and his mom had owned, and a six-pack of Coca-Cola.

"Welcome to Willett's Den." He looked at Cabe proudly. "Pretty neat, huh?"

Tommy stared, awed and envious. How wonderful it would be to have your own hideaway where Tallent and Grice couldn't find you. "Where'd you get those Cokes?"

"One of the ladies from the Baptist Church had an extra six-pack. She gave that to me when I helped her unload some clothes for us. Want one?"

"Sure."

Willett reached up and grabbed two cans, tossing one to Cabe. "Drink that and then I'll show you some more. There's some pretty cool old stuff in here."

Tommy opened his can and took a sip. It tasted wonderful. He hadn't had a Coke in months. Coca-Cola was a Jew industry, Sergeant Wurth told them. True Patriots didn't support Jew industries, so on special occasions Wurth provided them with pissy-tasting lemonade.

"Okay, Willett," Tommy teased as he drained his can. "Where's your secret weapon that will destroy Sergeant Wurth?"

"I wasn't kidding, man." Willett seemed miffed at Cabe's levity. "I really have got the goods on Wurth."

"Okay. So where is it?"

"Here." Willett set his Coke down and reached back into a fissure in the rock. Tommy cringed, thinking anyone would have to be crazy to stick their hand inside some dark crack in a cave, but Willett grinned, withdrawing something wrapped in a plastic sandwich bag. "This," he said reverently.

"What is it?"

He unfolded the plastic and withdrew a single unlabeled computer disk. He held it up to Cabe, his eyes serious.

"I'm not sure what Wurth is into, but it's big and bad. And all on this disk."

"What do you mean?" Cabe whispered, his palms already growing sweaty. "How did you get that?"

"One Sunday when Wurth sentenced me to copying the Bible, I picked the lock on his office door and copied this. He and the Troopers were all out playing baseball."

Cabe was stunned by Willett's audacity. "But how did you know what it was?"

"I didn't. I just wanted to surf the Net while they were outside playing. I sat down at his computer and all this weird military stuff about targets and assassinations was on his screen." Willett shrugged. "So I made a copy."

"Jesus, Willett." Cabe could barely speak. "Do you know how much trouble you could have gotten in?"

"Yep. I also know how much trouble it could get Wurth in." Willett carefully returned the disk to the sandwich bag. "That's why I keep it here. You're the only other person who knows about this, Tommy-boy."

"What are you going to do with it?"

"Someday I'm gonna smuggle it out of here and get it to the cops. Then I'm just going to sit back and watch AR and the rest of that old castle blow up around Wurth's ears."

Cabe grinned. "That would be pretty neat, wouldn't it?"

"I dream about it every night, Tommy-boy," said Willett as he restashed his treasure deep in the fissure of his den. "It's the only thing I want for Christmas this year."

CHAPTER 12

Several miles away from Russell Cave, Irene Hannah led Mary Crow into her kitchen, where the aroma of roasting turkey filled the air. Three newly minted pecan pies sat cooling beside the sink; an array of apples and carrots spilled from an overturned sack on the long kitchen table.

"We're cooking Christmas dinner," Irene explained with a laugh. "For us and our four-legged friends." Just then the bristly-haired gentleman who had flung open the front door walked into the room, having pulled on a bright red wool sweater. He smiled at Mary, the tips of his full gray mustache curling like little wings.

Irene put an arm around Mary's shoulders. "Hugh, we just got the most wonderful Christmas present we could possibly have! This is my darling Mary Crow. I adored her mother, and I've adored Mary ever since I pushed her, kicking and screaming, into law school. Now she's a tiger of a DA down in Atlanta."

"A prosecutor, is it?" Hugh's thick brows arched in amusement. "Then I'd best watch me p's and q's."

"Mary, meet Hugh Kavanagh, my next-door neighbor. Hugh's western North Carolina's premier horse breeder, tomato grower, and purveyor of hothouse snapdragons to every pricey restaurant west of Raleigh."

"Hugh." Mary extended her hand. "It's a pleasure."

"Aye." He grasped only her fingers, in the manner of Europeans.

"Hugh's from Ireland," Irene explained. "But he's been in the States for what, Hugh, forty years?"

"I came to New York in sixty-four." Hugh laughed. "I didn't move next door to Irene here until last spring."

Irene looked at Mary and smiled. "Okay, darling girl. Now that my heart's calmed down from the shock of seeing you, tell me why Santa Claus dropped you on my doorstep. I hope the news is something wonderful, like you've just married Jonathan or been appointed attorney general for the state of Georgia."

"Not exactly," Mary replied, edging away from the mention of Jonathan's name. She glanced at Hugh, wondering if Safer would want her to explain her mission to Irene in front of a stranger. Safer hadn't mentioned Hugh being a part of Irene's life, but perhaps he hadn't considered it important. Hugh seemed to sense Mary's hesitation. He smiled at Irene. "Why don't you take Mary down to the stable and check on Lady Jane? I'll mind the dinner until you get back."

"Would you, Hugh?" Irene's eyes danced. "I'd love to show her off for Mary."

"It would be an honor to be of service to two such learned ladies," Hugh replied.

Irene threw him a kiss, then pulled Mary out the back door.

"Does he live with you?" Mary whispered when they got outside. She hadn't overlooked Hugh Kavanagh's easy familiarity with Irene's kitchen.

"Oh, no." Irene tucked her arm through Mary's and led her across the patio, Lucy and the dog following. "We're neighbors and fellow horse breeders. He's a widower who loves to cook. I'm a widow who loves to eat. We get on nicely. That's his dog, Napoleon."

Mary turned. The big shepherd wagged his tail at her, but kept a wary eye on the goose. "Where's Chico? And when did you get Lucy?"

"Chico died in his sleep back in October. Then

a week later she hobbled up here with an arrow through her wing. I called the vet, who said it looked like someone had used her for target practice. She's been here ever since."

"Does she get along with the other animals?"

"She's crowned herself queen of the barnyard." Irene chuckled at the bird waddling regally behind her. "I can't figure out if she thinks she's human or we're all just lesser geese."

Past the grape arbor lay the rest of the farm. A red stable stood between two white-fenced paddocks, where more horses grazed. Two yellow cats huddled in the hayloft window, watching as low clouds scudded in from the north. Mary turned her face to the sky and breathed in. She could almost smell the icy tingle of snow on the breeze. Tomorrow might bring her first white Christmas in years.

"Now." Irene spoke in her bench voice, the voice that Mary knew would eventually ferret out anything the judge wanted to know. "Tell me the real reason you're here. Not in trouble, are you?"

"I'm not," replied Mary. "You might be, though."

"Me?" Irene frowned. "What did I do?"

"Irene, yesterday afternoon I got called away from my best friend's wedding and into my boss's office. A federal agent was sitting there with a briefcase full of some very troubling evidence."

Irene turned and spoke sharply. "If this is about Rosy Klinefelter, I know all about it. A bunch of Feds have been hounding me ever since Thanksgiving."

Mary blinked. "Doesn't it bother you that somebody might want to kill you?"

"Not nearly as much as the FBI bothers me. They wanted to assign two female agents to guard me around the clock. I think some are circling this property right now."

"But aren't you even a little worried?" Mary couldn't believe Irene's insouciance.

"Mary, if I got FBI protection every time someone threatened me, I couldn't do my job. Once you give in to fear, you're not worth a damn on the bench."

"But the Feds think this is real. They drove me up here to convince you to accept their protection."

"So that's why you're here? To talk me into having a bodyguard?" Irene started laughing.

"They suggested I bring this." Mary unzipped her jacket and exposed the Beretta. "That's how seriously they're taking this."

"My God." Irene stopped laughing as she saw the black pistol nudging up against Mary's left breast. "You actually go armed now?"

"Not usually. But after I convicted a guy whose family kept waiting for me in shadowy parking lots with piano wire up their sleeves, my boss gave me this. Said it might go against my moral code, but it would sure help him sleep better at night."

"I can't believe this. This is not like you, Mary."

"Irene, Rosemary Klinefelter was decapitated. It was horrible. I saw her picture. The Feds would like to spare you that fate."

"I've got plenty of protection around me." Irene's dark eyes flashed. "I've got thirty acres on a county road in the middle of the thickest forest in the Carolinas. I've got horses and chickens and—"

"Give me a break, Irene!" cried Mary. "Klinefelter got nailed in her own courtroom. One New York judge was stabbed in front of a Manhattan apartment. Another seemingly dropped dead at a Steelers game. They've killed eleven judges, Irene. One from every district except the Fourth. A flock of chickens and that stupid goose aren't going to save you."

"I don't care what will or won't save me, Mary." Irene's cheeks flamed with anger. "I'm a stubborn old woman, and I refuse to be part of a judiciary that has to be guarded. And Lucy is not stupid!"

With that, Irene stomped past her into the stable. Mary watched as she disappeared into the shadows, Napoleon and Lucy on her heels. With a helpless shrug of her shoulders, Mary followed. She needed to reason with Irene, not yell at her from the middle of a barnyard twenty feet away.

Inside, the stable was warm and dark, the air sweet, like hay. "Walk down here with me," Irene said softly, her anger already forgotten. "I want you to see something."

Mary followed her to a double-sized stall at the end of the corridor. Inside stood a small brown mare with a white blaze on her face. She raised her head and pricked her ears at Mary. Her belly was swollen as if she'd swallowed a truck tire.

"She's beautiful," Mary said. "But isn't she a little fat?"

"She's pregnant." Irene dug a lump of sugar from the pocket of her jeans and held out her hand. The mare thrust her long neck forward and nibbled it from her palm. "This is the brood mare I bought from Hugh. Her name's Lady Jane. Any day now she'll be having her sixth foal." Irene handed Mary a lump of sugar. "Here. Make friends with her."

Mary held out the sugar. Lady Jane stretched out again and sniffed Mary's palm. Her lips felt like velvet as they gently lifted the sugar cube from her hand.

"Shouldn't you be calling a vet or something?" Mary had never seen a pregnant horse before. She barely knew the protocol for whelping puppies, much less colts or fillies.

"Not unless we have problems. Hugh will be helping me out. Lady Jane will be safe here."

"That's great for her." Mary seized the chance to turn the conversation back in the direction she wanted it to go. "But what about you?"

Irene frowned. "Oh, Mary . . ."

"Do you know how many places you could be attacked from? What about—"

"Look around you," Irene interrupted. "I've got a footbridge that makes one person sound like a Roman legion. The guineas in the front yard shriek their heads off every time a cloud passes in front of the sun. Lucy follows me like a dog and Napoleon sleeps across the back door most nights. I have more bodyguards than I know what to do with."

Mary picked at a sliver of wood from the top of the stall door. She hated to mention it, but Irene left her no choice. "I walked across the bridge this morning. The guineas shrieked like banshees and Lucy honked right along with them. I banged on your front door three times. When nobody heard me, I came around and peered in the back door, Lucy honking the whole time."

Irene looked at her quizzically for a moment, then she understood. "You saw us? In front of the fireplace?"

Mary nodded.

At first Irene said nothing, then she threw her head back and laughed so hard that Lady Jane gave a sharp whinny, her ears flicking in alarm.

"Caught!" Irene howled. "In flagrante delicto, at the age of sixty-two!" Tears rolled from her eyes. "At least it was you, and not one of those FBI thugs!"

Although she wanted desperately to laugh with Irene, all Mary could think of was Rosemary Klinefelter. "Irene," she said softly, "if someone had wanted to kill you this morning, neither Lucy nor Napoleon could have saved you. You and Hugh would have died, and died horribly."

Slowly the laughter faded from Irene's brown eyes. "You really believe this might happen, don't you?"

"I'm scared that it could. Please let them guard you. If nobody gets killed during the holidays, they will have at least broken the pattern."

Irene gazed at Lady Jane as if pondering some point of law, then she turned back to Mary and shook her head.

Then she shook her head. "I'm sorry, Mary. I'd like to do it, if only to please you, but I can't. I can't live this long on principle and then fold my hand just because the game gets dicey. Please tell your friends that I'm a stubborn old goat who's probably not worth guarding, anyway."

"Irene, you don't understand—"

"I understand perfectly. Don't you see? For me to turn away from the rule of law in favor of rule by the gun would make me a coward. Worse—a fraud."

"No, it wouldn't."

"Sorry, Mary. You and I both know it would."

"Wait!" Mary insisted. "Let's reason this out." She walked to the stable door, frustrated, searching for a compromise. Suddenly she found it. She ran back to Irene. "If you won't let them stay with you, then let *me*. I've got a gun. I can guard you as well as they can."

"Absolutely not!" cried Irene. "If I'm in any jeopardy at all, I certainly don't want you here!"

"Too bad!" Mary crossed her arms and glared at her. "If you can live by your principles, then I can live by mine."

"That's unfair." Irene's voice sharpened in anger. "And unacceptable."

"How is it unfair? Unless you call Stump Logan to come out and remove me from your property, I'm here and I'm staying. And you can plan on me for the Rose Bowl Parade, 'cause me and my Beretta aren't budging anywhere till you go back to Richmond."

Irene looked at Mary. Several times she opened her mouth to speak, but each time she stopped. Finally she smiled. "Nice work, counselor. You've just beaten your old teacher at her own game." She gave a deep, courtly bow. *"O-stah."* She congratulated Mary in Cherokee.

"I learned from the master," Mary replied quietly. "But I'm not playing games."

"I know you aren't. I've seen that look on your face too many times before. I know when I'm licked." She reached over and took Mary in her arms. "Okay, darling girl. Merry Christmas. I won't sic Sheriff Logan on you. You can stay here and bodyguard me all you want. Bodyguard me until *you* feel safe again."

"Thank you," Mary whispered as she buried her face in the silvery softness of Irene's hair.

CHAPTER 13

"Anything going on?" Safer's voice broke the silence of the towering pines.

Mike Tuttle, a man reputedly well accustomed to the tedium of stakeouts, replied. "The boyfriend's still there. He slept over last night. Otherwise, the only new visitor is our little civilian helper."

Tuttle leaned against a tree and lit a cigarette. With his shaved head and green camouflage suit, he looked more like a Marine on maneuvers than an FBI agent staking out a target, but Finch, Safer's boss, had pulled him out of the Boise office expressly to help in this operation. Tuttle was supposed to be one of the Bureau's best.

"If there are any psycho groups within a hundred miles of you," Finch told him, "Tuttle'll sniff 'em out like a truffle hound."

To Safer, Mike Tuttle seemed arrogant,

bandy-legged, and not at all pleased with being assigned to the mountains of western North Carolina.

Tuttle glanced at Safer through his cigarette smoke. "Heard anything from her yet?"

"No." Safer pulled his collar up around his neck, suddenly aware of the silent cell phone in his shirt pocket. Mary Crow had had more than enough time to reason with Judge Hannah. She should have called an hour ago.

"So what's she like?"

"Who?"

"Pocahontas."

"You read her jacket."

"But what does she look like? I hear these hill-billies marry their own siblings up here. Come up with some pretty weird-looking offspring."

"She doesn't have that problem." Safer turned his back on Tuttle and looked into the forest, re-membering the brightness of Mary Crow's eyes and the straightforward way those eyes had stud-ied him. She'd been attractive enough until she'd walked out of that gas station and handed him that peach tart thing. Then she'd looked up and smiled, and suddenly it was all he could do to get back in the truck and drive them where they were going. Mary Crow was just another pretty woman until she smiled. Then she became radiant, making the truck seem smaller, leaving him sitting far too close to her.

"Think she can talk the judge into letting us on the property?" Tuttle took a deep pull on his cigarette, making the tip glow orange.

Safer shrugged, wincing at the memory of what a jerk he'd been about the peach tart. "She seemed pretty determined. But so's the old lady."

"I never knew any woman who wasn't determined about something." Tuttle didn't bother to hide the bitterness in his voice. "Usually it's grabbing money that doesn't belong to them."

Safer made no comment. Tuttle had complained more than once about an ex-wife who hauled him into court on a regular basis. His cell phone chirped and he pulled it from his pocket. "Safer here."

He frowned as the transmission turned Mary Crow's low timbre into a squawk. "Can you meet me at the bridge?" she asked. "I think we may have reached a compromise."

"What bridge?" Safer felt his heart beating faster. Idiot, he thought. All she'd done was smile, for God's sake. It meant nothing.

"Turn up Irene's driveway. You'll see me waiting for you."

"I'll be there in five minutes," he said, then clicked off the phone.

"Make any headway?" Tuttle flipped his cigarette butt into the trees.

"Maybe," Safer replied as he strode back to the Dodge. "I'll let you know."

★　　★　　★

He drove back to Upsy Daisy Farm, turning up the clay drive and bouncing over the bumps and potholes in the road. He rounded a sharp curve, and suddenly Mary Crow came into view, standing under a huge, bare sycamore tree growing beside one end of a suspension bridge that spanned a shallow rushing river. Slowing, he studied her as if he had a second chance to see her for the first time. She carried her medium-tall height proudly, her head held high. Her glossy black hair just brushed her shoulders, and though she sported the upscale jeans-and-down jacket look of a city woman on a country vacation, she seemed totally at ease leaning against a rickety bridge in the middle of a mountain farm.

He nosed the truck under the tree and turned off the engine. Before he could unbuckle his seat belt, she was standing beside the door. She looked different from when he'd dropped her off. Still serious but playful, like a tiger freed from the constraints of a cage.

"Hi, Safer." Once again she smiled that smile.

"What's going on?" He got out of the truck feeling like a schoolboy with his first crush, unable to take his eyes from her face. This was nuts. Who was this woman?

"There's good news and bad news."

"Start with the bad."

"She still won't allow you guys to guard her."

"So what's the good news?"

"She's allowing me to stay."

"Don't tell me *you're* supposed to protect her!"

"That's the plan. She doesn't want me here any more than she wants you. But she's agreed not to have me forcibly evicted from her property."

"That's the plan?" He slammed his hand down on the hood of the truck. "Jesus! Where does this crazy old bird get off? Didn't you explain to her how bad this could get?"

"I did. But she won't budge from her principles. And she can't make me abandon mine."

"Budge from her principles? Christ, you two make this sound like Judicial Ethics 101. Don't you know this is *real*? You saw that picture. Maybe I should have sent you in there with it!"

"It wouldn't have done any good."

"A nice long look at Judge Klinefelter's head in her lap might have convinced her that she needs somebody around with more than bright eyes and a target pistol."

"This Beretta is hardly a target pistol, Safer." Mary patted the gun nestled beneath her arm. "And I'm no stranger to criminals."

"You might be able to hit somebody standing still. The killer will come at you fast, like a shadow—"

"I'm sorry," she interrupted, her smile fading. "But me and my Beretta are all you get. It's still a better deal than you had when you dropped me off this morning."

Safer could already hear Finch roaring at him over the phone. What was it with these mountain people? Where did this idiot judge get off? Why would she allow this young attorney to put herself in such jeopardy?

"I can't let you do this," he replied, the words feeling like gravel in his throat.

Mary Crow laughed. "On what grounds can you stop me, Agent Safer?"

She had him there. She was a private citizen, on private property, carrying a gun she was legally entitled to carry. There was nothing he or the Bureau or even the damn Attorney General of the United States could do about it.

Rubbing his beard, he studied her. "You know she's maneuvered us both into this corner."

"Irene hasn't maneuvered anybody into anything, Safer," Mary replied evenly. "She doesn't want me here any more than she wants you.

She's just willing to put up with me." She gave an impatient sigh. "Look, one of Irene's mares is going to have a foal, so she's not going anywhere until she flies to Richmond on the fifth of January. So why don't you give me a ten-minute course on bodyguarding? If I'm on the inside with a gun and you guys have this farm surrounded, everything should be fine."

He glared at her, wanting to tell her that it wasn't going to be fine, and that it could well get very lethal very fast, but he didn't. What would be the point? Until he could call Washington and have them figure some way out of this, he would have to play along.

"Okay, Ms. Crow," he said, moving in behind her, standing so close that the spicy warm scent of her filled his nose and made him dizzy. He cleared his throat and spoke slowly, as if he were reciting the first page of a primer.

"The simplest way to kill a man is to rip out his eye. . . ."

CHAPTER 14

The snow Mary had hoped for did not arrive. In fact, Christmas Day dawned an anomaly in the damp cloudiness of a mountain winter. It glittered like a shiny jewel, with a cold aquamarine sky unmarred by the slightest wisp of a cloud. The fields of Upsy Daisy Farm glowed tawny in the sunlight, and from Mary's vantage point, just in front of the tree line that edged the woods, the whole farm looked like a page torn from a child's coloring book—blue sky, white house, red barn, golden fields.

"Pretty, isn't it?" Irene sat beside her on Spindletop, a dark brown horse that shook his head against the stricture of his bit.

"It's beautiful, Irene. I love it more every time I come here." Mary rode a little gray mare named Stella and smiled. "I *understand* it more every time I come here."

"That's because you're getting older." Irene chuckled. "In your twenties, you want bright lights and big cities. In your thirties, other things intrigue you. Come on. Let's go down to the creek."

Stella followed Spindletop with no urging from Mary. They picked their way down the hill until they reached the flat, unfenced pasture behind the barn. Then Irene picked up the pace. Though Mary had not ridden in a long time, she quickly remembered most of what Irene had taught her. Soon she and Stella were gliding over the fields in long, ground-covering strides. Mary had not much more to do than just stay in the saddle.

When Irene reached the stream, she gave Spindletop his head and let him drink. Mary eased up beside them to let Stella do the same. Early that morning they'd given the horses their special Christmas breakfast—an apple, pear, and molasses concoction that Irene added to their regular food. After they'd eaten their own breakfast, Hugh had returned to his farm and she and Irene had gone to the stable, saddling up Spindletop and Stella for a long ride. "They're fat as pigs," said Irene. "They needed a special Christmas breakfast about like I needed that extra slice of pecan pie. A little exercise will do us all good."

Now Irene looked at her as the horses sucked up long draughts of sweet, cold water. "So tell me. What's Jonathan doing while you're up here bodyguarding me?"

Mary had known this question was coming. She'd put off formulating an answer, mostly because she didn't know what to say—to herself or anyone else. "Jonathan and I aren't together anymore," she replied, the words sounding strange in her own ears.

"What?" Irene spoke so sharply that Spindle-top flinched. "When? Why?"

"He moved out last spring. He said he wasn't happy in Atlanta, but the fault was really mine."

"Yours?"

Mary looked at Irene with wistful eyes. "Work got crazy. We caught a man called the Dance Hall Demon—a guy who was romancing older ladies out of all their money, then killing them after he'd bled them dry. We had him on one count, then the cops dug deeper. Ultimately I indicted him for four different murders."

Irene whistled. "I heard about that. Wondered if you were in on it."

"I didn't work on anything else from last Christmas to Memorial Day."

"And Jonathan didn't like that?"

"He said he didn't like the city, but I think he

resented the hours and the pressure and the emotional ups and downs."

"And?" Irene pressed.

"And he hated the evidence files on the dining room table. The depositions I had to read each night in bed." She pressed her lips together and stroked Stella's neck. "Mostly, though, he hated the filth that rubbed off on me."

"Oh, Mary." Irene reached over and squeezed her shoulder.

"It's okay. I hung four murders on the Dance Hall Demon. Jonathan went out west and came back with a new girlfriend on his arm."

"You're kidding." Irene looked as if someone had just presented her with irrefutable evidence that the world was flat.

Mary nodded. "Ruth Moon. A full-blood Cherokee from Tahlequah, Oklahoma. She's pretty, she's smart, and she's trying to amend the Constitution to allow Native Americans in Congress."

The reins fell slack in Irene's hands. "I'm so sorry."

"Me, too," Mary replied softly and felt as bereft as she had the day she'd found Jonathan's note, telling her he was going back home to Little Jump Off. She squeezed Stella's reins hard and tried to think of something else.

"May I give you a piece of grandmotherly advice?" Irene leaned over and gently touched her shoulder again.

Mary nodded, not trusting herself to speak.

"Ride on," whispered Irene.

"Ride on?" Mary looked at her friend.

"Just ride on. Your road isn't close to ending. Who knows who you'll meet along the way?"

"But . . ."

"It's the only cure," said Irene as she turned Spindletop around and urged him forward. "Trust me. I know."

★   ★   ★

They rode the horses fast, then. Up through the woods, along the creek, finally around the whole perimeter of the farm. The warm sun on Mary's shoulders did seem to push Jonathan far away and relegate her heartbreak at Little Jump Off to something that happened to her in the distant past. Like so many times before, Irene Hannah had known the balm to soothe Mary's soul. As they rode down along the fence line that paralleled Lick Log Road, Mary saw two parked green vans with tinted windows. She grinned. She had no doubt that Daniel Safer was inside one of those vans, watching their every move.

"Hey, Irene," she called, pulling back on

Stella's reins. "Look. There are your friendly local G-men."

Irene slowed Spindletop to a walk as she eyed the vans, then her eyes began to sparkle with a devilish glee. "Want to show them what terrific horsewomen we are?"

"I don't know that I'm so terrific. I haven't ridden in a while."

"I'll ride up and do this trick Spindletop and I have been working on. When you hear my signal, ride up hard behind me. Think you can do that?"

"I'll try."

Mary watched as Irene turned Spindletop in a tight circle, then she began to race toward the van. When she pulled directly alongside it, Irene brought Spindletop to a skidding cow-pony halt. Faster than she could breathe, the horse reared up on his hind legs, his forelegs pawing the air. Mary looked on, astonished. It was the coolest move she'd ever seen anywhere outside a rodeo. Federal District Judge Irene Hannah on a rearing horse.

"Into the breach, my friends!" Irene cried as she waved at the vans full of Feds. "Charge!"

With that, Spindletop leaped obediently into a gallop, his tail flying out behind him as he sped up the hill. Mary followed on Stella. If she fell off now, she would be the laughingstock of

every cop between here and Washington.
Hunched over the saddle, she gripped the reins
tightly while Stella thundered after Spindletop.
When they reached the top of the hill, they
stopped. Slowly the driver's window of the second van rolled down. A single arm in a plaid
jacket sleeve emerged, gave a brief wave, and
then vanished back inside the vehicle. Mary and
Irene began to laugh.

"I think they enjoyed that," Irene said,
delighted.

"Good," Mary gasped. "Let's not give them an
encore. I'm not sure I could hang on."

"Me neither, actually. We can walk the horses
back to the barn. Maybe in a little while I'll
bring those boys one of my pies." She looked at
Mary, then shrugged. "After all, it is Christmas."

And so they walked, side by side, back to the
old barn, Mary once again content to cast her
sorrows on the hills of Upsy Daisy Farm.

★　★　★

Tommy Cabe did not wake up early on
Christmas morning. He had no illusions regard-
ing Santa Claus and not many more about
goodwill among men. He did have, that morning, a profound gratitude for the twenty-four
hours of Christmas liberty Wurth had given
them, and he honored the holiday by spending

the first part of it in warm, delicious slumber. Curled up on his cot, the scratchy wool blanket pulled to his ears, he floated through every Christmas he'd known—from the early, exuberant ones at his grandfather's farm in Kentucky, to the leaner, but still happy ones with his mother in Cherokee. Finally he landed on this one, and thought of the previous day, when Willett had shown him his cave. It hadn't been anything like he'd expected. True, it did smell a little bit, but it was also beautiful and mysterious. *It's cool inside, Tommy-boy. You can go flying inside your head!*

At the memory, his eyelids fluttered open. Blinding sunlight shone through his window, high in a crystal blue sky. It would be a perfect day to spend outside—cold, but bright. He and Willett could go back to the cave. Sitting up, he turned toward the cot next to his. "Hey, Willett," he called. "Wake up—"

Suddenly the words stuck in his throat. Willett's bed looked empty. He fumbled for his glasses.

"Willett?" he repeated.

Though his friend's bed was made up with the military precision Wurth demanded, Willett was gone. His battered Nikes were gone, his thin blue jacket was gone, even his Bulls cap, which he usually stashed beneath his mattress while he slept, was gone. Tommy Cabe peered down the long dorm room. All the rest of the Grunts still slept, each bed holding a boy deep in whatever dreams carried him away from Camp Unakawaya.

"Hey, Galloway! Young!" he called to the nearest sleepers. "Have you guys seen Pierson?"

George Young rolled over and groaned without opening his eyes. "Not since yesterday," he muttered before he covered his head with his pillow.

"Maybe he flew away." Harvey Galloway sat up and blinked sleepily at Willett's bed. "That's what he was always talking about doing."

"You didn't hear anything last night?" Cabe asked.

Galloway shook his head as he, too, settled back down to sleep. "Sorry, Cabe."

Tommy looked at Willett's bunk, stunned. They'd stayed up well past midnight, Willett alternately reading his airplane magazine and then rolling over to look out the window, goofily checking for Santa Claus. *Wouldn't it be cool if Santa Claus was real?* he'd said, his face shining with the wonder of a four-year-old instead of a teenager of fourteen. *Man, I wouldn't ask for anything but a lift out of this shithole. I'd never have to go to Attitude Realignment again!*

That was it, Cabe realized. Wurth had changed his mind. Wurth had decided that

Willett didn't deserve Christmas after all and had sent him to AR early.

"Fuck that!" Cabe cried aloud. Christmas was going to be Willett's last day of freedom for who knew how long. The two of them had planned to have some fun.

Tommy threw off his blanket and got to his feet. He'd talk to Wurth. He'd get Willett out of AR, even if he had to volunteer to take his place.

He dressed hastily, paying attention to the details Wurth held such store by. By the time Cabe reached the first floor of the castle, his cowlicks had been tamed, his teeth were gleaming, and his shirttail was well tucked in. Squaring his shoulders, he walked down the long hall to Wurth's office, his heart thumping in his chest like a rabbit's.

He lifted his hand and knocked on the door. Wurth answered immediately, his voice crisp with command. "What is it?"

Tommy opened the door. He'd been in Wurth's office only once, the first day he came here, but he remembered it clearly. A big, ornate desk faced the door, with red leather chairs set around it. Various flags stood around the room, mostly weird versions of Old Glory. A wicked-looking Ninja-type sword hung on the wall in an ebony sheath, and from one bookcase leered a human skull with a bullet hole in the very center of the cranium. On this morning, Sergeant Wurth stood behind his desk with a bald man in a black leather jacket, both of whom looked up from some kind of blueprint. Wurth's mouth drew down when he saw Tommy. "Yes, Cabe?" he snapped with impatience.

Cabe shuddered as he took two steps inside the room. It smelled of cigar smoke and coffee. Wurth looked at him with cold eyes.

"It's W-W-Willett, sir," Cabe said, mortified at the sudden girlishness of his voice.

"W-W-Willett? W-W-Willett P-P-Pierson?" Wurth mocked him.

"Y-yes, sir. He doesn't deserve to be in AR, sir. He was just trying to help me get m-my words out yesterday."

"And?" Wurth's eyes glittered like a cat's.

"And I was thinking maybe you would let me take Willett's place in AR. The whole thing was my fault, anyway."

"You're absolutely right, Cabe. It was your fault. But what makes you think Pierson's in AR?"

Tommy blinked. "He's gone, sir. His clothes are gone and his bed's made up."

Wurth rolled up the blueprint he and his friend were studying before he replied. "Willett's gone, you say? Well, isn't that just too bad."

Tommy frowned. He wasn't understanding this. Wurth had sentenced Pierson to AR. Wurth must have sent someone to get him in the night. Upchurch, maybe. Or maybe David Forrester had returned. "Sir?"

"Mr. Cabe, boys come and go out of this camp all the time. Sometimes their pathetic excuses for parents manage to wrangle custody back, other times the DHS places them elsewhere. The order can come down at any time, and they can be gone, just like that." Wurth snapped his fingers as if he were cracking a walnut.

"So DHS p-picked Willett up in the middle of the night? On Christmas Eve?"

"I can't discuss that with you, Cabe. All juvenile records are confidential." He planted his hands on the desk and leaned forward. "The only boy you and I can discuss, Mr. Cabe, is you."

"C-can't you even tell me where's he gone?" Tommy heard his already ridiculous voice begin to quiver. *Please, God, don't let me cry now.*

Smiling, Wurth shook his head. "Pierson is in much better circumstances, Mr. Cabe. Let's just say Santa Claus came last night and brought him a present. Now, would you care to talk about you?"

Tommy stood there, stunned. Wurth had just told him all he was going to about Willett. Now the attack had turned toward him. Wurth was probably going to say more terrible things about his mother, in front of this stranger.

"No, sir," Cabe answered meekly. "I'm fine, sir."

"Very well, then, Mr. Cabe. Have a Merry Christmas. Spend it wisely. You've got some de-merits to attend to, tomorrow."

"Yes, sir." With that he turned and walked out, trying to look like the Trooper he would never be. He closed Wurth's door behind him, his hands shaking with frustration and terror. Willett was in AR, he knew it. Willett had no relatives to demand custody of him, and the DHS wouldn't take a kid anywhere on Christmas Eve. Wurth had probably taken him to the basement early and just didn't want to admit it in front of that man.

I'll go down to AR right now, he decided as he hurried back down the hall, away from Wurth's office. *I'm sure as hell not going to let Willett spend Christmas down there all alone.*

CHAPTER 15

"What time have you got?" Wurth asked.

Wayne Tallent looked at the clock on the truck's dashboard. "Eleven forty-four."

"Twenty-three forty-four, Tallent," Wurth corrected. Would this boy ever learn the proper way to convey time? "Pick me up here at zero hours forty-five."

"Yes, sir."

"Do you know how long that will be, Tallent?"

"An hour, sir?"

"Okay. Get out of here."

Wurth thumped the side of the truck as Tallent pulled away, leaving him alone on the mountain road. He watched the red taillights blink and disappear around a curve, then he slipped into a thick green bank of rhododendrons.

He walked carefully, aware that the Feds were

patrolling the farm. He would have some hard questions to answer if they caught him sneaking up on Judge Hannah's house camouflaged, his face sooted as if he were part of a minstrel show. Not that the Feds would be paying much attention to her upper pastures and the slender trail her horses had worn to the barn. The Feds stayed in their two snug vans over the hill, keeping watch on the one long driveway that led to her house.

Still, he slipped through the trees, silent as a shadow. Getting caught would be the worst possible thing that could happen. Getting caught would only prove Dunbar right.

As always, moving through darkness invigorated him. The cold air tingled the back of his neck and amplified the tiniest sounds to thunder in his ears.

He thought of Irene Hannah, sleeping as he grew closer, unaware that she was now drawing the last breaths she would ever draw. How many targets has it been, he wondered as he neared the edge of the tree line that overlooked the pasture. At least a hundred in the past ten years. And how many boys have I instructed in my ways? Two for every state, at least. And Dunbar was worried that they had no control. Shit, David Forrester had simply gotten excited. *And he paid for it, too.* Wurth thought of the boy lying dead, his legs twisted like a doll's. Someday Dunbar was going to pay for that.

Cheered by that prospect, he looked down at the pasture below. The trail that ran along the tree line led all the way to the barn. Though the remnants of last week's snow had melted in the day's bright sun, he would have to be careful. Even the Feds could follow tracks in soggy mud.

Irene Hannah's house sat above the hollow in which the barn nestled. Neat and compact, it bore the look of a household snuggled down against winter—windows shut tight, no lights shining from within. A patio spread out along the back. Wurth nodded. *Perfect,* he thought. *I've got cover and a household sound asleep. I can get this done fast and be waiting when that moron Tallent shows up.*

Feeling suddenly buoyed upward by the chill breeze, Wurth slipped from behind the tree and onto the path the horses had carved, keeping to the shadows of the overhanging bushes as he crept toward the barn. The air was heavy with moisture, and once or twice his footsteps crunched when he stepped in a slushy puddle. Reaching the back side of the barn, he forced himself to slow down. Since Judge Hannah worked a farm, she might also sleep like a farmer—oblivious to storms, but keenly alert to any sound from her livestock. He did not need a barnful of neighing horses right now.

He kept low, easing beneath the stall windows, then turned the corner and looked up at the house. It remained a dark little cottage on the hill.

Thrusting his mind and body into a mode that had, over the years, become second nature to him, he padded forward, his noiseless strides more lupine than human. He reached the gate, slipped through it, then on up the hill, his passing marked only by a shadow on the ground. All the snow had melted up here. In one heartbeat he reached the edge of the patio; in the next he stood at the back door.

To her credit, the judge had installed two dead-bolt locks, but dead bolts did not trouble him. He had tools for dead bolts. He had tools for everything. He withdrew a slender steel instrument from his pocket, and in less than thirty seconds he'd turned them both. He smiled thinly as he eased the door open.

A warm breath of hickory-scented air caressed his face. Embers glowed orange from a fireplace, illuminating a bottle of Irish whiskey that stood on the table. Dishes—more dishes than one person could possibly use—were drying in a drainer by the sink. The judge had feasted mightily this holiday, Wurth decided. God had not let this merry gentlewoman be dismayed in the least.

Without a sound he made a swift tour of the downstairs, rifling through the papers on her desk, the Cherokee egg basket that held her outgoing mail, the pages of her appointment calendar. After deciding that she must spend most of her time working here, he headed up the broad, uncarpeted stairs, shifting his weight effortlessly to the balls of his feet as he climbed up to the second story, careful never to linger on one board too long. When he reached the top step he paused. The upper floor consisted of just two rooms, divided by a hall. A bathroom door stood ajar at one end. Judge Hannah would be sleeping in one of these rooms. Who, he wondered, might be sleeping in the other?

He slid his knife from his belt and crept down the hall until he stood between the two closed doors. One seemed no better than the other, so he turned left, remembering one of his teacher's old maxims—*Go in the way other men do not. At worst, you will only be mistaken.* Turning the doorknob, he cracked the door open by millimeters, lest a sudden rush of cool air wake the sleeper.

When his eyes accustomed to the light, he saw a single figure sleeping under a quilt. As he moved closer, his eyes settled on a 9mm Beretta dangling from the bedpost, holstered in the kind of brace women wore under their clothes. A bodyguard, he thought, smiling with surprise. Private? Or sent by Uncle Sam? He moved closer to the sleeper and gently lifted the covers with the point of his knife. The moonlight fell on a young female face. Her lustrous dark hair was tousled against the pillow; firm young breasts lifted the sheets. A jolt of desire shot through him. What a Christmas surprise this was! Did he dare?

No, a sterner voice cautioned him. Do the judge first. Save this one for later.

With an inaudible sigh he left the girl to her dreams. She lifted one hand to brush something from her eyes, then tugged her covers closer and turned away from him, burying her cheek deeper into her pillow. He watched her for a moment, then crept back into the hall beyond.

The old judge slept differently from her pretty young guard. Wurth opened her door to snoring so loud that he had to rush in, lest all the racket rouse the sleeping bodyguard from her dreams. Then he realized that the racket came not from Judge Hannah, but from the broad-shouldered man who slept with his arms wrapped around her. Though no pistol hung from the bedpost here, Wurth knew he was in much more danger.

Double the number of hostile eyes, reduce your chances accordingly.

Silently he skirted the male sleeper and crept toward the judge. Unlike her young friend, she slept in pajamas; her face turned toward her lover. Her hair was a cloud of silver, and though she smiled in her sleep, there was a strong Anglo-Saxon thrust to her jaw that no doubt gave every defendant in her courtroom pause. She looked of average height and weight, with a neck surprisingly straight for someone her age.

She moaned once in her sleep, then nestled closer to the whiskery fellow beside her, tucking her head just beneath his chin.

Wurth sheathed his knife and withdrew a loaded syringe from his pocket. This was perfect. She would feel a single tiny pinprick, then, fifteen seconds later, her heart would seize, then stop. She would die in her own home, in her own bed, nestled in the arms of her lover. Wurth smiled. Most old people would give anything to go like that. He uncapped the syringe and leaned over to inject the poison into the woman's flesh, then he stopped. With his needle poised just inches from its target, David Forrester's twisted body flashed before him. He heard the thud of a baseball bat slamming into his kneecaps, another one crushing his skull. Then he heard someone gasping in pain, then a single agonized cry that shrieked up to heaven. No, he suddenly decided, looking down at the sleeping judge. David had not gotten to die like this. Why should this woman be allowed to go so easily?

Moving like a magician skilled in sleight of hand, he recapped the syringe and returned it to his pocket. With a single step backward from the bed, he crept into the shadows and padded around the edges of the room, noting with a tiny penlight the books by her bed, the papers on her desk, the business cards by her telephone. By the time he circled to her bedroom door again, he'd learned everything he'd needed to know.

Sleep well, Judge Hannah, he silently bade her as he slipped back out into the darkened hall. *Enjoy your dreams. Someday soon, we'll meet again.*

CHAPTER 16

The raucous honk of a goose woke Mary up. She opened her eyes, for an instant unable to place herself in time and space; then she heard a horse neigh outside and downstairs, the slamming of a cabinet door. Yesterday was Christmas, she remembered. Last night she'd slept in her old room at Upsy Daisy—tucked into the narrow bed beneath the eaves, snuggled beneath a blue patchwork quilt. Lifting her head from her pillow, she saw her Beretta hanging over the end of the bed like a gunfighter's in some Hollywood western. First Christmas I've ever spent armed, she thought.

She threw the quilt off and padded to the bathroom, the hardwood floor frigid under her bare feet. Her thighs and buttocks felt like liquid fire, and every joint below her waist seemed to have been glued into one position. At first she wondered if she wasn't coming down with some kind of flu, then she remembered they'd ridden horses yesterday. All over the farm and up into the woods behind the pasture they'd galloped, the horses making long puffs of steam with their breath in the bright, cold air. Afterward Hugh had concocted some kind of turkey hash for dinner and opened a bottle of Irish whiskey. They'd roasted potatoes in the fire, then moved into the living room, where Irene had played her piano long into the night, Lucy honking a laughable accompaniment from the porch. Irene ran through her classical repertoire, then Hugh passed around the bottle and they'd sung songs and carols until Mary's eyelids drooped. Although she'd forgone the whiskey in an effort to stay awake, she'd stumbled up to bed exhausted, falling asleep to a sweet, slurred version of "Danny Boy."

Now she had an entirely different Danny boy on her mind. If Agent Daniel Safer could see her now, he would be furious. Bodyguards don't encourage their charges to drink whiskey. Bodyguards stay awake. Bodyguards know where their clients are at all times.

"Oh, shut up, Safer," Mary grumbled aloud as she flushed the toilet. "Irene's perfectly all right. No harm done." *Better not let it happen again,* an inner voice scolded her as she winced at her reflection in the mirror and brushed her teeth with cinnamon-flavored toothpaste.

She pulled on her jeans and a thick wool sweater and then clumped noisily down the stairs, lest she interrupt another tryst by the fire. When she reached the kitchen, however, only Irene was there, sitting at the table, reading the business section of the newspaper.

"Morning." Mary yawned, blinking at the dull light that licked at the windows. "What time is it? Where's Hugh?"

"Six A.M." Irene looked up from her paper and smiled. "He's delivering flowers in Raleigh. He'll be gone till tomorrow."

"Oh." Mary plopped down in the chair across from her. It had always made her sad that one day it was Christmas, and the next day it was business as usual. She guessed she liked her holidays to fade away gradually, rather than just end. "Thank you for a wonderful Christmas. I can't remember when I had so much fun."

"It was fun, wasn't it?" Irene stepped over to the stove and poured Mary a mug of coffee. "If Lady Jane would have had her foal, it would have been absolutely perfect."

"Have you checked on her this morning?"

"Twice, already. She's still pregnant. I'm on

my way to the stable to feed everybody. You want to come along?"

"Sure." Mary gulped her coffee while Irene stepped into a pair of green Wellingtons and stashed a small thermos in her eiderdown jacket. "Just let me get my gun," Mary said, draining her cup.

"We're only going to the barn."

"Doesn't matter. I'll be back in a flash."

She raced up the stairs, grabbed her holster, and strapped it on at the run. By the time she returned to the kitchen, Irene was halfway out the door, leading the way with her flashlight. The trees were just gray shapes in the mist, and the mountains looked like dark, sleeping giants. Mary smiled. *Udusanuhi*—the Old Men. *Dakwai, Ahaluna, Disgagistiyi.* Her mother's people had named them well.

"Do you remember who got fed what yesterday afternoon?" Irene flipped on the overhead lights when they reached the stable.

"I think so." Mary looked at the six equine heads that were peering at them over their stalls. "Spindletop, Banshee, and Stella get sweet feed and hay. Scooter and Dutchess get extra corn. I can't remember what you gave Lady Jane."

"Pregnant mare chow." Irene laughed. "Come on. The two of us can get this done fast."

She swung open a door to a room that contained several metal garbage cans full of grain.
With Mary glancing at a cheat sheet tacked to
the wall, the two women filled six different
buckets with varying ratios of corn to oats. They
delivered a bucket to each horse, along with a
pailful of fresh water. As the rhythmic crunch of
six horses serious about their food filled the
barn, Irene sat on a bench beside the tack room
and pulled the thermos from her vest.

"I'm out of Lady Jane's supplement," she said.
"I'll have to pick up some more when I go into
town."

"Did you say you were going back to
Richmond on the fifth?"

"Yep. We're ruling on an ICC case that week.
That's why I want Lady Jane to hurry up and get
on with it."

Mary knew better than to ask specifics; still,
she couldn't resist one more question. "This
case isn't a hot button for any lunatic fringe
group, is it?"

Irene chuckled. "No. In fact, on January fifth
the interstate trucking industry should send me
roses."

"That's a relief. I don't know what I'd do if
semis started chasing you."

Irene shook her head. "Mary, nobody's going

to come after me. I'm an old broad. My only claim to fame is being the lone liberal voice on the conservative Fourth Court."

"You're an important jurist, Irene. You could be appointed to the Supreme Court."

The smile faded from Irene's face. "Is that what this is all about?"

"Nobody knows what it's all about. That's what makes it so scary."

They waited for the horses to finish, then turned out all but Lady Jane. While the mare stayed in the little paddock next to the stable, nuzzling at the tiny green shoots of clover that sprouted even in the winter, the others galloped up the hill like schoolchildren freed at recess.

"They'll graze up in the woods for the rest of the day, then come back here around sundown." Irene smiled as the horses scattered up the hill. "See how totally not at risk we all are here?"

Mary gazed up into the mountains that ringed the farm, hoping that Irene was right. When the horses had disappeared into the tree line, she helped Irene muck out the stalls, then they walked back to the house.

"Are you going to work all day?" she asked as Irene slipped out of her boots by the kitchen door.

"All morning," she replied. "I've got a dental

appointment at two. And I'd like to stop and get those vitamins for Lady Jane at the feed store."

"A dental appointment?" Mary frowned. Safer had showed her how to rip out someone's eye, but he'd neglected to tell her what to do if Irene had to get a cavity filled.

"I've put off getting a crown as long as I can." She clacked her teeth together loudly. "I shouldn't be gone more than a couple of hours, though. Maybe we can go for another ride when I get back."

"Would you mind if I came with you?" Mary rinsed her coffee cup in the sink, abruptly aware of the gun beneath her left arm.

"To the dentist?" Irene looked mortified.

Mary shrugged. "I'm sure that's what Safer would want me to do."

"Well, okay. But if you bring that pistol, don't let anyone see it. Dr. Moreland's as old as I am. I don't want him any shakier with that drill than he already is."

Mary washed out the coffee cups while Irene went to work on her opinion. She put Hugh's mostly empty bottle of whiskey on top of the refrigerator and threw some stale biscuits out for Lucy. When she'd gotten the kitchen tidy again, she fixed a large pot of tea, remembering from her clerking days that Irene started the day with coffee, then switched at midmorning to Earl Grey tea. She smiled as she tapped on the door of the study, tea tray in hand.

"Irene? *Doyust zaditasti duli?*" Impishly, she phrased her question in Cherokee, wondering how much Irene remembered.

"I'd love some," Irene called, laughing. She looked up as Mary opened the door. "Wahdo!"

"Boy, I'm impressed. You've kept up!" Mary set the tray down on Irene's desk.

"Actually, it was a lucky guess," admitted Irene. "Other than you, I don't have anyone to speak Cherokee with."

"Me, neither." Mary poured Irene a cup of tea, counting the people with whom she could speak the language her mother had so proudly taught her. Beyond Jonathan, who only knew about three phrases, Irene was the only one left. Unless, of course, she counted Ruth Moon, who probably spoke fluently and wrote in the syllabary as well. Too bad she had so little to say to Ruth Moon.

"No Cherokees in Atlanta?" Irene asked as she took the cup Mary offered.

"None have introduced themselves to me." Mary poured herself some tea and walked over to one bookshelf. If Irene's house was her favorite house in all the world, then Irene's study was her favorite room. A massive rolltop desk sat on a faded sarouk carpet in the middle of the room, looking like a huge frog on a lily pad. The walls were covered floor to ceiling with bookcases, and the only spot not given to books was covered by an exquisite tapestry.

Mary's heart twisted as she looked at the weaving. She remembered the day she and her mother first met Irene Hannah. She'd come into Little Jump Off to buy fishing worms. Three hours later Irene and Martha Crow had become fast friends. The two women had discovered in each other a passion for books and art and the distaff mountain crafts—quilts and coverlets and the tapestries her mother wove. Her fishing trip forgotten, Irene Hannah had grinned at Martha with dancing brown eyes and declared, "I want you to weave me the mountains!" "But how big?" her mother had asked, flustered at Irene's expansiveness. "Just like this," Irene replied, spreading her arms wide.

The next day Martha had started weaving. It had been spring, and Mary and Jonathan had discovered a nest of wood ducks in the reeds beside the river. Six months later, as the grown-up ducks headed south for Florida, her mother finished it. Then Federal District Judge Irene Hannah had written out a check for a thousand dollars. It was the most money Martha Crow had ever earned for a piece of work. After Irene

had driven away with the tapestry in the back-
seat of her Mercedes, Mary and her mother had
piled into their old Chevy and splurged on a
steak dinner in town. Christmas had been more
than abundant that year, and Mary did not see
the worry lines in her mother's face again until
the next spring.

"That piece just goes on forever, doesn't it?"
Irene's voice broke the comfortable silence of
the room.

"Every time I see it I'm amazed all over
again."

"Your mother was an extraordinary artist. She
should have been rich and famous." Irene's
funny caned-back swivel chair squeaked as she
turned around. "Do you paint much anymore?"

"A little. I brought a set of pastels with me.
Maybe you and Lady Jane could pose."

Irene looked up at her. "Do you ever regret
my hauling you out of the studio and into the
courtroom?"

Mary thought of the dark, brackish paintings
she'd produced her first two years in college, after her mother's murder. "No." She smiled. "I'm
a pretty good prosecutor. As an artist, I would
have starved."

While Irene turned back to her work, Mary
moved around the room, looking at Irene's
books, smiling at the various mementos among

her legal tomes. A Japanese tea set, a Cherokee dream catcher, pictures—Phoebe on a Shetland pony, William in his Navy uniform, even a small snapshot of her, resplendent in her Emory gown, lifting her law school diploma in triumph.

When she came to a small cast-iron statue of a tree with six wedding rings dangling from the branches, she began to laugh.

"Remember Reuben Loveless? The guy with six wives?"

Irene nodded. "I sure do. Married six women without bothering to divorce a one. As I recall, five of the Mrs. Lovelesses were mighty pissed. The sixth one thought Reuben was just misunderstood." She turned to Mary and raised one eyebrow. "Remember the state of North Carolina versus Marcus Stephens?"

"Oh, lord, yes." Mary's cheeks flushed. "My first case to research. North Carolina real estate codes. I pored over those books for days."

"It was brilliant research," said Irene. "Too bad you just weren't looking in the latest books. . . ."

Mary shook her head. "I'm still mortified by that. You would have ruled for Stephens and been overturned in a heartbeat. And it would have been all my fault!"

"You were a kid." Irene laughed. "And I caught the error in time. Believe me, honey, worse legal errors have been made by grayer heads than yours."

"Thus ended my career as a dirt lawyer," said Mary.

"Honey, you were a criminal prosecutor right out of the gate. Anything less would have bored you."

"I don't think I've ever had as much fun as when I clerked for you in Asheville."

Irene chuckled. "You got a good education. We heard everything—murder, arson, kidnapping, embezzlement."

"Bigamy," added Mary.

"Ah, yes. I've still got most of those old files in my hall closet." She took a sip of her tea, then set the cup back in its saucer with a clatter. "You know, I remember seeing an old file of your mother's in that closet, a couple of months ago."

Mary looked at her, stunned. "You have a file of my mother's?"

"Yes. As I remember, it's nothing more than a transfer of deed and some letters she wanted to keep safe."

"Some letters?" Mary frowned. Other than her husband, Jack, all Martha's friends had been local, people she saw every day. She would have no need to write a letter to any of them.

"I think so." Irene looked at the papers on her desk. "How about I dig it out as soon as we come back from the dentist? I need to get back to work right now."

Mary wanted to ask if she could just get the file herself, but she said nothing. It would be a terrible breach of professional courtesy to rifle through another attorney's files.

"That'd be terrific," she said instead. She put her empty teacup down on the tray and left the study to Irene and her opinion, wondering what kind of files her mother's small, sad life could have left behind, and amazed that today, after thirteen years, she would soon find out.

CHAPTER 17

Sergeant Wurth had not been joking when he said serious work would begin after Christmas. Cabe had rolled out of his cot at 0700 hours, putting his glasses on with the crazy hope that Willett had returned. But the adjoining bed still sat empty, its unmussed linens tucked tight beneath the mattress. With a sad emptiness spreading inside him, Tommy ate cold cereal with his fellow Grunts, then reported in front of the castle at 0800. It was clear by the way Sergeant Wurth strode up and down in front of them that Christmas at Camp Unakawaya was over.

Yesterday it had been impossible to sneak down to AR. With all the Troopers prowling around in festive high spirits, it had been all Cabe could do to avoid Tallent and Grice. Ultimately he'd sneaked back up to the cave. He'd squeezed through the bars, grabbed the stolen flashlight, and threaded his way back to Willett's den. The four remaining cans of Coke and the photo of Tarheel remained where Willett had left them. Holding his breath, Tommy had thrust his hand inside the fissure that hid Willett's secret weapon, hoping wildly that his friend had escaped and was right at that very moment at some police station, loading those files onto a cop computer. But when his fingers curled around the plastic-covered disk, Cabe's heart sank. Willett was still somewhere at Camp Unakawaya. He would never have made a break for it without his disk. And anyway, Willett never would have left him without saying good-bye.

He stayed in the cave until late afternoon, when it was time to return to the castle for their annual Christmas dinner from the ladies of the Pisgah Valley Baptist Church. Willett had often raved about that meal, about how for once the Grunts got to eat the same food as the Troopers, real plentiful and all of it good. Cabe had looked for him before he sat down at the table, hoping Wurth might have released him from AR for the Christmas feast, but Willett was not there.

This morning Wurth made no mention of Christmas or Willett, but immediately assigned certain favored boys to certain favored duties.

Grice and Tallent and the rest of the Troopers were sent to start building some kind of platform in the gym. The Grunts got stuck with their usual jobs in housekeeping—the more promising boys getting kitchen duty or classroom mainte- nance. Lesser talents like Cabe, who had demer- its to work off, had to work outside. Though he usually hated the futility of sweeping dead leaves against a raw mountain wind, he didn't mind it today. Sweeping would give him free run of the place, and that meant he could maybe sneak down to AR.

He swept the wind-driven leaves away from the corners of the broad front porch, then moved on to the great porte cochere, listening to the snap of Wurth's huge quasi-American flag as it popped in the breeze. When his knuckles had grown red from the cold, Tommy decided it was time to risk a trip to the basement. Although any Grunt caught snooping around AR was liable to be sentenced to a long stretch there himself, Cabe didn't care. He was convinced that Wurth had sent Willett there early. As bad as Camp Unakawaya was, Cabe had never known anyone to just disappear in the middle of the night and not be heard from again.

With a hasty glance around, he shouldered his broom and strode to the back of the castle. Only he and another Grunt, who was picking up dead limbs from the tennis court, were out in this frigid weather. He stashed his broom behind a sprawling boxwood and raced up the steps to the mud room that opened into the kitchen. When he pulled the door open, warm, moist air instantly fogged his glasses. He took them off and wiped them on his jacket as he walked inside. Three other boys were washing dishes at the sink, their forearms enveloped in a cloud of steam.

"It's C-C-Cabe," Harvey Galloway mocked. "How many of those demerits have you worked off, C-Cabe?"

"I don't know." Cabe put his glasses back on. "Maybe two."

"Pierson ever show up?" Mike Abbot turned his ferret-like face toward him.

"No."

"I'm telling you he's dead," Galloway cried, as if Cabe had just walked in on an ongoing dispute. "You don't go off on Wurth like that and just cool your heels in AR."

"He's not dead, Galloway." Cabe said it flatly, trying to ignore the sick feeling inside him that Galloway might be right.

"Yeah, C-C-Cabe, as if you'd know." Galloway sneered back at him.

Abbot gave a nervous snigger and returned his

attention to the sink. Tommy stepped quietly through the kitchen.

"Where you going, Cabe?" called Abbot, catching him just as he was turning toward the basement stairs.

"To the john," replied Cabe. "It's too cold to shit in the woods."

The three boys howled with laughter. Cabe started toward the bathroom, but when the dishes began to clatter again in the sink, he turned quickly and slipped through the door that led down into the basement. He would have to move carefully, and he would have to move fast. At Camp Unakawaya there were limits to how long someone could sit on a john.

He tiptoed down the old stone stairs. The basement mirrored the creepy third floor, with lots of small plastered rooms lit by thin windows that began a few feet above ground level and extended downward. Even on bright days it remained dark, and Cabe always wondered if fungus wasn't the true ruler down here. Trying to ignore the feeling that malevolent spores were watching him from the shadows, he hurried down the T-shaped hall. When he reached the end, he turned left. The top of the T held AR—a series of tiny cells located beneath the upstairs dining room, no doubt arranged so the smell of food could taunt the hungry penitents as they languished in their cells.

He crept forward, keenly aware that time was passing, aware, too, that if he was caught here he would be in trouble like never before.

"Willett?" he whispered as he approached the first cell. He pressed his ear to the heavy wooden door. No sound came forth. Tentatively he put his hand on the doorknob and turned. The door swung open, revealing a tiny room, empty except for a single short stool squatting in the middle of it.

He moved on to the next door, again calling Willett's name, again getting no response. That door swung open easily, startling several huge pale roaches that scurried back into the shadows.

When he reached the third door he stopped. This was the last room. If Willett wasn't in here, then Willett wasn't anywhere. With a silent prayer, he leaned close to the door and whispered, "Willett? It's me, Cabe!"

He thought he heard a soft moan. When he tried the door it opened readily, but only revealed a small cell with a foul, stained mattress on the otherwise empty floor. Willett Pierson was not down here having his attitude realigned at all. He was not in his room, nor was he hiding in his cave. In that moment the sick feeling in Cabe's stomach grew heavy as a stone. Maybe Galloway had gotten it right; maybe Wurth couldn't allow insubordination like Willett's. Maybe Wurth had killed him and was betting that Cabe didn't have the guts to find out.

CHAPTER 18

At quarter past one, Irene emerged from her office. She and Mary went out the back door and headed toward a small red pickup truck that glittered in the sun.

"Do you still have your Mercedes?" Mary remembered the old brown tank of a car that Irene had careened through the mountains in ever since she'd known her.

"Yep. I save Miranda for the paved streets of Richmond. Out here, I drive this." Irene climbed behind the wheel of the little pickup.

"Are you one of those asshole truck drivers who go a hundred miles an hour and blind you with their headlights before they mow you down?" Mary pulled open the passenger door. Inside, Irene's truck looked no bigger than her Toyota.

Irene grinned mischievously. "They don't call me Haul Ass Hannah for nothing."

Mary tugged her seat belt tight. With a long rev of the truck's engine, Irene bore down on the narrow suspension bridge, zooming across before the sympathetic rumbling grew deafening.

They skidded down the driveway, then out onto the main road where Safer had dropped Mary two days before. How long ago that seemed, she thought, wondering what Safer had been doing. She didn't figure him for anyone who would call to wish them Merry Christmas, but he might have at least checked on them this morning. The cell phone, however, had not beeped a single time since he had stomped off, livid that she'd gotten the nod to guard Irene. Safer was weird, she decided as she looked at the dark green forest that pushed up against the pavement. But come to think of it, what Fed wasn't?

The twisting mountain road joined another, less twisting county road, and soon they were driving on 441, between vacationers toting skis to Wolf Laurel and Cattaloochee and long skidders hauling newly cut timber to the sawmills. Mary watched each vehicle they passed, looking for what, she didn't know. At Upsy Daisy, she felt confident in her ability to keep Irene safe. Out here in the real world, she was growing edgier by the minute. By the time they rolled into downtown Hartsville and pulled up at a sprawling old Victorian that had been turned into a small office building, she felt like she'd mainlined a half-dozen espressos.

Dr. John Moreland's reception room had once been the front parlor of the old home. Bright and sunny, it was now filled with two over-stuffed sofas and an array of aging magazines. Kenny G issued from the speakers overhead, while a heavyset Cherokee woman in a white hospital coat sat at the reception desk.

"Hey, Miss Irene," the woman called cheer-fully as Mary and Irene entered. "How you do-ing today?"

"Fine, Rebecca. How about you?"

"I'm okay. You bring along some moral sup-port?" Rebecca eyed Mary with suspicion.

Irene smiled. "Rebecca Taylor, this is Mary Crow. Mary clerked for me in Asheville. Now she's a top DA down in Atlanta."

Mary immediately recognized the look in Rebecca's eyes. She'd first seen it the day she started grade school. By the time she graduated from Cherokee High, she knew it all too well. *Tsalagi,* it said, *but not real Tsalagi. Skin too pale, eyes too light to be truly one of us.*

Rebecca Taylor's mouth drew down in a smirk. "DA, huh? You put away as many crim-inals as that New York lawyer gal on TV?"

"I've nailed a few," Mary replied. "In real life it's not that glamorous."

"Uh-oh." With a dismissive toss of her head, Rebecca turned her attention back to Irene. "Room two, Miss Irene. Doc'll be with you in just a minute."

Irene frowned as Mary fell into step behind her. "You're not going in the examination room with me, are you?"

"How long will you be in there?"

"I have no idea," Irene replied in the snappish tone she usually reserved for nitpicking attorneys. "Sit down and read some magazines. You're going to drive everyone crazy."

"Okay, okay." Chastised, Mary watched Irene disappear down a short hall. She sat down and thumbed through a two-year-old *Field & Stream,* then an *Outdoor Life.* Bored by the articles and not particularly compelled by photos of writhing muskellunge, she got up and gazed out the tall reception-room window. The bright December sun sparkled off the tinsel that hung from the streetlights. Across the street a woman emerged from Beckett's Bakery, one of their distinctive red-and-white cake boxes in her arms. Two little boys ran inside Roses' department store. It was amazing how many people were out on the streets. Anybody could be lurking out there. Anybody at all. She checked her watch. Irene had been in the chair fifteen minutes. Maybe she'd better see how she was doing.

With a glance at Rebecca Taylor, she walked back and peered into room two. A lanky, gray-haired man in a white coat stood reading an X ray. In the chair, looking like someone with numb lips, Irene raised her hand and waved. Everything was okay, Mary decided as she returned to the reception room.

"Not nearly as exciting as court, is it?" Rebecca Taylor raised one eyebrow scornfully.

"No, thank God. It's not." Mary sat down and opened another *Field & Stream*. She scanned an article about bow hunting and thought of Jonathan. Though he gave little notice to most official holidays, he always celebrated Christmas like a kid, buying presents, stringing up lights, passing out candy to the children who came into the store. Last year they'd drunk eggnog and exchanged his presents in bed. This year Jonathan was doing that with Ruth Moon. Mary felt a heaviness in her chest as she wondered what gift he'd given his new love. Tossing the magazine on the table, she went back to check on Irene.

"Any change?" Rebecca Taylor smirked as Mary returned thirty seconds later.

"Nope," reported Mary with a tight smile. She gave up on the magazines and looked out the window again. Two teenaged girls hurried into the video store; three old men gossiped in front of Comer's Drugs. A black dog trotted across the street. She glanced at her watch, then sat back down in the chair, determined to find something entertaining in *Dentistry Today.*

She turned the pages, the sun growing warm upon her back. She read one article on advances in tooth implants, then another on building a successful practice. As she started to read about how to soothe overly nervous patients, Irene appeared, upright, mobile, and ready to depart.

She scheduled her next appointment with Rebecca Taylor, then turned and jingled her keys at Mary. "Okay. Let's go."

Mary stood, grateful to shake off the warm drowsiness of the room. Rebecca Taylor did not look up from her desk as Mary strode into the hall beyond, zipping up her jacket as she did so.

"How's your tooth?" Mary asked as they climbed back into Irene's truck.

"I can't feel a thing now," replied Irene. Her bottom lip looked slightly swollen. "I might sing a different tune when this novocaine wears off." She started the engine. "Let's go to the feed store and hurry on home."

"Suits me," said Mary.

Irene started to back out into traffic, then she braked and pulled back up to the curb. "Damn," she said disgustedly. "I forgot those pain pills he gave me." She shoved the truck into park but left the motor running. "Wait here while I run in and grab them. Won't take me a second."

Before Mary could protest, Irene was halfway up Dr. Moreland's steps. Mary settled back in the seat with a sigh, glad that this little excursion into Hartsville would soon be over. She was beginning to understand why Safer always looked so sour. Bodyguarding was nerve-racking work.

Two teenaged boys on skateboards surfed down the sidewalk, their cheeks chapped from the wind. A sallow-faced woman parked a station wagon beside the truck; she and a little girl got out and scurried across the street to Beckett's Bakery. The truck's motor kept running; a high-pitched fan came on to cool the engine. Mary looked at the door of Dr. Moreland's office. Irene had been in there a long time. In fact, Irene had been in there more than long enough to grab a bottle of pills.

Mary switched off the ignition and flung open the door. In an instant she was running up the stairs, yanking the heavy, ornately carved paned door open. The old dentist was standing in his reception room, tying a red wool scarf around his neck while Rebecca Taylor was covering her computer with a plastic hood.

"Where's Irene?" Mary asked.

"I don't know," snapped Rebecca Taylor. "She got her pills and left."

"When?"

"Just a minute ago," said Dr. Moreland. "Tylenol with codeine. In case her tooth hurt tonight."

Mary stared at them, unable to speak.

"She's probably in the bathroom." Rebecca Taylor looked irritated at this little glitch in her own departure. "Sometimes dental work makes older people sick to their stomachs. She probably—"

Mary was out the door before Rebecca Taylor finished her sentence. There might be a lot of things that would make Irene Hannah sick to her stomach. Dental work wasn't one of them. With her hand gripping the Beretta, Mary flew down the long carpeted hall, passing the Masterson Insurance Company on her left, Jaxie's Beauty Shoppe on the right. The bathroom stood at the end of the hall. She pulled her gun and knocked on the door.

"Irene? Are you okay?"

She heard water running behind the door. *Thank God,* she thought. *She's in there. Maybe she had gotten sick.*

"Irene? It's Mary. Are you okay?"

Again, nothing but the sound of running water. Mary grabbed the doorknob and turned it; the door opened easily. Inside was a toilet and small pink vanity. A crushed paper towel lay on the floor, hot water ran steaming from the faucet. Irene Hannah was not there. But lying on the white tile floor, directly in front of the sink, was a single black feather from the wing of a bird.

CHAPTER 19

Turning, Mary ran down the hall, out to the end of the veranda beyond. The wide porch wrapped around the east side of the old house, stopping at the locked exterior entrance to the Masterson Insurance Agency.

She raced to the other side of the porch, running down wide steps that led to a short driveway. She followed that to the rear of the building, where two cars were parked near the exit. *Dr. Moreland and Rebecca Taylor are the only ones here,* she realized. *Whoever grabbed Irene took her out of the building, out the back door.*

She sprinted toward the alley that served as access to the parking areas behind the buildings on Main Street. Except for a single calico cat parading stiff-legged toward a trash Dumpster, it was deserted.

With a sick knot in her stomach, Mary turned

and ran back into the house, bounding into Dr. Moreland's office. The old dentist and Rebecca Taylor stood exactly as Mary had left them, their expressions a blend of bewilderment and alarm.

"I think that Irene Hannah may have been abducted from this building," Mary told them. "You two need to stay in this office."

"What do you mean *abducted*?" cried the receptionist, her eyes growing wide. "Who would have taken her?"

"I don't know," Mary answered. "But I'm calling the FBI to find out."

"Are you calling them right now? I've got plans tonight," Rebecca Taylor whined.

"Yes, you do, Ms. Taylor," replied Mary. "And I guarantee that one of them will be giving a long and detailed account of the day's activities to the FBI. I suggest that you don't leave this building. They like it a whole lot better if they don't have to come to you."

"Oh, dear." Dr. Moreland's voice sounded like a flute with a bad valve. "Poor Irene."

"Please sit down, Doctor," Mary told him. "Read some of your magazines."

Quickly she began to dig in her purse. That cell phone was in here somewhere. She found her wallet, her checkbook, then a lipstick and a pen. Where was the damn thing? She turned her purse upside down and dumped the contents onto the carpet. Only the things she'd already found fell out, along with a half-eaten roll of Tums. *Damn,* she cursed silently. *I must have left it on the table beside my bed. I was so worried about not forgetting the stupid gun, I walked off without that phone!*

Scooping her things back in her purse, she took a deep breath and tried to think, the eyes of Rebecca Taylor and Dr. Moreland upon her. Irene was gone. She had a gun and a truck, but no way to reach Safer. Dr. Moreland's phone wasn't programmed with the FBI's special code. What should she do?

She glanced at the window and thought of running down the block to Sheriff Logan's office. Safer had tipped him off about their concern for Irene's safety, but Stump Logan was a slow, deliberate county sheriff more accustomed to lost hikers than abducted federal judges. In the time it would take her to explain everything to Logan, she could have Safer right beside her, barking out orders to a trained staff.

She looked at the badly frightened dentist. "Dr. Moreland, I'm going to have to return to Irene's farm. I'll contact the FBI from there. They'll need to interview you and Ms. Taylor. I can't force you to stay here, but it would go a lot faster for everyone if you did." She turned to

Rebecca Taylor, who was still pouting at having to remain at work, off the clock. "Please lock both entrances to this building. And whatever you do, don't touch anything in the bathroom. That's where they grabbed her. It's now an official federal crime scene."

"Of course." Dr. Moreland nodded. "Rebecca and I will wait right here. We won't touch a thing."

"Thank you." With a single fierce glance at Rebecca Taylor, Mary walked out the door and back into the late December afternoon.

★   ★   ★

She drove back to Upsy Daisy in a fury, careening around the curves, roaring like a madwoman past a wobbling pickup loaded with firewood. Hunched over the wheel, she kept turning Irene's disappearance over in her mind. Why had the Black Feathers not just slipped the needle to her and let her go into cardiac arrest in the bathroom? Why take her someplace? Mary answered her own question. *To torture her.* To do to her what they did to Judge Klinefelter. But where in Hartsville would they take her?

Home? Mary wondered, her fingers turning to ice as she pulled into Irene's driveway. *Would they have the balls to behead Irene in her own home?*

Instinctively she pulled the truck off the drive, into a coil of laurel. She cut the engine and withdrew the Beretta from her holster. She'd always imagined that the act would make her feel ludicrous, like some overly dramatic TV cop, but the cold, heavy weight of the pistol felt good in her hand.

Keeping the gun pointed at the ground, she crept toward the house, slinking through the tall trees that lined the driveway. The sun had dropped below the mountains, bathing the farm in an amber light. A thin, gray haze hovered like smoke over the orange fields while the bulbous shape of an owl swooped through the bare, spidery branches above her head.

She moved forward, her footsteps crunching on the frozen earth. Rounding the final broad curve in the driveway, she waited in the last bit of cover, listening as the shallow creek kept up its low, throaty gurgle.

Nothing indicated that any strangers had visited Irene's house. No one had painted swastikas on the front door, no skinhead graffiti decorated the porch. Lucy and the guineas pecked for the day's last worms in the sparse grass on the far side of the house. Still, Mary sensed something different about the place, as if the air had somehow grown thicker.

She eyed the bridge, then slipped through the weeds to the creek below. She hated the thought of wading through the freezing water, but if anybody was lurking inside Irene's house, the wooden bridge would announce her advance like a drum roll.

Without bothering to remove her shoes or socks, she waded into the stream, gasping as the freezing water foamed up to her knees. She picked her way carefully among the slippery rocks to the cattails that grew on the other side of the bank. Gratefully, numb from the knees down, she left the icy water and began to crawl to the yard's edge.

She ran with her knees bent, sneaking onto the porch, garnering minimal notice by the worm-hunting guineas. She tiptoed past the front door and peered through the living room window. Though the interior of the house lay in shadow, she recognized the dark bulk of the grand piano and the Christmas tree. Grasping the doorknob through the pocket of her down jacket, she turned it slowly. The door opened without a sound. That surprised her. Had Irene locked it before they left? She couldn't remember.

Keeping to the shadows, Mary slid forward and closed the door behind her. The comforting tick of Irene's old grandfather clock broke the house's silence, and the aroma of the bacon they'd fried that morning still lingered in the quiet air.

Normal, Mary thought, her edginess growing. *Everything looks just like it did when we left.*

She tiptoed down the hall, turning lights on first in the living room, next the dining room, then the huge old kitchen. Everything looked normal—dishes drying in the drainer, Hugh's whiskey on top of the refrigerator where she'd put it herself. Mary moved back down the hall toward the staircase, this time stopping at Irene's study. If anybody wanted to decapitate the Fourth Circuit judge on her own turf, they would have done it here, right behind this door.

Again she grasped the doorknob through her jacket. For an instant she paused, longing to close her eyes. She often did that with crime scene photos, hoping in vain that if she didn't look at the slit throats and savaged vaginas that maybe the women wouldn't be dead; maybe they would still be alive somewhere, shopping for clothes or drinking coffee with their friends. As much as she wanted it to, it never worked. Once her eyes took them in, they were gone. No more coffee, no more new shoes. In that instant they became dead people; just new victims in the system she served.

She took a shaky breath, then opened the

door. With trembling fingers, she reached for the light. When the bright colors of the room hit her eyes, relief hit her like a blow. Irene's great haven of law and order looked just as they had left it. Her beloved old desk still stood in the middle of the room, covered with the variously colored pages of the legal profession. The case-law books she'd been studying lay open where she'd marked their pages, a half-drunk cup of tea rested on the table by the phone. Martha Crow's beautiful tapestry still hung on the wall, the old sarouk carpet still covered the floor. Mary took in all these details, struggling to grasp what it all meant. With a sinking in her chest, she knew it in an instant. Whoever had taken Irene had not brought her back here. Whoever had taken Irene had taken her someplace else.

Swiftly she backed out of the study and hurried upstairs. Nothing up there had been touched, either. She dug Safer's cell phone out of her backpack and punched in her mother's birthday. Moments later, she heard Safer's crisp greeting.

"Agent Safer," she said, her voice sounding as if it were coming from the depths of a barrel. "You need to get over to Upsy Daisy Farm. Someone has kidnapped Irene Hannah."

CHAPTER 20

Seven minutes later the green vans screeched to a halt a yard away from the bridge. Mary watched from the porch as three FBI agents leaped out, led by Daniel Safer. Safer had sounded more alarmed than furious when she'd told him what had happened. He requested only that she remain where she was, if she felt safe. That was not a problem. No one was in danger here at Upsy Daisy.

"Are you okay?" Safer asked now, his dark eyes intent as his men went past her into the house.

"I'm fine."

"Anything inside?"

"Nothing. I don't think anybody's been here since we left."

"Have you touched anything?"

"Nothing but the doorknobs of the downstairs

study and the small bedroom on the second floor. They grabbed her at Dr. Moreland's dental office in town. That's where you need to be looking for prints."

"Mike Tuttle's on his way there now. We'll dust here, anyway. You want to come inside?" he asked softly.

Mary shook her head. "I'm going down to the stable. I need to check on Lady Jane."

"I'll meet you there as soon as I see what's gone on up here."

Nothing, thought Mary, as Safer disappeared into the house. *Nothing has gone on in there at all.* Drawing her gun just the same, she hurried around the house and through the backyard. Opening the gate, she ran down to the stable.

The dying light cast the interior of the stable in a network of dense shadows. She hesitated, wondering if perhaps whoever had taken Irene had brought her here. She curled her fingers tighter around the Beretta and smiled. If Irene's abductor was hiding in here, so much the better. She would kill him. And she would feel happy while she did it.

Squaring her shoulders, she stepped inside. The only noise she heard was from doves cooing from the hayloft over head, but she gripped her pistol with both hands and held it straight in front of her. Slowly she walked down the center aisle. The first two stalls were empty. Peeking into the crack of the feed-room door, she saw that it contained nothing more than barrels of grain. She inched along, checked the stall on her right, then turned and looked at the foaling area. Empty. Except for her and the doves, nothing alive and breathing was in this barn.

Suddenly a hand gripped her shoulder. She whirled, her finger tightening around the trigger.

"Hey!" a voice cried. Someone grabbed her right arm and twisted it behind her back, then gathered her in an awkward embrace.

She knew it was Safer before she saw his face; she could smell the laundry soap in his shirt, feel the tautness of the muscles in his chest. Shaking with nervous exhaustion, she leaned against him. The day that had started so happily this morning had, in the last two hours, turned into a nightmare.

He held her for a moment, then he let her go. "Are you all right?"

Mary nodded as she stepped back and slid the Beretta in her holster. "I just need to find the horses."

"Why did you leave Judge Hannah alone?"

Safer's question cut her like a knife. "She ran back inside the dentist's office, to get some medication. She left me in the truck with the motor running. I guess I thought she would be safe for thirty seconds."

"Why didn't you call me immediately?"

"We left for town in a hurry, already late. I was so concerned about carrying this," she touched the handle of her gun, "I forgot the stupid cell phone."

He looked like he was going to scold her; his eyes blazed. Instead, he said, "Tell me everything."

Mary explained exactly what had happened. She'd gone first to Moreland's office, then the bathroom. She'd found the black feather lying in front of the sink. "I told the dentist and his assistant not to touch anything." Mary remembered the thin, sullen line of Rebecca Taylor's mouth. "I think they understood."

Safer studied her for a moment, his dark eyes boring into her. Then he shook his head. "I knew this wasn't going to work."

"Oh, really? Well, where were you? And where was your little surveillance team?" Mary demanded, stunned. "I thought you hotshots had everything covered."

"I stayed here with the vans. Mike Tuttle was behind you the whole time in the truck."

"Then why didn't he see Irene go back inside that building?"

"One of Logan's deputies tried to ticket him

for being double-parked. By the time Tuttle got the deputy straightened out, you'd pulled back into traffic, headed here. Mike figured everything was okay."

"Didn't he see that I was alone in the truck, driving like a fiend?"

"You had a tinted rear window. And you drove no worse than the judge did on the way to town." Safer's tone was grim. "Come on. Let's go back to the house. I need to get your prints, so we can separate yours from everybody else's."

They crossed the paddock in a furious silence. Every window of the house now blazed. Mary could see the crime scene investigator moving around inside, gathering clues that might lead them to Irene. Suddenly a figure appeared in the floodlights that illuminated the patio—tall, male, khaki-shirted with a white Stetson hat. Mary knew that the man's eyes would be gray, his mouth thin, and his face creased with deep lines of worry around his mouth and between his brows.

"Hello, Mary. Agent Safer," the man called as they came closer.

"Sheriff." Mary gave a tense nod.

Stump Logan turned to Safer. "You want to fill me in on what's going on out here? Them boys of yours aren't too cooperative."

"Judge Irene Hannah disappeared from her dentist's office at approximately three o'clock this afternoon, mostly because one of your deputies was trying to cite my second-in-command for a parking violation." Safer talked as if his jaws were wired together.

"There was a slight misunderstanding between them. Son, you need to let me know if you're bringing your investigation to Main Street of my town."

Safer did not blink from Stump Logan's accusing gaze. "I don't *take* my investigations anywhere, Sheriff. I go where they take me."

"Uh-huh." Logan cast a sideways glance at Irene's house. "You guys dusting now?"

Safer nodded.

"Mind if I go in and have a look?"

Though Logan had phrased his request politely, Mary knew the pissing contest had started. *This is my county, you candy-ass Yankee boy,* is what Logan really said. *Just try to keep me out of an ongoing investigation.*

"Please." Safer pulled a pair of latex gloves from his back pocket and tossed them at Logan. "In fact, why don't we discuss this situation further? Inside."

Logan caught the gloves and turned toward the house. Mary sat down on the edge of the patio.

Safer looked at her. "Aren't you coming?"

She shook her head, suddenly weary of cops and G-men and the constant, bitter turf wars of law enforcement. "You and Sheriff Logan can hash it out on your own. I need to go feed the horses."

"Whatever." Safer snapped as he turned and followed the chief crime officer of Pisgah County, North Carolina, into Irene's home.

Mary gazed up into the sky. God, how could everything have gone wrong so fast? Why hadn't she just gone back to Moreland's office with Irene? Irene would have been irritated, but hell, at least she might still be here.

Mary got up and walked back to the stable. Where just minutes ago it had been devoid of anything resembling a horse, now Irene's entire herd of six all stood at the back paddock gate, each looking at her, ears pricked and tails swishing.

"Okay, guys," she told them softly, touched by the simple, innocent expectance of their gaze. "Tonight, dinner's on me."

She doled out each one's ration of grain, then opened the gate to let them into the stable. Each knew exactly where to go. They didn't fight, they didn't complain, nobody tried to shove their way into another's stall.

"Maybe this is what Irene loves about you so,"

she whispered as their quiet, rhythmic crunching filled the stable. "Whatever scrapes happen in the pasture, you guys work it out. As long as you have a bucket of oats and a warm place to sleep at night, everything is okay.

"Wonder why everybody can't take a lesson from that?" she murmured as she rubbed Lady Jane's silky mane and wished that somehow she could just relive the afternoon all over again.

CHAPTER 21

"Where's C-C-C-Cabe? I been looking for him."

Tommy Cabe snapped Captain Nigel Dempsey's diary shut and double-checked the lock on the bathroom stall door. Fear sluiced through him like shit through a goose. The toilet next to his flushed, then fat bare feet scrambled out, fleeing to the far end of the bathroom. Loftin, Tommy thought. Little chickenshit.

"C-C-C-Cabe?" the voice called again, high and whiny, like a girl's. "Where are you, boy? I been looking for you all day. I got some news about Wilma!"

The usual chatter of the Grunts died, leaving the bathroom in a dank silence broken only by the sound of water dripping. Tommy considered pulling his feet up and squatting on the toilet to hide, but it would be pointless. They already knew he was here.

"C-C-C-Cabe? Are you missing Wilma in there? Or did all that stuff Wurth said about your mother make you sick? Are you having di-di-diarrhea?"

He heard giggling as other bare feet hurried past his stall. The wide, fleshy ones would be Ledford's, the narrow ones Galloway; Abbot was the one missing a toe. All were pattering away. Not pattering off to help him, just pattering far enough to keep out of harm's way and still enjoy the show. *Bastards!* he thought, his throat swelling with tears. *Damn bastards!*

He stared at the floor as the sound of heavy, cadenced footsteps echoed off the tile walls. Suddenly not one, but two pairs of feet shod in steel-toed boots came into view. Tommy's heart sank. Tallent and Grice. The two Troopers who despised him most had come to call.

"C-C-C-Cabe!" One of them pounded hard on his stall. "What are you doing in there, boy? Shovin' in a tampon?"

Nervous laughter echoed as the rest of the Grunts gathered at the far end of the bathroom, listening and laughing. Tommy held the old diary close against his chest, wishing he could turn into Willett or even toothless old Captain Dempsey. *They* never took any shit off anybody.

"C-C-C-Cabe!" This time the pounding was thunderous; the second Trooper had joined in.

He wiped himself and stood up. When Willett was here he ran interference for Cabe, usually managing to befuddle Tallent before too much happened. Tommy's ally, though, was gone. Now nobody stood between him and his torturers.

He sighed. He may as well go out and get it over with. The sooner they finished with him, the quicker he could crawl into his cot and fig-ure out where next to search for Willett. As he pulled up his pajama pants and flushed the john, he wished with all his heart that he was six feet tall instead of five feet eight inches; wished he weighed 200 instead of 124. But that was not going to happen, at least not soon enough to help him now. He wondered what it would be tonight—a simple beating or the wienie games? The first, he hoped. Bruises faded over time. That stuff with the wienies stayed with you forever.

"C-C-C-Cabe!" The pounding began again. Squaring his shoulders, he shoved back the bolt on the stall door. The crack echoed through the tiled room as the door swung open. Just as he'd figured, Tallent and Grice stood there grinning, their eyes fever-bright with malice.

He stepped out from the stall, the old diary pressed to his side. The other boys stood silent, huddled and watching. Galloway tried to smile;

McCall stood with hands clasped in front of him, trying to protect himself any way he could. Only fat, dumb Darrell kept his head lowered, his gaze fixed on the floor. Darrell knew what was coming. He'd been wienied before, a time or two.

"Wh-what do you know about Willett?" Cabe forced himself to look up into Tallent's pink, piggy face.

"He sends you all his love," Grice said in a high falsetto.

"Yeah," Tallent snarled. "All the way from hell, which is where Willett is. Too bad he won't be around to protect you no more."

Before Tommy could spit out a word of protest, Tallent slapped him, snapping his head back against the bathroom stall, sending his glasses flying. Tommy heard them land, somewhere under the sinks, then someone snatched the diary from his hands. He heard Tallent and Grice laughing.

"Look at poor little C-C-Cabe. Got his thick old glasses broke again. He really needs his Wilma, now."

"What's this old shit you're reading, Cabe?" Tallent mocked, opening the diary. "Looks like Abe Lincoln wrote it."

Cabe tried to grab the book back, but Grice snatched it away and threw it back into his stall.

He felt a fist pummel into his gut. He doubled over, a dark red curtain shimmering down over his eyes.

"What do you mean reading in the john, C-C-Cabe?" Tallent demanded. "Don't you know that's bad manners? Or didn't your mom, the whore, teach you no better?"

"You go to hell!" Cabe cried, trying to stand upright long enough to take a swing at Tallent's face, wishing he could kill both of them.

They dodged easily away from his blows, laughing and sniggering. Pretending to be afraid, they danced around him, cuffing at his face. Ruthlessly they grabbed him and spun him around. Grice jerked his pajama pants to his knees, then held him down, bent over at the waist. He squirmed hard to get away, but Grice was too strong. When his pajamas fell to his ankles, Tallent began swatting his bare buttocks. They beat him with their open hands, slapping him as they would a woman. The other boys laughed nervously as he slipped and fell to the floor, but Tallent and Grice just pulled him up and started all over again.

"No more Wilma now, C-C-Cabe," Tallent sneered. "Nobody left standing between you and me." He unbuckled his belt and pulled it from around his waist. "But don't worry, Cabe. We're doing you a big favor. We're teaching you to be more of a man than little Wilma ever could be. You'll thank us someday."

That's absolutely right, Tommy Cabe thought, squeezing his eyes shut against all his pain and humiliation. *Someday I will thank the living shit out of you,* he vowed.

CHAPTER 22

The moon had risen above the mountains by the time the horses finished eating. One by one they crunched the last of their oats, took long slurps of water from their buckets, and settled down to sleep. Mary leaned against the foaling stall, watching Lady Jane turn in a circle like a dog, finally finding a position that suited her. As the little mare with the huge belly arranged herself in the straw, Mary heard a noise behind her. Instinctively she whirled around, then she recognized Safer's silhouette in the doorway. He held what looked like a camera bag in his right hand.

"Hey," he called softly. "How are you doing?"

"Okay," she lied, her shoulders relaxing. "I just finished feeding the horses."

"I still need to get a copy of your prints." He held out the bag. "And a statement."

"Sure." Her heart gave a little thump of disappointment. She was hoping he'd say something different—what, she didn't know. Maybe that they'd found Irene, or that she wasn't such a fuckup as a bodyguard. But no words of comfort left Safer's mouth. Why should they? He was here to track a killer, not ease her guilt.

He glanced at the dimly lit rafters of the hayloft. "Maybe we'd better go back up to the house, where we can see better."

"Let's try the tack room. Irene's got a little office in there."

She opened a door and turned on an overhead light. Safer followed her into a small room where, along with an extensive array of saddles and bridles, Irene kept a battered couch, a desk, and a dorm-sized refrigerator that held medicine for her horses.

Safer sat down on the couch. "Smells like a shoe store in here."

"All the leather," Mary explained, watching as he pulled out a small tape recorder and something that vaguely resembled a kid's set of watercolors.

"What do you want to do first?" He looked at her almost shyly. "Statement or prints?"

"You choose." She sat beside him on the couch. He turned on the tape recorder and handed it to her. Holding the microphone close to her mouth, she recounted everything, from finding the black feather in the bathroom to calling Safer on the cell phone.

When she finished, he rewound the tape and switched the recorder off.

"Thanks," he said softly. "I know that wasn't easy."

"Statements never are." Blurry-eyed, she stared at the mahogany-colored saddles. "I've made enough to know."

Safer put the recorder back in his bag and opened his set of watercolors, which turned out to be a fingerprint kit. Ten little pots of smooth black ink next to ten little squares of fingertip-sized white paper. Balancing the kit across his knees, he reached over and took her right hand. "Sheriff Logan thinks I ought to put you in charge of the investigation and go back home to D.C."

Mary felt her face grow hot. She despised being the subject of cop gossip. "Let me guess. He told you I tracked a crazy man for three days through the forest, then smashed another man's head in before I pushed him into a nest of rattlesnakes?"

Safer's hand on hers felt like warm silk. "I believe it went something like that," he said quietly, keeping his eyes on his work as he printed her left ring finger.

"Did he tell you that the man deserved it?"

"No." Safer stroked her finger before he pressed it into the ink. "I figured that out on my own."

For a moment, neither of them spoke. Safer handed her a tissue and reached for her right hand.

"You know what else he told me?" Safer asked. "He warned me that you were trouble. Said you had the perfect name—that death was your bread and butter. Just like a crow."

For the first time, Mary could see the true color of his eyes—not black, but dark, dark brown, like feldspar flecked with quartz.

His surprisingly gentle fingers guided hers across the ink and onto the paper. In the silence that sprang between them, his movements became almost languid, as if he wanted to prolong the process as long as he could. When he finished he looked at her hand, cupping it in his as if it were made of glass.

"What do you think?" she asked impulsively. "Is this the hand of a reveler in death?"

He looked at her with a fierceness that took her by surprise. "I think you and I might be cut from the same cloth," he whispered, his voice like sand.

She stared at him, astonished. He started to say something else, but the cell phone in his pocket beeped. He sat back on the couch and closed up the print kit, offering her another tissue as he answered the phone.

"Safer here," he said, his voice once again crisp and perfunctory.

He listened for a moment, then switched off with a brisk, "I'll be right there." Quickly he repacked his bag and stood.

"I've got to get back to the house." He spoke awkwardly, as if embarrassed by the words he'd said moments before. "Why don't you come, too? Logan's gone. And it's warmer up there."

"Thanks," she replied. "But I want to stay out here awhile. Make sure the horses are okay."

"Sure." He dipped his head and shouldered the fingerprint bag. "I'll see you later, then."

She watched him stride back to Irene's empty house, then she checked the horses one final time. Four stood dozing on their feet, while Lady Jane and Stella lay curled up in their straw. Mary stopped to see if the mare exhibited any signs of imminent labor, but Lady Jane seemed like just another tired horse, sleeping with her front legs tucked neatly beneath her like a deer.

All at once she, too, felt weary beyond be-lief—tired as if she'd crawled all the way from Atlanta on her hands and knees. Yawning, she returned to the tack room, where she found a large blanket along with several smaller, thicker ones that Irene used as saddle pads. Hoisting the lot over her shoulder, she climbed up to the hay loft, her legs feeling like lead. She kicked all the loose hay in front of the loft window and spread it out on the floor. Over that she placed the saddle pads and spread the larger blanket. With a brilliant winter sky overhead, she lay down and burrowed into the fragrant hay. All the lights in Irene's house still blazed. The two green vans still sat in the driveway. Safer and his Feds were working this case, busy as bees in a hive.

She supposed she should go back up there, but cops got irritated when someone wandered into the middle of an investigation. What could she do, anyway? If it hadn't been for her, Irene would be there right now, playing her piano.

Her eyelids grew heavy and she began to drift in and out of a dream about Irene and Jonathan and his new love, Ruth Moon. She was floating, following them all down a long hall, only they were running and she was helplessly floating, insignificant to them as a dust mote in the air.

★   ★   ★

The next thing she knew she was sitting up, chilled and itchy. The prickly hay had lost its warmth and the Beretta had rubbed a sore place under her arm. The horses slept below her, Spindletop snoring as loud as any human sleeper. Tilting her head, Mary realized something else. Music was floating through the night air. Notes from a piano, bright and clear as stars.

"She's back!" Mary cried, flinging the horse blanket off. "They found her!"

Without stopping to think, she raced headlong down the hayloft stairs, tearing through the stable and up the hill to the house. The lights in the kitchen had been turned off, but she could see a glow from the living room. Irene had sent the Feds home and was playing the piano! She flew through the grape arbor, across the patio, up to the back door. She tugged on it, but it did not budge. She ran around to the front of the house, where golden light poured out onto the porch as golden notes poured into the air—fast, bright, Bach-like melodies. Mary's heart soared as she leaped up the front steps. Irene was home and playing music!

The front door, too, was locked. As the music accelerated, she raced to the window. Grinning, she pressed her nose against the cold glass, waiting to catch a glimpse of that familiar silver head bobbing over the music. Then her heart fell. Though it was Irene's house and Irene's piano, it was not Irene playing. Safer sat at the old Steinway, pounding the keyboard as if the secret to

Irene's disappearance lay hidden in the ivory beneath his fingers.

"Oh," Mary whispered, her joy seeping away like air leaking from a balloon. "It's you." When Safer came to the end of the piece, she tapped on the window.

He looked up, startled, then rose from the piano bench and unlocked the door. "I thought you were asleep in the hayloft."

"I heard you playing. I thought you were Irene."

"I'm sorry," he replied, his voice instantly full of regret. "I didn't mean for you . . ."

"It's okay." She walked past him into the living room. "Forget it."

He closed the door and returned to the piano while she slumped into an armchair. He began to play again. This time the tune was softer but sad, in a bittersweet way. As she closed her eyes and listened, she had to admit that whatever Safer had or hadn't accomplished as an FBI agent, he could certainly play the piano. He finished the first song, then began another. This one she knew—she'd heard a girl sing it one night when she and Jonathan went to a piano bar. She smiled, the lyrics echoing in her head. *"When Sunny gets blue, her eyes get gray and cloudy, then the rain begins to fall . . ."*

She drifted away, immersed in the music until

the last notes faded into silence. When she sat up and opened her eyes, Safer was staring at her, his dark gaze again inscrutable.

"You play well," she said, embarrassed that he had caught her in such an unguarded moment. "That's a nice tune."

"It seemed to fit the moment," he replied.

"Do you always play the piano in the middle of an investigation?"

For the first time since she'd met him, Safer almost laughed. His cheeks rounded and she caught a flash of straight, white teeth through his thick beard. All her lovers had either been clean-shaven or, like Jonathan, grew little facial hair at all. *What would it be like,* she wondered, *to have Safer's beard curling around my fingers?*

"When I'm trying to figure something out," he said, tinkling out the melody to "Stardust."

"What are you trying to figure out now?"

He nodded. "The pattern. Irene Hannah's the twelfth judge in twelve months, but none have had exactly the same MO. Klinefelter was beheaded, Hannah was abducted."

"But there were black feathers at the last two crime scenes. They must be some kind of signature."

Safer started a Bach minuet. "But why didn't they just stick the feather in her mouth and kill her, right there in the bathroom? They could have poisoned her easily. Hell, they probably had enough time to chop off her head."

Mary's stomach tightened so at the thought of Irene being decapitated that she had to cover her mouth with her hand.

"I'm sorry." Safer quit playing. "I keep forgetting how much she means to you. It was pretty cool what you guys did yesterday."

"Yesterday?" The day before seemed to Mary like a distant memory.

"You know, Christmas afternoon. That horserearing thing."

"Yeah," agreed Mary. "That was pretty cool." She stared at the Christmas tree for a moment, then she turned back to him. "Have you increased the protection on the other judges?"

He nodded. "The entire federal judiciary is on full alert. Everybody's got some kind of guard on them." He frowned at the keyboard and played a single note. The sound echoed in the silence. "I just can't figure out how the hell they knew Judge Hannah was going to be at the dentist's this afternoon."

Mary thought of smug Rebecca Taylor. "I assume Dr. Moreland checked out."

"Everybody who works in and around that building checks out, although the dentist's receptionist did accuse you of trying to intimidate her."

"Then somebody who blends in very well in Hartsville must have staked us out," said Mary.

"That's what it looks like."

"Damn." She pressed her fingertips against her forehead. "Why didn't I just get out of the truck and go in with her?"

"Look." Safer leaned forward. "Don't go to the land of coulda-woulda-shoulda. You're a female civilian. You did the best you could. Considering what happened, you did a great job."

Mary swallowed hard, trying to loosen the guilt that felt coiled around her throat. "Don't baby me, Safer. You know as well as I do that if I'd stayed with her, this wouldn't have happened."

"Maybe. But maybe it would have, anyway. Maybe it would have been worse."

"Worse?"

"Maybe they would have eliminated you and taken her just the same."

She sighed. "Yeah. Maybe."

He played a complex jazz chord, mournful and full of longing. As he let it fade into silence, she felt as if everyone she'd ever loved had gotten into a boat and sailed away, leaving her alone, to inhabit an island that ships rarely visited. She heard the piano bench squeak as he stood up. He walked toward her, his footsteps muted on the worn carpet.

"They've cleared your room. Why don't you go back upstairs and get some rest?" He touched her shoulder. "It's almost three A.M. There's nothing more either of us can do now."

"What about later?" she raised her head and looked at him.

"Later we'll find out what the lab comes up with," he said impassively. "Then we'll go from there."

CHAPTER 23

Far beyond the reach of Safer's piano, the bare
limbs of maple trees sang in the darkness, played
by a winter wind that whipped and eddied
across the Little Tennessee River. Ruth Moon
stood naked in the bedroom she shared with
Jonathan Walkingstick, staring out into the inky
darkness, shivering as a frigid whisper of air
seeped in beneath the drafty window. For hours
she'd lain awake, gazing at the North Star, trying to pinpoint the vague sense of unease that
had crimped her sleep ever since she'd first
shaken hands with Mary Crow.

At first she thought it was simple jealousy—
Mary was pretty; Mary was smart. Mary walked
through Little Jump Off with a grace she, Ruth,
would never possess. But there was also a darkness about Mary Crow. She had a sadness that
sucked people up. Jonathan had only now begun

to heal from the wounds she had inflicted upon him. Only now did his mouth begin to turn up in a real smile. Only now did he love Ruth with ardor of their own making, instead of passion remembered for the woman he'd left behind. How could she let that woman come back into his life—into their life—to gnaw at his gut once again?

She turned from the window and studied him, lying on the bed behind her, sleeping on his back, his face and body open to the night around him. How she loved him. How she longed for him to look up and say to her *You have become my love. I want you to become my wife.*

"*Udolanushdi.*" She whispered his name in Cherokee, speaking in the Atali dialect she'd grown up with. "I'm going to protect you."

She closed her eyes as wind rattled the window, then she tiptoed to the bed. In her hand she held three seeds, all from the same red apple. Moving without a sound, she pulled the blankets from him, exposing his nakedness to the cool air. Soon he would awaken. She must hurry. She placed the largest seed between his feet, then the next largest over his head. The smallest, a mere dot of a seed, she put ever so gently on his heart, so perfectly that she could see the tiny brown drop throbbing with his heartbeat.

"Selu," she whispered. "Keep this man safe. Safe for me, safe for the purpose he was intended. Above all else, keep him safe from the one from the south, the one who would steal his soul."

At that word, Jonathan began to stir, lifting one hand to scratch at the tickle on his chest. Hastily she gathered the apple seeds up and placed them in her special box on the dresser, the one she'd brought all the way from Oklahoma. Then she hurried back over to the bed.

"Ruth?" Jonathan lifted his head and gazed at her, groggy. "What's wrong? Are you sick?"

"No," she replied, lying down beside him. She pulled the blankets back over both of them and rested her head on his chest. How she loved his smell, the texture of his skin. "I was just looking at the stars."

Laughing, he wrapped his arm tighter around her and kissed the top of her head. "Any one of them in particular?"

"I was thinking about what you told me about Polaris."

"Polaris? What about it?"

"That in twenty-six thousand years it will no longer be the North Star," she answered. "Lyra will be."

"Lyra Two, actually."

"That makes me sad," she whispered, knowing it was crazy to care about some icy ball of gas light-years away. "I mean, Polaris has always been the North Star."

"Things change," he replied, yawning. "Shit happens."

"I guess you're right," she said with a secret smile, suddenly cheered by the notion that if something as vast as the cosmos could change, then surely so could the desires of a human heart.

She kissed him, then she straddled him, placing his hands on her thighs. "Do you think a lot about Mary Crow?"

"Some, I guess," he replied, his voice carefully neutral. "I wish I could figure out who she came up here to visit."

"Maybe she really came to see you." Ruth threw out that notion like bait, to see what his response would be. "Maybe she just got scared and told me a lie."

"Mary?" He laughed softly. "No," he added, after a pause that lasted a jot too long. "Mary wouldn't get scared over seeing you."

Ruth guided his hands slowly up to her belly. "You know, I was surprised she was so light. The way you spoke of her, I assumed she was a full-blood."

"No." He cupped her breasts and squeezed them in the way she loved. "I've seen pictures of her father. He was tall and blond."

Ruth giggled. "A cowboy in the woodpile, huh?"

His caresses stopped. "No. That wasn't the case. Her mother never loved anyone else after her husband died. I don't think Martha even had another date."

"I'm sorry. I didn't mean that the way it sounded. I'm just surprised you would ever be with someone like that."

"Like what?"

"I don't know. . . . You're more *Tsalagi* than any man I've ever known. It just seems that you'd be happier with one of your own kind."

"Ruth, I grew up with her," he said, a trace of huskiness in his voice. "Who could be more of my own kind?"

"Nobody, I suppose." She lay down on top of him, pressing herself into the concave curve of his belly. "Let's not talk about her anymore."

"Fine with me." He wrapped his arms around her and kissed her, threading his fingers through her hair and holding her head tightly in his hands. When she felt him grow hard she scooted down and lowered herself onto him, moving her hips with his. In a few moments he came with a cry and shudder, then she did the same, hot little jolts of bliss fusing and circuiting and cross-circuiting inside her. As her pleasure faded and their breathing slowed, she kissed him, but felt a distance between them. Suddenly she grew uneasy all over again. It was as if some invisible beast was circling their home, just waiting for the right moment to spring. As she felt him slip into sleep beneath her, she again turned her face to the window, where Polaris twinkled in the winter sky.

She sighed. In twenty-six thousand years Polaris would be a has-been. She turned that thought over in her mind and wondered if, when Lyra Two assumed the title of North Star, Jonathan Walkingstick would still be in love with Mary Crow.

CHAPTER 24

For the remaining hours of the seemingly endless night, Mary Crow lay awake in the upstairs bedroom, listening as the wind rattled her windows, reliving each hour of the day a hundred times over. Why hadn't she remembered that cell phone? Why hadn't she called Safer to tell him they were going to the dentist? Why hadn't she just gone back inside the building with Irene? *Because you thought she would be safe,* she told herself in disgust.

She thought about Irene, remembering Christmas Eve, when the tall red candles on her dinner table had reflected the pure happiness on her face. And Christmas Day, when she'd reared up on Spindletop, quoting Shakespeare. Just twelve hours ago they'd laughingly conversed in Cherokee. Now she was gone. All that happiness was over.

While she thought of all that had transpired between them these last three days, a single sentence Irene had uttered yesterday kept popping into her head. *I have one small client file with all your mother's legal business in it.*

One small client file in Irene's closet. One small, last link to her mother. Mary stared at the ceiling until the shadows blurred before her eyes. The client file still belonged, theoretically, to Irene. But as Martha Crow's sole heir, the file also rightfully belonged to her. There would be no problem if Irene were here, she was going to give it to her anyway. But Irene was gone and the file could now reasonably be considered part of her estate. Though it would be a breach of every personal and professional standard she honored, she was going to see that file. Otherwise, who knew how long it might be before she would get another look at it.

Forgive me, Irene, she whispered when she heard the clock downstairs chime five. *But I know you'd understand.*

Slipping from beneath the quilt, she pulled on her jeans and sweater in the dark. She left her shoes under the bed, but grabbed a tiny flashlight key chain from her purse and tiptoed down the hall to the head of the stairs. The gleaming oak floor felt cool and slick beneath her bare feet. Downstairs, the house was wrapped in a dark silence broken only by the sonorous ticking of the old clock. Holding her breath, she began to creep down the steps with exquisite care, easing down each riser as if it were made of glass. After what seemed like decades she reached the bottom and peeked into the hall. To her left, the windows in the living room were small squares of cold light, illuminating the dark silhouette of the Christmas tree. She turned her head. The banked fire cast the kitchen in a dim glow. She could have sworn she heard the faint rattle of pages turning. *Safer,* she thought. *He's reading in the kitchen.* She was hoping he'd be stretched out and snoring on the sofa, but it didn't matter. She had only one chance to get this file before Irene's papers were sealed, and she was going to make good use of it. Turning, she looked across the hall. Though the Feds had dusted the whole house, they hadn't cordoned off any rooms with tape. The door she needed, the closet door, stood not five feet away. If Irene had left it unlocked, she would be in business.

With a final glance toward the kitchen, she inched across the hall. One floorboard gave a long, complaining squeak. She froze, heart thudding, waiting for Safer to appear in the doorway, but he remained in the kitchen. She inched forward. Finally she reached the closet and grasped the doorknob, turning it as if she were cracking a safe. She heard one tiny, metallic *click,* then pulled it open. Moving like a shadow, she wedged herself in between a heavy wool coat and something wrapped in dry cleaner's plastic and closed the door behind her.

She stood still, listening for Safer to come rumbling down the hall to investigate, but the house remained quiet. A cord from the light fixture on the ceiling batted against her cheek. She was tempted to switch it on, but opted for the tiny flashlight on her key ring instead. She felt ridiculously exposed. If Safer opened this closet and found her here, she would have no excuse.

Squeezing through the coats to the back of the closet, she flashed her light along a row of cardboard packing boxes labeled XMAS DECORA-TIONS. Finally she found what she sought. A squat, two-drawer file cabinet sat in the rear corner of the closet.

She dropped to her hands and knees and fumbled over several pairs of riding boots. Holding the flashlight in her mouth, she opened the top drawer of the file. It opened willingly, but with a loud, grating screech. She froze, her pulse thumping in her ears. What could she say if Safer opened this door? *Don't let him hear me,* she prayed. *Don't let anything keep me from getting this file.* She grasped the file drawer so tightly her fingers started to tingle. Finally, holding her breath as she lifted the drawer from its squeaky rollers, she pulled it toward her. She remembered Irene's filing system well—logical, but quirky. Sometimes she filed things under litigants' names, other times under the type of litigation involved. Smiling at the eccentricities of the system, Mary rifled through the first drawer.

She found it exactly where anyone would have put it. In the alphabetical files, under the C's, between Crane and Crudup. A discolored manila folder, older than the others. She pulled it out. *Crow, Martha.* The name had been scrawled across the top in Irene's own flamboyant hand.

Quickly Mary opened the file. Inside were copies of her mother's birth certificate and marriage license. Her light flashed across a bill of sale for a tiny piece of property Martha had sold to a man for a tobacco barn, a copy of Mary's birth certificate, and finally, an oversized envelope from the Department of the Army.

Department of the Army? Frowning, Mary bent closer and opened the envelope. It contained three letters—one business-sized, on Army letterhead; the other two smaller envelopes with red-and-blue-striped margins, the word FREE printed where a stamp should have gone. Square, angular printing like an architect's hand addressed both letters to "Martha C. Bennefield."

"Good grief," Mary whispered, the letters trembling in her hand. These were from her father, from Vietnam.

At that instant, she heard a noise. She switched off her tiny flashlight and listened. Safer's voice came from the hall. He was walking into the living room from the kitchen. She could tell by the crisp way he talked that he was wide awake and on his cell phone. She needed to get out of this closet, now.

Swiftly she stuffed all the letters in the back pocket of her jeans. If the Feds impounded these files, she might never see them again. Of course, if they found that she had hidden them upon her person, she might be disbarred and put into prison. But she didn't care. These letters had nothing to do with Irene Hannah's abduction, and everything to do with her.

Listening at the door, she heard Safer's footsteps pause, then continue toward the living room. Though he still talked on the phone, he began to diddle on the piano, tinkling out a somber, distracted rendition of "Jingle Bells." Then the music stopped. She heard his footsteps cross the room and he walked back down the hall, past her door, heading once again to the kitchen.

Now, she thought. *Now!* She turned the knob and cracked open the door. Safer talked from the kitchen, but no one was in sight. She leaped into the hall and closed the door softly behind her, her heart racing as if she'd run a mile. For a moment she stood there, waiting for Safer to appear, demanding "What were you doing in that closet?" But he didn't. She stood alone in the empty hall.

Stashing her key ring in her jeans pocket and pulling her sweater down to her hips, she turned to go back upstairs, then she heard Safer's voice ring out.

"Ms. Crow?" he called, sounding surprised. "Is that you?"

"Yes." She hurried into the kitchen before he could peer out into the hall. "It's me."

He stood at the sink, pouring a cup of coffee, the cell phone glued to one ear. Overnight his team had turned Irene's kitchen into a crime lab. A bank of laptop computers, fax machines, and cell phones covered one end of the old kitchen table, while topo maps and files marked FBI covered the other. One tall, thin agent sat sneaking little glances at Mary over a laptop computer, at the same time rattling in a bag of barbecued pork rinds. When she came into the room Safer held up the carafe of coffee.

Yes, she nodded, she would like some. Without missing a beat on the phone, he retrieved another cup from the cabinet and began to pour. She had just opened the refrigerator when she heard someone knocking. She turned. Two men stood at the door. One was young and bald, and looked as if he was force-fed a steady diet of sour apples. The other was old, mustached, and looked as if he'd just been blinded in the headlights of someone's car. One man she did not know; the other was Hugh Kavanagh.

"Oh, no," Mary whispered. Hugh had been gone since the day after Christmas, making his flower deliveries in Raleigh. Now he was back, collared by some federal thug. She hurried to open the door.

"Hello, Mary," Hugh said. Napoleon stood behind him, grinning up at Mary and wagging his tail.

"Step aside, please." The short man escorted Hugh into the kitchen, his hand on his elbow. He kicked the door shut with his foot, slamming it in the dog's hopeful face.

"Hugh." Mary reached to hug him. "I'm so glad to see you."

Jerking his elbow away from the officer, Hugh

stood stiffly in her embrace. "Would you mind tellin' me what the bloody devil is goin' on? I was out checkin' on Lady Jane and this stupid git hauls me up by me collar like I'm some hooligan on the street."

Mary shook her head. This was awful. This was unforgivable. "Hugh, I need to tell you something—"

"*You* don't need to tell him anything, lady," the short man cut in. "He needs to tell us quite a bit."

"Who are you?" Mary demanded, anger warming her face.

"Mike Tuttle." The little man whipped out a badge similar to Safer's. "FBI."

"Look, Agent Tuttle, if you think this man had anything to do—"

Suddenly Safer was at her side. He jerked his head at Tuttle, brusquely motioning him away, then he extended his hand to Hugh.

"Good morning, sir," he said, his voice kind. "I'm sorry about all this. I'm Daniel Safer."

Hugh blinked up at him through his glasses. "Hugh Kavanagh, sir. Wexford Farm. I repeat my earlier question. What the bloody devil is goin' on?"

With a glance meant to silence her, Safer locked his eyes on the stocky old Irishman. "I'm afraid we've got some bad news, Mr. Kavanagh. Yesterday afternoon—"

"It's Irene, isn't it?" Hugh stared at Mary, unbelieving.

Mary nodded.

"Mother of God! What happened?"

"We don't know yet exactly what happened," replied Safer. "But we think Judge Hannah's been abducted."

"When? Where?" Hugh peppered them with questions, struggling to make sense of the incomprehensible.

"We were downtown at her dentist's office," Mary explained. "She ran back to get some pills she'd forgotten. I waited in the truck. When she didn't return I went inside to see what had happened. She was gone."

"Gone?"

"Mary called me almost immediately after it happened," Safer added. "We have no evidence that Judge Hannah's been hurt or killed. But we do suspect an abduction."

Hugh frowned, as if he found Safer's beard and blue jeans lacking in investigative presence. "Then if you sods are the FBI, why haven't you found her?"

"Actually, I was hoping you might help us out, Mr. Kavanagh. You know a lot about Judge

Hannah that Ms. Crow and I don't. Maybe you could answer some questions for us."

Hugh glared at Tuttle. "Ask away, boys. I've got nothin' to hide."

Mary poured everyone coffee and sat down beside Hugh at the cluttered table. In the time-honored tradition of all interrogators, Safer and Tuttle started soft, hoping to gain trust before the questions became sharper and more pointed. Name. Occupation. Relationship to the victim. Hugh sailed through the first questions, un-abashed that he was Irene's neighbor, farm con-sultant, and bed partner nine nights out of ten. By the time Mary freshened Hugh's coffee, Tuttle had picked up the pace. When did you last see the judge? Do you own any weapons? Can you account for your whereabouts during the last forty-eight hours? When Tuttle began hurling the questions like darts, Mary glared at Safer. Hugh fumbled on his answers; any sev-enty-year-old man who'd just found out that the woman he adored could have been murdered certainly would. And any cop knew that only criminals could supply witnesses to corroborate how they'd spent every minute of every day.

She knew Hugh was telling the truth. She could only hope Safer shared that conviction. When he finally halted the questioning, she put one arm around Hugh's shoulders and hugged him.

He turned and looked at her, his eyes brimming with accusation. "You were sent to guard her, Mary Crow. Why did you leave her alone?"

"I have no excuse, Hugh. I thought she would be safe in the thirty seconds it takes to run inside. I was wrong."

As the ruddiness drained from his face, Hugh seemed to age before her eyes. His shoulders slumped, his head bent low. Finally he muttered something under his breath and wobbled to his feet. "I'll talk to you later. Enjoy your morning," he said, his voice close to cracking. "Right now I need to go."

Safer stood, too. "We appreciate your cooperation, Mr. Kavanagh. Would you be willing to talk to us again? Maybe at your house?"

"I live a mile down the road." He pointed toward the barn. "That way. But then, you already know that, don't you?"

Walking like a very frail man, Hugh turned away from them. Napoleon leaped to his feet as he opened the door, his tail wagging.

"Come on, lad," Hugh muttered as he stepped outside. "Let's get us some fresh air."

CHAPTER 25

Mary finished the last of her coffee. It tasted cold and dark, its bitterness mirroring her mood. "So what do we do now?"

Safer held his notebook in front of her. "Read my notes. I've been on the phone with Washington most of the night."

Mary scanned the chicken scratching that passed for Safer's handwriting. She struggled to decipher the six pages of code names and doodles, but only three words and a circled number looked at all familiar.

She frowned. "Why did you write *New Year's Eve*? Is that significant?"

"If Judge Hannah isn't already dead, we're thinking maybe someone or some group could have kidnapped her to make a statement. What better time to grandstand than New Year's?"

Mary turned her gaze back to the paper, not

knowing how to reply. That Irene might not be dead was wonderful; that Irene might be a political prisoner facing some kind of end-of-the-year execution made her ill inside. She looked at the number 4413, which Safer had circled three times. "What does Delta four-four-one-three mean?"

"Your flight from Asheville to Atlanta. It leaves this afternoon."

"Dream on, Safer. I'm not leaving here until one of us finds Irene."

"Ms. Crow, I—"

"You brought me into this. You can't make me go." She glared at him.

"Yes, I can."

"How? I know the law, Safer. I'm a private citizen."

"A private citizen smack in the middle of an ongoing felony investigation, Ms. Crow. I'll get four federal marshals to come and escort you, with weapons drawn if need be, to the airport and onto your plane." He scowled at her. "We've got a few judges in our back pockets, too."

"Safer, you seem to have forgotten your ongoing felony investigation is centered on a horse farm. Irene's got stock that need to be fed twice a day, and a mare that's about to foal—"

"And you're a highly successful criminal prosecutor who's lived the last dozen years in an Atlanta condo without so much as a pet gold-fish," he reminded her coldly. "We don't need you to take on the role of ranch hand now."

"I could help you guys out on this. The FBI could use something in the win column right now."

"This isn't my decision, Ms. Crow," said Safer.

"So you're just crating me back to Atlanta?"

"Like I told you, I didn't make this call." His eyes reminded her of dark rain clouds that crackled with electricity.

She turned and rinsed her coffee cup in the sink, watching the pale brown water swirl down the drain. She had just begun to think that Safer might be different from the other Feds she'd known, but she was wrong. He was no kinder than the rest; he would have her carried onto the plane if he had to.

"So when do I go?"

"The plane leaves from Asheville at three-fifteen."

"Good. At least I'll have time to feed the horses."

"Feed what you like," replied Safer. "Just be packed up and ready by noon."

"Not a problem," Mary snarled as she turned her back on him. "Not a problem at all."

★　★　★

She strode angrily to the barn, her footsteps
crunching through the frosty grass. Hugh had
already fed the horses, but in his anger had neglected to clean out their stalls. With Lucy honking beside her, Mary speared up the soiled straw
and manure with a pitchfork. Though the physical labor should have made her feel better, it
mostly just chilled her molten anger into a hard
lump of resolve. If Safer thought he was putting
her on a plane to Atlanta, he was in for a surprise. As she dumped the last wheelbarrow full
of horse droppings into the muck pile, she
froze.

Good lord, she thought. The letters. In the
midst of everything else, she'd forgotten all
about them. Swiftly, she rolled the wheelbarrow
back into the stable and climbed the hayloft
stairs. Sitting down on the bed she'd fashioned
the night before, she pulled them from the back
pocket of her jeans.

"Okay, Mom," she whispered. "Why did these
mean so much to you?"

Setting aside the two personal letters, she
opened the official communication from the
Department of the Army. It was dated 12
November 1987, on letterhead from the U.S.
Army Judge Advocate's Office.

Dear Mrs. Bennefield:

I regret to inform you that after careful and deliberate investigation, we have found no substantive evidence to warrant any further action concerning the death of Jackson W. Bennefield, your late husband, while on active duty in the Republic of Vietnam. Though Sergeant James F. Green's suspicions have merit, given the circumstances and the passage of time, we find them to be unprovable. Enclosed are the two letters which you graciously allowed our Legal Department to analyze.

Sincerely,
Major Richard R. Rhodes, U.S.A.

Mary read the letter twice. What were they talking about, Sergeant Green's charges? Her father died in 1971, when he stepped on a land mine in Vietnam. She opened the first of the personal letters. It was written on two pages torn from a spiral notebook, thick reddish dust still lining the creases.

17 July 1970

To My Sweet Dream Baby

Boy, I used to think Atlanta was hot, but it's nothing compared to this. We've been humping through the bush for the past five days and have just made it back to an artillery camp near Song Be. Got a hot shower and a beer, plus a couple new pairs of socks, which made me feel almost human. Somebody said we'll get to stay here for a whole week. Clete's eye has recovered from our fistfight. We shook hands and everything's okay. He and Bobby found a field they'd cleared of mines and the three of us started tossing a football around. Clete always has to play quarterback, his old position in high school. The Gooks all watch us like we're nuts. How's Mary? Saying any more words yet? She'll probably be jabbering like a magpie by the time I get home!

If you get a chance, could you send some more Lifebuoy soap? And make me a tape of some good music! Doors and the Stones, if they've got anything new out. Can't stand this Army radio shit.

Well, now that I've asked for the moon,

I'll sign off. All my love forever and ever. Bookoo kisses for our little Mary.

Your nummah one husband,
Jack

Ps. Clete says to tell you hi!

Her eyes blurred with tears as she read the lines her father had written some thirty years before. She felt as if a vibrant young stranger had leaped from the paper and stuck out his hand, saying, "Hi, Mary. I'm your old man!"

She opened the last envelope. The letter was dated just two days later than the first, but read much the same—her father complaining about the rain and a terrible batch of C rations that contained nothing but tapioca pudding, a dish he apparently despised. He inquired about some weaving of Martha's and asked if Mary could say "Daddy" yet. He was anxious to come home, counting down the 106 days he had left. Then:

I guess Clete is still pissed about us. Sometimes he drills the football into me pretty hard. But he and Bobby scope out the safe fields and they always ask me to play, so I guess you and me being married doesn't bother him all that much. He's changed a lot since we've been over here.

I guess we all have, but both Clete and Bobby have turned into real bad-ass dudes. Sometimes I think they enjoy the things we have to do. I'd much rather smoke a little dope and cross off the days on the calendar.

The letter ended as the other had—love to little Mary, and to Martha. In this one he'd even instructed Martha to give his dog, Jeb Stuart, a bone.

"What the hell does all this mean?" Mary murmured, her thoughts spinning as she spread all three letters out across the blanket. The first letter, postmarked six months before her mother's murder, indicated that a Sergeant Jim Green had thought her father's death something beyond a simple KIA. The second two, which her mother had forwarded to the Judge Advocate's Office, spoke of Bobby and another person named Clete, who apparently knew her mother, too. But who were they? It sounded like this Clete had a problem with their marriage. Her mother had told her the story of their courtship a thousand times—that Jack had come up to hunt one October when he was on leave from Fort Bragg. He'd gone into Little Jump Off to buy shotgun shells, and three days later he still sat there in front of the fireplace, his shells unbought, squirrel or bear or whatever he'd planned on hunting completely forgotten. *Jack always sang "Sweet Dream Baby" to me,* her mother used to say with a laugh. *But he was my dream, too.* By the end of his leave Martha had accepted his proposal; at Christmas, they'd married. In all the times her mother had recounted that story, not once had she mentioned any rival for her affections named Clete or Bobby. Her grandmother would probably know all about this, but Eugenia was dead. There was no one left to ask anymore.

Mary stared at the letters, wondering if Irene might know what this meant. Even if she wasn't familiar with the JAG inquiry, she might know who this Clete was. After all, she'd been her mother's attorney, as well as her close friend. Her mother might have confided in Irene about something this important. Suddenly she heard a noise outside, a roaring from the sky. She looked out the window. A small blue-and-white helicopter was landing in the front field. Safer and Tuttle walked toward it, their jackets whipping in the stiff rotor-wind.

"I bet they've come to fly me to the airport," Mary said aloud as she stood up and stuffed the letters in the back pocket of her jeans. "Well, you can forget about that, Safer. This girl's got other plans."

CHAPTER 26

Of all the rooms in his castle, Wurth liked this one the best. Spacious, with a twelve-foot ceiling, it took up one entire suite on the second floor and served as his private dojo. LeClaire's famous poster of the new Jerusalem did not hang here, nor did any of Dunbar's silly charts describing the superior size and weight of male Caucasian brains. Wurth's studio was devoid of anything other than the flag he'd earned in Japan, years ago. Huge and red, it covered one entire wall of the room, and consisted of the word *kyoushu*—assassin—written in black kanji on a circle of white. Along the right side of the flag hung a long knotted cord of black silk. Each twist in the rope meant that someone's life had ended by Wurth's hand; he'd lost count of their number back in '79.

Under the flag stood a black credenza that bore

an array of mementos. A folded Stars and Stripes, the flag he'd given the best years of his life to; a framed collection of the ribbons that once bedecked his chest. An old photograph of four young men grinning in combat greens stood among several newer pictures of himself and his Troopers, young men exuberant with the same esprit de corps that had gleamed from his own eyes, so many years ago.

He picked up a photo of a grinning David Forrester, taken on the day he'd become a Feather Man. Wurth traced around the boy's image with his little finger and smiled. Only 2 percent of all the troops in the Army could ever hope to become Feather Men. Only that few could bring themselves to kill in that soundless, seamless way, where the act of murder bound two people as intimately as the act of love. The lunkish boys Dunbar sent him could kill, but only with a rifle or a small array of organized crime tricks. David Forrester had been the lone one capable of creeping up and slipping a knife into someone's kidney or a needle into their heart. Then, when he'd earned his black feather, Dunbar had him beaten to death like a dog.

"Someday you'll pay for that, Dunbar," Wurth whispered as he replaced the picture, blowing away a small speck of dirt from the glass.

"Someday you're going to learn a whole new meaning for the word *reliable*."

Striding to the door, he turned on a panel of huge lights that stretched down from the high ceiling, illuminating a tall mannequin in the center of the room. Built of bamboo and painted black, it was six feet tall and poseable, much like the small models that art students use to study anatomy. Its arms and legs could be extended, and the bulbous black head could be totally removed. Wurth gave a wistful smile. David had mastered *Iaido* with astonishing speed, he had the awesome natural talent of a true *kenjutshushi*. Wurth wondered if his old arms could still do as well.

Though he, himself, had probably eliminated a hundred people in the last ten years, he had not taken a head since the mid-1980s. Back then he'd been good; better than any other American. He was invisible, undetectable. He could leave lots of blood when he wanted to, almost none when he didn't. But that had been almost fifteen years ago. Though he'd kept his body exquisitely toned, time took its toll. Reflexes slowed, strength ebbed away. Today, he would consider himself lucky if he could do half as good a job as David Forrester.

He crossed the room and pulled over a large

cardboard box he'd left beside the door. Inside were eight pumpkins, each roughly the size of a human skull. He removed the mannequin's head and replaced it with one of the pumpkins, then stepped back. The thing looked ridiculous, a bony black scarecrow with a fat orange head. David had found that funny, the first time. Then, when Wurth explained that until you could slice a pumpkin all the way through with one blow, you could never slice through a human neck, the boy had ceased laughing. David's first boxes of pumpkins had been horrible— hacked into pieces as if they'd been the victims of Halloween carvers gone mad. Then, midway through the fourth box, he began to catch on. He mastered the technique, then added his natural speed to cut through first the spine, then the soft tissues of the throat.

"Why cut from the back?" David asked one afternoon, when his sweat gave the muscles of his chest the sheen of satin.

"You want to cut the hardest part at the beginning of your stroke," he'd replied. "Also, it's kinder. We are assassins, not monsters."

No, he thought as he stared at the pumpkin head. They weren't. David had not been a monster, and neither was he. The monsters out there sat in the Apostle room, underground in California. He looked up at the orange-headed mannequin and smiled. "You want to see how reliable I am, Dunbar? You just watch."

He walked back to the credenza, pushed one of the sliding drawers open, and withdrew a long, heavy bundle wrapped in red silk. Untying the golden cord that bound it, he spread it out carefully.

They were all there, their blades glistening silver in the bright light. Two Honshu razors that were good for vocal cords and veins, a crotchet for the soft tissues of the mouth. An old French bodkin was his secret for any script to be written across their bellies; a heavy-handed Bowie for the joints of thumb and finger. A Japanese *ryoba,* for ears and the tough ligaments of the jaw. He had more, of course, others from around the world, still others he'd forged for his own purposes, but these before him were the ones he loved the most. These he came back to over and over again. As the few basic colors on a painter's palette could render most of the colors in nature, these knives, along with his syringe, could accomplish the tasks of a Feather Man.

Carefully he withdrew his favorite, an ancient *hira zukuri* and refolded the silk, putting it back in the credenza. He hated to expose his pets to light and air unless he had to. They stayed much happier wrapped in their dark silk cocoon. Much sharper, too.

He walked toward the mannequin, swinging the *zukuri* in a wide arc in front of him, loosening up. When his muscles felt limber he pulled the sword from its scabbard. The edge of the dark steel blade glowed blue in the light. He wrapped his right hand around the handle, close to the hilt, then positioned his left hand just beneath it. Extending his arms, he lifted the heavy sword out in front of him. When the tip of the blade hung motionless as a raindrop, he smiled. Good, he thought. He still had the muscle. Still could maintain the control.

He then turned his gaze to the pumpkin-head, seeing not the simple topography of a giant squash, but Richard Dunbar's overly styled hair and jittery black eyes. Richard Dunbar, puppet master. If the next few days worked out the way he'd planned, Dunbar was going to find out what it felt like to have a Feather Man jerk his strings.

"Yeeaaahhhhh!" He leaped forward so swiftly the *zukuri* was just a blur of light. He felt the faint resistance of the blade as it entered the thick skin of the pumpkin, pushed through the slimy middle, then sliced through the other side. As he ended his stroke, with the tip of his sword high, there seemed to be the smallest sigh from the pumpkin itself, as the top part re-settled down on its lower half. Wurth looked at it and nodded with satisfaction. He'd cleaved the thing in two and yet had not even jostled it from the neck of the dummy.

"Get ready, Dunbar," he murmured as he rubbed the blade carefully with a silk cloth. "Soon we're really going to have some fun."

CHAPTER 27

"So who's taking care of Irene's animals?" Mary asked Safer as they hurried down the airport concourse, her backpack in hand.

"Kavanagh said he would be there this evening."

"Is he still at the top of your suspect list?"

"No," Safer replied in the muffled tone cops use when they're embarrassed. "He checked out okay."

Mary hid her grin of satisfaction. She could be right about a lot more things, if Safer would only give her the chance. But the Feds didn't want to do that. Washington had said no.

"Look, Safer, before I go back to Atlanta, at least tell me where things stand."

"No print matches in the building, no saliva or blood on the feather, no reports of a headless body anywhere in the Carolinas, Georgia, or

Tennessee." He lowered his voice as they walked. "Tuttle thinks someone killed her and dumped her in the woods. Krebbs, my computer junkie, likes the conspiracy theories. He thinks they're keeping her alive until New Year's."

Mary looked at him. "What do you think?"

"I'm inclined to agree with Krebbs." He gave a grim smile. "But then, I've always been an optimist."

"Gosh, I forgot to take off my gun," she cried as Safer handed her backpack to a handsome gray-haired man in a Delta uniform.

"I've explained the situation to them," Safer said quietly. "Mr. Simmons will take care of it. He'll see that you get through here and at Hartsfield without setting off all the bells and whistles."

"You think of everything, don't you?" Mary watched Mr. Simmons lumber off with her pack.

"I wish." Safer looked at her with rueful eyes. "If I had, Judge Hannah would still be writing opinions and feeding her horses. And we wouldn't be parting like this."

For an instant, Mary didn't know how to respond. That Safer had considered their parting at all took her by surprise.

Suddenly his cell phone beeped. He pulled the

thing from his pocket and turned his back to her. Something was happening; she could tell by the way his shoulders tightened.

"Safer, what's going on?" she called as the line began to inch forward.

He shook his head, listening intently to whoever was talking. In a moment he switched off his phone and turned. "No news, but I've got to go just the same," he told her. "Listen—thanks for all your help. It was a real pleasure working with you."

For a moment he looked at her with that all-seeing gaze of his, as if he suspected her of some subterfuge he couldn't quite pinpoint, but she just nodded her head docilely and moved on toward the gate.

"Have a good flight," he called, his brows drawing down in a frown.

"Thanks." She gave him a small wave, then watched him walk away. As he turned the corner, a dozen people straggled off a prop-jet from Charlotte. With a hasty glance at the Delta gate agent, she ducked out of line and joined them, tromping along with them down an escalator. Ahead of her she could see Safer leaving the concourse, the sun shining on his dark hair as he hurried to the parking lot.

As the travelers chattered along toward the

baggage claim, she slipped into the women's rest room. She knew immediately that she'd made a mistake. *When that Simmons figures out I've gone, this is the first place he'll look.* Quickly she backed out the door. Where could she hide? They would search the restaurant and bar; everyplace else in the small airport was brightly lit and absolutely exposed. Renting a car would take too long—she'd be spotted before they gave her the keys. Shit! Where could she go? She looked back out into the terminal. This time a huge wave of people were coming down the escalator, the men sporting crimson fezzes bedecked with rhinestones and the women wearing yellow tour badges on their coats.

Shriners, thought Mary, remembering a picture she'd seen of Jim Falkner in a similar getup. *The loyal brothers of the mystic Shrine are on holiday.* She ducked her head and strode into the middle of them, scooting in between Mitzi Johnson and Lorene Miles, who were gleefully discussing someone named Barbara's liposuction-gone-wrong. Though Mary's was the youngest, darkest head among the bunch, she was hoping the eye-catching fezzes would deflect all attention away from her.

Walking on the heels of the two women, she skirted the metal detector and moved on to the baggage claim. A dapper young man wearing a dark green blazer stood waiting for them.

"Good afternoon, everyone! I'm Ron, from the Grove Park Inn, and I'd like to welcome you all to Asheville! Our tour bus is outside, ready to go, and as soon as you get your luggage we'll be on our way!"

Mary's heart leaped as she looked outside to see a huge bus, its diesel engine merrily polluting the air. This was even better than she'd hoped. If her luck held, she might be able to catch a ride all the way into Asheville.

She looked around, searching for Mr. Simmons. She didn't see him, but she knew she'd attract attention if she just stood here while everyone else grappled with their luggage. Holding her purse close to her side, she strolled casually to the souvenir shop, as if she were a woman whose husband took charge of the tiresome little necessities of travel, like tickets and bags.

Inside, she searched for something that would help her blend in with the middle-aged Shriners. Five minutes later she emerged wearing sunglasses and a red Asheville Tourists baseball cap. It was not the greatest of disguises, but it was something. If she could just slip into the next group of Shriners headed for the bus, she might be able to sneak past Ron, who was checking off names at the door.

She hesitated a moment to reconnoiter. Two redcaps hustled among the Shriners, loading luggage into the belly of the bus. Just inside the main entrance to the airport, a tall, gray-haired man stood unobtrusively scanning everyone who left the building.

"Helloooo, Mr. Simmons," Mary whispered, recognizing him immediately. "Nice to see you again."

She ducked behind an Asheville Chamber of Commerce display. Simmons seemed mostly concerned with the front of the airport, only occasionally glancing in her direction. If she could just worm her way into a little knot of the red fezzes . . . She waited until three men started toward the door, then scurried out to join them.

She stayed a half-step back from the trio, walking with her head up, but turned away from Simmons. As the group moved into the pale afternoon sun, she caught snatches of the men's conversation—something about getting in some good golf and trying to avoid the Christmas Tour of the Biltmore Estate. As they approached the bus, Ron of the green blazer looked up and grinned.

"Hello, folks. Welcome to the Grove Park Inn. Could I have your names so I can check you off my list?"

"Perry," the first man said. "Say, buddy, is there any golf around here?"

Mary glanced over her shoulder as Ron replied. Simmons was staring in her direction.

"Griffin." The second Shriner pointed to his name on Ron's list.

Mary looked again. Simmons was walking her way! She had to make a move, and make it now.

"Montgomery," the last man said. He started to point to his name, then Mary bumped into him.

"Excuse me," she said sweetly, beaming at Ron as she squeezed past Mr. Montgomery. "My husband's already checked us on the bus. I've got some medication for him that he needs to take right this minute!"

Ron looked at her for a moment, then smiled. "Of course, go right on board."

She skipped up the steps. A few people looked up at her curiously, but most chattered away with their seatmates, happy to be on vacation. She walked down the aisle, looking out the smoked-glass windows to see where Mr. Simmons had gone. He was still headed her way.

"Come on," Mary urged as she sat down in a seat by herself. "Let's get this show on the road."

More Shriners boarded the bus. Simmons drew closer, now peering in the windows. Mary shrank down in the seat and pulled her cap low, pretending to be napping. She felt a jolt and opened her eyes. An overweight couple had plopped down in front of her. She saw that the bus driver was ready to go, but Mr. Simmons was now talking to Ron. With her heart beating madly, she watched as Simmons gestured, indicating someone's height. Ron shook his head. Simmons said something else and nodded at the bus. Ron pointed to the passenger list and shrugged. She shrank down lower in her seat. If Ron let Simmons on this bus, she would be a goner. . . .

Mary peered toward the front of the bus. Ron hopped on board, his cheeks rosy from the wind. She braced herself, knowing Simmons would follow, and she would be discovered. But the doors closed. She lifted the brim of her cap and peeked out the window. Simmons was walking back to the airport as the bus driver released the air brakes and began to roll toward the highway.

After a half-hour ride where several bottles of Scotch were passed up and down the aisle, they arrived at the inn. As the bus pulled up to the sprawling old resort, Ron stood up and again welcomed everyone to Asheville. "Ladies and gentlemen, if you will gather in front of the stone fireplace to the left of the lobby, the concierge will direct you to your rooms."

As the Shriners got to their feet, Mary once again tugged the cap down low over her eyes, then attached herself to the first group getting off the bus. Ron had already hurried inside the building, weary, no doubt, of the vacationers' increasingly tipsy good humor. Still, she stayed with her little cluster of red fezzes as they entered the building. The lobby was cavernous. Two fireplaces, each big enough to barbecue a steer, commanded both ends of the room, each burning a long, fat log of aged oak. As her fellow travelers wobbled over to the wide hearths, Mary quietly slipped away, slinking down a hall that offered a long row of split oak rockers in front of a bank of pay phones.

Grabbing a directory, she flipped to the Yellow Pages. In a moment she'd found what she was looking for—a used-car dealership that advertised rentals. It wasn't the most surreptitious way to go, but it was the best she could do. When Safer found out she'd given him the slip, he would think Hertz or Avis. By the time he came up with Bingo's, she would have long since driven to her destination. She wrote down the address, then called the first of Asheville's half-dozen cab companies.

"Ten minutes," the dispatcher said.

"I'll be waiting out front."

She hung up the phone and walked back out to the lobby, where the Shriners were squabbling over their rooms, a covey of scarlet fezzes massed in front of one fireplace. Swiping her baseball cap off her head, she sat down to wait for her cab. So far she had escaped being deported to Atlanta. Now, if she could only make it to her destination before Safer tightened the net around her.

CHAPTER 28

Mary steered the rental car through a series of hairpin curves. A bright red taxi cab had picked her up at the Grove Park Inn, and she directed the driver to take her to Bingo's Used Cars on Tunnel Road. Half an hour later, Bingo Davis handed her the keys to a 1985 gray Celica with an odometer that read over 225,000 miles.

"This is it?" The car looked like it had finished dead last in a long line of demolition derbies.

"You said you didn't want nothin' flashy," said Bingo, a beefy, red-haired man who wore a short-sleeved Nascar T-shirt even though it was spitting snow. He patted the car's hood. "She ain't purty, but she'll go like a sumbitch."

Mary got in the car. Though it stank of cigarette smoke and old french fry grease, the engine was surprisingly quiet. "I'll have her back in a couple of days." She waved once at Bingo, then she turned onto I-240, merging into the westbound traffic.

Now, as the little coupe buzzed deeper into the mountains, Mary cracked the window and greedily breathed in the Nantahala's winter smell. Cool pine and damp cedar overlaid the pungent tang of iron-rich earth. She knew it as well as she knew the jumble of aromas that made up Little Jump Off Store. *Jonathan,* she thought. *Why is Ruth Moon here? Is it truly finished between us?*

A rabbit bounded across the road. Skidding around a curve, Mary followed the Little Tee River for a hundred yards, then the store's single electric sign illuminated the darkness as if it were the last outpost of civilization before the world reverted to its true self of wildness and unrestrained growth.

Mary pulled into the parking lot. Two battered pickup trucks nudged against the building, one with North Carolina license plates, the other with Oklahoma. Ruth Moon, Mary thought, dread weighting her chest. She and Jonathan were probably eating supper right now, no doubt cooing at each over a basket of bean bread Ruth had baked herself.

She got out of the Toyota and crossed the lot, her footsteps crunching in the gravel. Lights blazed from inside the store. *Maybe Ruth Moon and Jonathan keep it open all the time now. Organizing the Cherokees into political action committees. That wouldn't be so bad,* a cold voice whispered inside her head. *At least they would be upright and clothed. Not naked and touching each other.*

She shook that image from her brain and walked up the steps. She hated dropping in on anybody unannounced, but tonight she had no choice. She peeked in the window. Inside, she could see the fireplace and the Christmas tree and Ruth Moon's REPIC poster, but there was no one behind the counter. Softly she tapped on the door, her fingers like icicles.

Nothing happened. She tapped again, louder, hoping she wasn't interrupting another Hugh-and-Irene moment. All at once she saw a blur of motion as Jonathan came down the stairs, barefooted, but dressed in jeans and a light blue work shirt. She almost laughed in relief at the sight of him. Given Ruth Moon's political proclivities, she had almost expected him to appear in buckskins and war paint. But he looked much the same as when she'd seen him last—tall and lean, his dark hair tied in a ponytail. She watched his face through the glass panes of the door, smiling as he registered shock, then gladness, then a new, hesitant emotion she couldn't identify. He unlocked the door and pulled it open. The light and warmth from Little Jump Off enveloped her like a cloud.

"Mary!" he cried. "Ruth said you'd come by. Why didn't you leave a number where I could reach you?"

"Hi, Jonathan." She watched as his old familiar smile once again crinkled his eyes. He was surprised to see her, but very pleased, too. How well she could read his face. How deeply did she miss it.

"Come on in!" He held his arms out to her. She stepped forward, was almost about to touch him, when another voice resounded through the room.

"Jonathan? Who is it?"

Before either of them could say another word, Ruth Moon appeared at the top of the stairs, clutching a white napkin in one hand. Her eyes widened slightly when she saw Mary, but then she smiled as she hurried to stand beside Jonathan.

"Mary," she said, her voice like honey. "How wonderful to see you again. Jonathan was so happy that we'd finally gotten to meet!" Her eyes glittered. "How's your old friend?"

"Yeah," Jonathan said. "I couldn't figure out who you would spend Christmas with."

"Irene Hannah," said Mary.

Jonathan's brows lifted. "You spent Christmas with Judge Hannah? Over at Upsy Daisy?"

Mary nodded. "I need your help, Jonathan. Something terrible has happened."

"Wait right there," he said, turning immediately to the check-out counter. "I'll get my coat."

"No, it's not like that. Let me explain. . . ."

"Have you had supper, Mary?" asked Ruth Moon.

Mary shook her head.

"Then come join us," she invited, looping her arm through Jonathan's. "I'll set an extra place and you can tell what kind of trouble you're in."

★   ★   ★

An hour later, with a pile of delicate trout bones making a slender modernistic sculpture in the middle of the kitchen table, Mary had told the story of Irene Hannah's abduction. She told them about waiting in the truck for Irene to return with her medicine, then going inside to find her gone.

"So this Agent Safer doesn't know you sneaked back up here?" Jonathan had listened to her without interrupting, while Ruth Moon had questioned her at every turn, as if testing the veracity of her story.

"He's pretty smart. I imagine he's figured it out by now."

Ruth Moon put three slices of lemon pie on the table. Mary noticed she'd fixed it without meringue, the way Jonathan liked it. She asked, "And the only clue you have is a black feather in the bathroom?"

Mary nodded. "That's all they had this morning."

"And they have no idea who might have taken her?" Jonathan took a bite of pie.

"Somebody with a case against a sitting federal judge." Mary didn't mention that eleven other judges had already been murdered and that some group might be saving Irene for a bizarre New Year's Eve celebration. "The FBI is afraid that it might be part of a much broader conspiracy."

"And wouldn't that be just too bad?" Ruth Moon's words were so laced with acid that Mary and Jonathan both looked up. Long seconds passed in awkward silence, then Mary spoke.

"Look, Ruth. I've sworn to defend the U.S. Constitution and the federal government. If you've got a problem with that, then maybe I've come to the wrong house."

"I'm sorry." Ruth rearranged the knife and fork on her plate. "That came out wrong. It's just that I've got a few issues of my own with the U.S. government."

For a moment Mary gazed at her in reluctant admiration—the upward tilt of her dark eyes and the defiant jut of her chin were undeniably attractive. Ruth Moon was pretty, intelligent, passionate, and diametrically opposed to everything Mary represented. Suddenly she realized she'd been a fool to come here. Jonathan belonged to this woman now, and she wasn't going to loan him out as a white knight on demand. Mary wiped the corners of her mouth with her napkin and rose from her chair.

"Thank you so much for dinner," she said, smiling. "It was delicious. But I think it's time for me to leave."

"No, Mary, don't go." Jonathan grabbed her hand. "Ruth is from Oklahoma—she doesn't understand how much Irene Hannah means to you."

Ruth Moon read the expression on Jonathan's face and instantly retreated. "Mary, I'm in favor of rearranging Congress. Not of abducting innocent people. If Jonathan wants to help you, of course I will, too." Ruth smiled as if her shoes had grown suddenly too tight.

Mary studied her, not totally convinced by her quick change of heart, but she sat back down. As much as she mistrusted Ruth Moon, what else could she do? She was stuck. She had to find Irene Hannah, and she desperately needed Jonathan's help to do that. If he and this woman now came like a matched set of earrings, then she'd just have to deal with it.

"Anyway," Mary looked at Jonathan and began again, "I figured if anything was going on up here, you'd know about it."

"Where does this judge live?" asked Ruth.

"About fifteen miles away," said Jonathan.

Mary pressed on. "Do you know of anyone who might have a grudge against Judge Hannah? Legally, she's come down hard on the timber industry, and the NRA certainly doesn't regard her as a friend. Any Second Amendment storm troopers around here?"

He shrugged. "Everyone with a squirrel gun spouts that 'pry my gun from my cold, dead fingers' line every chance they get."

Mary sighed. That macho boast rang hollow for her—she'd seen too many weeping mothers kissing the cold, dead fingers of their murdered children.

"Any militia groups or white supremacists in the area?" Unconsciously Mary fell into the voir dire rhythm she used when she questioned prospective jurors.

Jonathan shook his head. "None that I know of. But it's the mountains. Strange individuals riddle these hills."

"Anybody strange enough to kidnap a federal judge?"

"I don't think so, although everybody gets pretty surly around April fifteenth."

"Wait a minute." Ruth Moon frowned at Jonathan. "Remember those files I cleaned off that hard drive a few weeks ago?"

Jonathan took a sip of sassafras tea. "The Hot-N-Ready Honey file from the insurance agency?"

"No, these were from Sergeant Wurth's computer. I told you about it—America something or other." Ruth looked at Mary. "Jonathan picked up some computers from this ex-Army guy who's running a camp in the middle of what used to be *Tsalagi* land, and he's spouting all this flag-waving patriot stuff."

Jonathan snorted. "Sergeant Wurth's okay, Ruth. Hell, he *gave* you three computers."

"Who's Sergeant Wurth?" Mary leaned forward. A lot of roads seemed to be leading her back to the Army today.

"This Vietnam vet. He turned the old Frieden Sanitarium into a summer camp called Unakawaya," explained Jonathan. "He keeps about a dozen foster-care boys there all year.

Stump Logan takes all his high-risk juvies up to Wurth to be remolded into upstanding young men."

"Upstanding young *white* men," muttered Ruth Moon. "Wurth doesn't take any boys of color."

"Ruth, the only other boys of color around here are Cherokee boys, and we take care of our own. Give the guy a break."

"But I thought that old place was about to fall down." Mary had never seen the Frieden Sanitarium, but she remembered when some kids in her high school broke into it one night, wanting to test their courage in a haunted house.

"Wurth's dumped a lot of time and money into it. I've heard he works those DHS kids pretty hard."

"Could this Wurth have a grudge against the judiciary?" Mary asked.

"The one time I saw him he was teaching a bunch of kids how to put in a Japanese garden. That sounds like a pretty mellow kind of guy to me."

"But didn't he tell you he was some kind of black belt in something?" insisted Ruth Moon.

"He said he was an ex-Ranger."

"See?" Ruth pressed her point. "That's something."

"Yeah, but what white supremacist worth his salt would waste his time showing boys how to prune bonsai trees? Anybody who would kidnap a federal judge would have kids going at each other with pugil sticks and making bombs in the basement."

"I guess you're right," said Mary, the scent of a trail evaporating as quickly as it had materialized. "There's nobody else around here that you can think of?"

He closed his eyes. After a few moments, he looked at her and shook his head. "I know most of the territory within a fifty-mile radius of Upsy Daisy Farm. If anything that big was going on, I'd have heard something."

They finished their pie and talked for a little while longer. When Ruth Moon rose to clear the table, Mary knew the time had come to leave. Using her rusty Cherokee, she thanked Ruth for her hospitality, then she started down the stairs into the darkened store.

"Where are you going tonight?" Jonathan asked, following her.

"I don't know." Mary shrugged. "Maybe over to Cherokee. Some of their motels are probably open."

"Why don't you stay here? I'll make up the cot in front of the fire."

She looked up at him, feeling awkward. A

year ago they would have been curled up together, in his bed upstairs. Now he wanted to
prepare a cot for her, thinking that just the fire
could keep her warm.

"I don't think that would be such a good
idea," Mary said.

"I can hide you so this Safer character could
never find you." Jonathan touched her arm
awkwardly. "It'll be okay, Mary. It's late and it's
cold. Stay here with us tonight."

Us, she thought. No longer him. But us. She
looked at his eyes, his mouth. How she would
love to say yes and allow him to hide her in his
room where he kept his bed shoved beneath the
window so he could look at the stars. How she
would love to take off her clothes and wrap herself in his warmth. But she could not do that.
He had another woman in his bed now. He had
made a life for himself without her.

She smiled. "Thanks, Jonathan. I appreciate
the offer, but . . ."

"Then sit down. It would be wrong for you to
leave. I'll be right back." He was already bounding up the stairs.

She sighed, realizing he had invoked the tradition of hospitality that all *Tsalagi* honored. Now
it would be insulting for her to refuse. She sat
down in one of the rockers by the hearth. Although the little fireplace was probably one-

twentieth the size of the ones at the Grove Park Inn, Jonathan always burned wild cherry wood at Christmastime, so the whole store smelled like budding flowers. As she looked into the flames she grew drowsy, then suddenly both Jonathan and Ruth Moon reappeared, Jonathan with the cot, Ruth Moon carrying an armful of sheets and blankets.

"I really didn't mean for you to do this—" Mary jumped up from the rocker.

"It's okay," Ruth assured her as Jonathan unfolded the cot. "We're happy to have you."

All three of them worked on the cot, finally arranging it in front of the fire with sheets and two wool blankets.

"I guess you remember where the bathroom is," said Jonathan, shifting on his feet.

"Right next to the ice-cream freezer," Mary replied, equally ill at ease.

"Help yourself to anything you need down here. Toothbrush, toothpaste, Ding-Dongs."

"Thanks, Jonathan." Mary had to laugh. "If I get hungry I'll hit the Ding-Dongs first."

"Come on, Jonathan." Smiling, Ruth Moon grabbed his hand. "Let's go to bed and leave Mary alone. I'm sure she must be exhausted."

"Right." Jonathan looked at Mary as Ruth dragged him toward the stairs. "Call me if you need anything."

"Thanks." She smiled. "Good night."

With a helpless shrug he turned, and Ruth pulled him up to their bedroom. Mary stood and watched as they disappeared upstairs, then she sat down on the little cot and started to take off her clothes, getting ready to sleep alone.

CHAPTER 29

Tommy Cabe switched off his flashlight and peeked out from the blanket that covered his head. He'd been reading Captain Dempsey's diary, and if everything Captain Dempsey had written was true, then Willett had been right about the third floor. It had been a place of pain, where some German doctor named Boehr had tried to make fake body parts for the maimed soldiers who'd lived here. No wonder those rooms looked so creepy, Cabe thought, shivering as he slipped the diary under his mattress for the night.

He sat up in the dark room, his ears keen to the noises around him. Galloway had finally stopped tossing on his mattress, and the rhythmic squeaking of Abbot's cot as he jerked off had long since died away. Now Cabe heard only the soft snoring of ten Grunts on ten cots, escaping Camp Unakawaya the only way they could. He sighed. He'd searched every inch of this camp for Willett—even sneaking into the Trooper quarters, in case they were holding him hostage—and had come up with nothing. Now there was only one place left to search. The third floor. If he didn't find him up there, then he could only guess that Galloway must have been right.

He rose from his bed, trying to keep his weight off his exquisitely tender buttocks. Since his encounter with Tallent and Grice in the bathroom, every movement made him hurt, and he dreamed constantly of when he would make those two kneel and bare their asses before him.

Bastards, he thought, fighting back a boiling anger. He needed to be cool now, not hot. Clever instead of angry. "Act smart," he reminded himself in a whisper. "Act like Willett."

He pulled on a pair of socks and tiptoed to the door. The old linoleum floor crackled as he walked, but none of the other Grunts stirred. The outside hall was laced with shadows, illuminated by a stark winter moonlight that poured in the dormer windows.

He and Willett had explored much of the third floor. They'd seen dusty, leather-topped tables with straps to hold people down, and dentist chairs with electrical wires attached. Those rooms had scared Willett, who claimed that anybody who got strapped to that stuff would get up with a whole new definition for the word "pain."

Keeping to the shadows, he turned left. At the end of the hall was the scene of his humiliation, the bathroom. What Cabe knew that most didn't was that in the narrow locked closet where Wurth kept cleaning supplies was a small window that opened onto an ancient fire escape.

He tiptoed into the bathroom and opened the door of every stall to make sure nobody had their feet up, hiding. After he was satisfied the room was empty, he crept over to the closet. From a string around his neck he pulled a small tool he'd fashioned from a ten-penny nail. When Wurth had confiscated his little Barlow knife the day he'd arrived, Willett had showed him how to make this instrument, calling it a "Carolina church key." Frowning with concentration Tommy worked the slender piece of metal into the lock. This little pick had served him far better than his Barlow, and he'd made it mostly all by himself.

When the lock slid open, he slipped into the closet. Moonlight glowed dimly through the white-washed windowpanes. He unlatched the old hasp and quietly lifted the window. Frigid air raised instant goose bumps on his arms, and his breath made little puffs of smoke. Below him, the back acres of the camp rolled like a carpet into the blackness of the forest. Far away he heard an owl; then, all at once, a car engine growled. Curious, he thrust one leg through the window and wiggled out onto the fire escape. Craning his neck as far as he could, he saw the broad, low taillights of a big sedan—first bright red, then white as the car backed up once, then took off down the driveway.

"Shit," he whispered. "That's Logan's cruiser!" Had the sheriff just dropped off another poor kid to be raised by Sergeant Wurth? In a way Tommy wouldn't mind if he had. A new kid would mean fresh meat for Tallent and Grice. A new kid would take the heat off him.

But he could do nothing about any new kid now. Right now he just wanted to find out if Willett was still alive. Shivering with the cold, Tommy held the rusty railing with both hands and began to ascend the steps, the whole skeletal structure wobbling as he climbed. When he'd scaled two flights of ten steps each, he raised a window on the third floor, one he and Willett had discovered was never locked.

He stepped into another bathroom, this one so humid that the air felt almost too thick to breathe. He tiptoed across the sticky tile floor and peeked out into the hall beyond. Usually it was dark and silent as a tomb. Tonight, though, he heard voices murmuring from the far end. *Damn*, he thought, his heart starting to pound. *Why didn't I look up here first?*

Hastily, he left the sanctuary of the bathroom, slithering through the dense shadows along the wall, his breath coming fast and hard. He'd made it halfway down the hall when a sudden loud shriek ripped through the silence.

It startled him so he jumped into a doorway, banging his head against the old door. By the time he'd figured out where the first sound had come from, two more screams split the air, the last followed by the low rumble of nervous laughter.

His heart was beating like crazy now. He hadn't heard shrieks like that since the day he'd watched his grandfather castrate hogs.

Pressing himself into the doorway, he listened. Over the rumble of voices he heard Wurth's deep, crisp tones of command. "This knife cuts like this," Tommy heard him say. "If you use it this way, the blood will never obscure your vision."

Tommy heard another scream, this one so awful that he clapped his hands over his ears. He wanted to run, to hide. As much as he despised Tallent and Grice, he'd never feared for his life with them. Right now it sounded like someone was torturing Willett to death.

The door opened. Cabe shriveled back against the wall. Upchurch burst out of the room. He was followed by another Trooper named Rogers, a sallow young man with a shaven head.

"Can you believe what he's doing in there?" Upchurch closed the door before he spoke, looking as if he might vomit.

Rogers's voice held the faintest tremor. "This Feather shit is pretty bad."

"You ought to see what he's going to do next," Tommy heard Upchurch say. "Come on. We'd better go get his bag."

"Let's take our time." Rogers gave a skittish laugh. "I kinda need some air."

Tommy watched as Upchurch and Rogers sauntered down the hall, their footsteps languid as the sound of sobbing came from behind the closed door. All at once he felt hot and strange, like the time he'd accidentally interrupted his mother and one of her boyfriends.

Then the sobbing abated, leaving the corridor in an ominous silence. For a moment he wondered if Upchurch and Rogers hadn't bugged out entirely, then he heard their footsteps approaching. Now was his only chance to see what they were doing to Willett.

He darted up to the next doorway. If Up-church and Rogers opened the door wide enough, he might be able to see inside. As the pair came into view, he saw that Rogers now carried a small case. It looked like an old doctor's bag. Cabe fought back a shudder as they glanced once at each other, then opened the door.

He pressed forward as they went inside. Most of the Troopers were gathered around what looked like an examination table. Wurth had some kind of white apron strapped on, while Tallent and Grice and the others gaped at a lump beneath a blood-speckled sheet. Cabe leaned from the doorway to get a better look. As the door swung open to its widest point, he caught a glimpse of a head of silvery gray hair. He blinked in amazement. It wasn't Willett they were torturing! It was some old woman!

He stood like a statue until the door closed, then he turned and fled. He knew he should move with caution, but he didn't care. Every-thing inside him felt on fire. What was going on? What had they done with Willett? Who was the old lady? Was Sheriff Logan now delivering old women for Wurth to cut to pieces?

Fighting hot tears, Tommy jerked open the bathroom door. *This place has been fucked from the start,* he thought. If he didn't get out of here soon all Wurth's vileness would become his. He would not grow up to be a good man like his grandfather, but someone like Wurth, who sliced up boys with his tongue and old women with knives.

Hurrying to the window, he scrambled out onto the fire escape and breathed in the frosty night air. As his head cleared he looked up to see a single star shooting across the black sky. He realized then without tears, that he would never see Willett again. His only friend had become, in that moment, one of Unakawaya's ghosts. The stones of this castle would forever keep Willett's fate a secret. All Tommy could do now was try to escape this awful place and take the memory of Willett with him. He only hoped he could do that and still remain alive.

CHAPTER 30

"Does she always sleep like that?" Ruth Moon backed away from Mary Crow, who during the night had switched from the cot in front of the fire to the rocking chair, where she now slept upright, her Beretta clutched in her hands.

Jonathan leaned over Mary and gently took the pistol away. "Her mother got killed about ten feet away. I imagine that would make anybody a little skittish."

Mary's jaw hung slack; a small drop of saliva had collected in the corner of her mouth. With a single, tender gesture, Jonathan reached under her chin and closed her mouth, his strong hand cupping her jaw. "I should have stayed down here last night. There are too many ghosts for her in this room."

Ruth didn't say anything else. She turned and

walked back up the stairs, unwilling to stand there and watch her lover stew over Mary Crow. She sat down at the kitchen table and poured herself a cup of coffee. In a few moments Jonathan padded back up the stairs, carrying a package of chocolate Ding-Dongs.

"Is she still asleep?"

He nodded, opening the cellophane and cramming half a Ding-Dong in his mouth. "I wonder what made her draw that gun."

"Probably some weird mountain noise." Ruth remembered her first weeks at Little Jump Off. She'd grown up in the flat plains of Oklahoma, where sound radiated out into the air. In the mountains, noise seemed to have a life of its own, careening from one spot to the next, amplified by moisture and altitude. Up here, a simple bullfrog could sound demonic; a prowling tomcat like the devil himself.

"Yeah. I guess." Jonathan finished one Ding-Dong and started another.

"Are you still going up to Asheville, to get those computers?"

"If you want me to." He grabbed his mug from the dish drainer and poured himself some coffee.

"They need us to get them before the end of the year. They want to write them off their income tax."

"Then I'd better go today," said Jonathan. "I'm taking three guys out fishing tomorrow."

"How long will you be gone?" Ruth hated to be left alone at Little Jump Off. Though she would never admit it to Jonathan, she understood perfectly why Mary Crow had slept with a gun in her lap. Ghosts hovered around Little Jump Off like smoke around a fire.

"I'll be home on New Year's Eve. They want to get back to Greenville to party."

Jonathan finished his Ding-Dongs, then put on his socks and boots. Rising, he grabbed his jacket and scooped his car keys off the table. "Okay, then." He leaned over and kissed her on the mouth. "I'll see you around noon."

"What about Mary?" She looked up at him.

"Just let her sleep," he replied, then added, "but keep an eye out for that G-man. Wake her up if somebody strange comes by."

He smiled at her, then he was down the steps and out the door, off to pick up the year's last computers.

★　★　★

Ruth busied herself in the kitchen, washing dishes with great gusto, hoping the clatter might wake Mary up. She had to open the store at nine, and it would be difficult to conduct business with someone snoring in a rocking chair.

She had just turned to put the dishes back in the cabinet when Mary appeared at the top of the stairs, her clothes rumpled, her hair uncombed.

"Hi," she said, her voice grainy and soft.

"Good morning." Ruth smiled. The famous Atlanta prosecutor seemed lost and bewildered. "Did you sleep okay?"

Mary shrugged, looking embarrassed. "Not really. I kept imagining all sorts of noises."

"Would you like some breakfast? Some eggs or toast?"

"Coffee and toast would be wonderful, if it's no trouble."

"Not at all." Ruth started another pot of coffee and dropped two pieces of bread in the toaster. Mary sat down at the table, sleepily gazing at the *Hartsville Herald* crossword puzzle that Jonathan had worked earlier.

"So what kind of noises did you hear?" Ruth snagged the slices of toast as they popped up, wondering if Mary heard the same late-night sounds she did.

"Footsteps," Mary said softly. "On the porch." She looked as if she wanted to say something more, but instead she rubbed her eyes, as if trying to rid herself of some lingering bad dream.

Ruth poured her a cup of coffee and put the toast in front of her, along with a jar of apple butter and a small pitcher of cream. Mary slathered the apple butter on the toast, but drank her coffee black. She ate neatly, but fast, as if she were ravenous. When she finished, she looked at Ruth and smiled. "That was delicious."

"Want some more?"

"No. Thanks."

Ruth removed the empty plate to the sink. Coffee and toast perked most people up, but Mary Crow still huddled at her table like some kind of refugee. "You're welcome to take a shower if you want," Ruth said.

"Would you mind?"

"Not at all. I'll get you some clean towels."

She rummaged in Jonathan's closet, then put two clean towels and a fresh bar of soap in the bathroom. When she returned to the kitchen, she found Mary looking at one of her computers.

"What was that guy's name we were talking about last night?"

Ruth frowned. "I'm not sure who you mean . . ."

"The ex-Ranger. The one with the boys' camp."

"Sergeant Wurth. Camp Unakawaya."

Mary raised one eyebrow. "You know what 'unakawaya' means in Cherokee?"

"White wolf."

"Mmm." Mary tapped one finger on the monitor, watching the pixel display bounding across the screen. She looked up at Ruth. "Is there any way we could look up this Wurth on the Internet?"

Ruth shrugged, secretly flattered that the great Mary Crow had taken her suspicions seriously. "I guess we could get online and find his address and phone number."

Mary glanced at Jonathan's crossword puzzle. "Think we could access the newspaper's files?"

"Probably," said Ruth. Mary grinned, as if she'd succeeded in persuading her to join in some bit of mischief. Suddenly Ruth found herself grinning back, pleased to be included as an accomplice. "Why don't you go take your shower and I'll see what I can pull up."

"Would you mind?"

"Not at all," said Ruth, now eager to join the adventure.

"Thanks. That would be terrific." Mary brushed past her and walked into the bathroom. As Ruth logged on to the Internet she heard the toilet flush, then the shower came on. She felt strange, having the woman she'd invoked Selu over bathing in her own bathroom, but she put it out of her head and concentrated on the task before her. She'd never aided in a criminal investigation before.

By the time she accessed all the Robert Wurth

articles from the *Hartsville Herald,* Mary sat beside her, warm and damp, her dark hair slicked back behind her ears. Both women watched as three little coffin-shaped icons appeared on the screen, inscribed with the dates 2–87, 7–93, and 10–95.

"Try 1987 first," suggested Mary.

Ruth clicked her mouse. Seconds later, an image appeared.

"Sergeant Robert Wurth Returns Home." Mary read the headline above a photograph of a smiling man standing in front of a tall iron gate. The man wore an Army uniform and even in the old photo had light, piercing eyes that stared from beneath heavy brows.

"Sergeant Robert Wurth has recently reopened Frieden," the article went on, "the sanitarium built in 1920 by Baron Ernst von Loessing, as Camp Unakawaya, a summer camp for boys. Sergeant Wurth, retired from the U.S. Army, grew up in the area and is a 1964 graduate of Hartsville High School. 'I hunted all over the Frieden land when I was a boy, and have always thought of it as home. When the old place came on the market, I jumped at the chance to buy it,' said Sgt. Wurth.

"Wurth plans to open Camp Unakawaya this June, adding archery and riflery to the program as soon as possible."

Ruth went next to the July '93 article. The photo showed Sergeant Wurth grinning with those same cold eyes, a rifle in his arms. This time he was flanked by several other young marksmen. "Camp Unakawaya Rifle Team Takes Top Trophies," read the headline.

"For the first time, a rifle team from a local camp has swept the field in the statewide Sporting Guns Competition," said the article. "Coached by camp owner Robert Wurth, the Camp Unakawaya marksmen hail from seven different states. 'We work hard at Unakawaya to provide a good, safe shooting experience for our youngsters,' said Wurth. 'We've got some very keen-eyed young men.' Camp Unakawaya, formerly the Frieden Sanitarium, was converted into a boys' camp in 1987. The riflery program was added the following year. The camp also offers archery and an outdoor survival program."

Mary frowned at Ruth Moon. "It's beginning to sound like a junior-grade Parris Island, isn't it? Let's pull up the last article."

Ruth again clicked her mouse. Another picture flashed on the screen. This time Wurth was accepting a check from a cluster of men who looked like a well-fed Chamber of Commerce.

"Camp Unakawaya Changes Its Mission," the headline read.

"Camp Unakawaya, owned by Sgt. Robert

Wurth, has just announced the inclusion of permanent year-round foster care to its summer camp for boys," the newspaper reported.

Mary sat up straighter in her chair.

" 'We've just received a major grant from the FaithAmerica Foundation to augment our regular camp program with a residential camp for at-risk boys,' explained Sergeant Wurth. 'The number of abused and neglected boys here, in these mountains, is growing every day. Frieden Sanitarium's original mission was one of service to our fellow man. We're just following that tradition in a slightly different way. With our programs, we hope to turn these delinquents into productive and law-abiding young men.' "

"Look." Ruth pointed at the screen. "It's that TV preacher. Gerald LeClaire."

Mary squinted at the picture of Wurth shaking hands with a doughy-faced man with a broad grin. "I've seen that guy before," she said thoughtfully. "On television, at my grandmother's house. Her nurse, Jonelle, loved the FaithAmerica hundred-voice choir."

"I read somewhere that he makes six million dollars every year on prayer requests alone."

Mary continued to stare at the picture, then she pointed to one of the men standing behind Wurth and LeClaire. "I'll be damned," she whispered. "That's Stump Logan!"

"Who's Stump Logan?" asked Ruth.

"Hartsville's friendly local sheriff," Mary said grimly. "That man's passion for parking tickets may have cost Irene her life."

"That's everything from the newspaper," said Ruth. "You can stay up here and dig deeper, but I promised Jonathan I'd open the store on time."

"That's okay." Mary smiled at her as she rose from her chair. "This has been a great help, but I've got to get going myself."

"You do?" Ruth felt an unexpected twinge of disappointment. It was fun having Mary Crow here, chasing bad guys through cyberspace. "Where are you going?"

"I'm not sure." Mary shook her head. "All I know is that I've got to keep searching for Irene. Wherever that trail takes me is where I'll go."

CHAPTER 31

Mary stood behind the Little Jump Off counter, thumbing through the Pisgah County phone book while Ruth Moon sacked up a box of crackers and four cans of sardines for two men who were going fishing. Mary shivered as she waited for them to leave; she regarded fishing as a pleasant way to waste a summer afternoon. To sit for hours by icy water with a cold wind stinging your face seemed closely akin to torture.

She found the number she was looking for. When the fishermen were safely out of the store, she picked up Jonathan's old rotary phone and dialed it. Moments later, Hugh Kavanagh answered, his brogue sounding gruff as Irish gorse.

"Hugh? This is Mary Crow." She knew Safer had probably bugged his line, so she would have about twenty seconds to find out what she needed to know. The Feds could trace any call lasting longer.

"Mary Crow?" Hugh paused, confused. "They told me you went back to Atlanta."

"No. I'm here. Can you tell me what's going on? What's the FBI doing?"

He snorted. "Not a bloody lot. Mostly they sit on their bums in her kitchen drinking coffee and pecking on those damn computers."

Figures, Mary thought, the hand on her watch sweeping through the seconds. "Any news of Irene?"

"I asked this morning when I turned out the horses. The tall one with the beard told me they hadn't found a thing."

"Thanks. I've got to go. I'll talk to you later."

"Mary, what's going to happen? I didn't know—"

She hung up at eighteen seconds, cutting him off in midsentence. "Sorry to be rude, Hugh," she whispered as she put the receiver back in its cradle. "But I couldn't have told you a thing."

"Any news on your friend?" Ruth Moon stood at Mary's elbow, unabashedly eaves-dropping.

"Not as of this morning, if they told her friend Hugh the truth."

"So what are you going to do?"

"I'm not sure."

"You're welcome to stay here," Ruth offered. "We could get back on the Internet again."

Mary walked over to the fireplace and gathered up her coat and purse. "I think I'll just do some snooping around by myself."

"Jonathan should be back in about an hour. Don't you want to wait for him?"

"Just tell him thanks—and thank you, for all your hospitality." Over the morning, she'd almost grown to like Ruth Moon. She'd been helpful, considerate, and more than adept on that computer. If the circumstances were different, they would probably be good friends. Mary smiled and extended her hand. "Maybe I'll drop back by, the next time I come up here."

"Good luck." Ruth shook her hand. "I hope you find your Judge Hannah."

Mary smiled. "I do, too." Mary paused to glance at the front corner of the store, then she opened the door and stepped outside.

She wiped a thin crust of snow off the windshield of the Toyota before she got inside. The engine started easily, and she had to admit that whatever Bingo didn't do to his interiors, he at least kept his engines ready to roll. With a rev of the motor, she gave Little Jump Off Store a final glance and pulled out onto the highway beyond. She hadn't told Ruth Moon, but she knew exactly where she was going. Something was odd about an ex-Ranger starting a camp, winning all sorts of elite shooting trophies, then opening his program to a bunch of foster kids. It could, of course, be a curious coincidence, but her years in the courtroom had taught her to pay close attention to coincidence. If Wurth had some kind of weird agenda, a camp like that would be the perfect setup. Big enough to hide a federal judge, but small enough to fly below the FBI radar.

Mary heard Jonathan's voice in her head, chiding her, telling her she was grasping at straws. "Of course I am," she answered aloud. "But you'd be amazed at what winds up in my hands."

★   ★   ★

Camp Unakawaya lay northeast of Hartsville. She skirted the town to avoid any Feds, then drove into the mountains along a bumpy two-lane road that snaked beneath a high canopy of trees that waved gray, skeletal fingers as she passed, whispering sibilant greetings to the icy wind. As she twisted up the highway a Cooper's hawk swooped in front of her, nothing more than a high-pitched whistle and a blur of speck-led feathers.

Driving higher, she switched on the radio. A distant dance-band station bounced its signal through the mountain static—Doris Day singing "My Secret Love." Mary shook her head. On overcast days, mountain radio was laughable—stations from all over the country came in erratically, so in the space of a fifteen-minute trip you could hear everything from Ella Fitzgerald to Britney Spears without ever touching your dial. She sped, listening to Doris Day. Though finding Irene never left her mind, part of her felt more alive than she had in a long time. For once she was not stuck indoors, in a courtroom bound by law and precedent, hurling words at surly defendants and their pompous attorneys. For once she was hunting no less earnestly than that hawk, seeking her prey with all her senses sharp as knives.

"Maybe this is what crows were meant to do," she whispered aloud. "Maybe I should have taken this path years ago."

Suddenly a small brown arrow-shaped sign on the left shoulder of the road read "Camp Unakawaya."

She drove on, passing what seemed like miles of a low stone wall, then finally turned onto a gravel drive that twisted between two crumbling stone pillars nearly invisible beneath a huge tangle of thorny vines. A rusted wrought-iron archway connected the two pillars, the word "Frieden" worked gracefully inside, tendrils of the vine curling around the rusted letters.

"Pretty creepy," murmured Mary as she passed beneath the archway. She looked at the field-stone wall that lined the drive, holding back thick woods that coiled behind them. She caught only the barest glimpses of straw-colored fields through the crowd of massive oaks and maples. After the driveway traversed acres of forest, a wide bridge spanned a lake of churning gray water. An old-fashioned wooden diving platform caught her eye; when she turned her gaze back to the driveway, she gasped.

At first she thought she must have taken a wrong turn. The building in front of her looked nothing like any camp she'd ever seen. Massive, constructed of hewn stone, it stood dark slate and mossy with age, sprawling like some me-dieval manor house, with turrets and chimneys sprouting at odd angles across the roofline. It looked as if it belonged not only to a different age, but to a different continent, incongruous as a woman coming to a barn dance in satin and pearls.

The driveway curved into a huge porte cochere that extended from the front of the house, passing below rows of small leaded-glass windows running the length of the structure. As she drove closer, Mary saw that Frieden had not worn its years well. Moss stained the stone foundation, and one long, elaborate network of gutters had pulled away completely from the house. Though a section of the roof looked recently repaired, around the lower eaves several of the slate tiles were missing and a walnut sapling sprouted from one chimney. It occurred to her that Sergeant Wurth may have had the money to buy Frieden, but its maintenance was stretching him thin. *That might account for his cozying up to Reverend Gerald LeClaire,* she thought. *Maybe Wurth houses his foster kids on the cheap and spends his FaithAmerica dough just trying to keep up with this place.*

She pulled under the porte cochere and got out of the car. A number of teenagers were at work around the property. Several strapping young men wearing handsome leather flight jackets were carrying plywood into what looked like an old gym. A thinner, younger boy clad in jeans and a worn cotton jacket bent over a broom, sweeping dead leaves off the porch. Despite the activity, there was an eerie quietness about the place, as if all the former Frieden residents still hovered over their old domain.

Broad stone steps led to the lodge, and a huge American flag snapped in the cold wind. As she crossed the chipped tile porch, the boy with the broom turned and stared at her, his brows lifting in alarm.

"Hi," Mary called, smiling. "Could you tell me where I might find Sergeant Wurth?"

The boy pushed his glasses back on his nose as he blushed tomato red. "I think he's at the g-gym," he replied, nodding over his shoulder.

"Down that way?"

Nodding again, the boy looked increasingly flustered, as if he were afraid.

"I wanted to ask him about his camp," Mary explained. "See if he had any room left this summer."

The boy leaned his broom against the outside wall of the castle. "G-go on inside. I'll see if I can f-find him."

He opened the door and stepped into the castle. Mary crossed the threshold behind him. When she entered the foyer, she blinked. While the lower half of the room was paneled in a somber chestnut, the upper half was a riot of color, with flags of every state hanging from the vaulted ceiling. Light from the diamond-paned windows illuminated the fields of red and white and blue. Mary picked out Georgia's old version of The Stars and Bars, North Carolina's big "NC," and the mystical crescent moon of South Carolina.

She frowned. Though the flags looked festive, she found the foyer oddly oppressive, as if she were trapped in the middle of an old Teutonic hunting lodge.

"C-come on," the boy said, pointing toward an even larger room to their right. "Wait in here. I'll g-go get the sergeant."

He ran back out the front door, leaving her in a white plaster room with long floor-to-ceiling windows that could be raised high enough to allow passage out to the porch beyond. In the middle of one wall rose a huge fireplace; over that was hung a portrait of a handsome young man in a World War I Army uniform. A ballroom, Mary thought, fighting the urge to run and see how far she could slide along the glossy smoothness of the ancient wooden floor. She shook her head. A grand salon in the middle of Appalachia. The mountains never ceased to amaze her. She moved closer to the fireplace, looking up at the old painting.

The door opened behind her. She turned. A man of average height stood there, dressed in a khaki army uniform and a brown leather jacket. His dark hair was buzz-cut, and his pale blue eyes bulged, giving him the air of a ferocious bulldog. His face and features were even, but he looked impatient, as if he were enduring some frivolity for which he had no time.

"Good morning," he called, his voice brisk. "I see you're appreciating our artwork." He nodded at the portrait over the fireplace.

"It's very well done," Mary replied. "A relative of yours?"

"No. It's Helmut von Loessing, the son of the man who built this house. He was a German infantry officer. That painting was done before he left for France." The man stepped forward, extending his hand. "I'm Robert Wurth. How can I help you?"

"Oh." Mary tried to sound delighted. "You're the gentleman I'm looking for."

"And why is that?" Wurth looked at her as if he were measuring her for a dress.

"I'm trying to find a summer camp for my nephew, and someone suggested that I drop in and have a chat with you." She glanced around the grand room and feigned embarrassment. "I'm sorry if I intruded. . . ."

Wurth grinned. "Visitors don't wander in here often, but we're happy when they do." His eyes narrowed. "Who did you say sent you here?"

"Uh, the guidance counselor at my nephew's school. Teddy's recently gotten interested in riflery, and the counselor told me that Camp Unakawaya was the best camp in the country for young marksmen."

"And what did you say your name was?"

Mary felt his eyes boring into her. "Mary Crow. From Atlanta. I'm up here on business. I would have called, but I took a chance and just stopped by. Are you completely full for next summer?"

"Actually, we are, but we might be able to squeeze your nephew in. How old is he?"

"Twelve. Teddy Bennefield's his name."

"Bennefield?" Wurth cocked his head as some long-ago tumblers apparently clicked in the vaults of his memory. "That name seems familiar, somehow." He gazed at the floor, then shrugged. "You meet so many people running a camp, sometimes all the names sound familiar."

"I'm sure they do."

"Wait right there, Ms. Crow."

Wurth strode back through the foyer and down a dark hall beyond, his footsteps crisp on the highly polished floor. He was gone so long that Mary wondered if he'd forgotten about her. Then she heard his footsteps drawing closer. In a moment he stood in front of her again, holding a large white envelope.

"This is our camp brochure, an application form, and all the permission slips your nephew will need." He handed her the envelope, then his eyes flicked over her again. "How would you like to go on a private tour?"

"Right now?" Mary stalled, wondering if going anywhere alone with this stranger was the best idea.

"Absolutely," Wurth replied, his lips stretching in a cold smile. "I've already had one of my boys pull up the golf cart."

"Well . . . I suppose I could . . ." Mary returned Wurth's smile as they walked back into the foyer. *It'll be okay*, she told herself. *There are people around here. And you're armed.* She was comforted by the Beretta nestling under her jacket.

On the porch, the same gawky boy worked his broom. "Cabe, I want that spotless," Wurth snapped as they walked toward the golf cart.

"Yessir." The boy kept his eyes on the floor. "N-not a problem, sir."

"He looks kind of cold in that thin jacket," Mary remarked, huddling into her own warm parka.

"He's got a better one he could wear," replied Wurth. "Kid keeps his nose stuck in a book all the time. He probably doesn't even know it's winter."

Mary shivered as a raw, cold wind slapped her face. "That seems like it would be hard to miss."

They climbed into the waiting golf cart and drove off toward the lake, Wurth giving a running commentary about his camp.

"I've run Unakawaya for almost fifteen years. Each summer we have three month-long sessions for fifty boys. We teach swimming, riflery, outdoor survival, and traditional American values."

"Traditional American values?" Mary echoed.

"Yes. Did you know that statistically, by the time your nephew's thirteen, he will have experimented with marijuana, acid, PCP, and cocaine?"

"I didn't know that."

"Well, it's true. Even when a boy comes here without having experimented with drugs, he can't do a single pull-up. His fingers might be callused, but not from work, or even baseball. From computer games! American boys today spend far too much time on their butts, gaping at screens. Camp Unakawaya puts an end to that."

"Don't the boys go back to their old habits when they return home?" Mary asked mildly.

Wurth shook his head. "Not according to the mail I get from their parents. They're amazed at the changes we work in just thirty days."

"I bet they are," she agreed.

They zipped down to the lake, then turned and drove back around the side of the castle. In the sunlight Mary could see what sad repair the huge old sanitarium was truly in. Many of the windows that lined the two smaller wings of the main house had been boarded up with plywood, and the mortar around the top of all the chimneys was crumbling away. Lanky hemlocks huddled close to the house, stretching up to the roof, where various shades of speckled mold grew on the mottled slate tiles.

"Do the campers stay in this castle?" Mary asked Wurth.

"No," he replied. "I keep my foster boys in there."

"But the place looks so old. Is it safe?"

"It's all right. Originally, this was just a log internment camp for German merchant seamen in the First World War. One of the prisoners was a cousin to the young man whose portrait you saw. He wrote his family so glowingly about the mountains that after the Armistice, his rich uncle bought the place from the government and built his own sanitarium for his son. Hired a hotshot German doctor to treat his boy. Other young veterans heard about it. Pretty soon this place was a regular United Nations."

Mary grimaced. "For the maimed and disfigured?"

"Regrettably." Wurth's eyes scanned the old building. "Not too many of them ever made it back to Europe. But at least they had a comfortable place to die."

"So how did you wind up with it?" Mary pressed further, trying not to sound like a prosecuting attorney.

"I bought it when I left the service," explained Wurth. "I grew up in Hartsville and knew the place well. I turned it into a summer camp that first year and haven't looked back since. Down here you'll see our cabins."

He puttered down a lane canopied by pine trees and dotted with Camp Unakawaya cabins. Each was a single-room log structure nestled under the shadows of the trees. As Wurth drove past, Mary examined each one in the manner she'd learned from the cops in Atlanta—looking for car tracks in the dirt, an open door, any signs of habitation. She saw none. She could tell by the deep drifts of orange pine needles around the doors and windows that the cabins had been shut up tight last fall, and nothing had disturbed them since. Still, in that castle, there must be a thousand different places where you could hide someone.

"These look nice," she said neutrally as Wurth drove into a deserted cul-de-sac. "Do they have indoor plumbing?"

"They do," Wurth said proudly. "And electricity, too. Von Loessing was way ahead of his time. Hooked the place up to a water-driven generator and put all his wiring underground.

That wasn't commonly done up here until almost fifty years later. Come on. We'll go inside this one."

"That's okay, Sergeant Wurth," she said. She felt an odd, tight feeling in her chest. "I'm sure you must have other things to do. . . ."

"Not at all." He turned the golf cart in a tight circle and parked in front of the last cabin. "I'm very proud of Camp Unakawaya."

"I'm sure you are. But I really don't have the time right now. As I told you, I'm here on business."

"I know." Grinning, he leaned toward her. At first she thought he was trying to kiss her, but before she could move, before she could even breathe, he pinched a nerve in the side of her neck. Shocks of pain shot all the way down her leg. She struggled to get away but he gripped her tightly with one hand and unzipped her jacket with the other. She watched in horror as he extracted her Beretta, laughing in her ear as he did so, his breath hot and vaguely sour.

"You don't know this, Ms. Crow, but we've met before," he told her. "Irene Hannah's house, Christmas night. Second bedroom to the right of the stairs. Like most women, you're quite beautiful when you're asleep."

The rest happened fast. He forced her out of the golf cart and into the cabin, her own gun pointed at the base of her skull. She wanted to weep, not from fear, but because her own incompetence had led her into the oldest trap of all. She would not be saving Irene. She wouldn't even be saving herself. Her boss, Jim Falkner, had been absolutely right. She really didn't have any business doing this at all.

CHAPTER 32

"What time are you meeting your fishermen?"

Ruth Moon stood in the doorway of Little Jump Off Store, drinking a cup of coffee as Jonathan packed two bows and a quiver of arrows in the back of his truck. It was just moments after dawn on Saturday morning, and Polaris, still the reigning North Star, was beginning to fade overhead.

"Seven o'clock," he replied. He looked ghostly in the dim light, working in faded jeans and a white thermal undershirt. Ruth drew her shawl closer around her shoulders. She hated to watch him prepare for a trip, and this morning the idea of his going anywhere made her feel particularly nervous and unlucky. She thought of Mary Crow, sleeping yesterday with her pistol in her lap.

"I need to get going pretty soon." Jonathan

looked at her and smiled. "What are you going to do while I'm gone?"

"Mind the store, I guess." She shivered beneath her shawl. "I may close early tonight and drive down to Wal-Mart."

"What do you need at Wal-Mart?" He buttoned his old Army jacket over his undershirt. "We live at a general store."

"Oh, just a couple of the very few items Little Jump Off doesn't carry." She felt her smile wobble. "Aren't you going to eat any breakfast before you go?"

"Just my usual."

She turned and walked inside. She didn't much care for working at Little Jump Off. She didn't know either the merchandise or the clientele very well, and as helpful as she tried to be, the customers always regarded her as a poor substitute for Jonathan. Still, if she manned the cash register she could add a few more dollars to their thin pockets and she might recruit some more people for REPIC. She hopped up on the stool behind the counter while Jonathan poured himself coffee and scooped up a package of Ding-Dongs from the snack food display.

"You're going to turn yourself into a diabetic like that," she warned, amazed at the amount of sugar these Eastern Cherokees consumed.

He shrugged. "It's just the hillbilly version of a double latte and a chocolate croissant."

She couldn't watch as he licked the chocolate crumbs from his fingers. The sight of food sickened her.

"Have you heard from Mary?" She knew he hadn't, but she wanted to hear him say so.

"No."

"You don't think she could be in any trouble, do you?"

"I think she's way out of her league if she's gotten involved in an FBI investigation. Those boys play rough."

Ruth cocked her head. "How do you know?"

"I lived here when they were beating the bushes for Eric Rudolph." Jonathan tossed the Ding-Dong wrapper in the garbage can.

"But they wouldn't let Mary get hurt, would they?" Ruth's heart beat faster. She knew she should be wary of Mary Crow, but she had enjoyed her company yesterday. She was now sorry she'd ever brought her to Selu's attention. That was always risky.

"They would try their best to keep her safe," Jonathan answered. "But they stay pretty focused on their own objective." He glanced at her curiously. "Why all the sudden concern about Mary?"

She knew she should say, *Because I helped her look up Sergeant Wurth on the computer,* but the words stuck in her throat. "I guess I'm worried that we haven't heard from her."

"Oh, I wouldn't worry too much about that." As Jonathan poured himself another cup of coffee, she noted the barest trace of bitterness in his voice. "Mary takes care of herself pretty well."

Ruth walked over and wrapped her arms around him. She needed to feel his warmth. Maybe she was mistaken about Mary being in trouble. Maybe Mary Crow had just given up on her old friend and driven back to Atlanta.

"Want to go upstairs and tell me good-bye?" She nibbled his earlobe.

"I can't." He laughed and kissed her. "Those guys from Greenville are probably already waiting."

She let go of him, astonished. Most men she knew would stop everything short of brain surgery for a good fuck—they certainly wouldn't let meeting up with a pair of fishermen keep them out of bed. But then, Jonathan was not most men. "When will you be back?"

"In time to celebrate New Year's. I promise." He kissed the top of her head. "Are you okay? You look kind of green around the gills."

"Just a little tired." She walked back over to

the stool. "Not used to getting up so early, I guess."

"Welcome to my world." Jonathan grinned. "See you day after tomorrow."

"Be careful," she called as he went out the door, wanting suddenly to add more. The feeling she'd had of something lurking out there returned. Although she had no words for it, she saw it as a wolf with sharp teeth and keen eyes slinking through the trees, just waiting for the chance to tear them apart.

★   ★   ★

Miles away, an older wolf of a different sort peered through the shaggy green branches of a hemlock tree. Short and bandy-legged, he stood with a gray tweed cap pulled low across his forehead and watched the lights flickering from the windows of Irene Hannah's kitchen.

"Bloody jackasses," Hugh Kavanagh muttered. "Useless as tits on a bull!"

Hugh had made it his habit for the past two mornings to walk over from his farm shortly after sunrise and station himself with a pair of binoculars on the hill above Irene's stable. The elevation afforded him a perfect view of her house, and the evergreen hemlocks provided him cover. Since Thursday morning, the farm

had served as ground zero for the FBI investigation. Although the search had looked impres-
sive, with undercover surveillance vans and
heat-seeking helicopters, Hugh knew that
Irene's disappearance remained just as big a mystery this morning as it had been three days ago.

He'd watched the place so long, he'd nick-
named most of the agents. Abe was a tall, thin
agent with a face that looked as if it had been
hewn from oak. He stayed hunched over the
computers all day, munching chips from a cellophane bag. Blackbeard was the muscular, serious
lad who seemed to fancy Mary Crow. The short
little twit who'd collared him in the barn he
called Scab. Those three foostered in and out of
the place night and day, mostly tramping around
in each other's footsteps. No wonder they
couldn't find anything.

Still, he lingered beneath the tree, on the off-
chance that they had found Irene. He knew she
would demand to see her horses first. After all,
she had a pregnant mare to look after.

He squinted down at the house below. Lucy
the goose slept on the back steps, a ball of white
feathers with her head tucked beneath her wing.
One of the barn cats crouched on the edge of
the patio, staring at something in the grass. The
cat flicked its ears, then both animals—goose
and cat—leaped into the air as Blackbeard thun-

dered out the door, cell phone plastered to his ear. Back and forth across the patio he stomped, stabbing the air with his index finger.

"Not got her yet, have you, boy?" Hugh whispered mournfully, feeling his heart droop with disappointment. Every morning he'd come up here longing to see his dear Irene tromping out in her green Wellies, feed bucket in hand. How happy he would be then! How fast he would run down this hill!

"You're a bloody fool, Kavanagh," he scolded himself as he watched Blackbeard take one final frustrated lap around the patio, then slam the door behind him as he went back inside.

With a deep sigh, Hugh turned and walked along the edge of the tree line down to the barn. *Not today, old man.* The words whispered in his head. *Maybe not ever again.*

In the stable, he switched on the lights. Five of the horses were already standing up with their ears pricked, peering at him expectantly over their stall doors. The large foaling stall where Lady Jane stayed looked empty.

"Uh-oh." He hurried down to the end of the passageway, half expecting to see the mare lying on the straw with a brand-new foal curled up beside her. Instead, when he peered over the door he found Lady Jane restless and agitated, pacing a circular path in her straw. Her nut-brown coat glistened with sweat and she was huffing as if she'd just galloped miles.

"I'll get these others fed and turned out, girl," Hugh promised softly, reaching over to pat the nervous horse. "You're going to be a mama soon."

"What the hell do you think you're doing?"

The gruff words hit him like a truncheon. He thought he recognized the voice of Scab, the bald one who was not quite a full shilling. He turned around slowly. Sure enough, the little man stood there, his face in a fierce scrunch, his hands balled into fists.

"I'm doing what I was asked to do two days ago, boy," Hugh replied. Holy Mother, how these Americans loved to swagger like John Wayne. "Taking care o' these horses. If you're interested, this one's about to foal."

"What were you doing on the hill with those binoculars?" Scab closed the distance between them. His blue eyes glittered as if he'd found Hugh hiding both Irene Hannah and Eric Rudolph out here in the straw.

"Watching you sad lot of bloody fools."

"What for?"

"Because I need to see if you've found her."

Scab pushed his face into Hugh's, forcing him backward. "So what if we have, old man? The judge is going to have more important things to do than come running down here to see you."

Hugh looked at the young rotter, longing to curl his right hand into a fist and bust his pointy nose into next Tuesday. Thirty, maybe even twenty, years ago he could have knocked this one down with one hand tied behind him. Now he wasn't so sure. His joints hurt like fire most mornings and climbing up that hill to the hemlocks got harder every day. He sighed. He was old. He just wanted his sweet Irene to come back to him, so they could raise this little horse Lady Jane was about to have and enjoy what time they had left together.

"Aye, boy," he finally murmured. "I'm sure she does."

"Then stay the hell away from that hill," Scab muttered as he grabbed Hugh's binoculars and hung them around his own neck. "This is a classified government investigation."

"Aye." Hugh rolled up his sleeves. "That I'll bloody well not forget." He watched as Scab stomped out of the stable, then he knelt beside Lady Jane, ready to attend the heaving mare with the practiced hands of a County Wexford man.

★   ★   ★

"Where the hell have you been?" Daniel Safer demanded as Mike Tuttle walked through the kitchen door, a pair of German binoculars hanging around his neck.

Tuttle laughed. "Just hassling that old Irish fart. Got to get your kicks where you can, up here in the boonies."

"Take those binoculars off. They're private property."

"They're Zeiss binocs," Tuttle protested. "That old asshole's spying on us with them."

"I said take them off, Tuttle." Safer's tone sharpened.

Krebbs raised his eyes from his computer screen, watching the exchange between the two men. Tuttle glared at Safer, then, with a shrug of his shoulders, removed the binoculars. "I wasn't going to keep them," he muttered.

"You lay off that old guy," Safer told him. "If it wasn't for him, you'd be the one out there shoveling horse shit."

Tuttle opened his mouth to speak, then thought better of it. He yanked out a chair and sat down, his body stiff with anger. "Okay, big Dan. What's our schedule for the day?"

Safer glanced at his watch. It was 6:27 A.M. Friday, December 29. In the past sixty-three hours since he'd gotten the first call from Mary Crow, he had found nothing. The roadblocks Logan and the North Carolina State Police put up had yielded only drunk drivers; their door-to-door search of Hartsville had only embar-

rassed a few errant spouses who were dallying
where they weren't supposed to dally. When the
operations manager for Delta Airlines had called
and confessed that Mary Crow had somehow
given them the slip, Safer had to go take a walk
to cool off. This was Eric Rudolph, volume
two, only worse. The mountains were doing it
to him once again. He knew as well as everybody that with each passing minute, their
chances of finding Judge Irene Hannah faded.

He looked down at the huge map of western
North Carolina spread out before him. "Tuttle,
I want you to meet up with the rest of the guys
in Hartsville and divide into two-man teams.
Rice has the list of everybody we've done business with up here. Assign each team to one of
the surrounding counties—Cherokee, Clay,
Macon. I want you to lean on everybody—
blockaders, dopers, klansmen, cockfighters. Ask
them if they know anything about Judge Irene
Hannah or Mary Crow. If they do, offer them
anything they want in exchange."

"Are we now listing our civilian helper as of-
ficially missing?" asked Tuttle.

"Mary Crow's an officer of the court and a
part of this investigation. She hasn't been seen in
forty-eight hours. That's considered missing in
anybody's jurisdiction." Safer glared at Tuttle.

"Now get going and let me know what you find out."

Tuttle stood and put one hand on the binoculars. "Can I take these with me?"

"No," Safer snapped. "Leave them here."

With an angry glare, Tuttle stomped out, slamming the door behind him.

"Thanks, Daniel," said Krebbs, rattling his bag of pork rinds. "He was beginning to get on my nerves."

"Everything's beginning to get on all our nerves." Safer frowned over at Krebbs. "Have you gotten anything off those computers?"

"Nothing beyond bureau updates every fifteen minutes," replied Krebbs. "The good news is that all the other federal judges are safe and accounted for. No action in any of the other twelve districts."

"And the bad news?"

"The bad news is that there's no other news. Our scanning program Carnivore hasn't intercepted any kind of weird E-mail correspondence."

"What about websites?"

"Same old neo-Nazi, white-supremacist, anti-satanic government shit. No new buzz from the hate mongers."

"Then it must be one guy." Safer chewed the end of his pen. "One extremely lucky, amazingly well-organized killer with some kind of monster grudge."

"The profilers say no," said Krebbs. "No consistent pattern either in the MO or the victims."

"Then who the fuck is it?" Safer tossed his pen down on the table.

"I still like a group, on New Year's Eve."

"Tell me why."

"The killings have been on or near American holidays, which implies a political statement. They've been virtually indistinguishable from accidents or random crime, which implies intimate knowledge of the victims. Plus, they've zigzagged all over the country. Judge January drowns in California, Judge February has a coronary in Maine. An individual couldn't leave California, get that familiar with the guy in Maine, then move on to kill the judge in Alabama in March."

"Sure he could," said Safer. "He'd be racking up some big-time Sky Miles, but it could be done."

"It's *possible*," Krebbs granted. "But look how much easier a group of just two or three well-trained guys could do it."

"But nobody's bragging out there." Safer nodded at Krebbs's computer screens. "Conspirators should be crowing like roosters over this!"

Krebbs shook his head. "The biggest bark isn't

always the worst bite, Daniel. The guys who'll bomb your federal buildings don't end their names with dot com."

"So you're saying it's a conspiracy that's going to act when the ball drops in Times Square."

"That's the only thing that fits what's gone on before." Krebbs crunched down on a pork rind. "We just have to figure out who they are some-time within the next two days."

"Thanks, Krebbs," Safer said bitterly. "Next time tell me something I don't already know."

CHAPTER 33

Mary was floating. She lay suspended over a dark landscape, detailed and horrific as any Bosch painting, watching the women she loved doing unspeakable things. Her friend Alex laughing as she beat a dog. Irene lying naked on her desk, masturbating with the barrel of a gun. Her own mother looking up from something's body with a sharp-toothed, malevolent grin. Mary tried to turn her head, tried to close her eyes, but the images remained, mocking, obscene.

Then she sensed movement around her. Something was coming, something that would rip her to pieces. She needed to scream, to scare it away! She opened her mouth to yell, but she felt weighted down, as if tons of earth covered her. She tried to speak but nothing came out. Tightening every muscle, she forced a scream up from her chest and out her mouth, opening jaws that felt welded shut. Suddenly her eyes flickered open; the crushing weight was gone. She awakened.

At first she could only blink at the blazing light that glared down upon her like an enormous eye, then she raised her head cautiously. Her clothes were gone, replaced by thick black pajamas similar to the outfits worn by karate students. Tight leather straps bound her to a metal examination table. Although everything spun before her eyes, she realized she lay in some kind of theater where tiers of empty seats rose around her, only to disappear into the dense shadows beyond the blinding light.

She lowered her head, nauseous, sorry that she'd looked up and started the room spinning. Grasping the solid edges of the table, she tried to anchor herself in time and space. She remembered eating toast at Little Jump Off, then driving somewhere and talking to a man with diamond-sharp eyes. *Christmas is coming,* she thought. No, wait. Christmas had come. She'd spent Christmas at Irene's, then Irene—! In a rush, it all came back. She'd driven to Camp Unakawaya to look for Irene, and Sergeant Wurth had forced her into that cabin! She'd expected to be shot, or decapitated, but instead all she'd felt was a tiny prick on her neck and the world began to smear and drip around the edges as her knees buckled. The last thing she remembered was looking at her own reflection in the polished toe of a black leather boot.

Past that, she recalled only sensations. Arms carrying her, hands jerking her clothes from her body. It seemed like Irene had been there, but she couldn't be sure. Where was she now? And where was Irene?

Suddenly she sensed the presence of someone else in the room, someone behind her, just beyond the puddle of bright light.

"Hello?" Her voice rang hollow in the glaring emptiness. "Is somebody there?"

Not a sound broke the silence. She struggled to lift her arms and legs, but the straps held her tightly.

"Please help me!" she called, raising her head, certain somebody was standing just inches away. "Please come and untie these straps."

Again she heard nothing. She listened for another moment, then she flopped helplessly back on the table. She must have just imagined someone was there. God knew, she'd imagined a lot, lately.

"No," she told herself aloud. "You haven't imagined anything. Wurth kidnapped Irene and now Wurth has kidnapped you. You just have to figure out what to do about it."

She heard another noise behind her. A shuffling of feet. Someone *was* there!

"Hey," she cried. "Please help me get out of here!" She twisted her head as far as she could, but all she saw were shadows. Still, she was certain she could hear the faint wheeze of someone's breathing.

"At least tell me where I am," she pleaded. "Tell me how long I've been here!"

She strained to listen with every cell in her body, then, to her enormous relief, a young male voice floated out of the darkness. "It's D-December 30. You're on the third floor of Camp Unakawaya."

"Please help me get loose!" she cried, twisting, desperate to see who stood behind her.

But her bindings made it impossible to see, and suddenly all she heard were soft footsteps, hurrying away.

"Don't go!" she begged. "Please wait! Please—"

The click of a door closing cut her off before she could utter another word.

"Damn!" she fumed, struggling against the leather straps. She'd gotten it right. She was at Camp Unakawaya and someone had been standing there watching her. If only they would come back. She had to convince them to turn her loose!

As she tried to work free her right arm, she heard a different noise. Nothing discreet about this—it sounded like a lot of people, all walking with a purpose. The sound rumbled closer, then the door opened. All at once the whole room was bathed in light.

"Ms. Crow." A deep voice called out from behind her. "How wonderful that you're awake!"

She craned her head toward the voice. Wurth came into view just behind her, leading a pack of young men. His eyes seemed almost transparent as his thin lips stretched in a grin.

"Where's Judge Hannah?" Mary demanded.

"Both of you are our guests at Camp Unakawaya." Wurth walked over and put what looked like a doctor's bag on the table beside her. "And we're honored to have you. You're a terrific tracker, Ms. Crow. If the situation were different, I would put you on my staff."

"If the situation were different?" Mary watched as six young men, all in khaki uniforms identical to Wurth's, clustered around the table. They watched, happy and wide-eyed as Wurth rummaged in his bag. In a moment he'd unrolled a piece of red silk across her stomach, revealing several different kinds of knives. Some glittered like the elegant instruments of a surgeon; others reminded her of butcher's tools.

"If you believed as we did," he told her, "then you could teach my boys here. But since you don't, I'll have to use you in a different fashion."

"Like how?" Mary's heart was beating so fast, she thought it might fly out of her chest.

"Oh, I'll think of something." Smiling, Wurth retrieved another instrument. It consisted of a number of stiff, thin wires sprouting from a single handle, each with a tiny, razor-sharp barb at the end. It glittered with a kind of lethal beauty in the bright light above.

"Upchurch, can you tell Ms. Crow what this is?" Wurth asked a harelipped boy who stood next to Mary's right knee.

"It's a *muchi,* sir," Upchurch replied.

"And what do we use the *muchi* for, Mr. Spooner?"

"External tissues," recited Spooner. "Where nerve endings are close to the surface."

"And to what end, Mr. Grice?"

"Uh, when the goal is intimidation?"

"Right, Mr. Grice." Wurth handed the instrument to the boy. "Since you know what the *muchi*'s used for, would you like to demonstrate how it works?"

"Sure."

A smug grin spread across Grice's face. Taking the stiff little whip from Wurth, the boy looked down at her once, then he tightened his grip on the handle and swung it at her face. Instantly she felt as if a dozen yellowjackets had stung her all at once. Before she could make a sound Grice swung the thing again. Tendrils of hot pain lashed through her.

"Since you tried to infiltrate my operation, Ms. Crow," Wurth said, "I'm going to use you as a teaching example. With your help, these young men are going to learn how to use all the instruments in this bag. I wish I could promise that you won't feel a thing, but the fact is, Ms. Crow, you will feel quite a lot."

"And I will remember everything, Mister Wurth." Mary looked up at him through eyes already stinging with tears and blood, determined that she would never give Wurth and these boys the pleasure of hearing the screaming inside her own head.

★   ★   ★

"Where are you going in such a hurry, Cabe?" Galloway looked up from the mountain of potatoes he was peeling.

"Out," called Tommy over his shoulder as he hurried through the kitchen.

"Out where?" Galloway persisted.

"J-just out. Out to sweep. Out to whittle my demerits down. Out to get away from assholes like you."

"Oooooh!" teased Abbot. "Better watch out. C-C-Cabe's mad!"

No, Abbot, Tommy thought as he ignored the laughter of the other Grunts and raced out into the late afternoon sun. *I'm not mad. I'm fucking terrified.*

He hustled around one corner of the building, away from the kitchen windows. He didn't want Abbot or Galloway to see where he was going. After he'd sneaked out of the amphitheater he'd gone straight to his cot in the Grunt dorm, his stomach churning. This place was more fucked up than he had ever imagined. First Willett, then that old lady, now that pretty woman who'd smiled at him the day before yesterday. If he didn't get out of here now, it would be him next. He hastily stashed what few personal things he had in the pockets of his cargo jeans and put on the warmest jacket he could find. He was busting out of Camp Unakawaya. They would not find him here in the morning, dead or alive.

First, though, he needed to get one last thing. Working his way to the far end of the castle, he glanced around to make sure no one was watching, then he sneaked past the cabins and sprinted up into the woods beyond.

Help me, he heard the pretty woman's plea echo in his head. *Please untie these straps.*

Sorry, lady. There was nothing I could do, he told himself as he leaped over a rotting log.

Help me. Please don't go.

"I have to, lady," he answered aloud. "If I don't go now, I'll be next on that table."

He ran on, trying to shake her words out of his head. Just a few hundred more feet up this ridge and he would reach Willett's cave.

With his lungs on fire, he wiggled inside the old gate. He knew the way so well that he no longer kept the flashlight inside the mouth of the cave. He felt his way through the passage keeping one hand on the wall, then, when his fingers touched a tiny trickle of water, he knelt and crawled to the right. Moments later he stood in Willett's den. He grabbed the flashlight from behind a rock and turned it on. Everything looked the same—the cans of Coke, the lone photo of Tarheel. He glanced at the photograph then plunged his hand inside the little fissure and pulled out Willett's disk. If he was taking his one chance to get out of here, he sure as hell wasn't going to leave this disk behind. If he made it to some town, he would give it to the cops. Maybe it would bring Wurth down and maybe it wouldn't. All he knew was that he had to give it to somebody, for Willett's sake.

Stashing the disk in his jacket pocket, he scrambled back into the passageway beyond, then stopped abruptly, suddenly feeling more frightened than he ever had in his entire life. What was wrong with him? He should have tried to help that woman. He should have unstrapped her and tried to sneak outside with her before Wurth got there. His grandfather would have done that. Captain Dempsey would have done that. Even Willett would have tried to do that. Why hadn't he?

"Because you are a coward," he admitted miserably, his self-condemnation echoing up into the rank darkness. He thought of Tallent, beating him now most every night, of Wurth abusing him with words, of the other Grunts laughing at his stutter. That was the life of a coward. As bad as that was, though, what he felt now was much worse. To ignore someone begging for your help was beyond cowardice. It was something else, entirely.

"Vileness," he whispered, the word leaving his mouth so softly, it could have been whispered by the cave itself. "Anybody who would not try to help that woman is vile."

He shivered in the dampness, remembering the way Upchurch and Rogers looked when he'd seen them that night on the third floor. They were vile. And though his grandfather could probably understand cowardice, the old man would never respect someone vile. Tears stung his eyes. As much as it made him shake inside, he would rather die a coward than be vile, than be one of them.

He crawled back into Willett's Den and returned the disk to the fissure. Willett's secret weapon would have to wait. Right now he had to go back to Camp Unakawaya. He had fallen into vileness once in the amphitheater. He now had to prove to himself that he would never do it again.

CHAPTER 34

"If I knew anything, I'd tell you, Dan'l. It ain't right for a man to do a woman like that." Mooney Garvin sat down on the log beside Daniel Safer. New Year's Eve was a big "pullin' off" day for Mooney, and a cardboard box filled with topped-off Mason jars lay at his booted feet. Digging one of the jars out of the box, he unscrewed the lid and passed a pint of the clear liquid to Safer.

Though Safer really didn't have time to sit and sip corn liquor, he raised the jar to his lips. He didn't want to offend Mooney by seeming unappreciative, and there was a raw, cold dampness in this little cove that pierced him to the marrow. He knew from experience how quickly the liquor would take care of that.

He took a small sip. Mooney's 'shine was so highly proofed, it felt like lighter fluid on his tongue. He swallowed slowly, amazed as always at how smoothly the alcohol slid down his throat. One of the pleasures of his mountain assignments had been to make the acquaintance of Mooney Garvin, coon hunter, gossipmonger, and master distiller. Mooney knew most of what went down in these woods, and most everybody responsible for it. And unlike most other mountain folk, if he felt the cause was right, Mooney would spill whatever beans he had.

"Are you sure you haven't heard of anything going on?" Safer handed Mooney back his whiskey, grateful for the heat that spread from his gut outward, chasing the chill from his bones.

Mooney took a swig, then a second one. "I heard that Royce Lunsford beat up some Mexican for starin' at his girlfriend's titties. Beyond that, I ain't heard nothing but hound dogs and them Piney Mountain Methodists singing Christmas carols."

Safer drummed on the log as he regarded the still that Mooney had built into a shallow overhang of a mountain. Covered on three sides by thick limestone walls and at the entrance by a growth of scrubby laurel, the still was invisible to prying eyes. Just like most of the shit going on up here, Safer decided. For the past forty-eight hours, Tuttle and his crew had scoured the

surrounding counties for Irene Hannah and
Mary Crow and had learned nothing. The
cockfighters didn't know. The klansmen were
all excited about some rally in South Carolina.
Even the local dopers had looked at them
blankly when offered mulligans in exchange for
information.

Now Mooney Garvin, the king of the moon-
shiners and the one man who knew everything
afoot in western North Carolina, had nothing
to say.

"Whatcha gonna do?" Mooney studied Safer,
his pale eyes rheumy with age.

"I don't know." A flicker drilled a tree somewhere in the woods. Safer thought of Mary
Crow. Where had she gone when she left the
airport? What the hell had happened to her?

"I know what I'd do if I was you." Mooney
rubbed his chin whiskers—a cluster of stiff
white wires protruding from skin that looked
like the leather of Irene Hannah's saddles.

"What?"

"If I thought that judge lady was up here, I'd
get me somebody who knows these woods. You
Washington boys rely too much on them computers. You need somebody who's got woodsy
eyes."

Safer gave a rueful smile. He'd had someone

like that, but he'd stupidly dropped her off at the airport four days ago. "So you come with me, then," he said to Mooney.

"I'm too old and down in my back. You need somebody young and strong." Mooney nudged his moonshine box with the toe of his boot.

"Who?"

"Most of the old boys I know are either moved away or in jail. There's supposed to be an Injun feller named Walkingstick who's right good."

"Where would I find him?"

"I heard he takes people out from a store over on the Little Tennessee River." Mooney lifted one bony arm and pointed over the ridge. "Five miles or so west of here, on the county road."

"You think he'd talk to a federal agent?" asked Safer.

"I don't know." Mooney chuckled. "Them Cherokees punch a different clock from the likes of us, if you know what I mean."

Safer sat there, watching the already gray sky lower until it obscured the tops of the mountains. Finally he stood and gave the old man's thin shoulder a pat. "I guess I'd better get going, then. Thanks for all your help."

"You want to take a couple a' these with you?" Ever anxious to make a buck, Mooney nodded at the cardboard box full of jars. "I'll sell out pretty quick today," he warned, "everybody goin' to them parties tonight."

"Sure." Safer wished he could hole up with some corn liquor and just drink away Mary Crow and Judge Hannah and the whole fucking disaster of the past four days. "They might come in handy later on."

"I'm sorry, Dan'l," Mooney shook his head as he handed Safer two jars of corn liquor in exchange for a twenty-dollar bill. "I wish I could help you out."

"I know you do, Mooney." Safer walked to the truck and stashed Mooney's liquor under the seat. He turned back and held out his hand. "You take care now, buddy. Have you still got your free pass?"

"Right here!" Mooney withdrew a tattered business card from the pocket of his coveralls. On it was printed Safer's name and phone number. Mooney looked up at him and grinned. "I ain't seen any of them ATF boys in a while, but I'll sure use this if I do."

"Tell them to call me before they start busting anything up. You want a lift back to your cabin?"

Mooney shook his head. "Keep your ass low, Dan'l," the old man cautioned as Safer climbed in the truck and started the engine. "And your powder dry."

"Happy New Year, Mooney."

The old man stuck the card and the twenty dollars back into his coveralls. Safer had started to bump down the old logging road when he heard Mooney's distinct mountain holler. "Hold on, Dan'l!"

He stopped as the old man got to his feet, moving as if all his joints had been glued together. He hobbled over to the truck and held on to the door handle for support. "I just thought of somebody you might ought to investigate!"

Safer killed the engine. "Who?"

"Feller named Wurth. One of them Vee-et-nam veterans. Meanest sunuvabitch in six counties. Runs a camp over by old Russell Cave."

"Okay." Safer pulled a notepad from the visor. He knew from experience that when Mooney spoke, it was always best to take notes. "You know the name of this camp?"

"Unaka something or other. U-N-A-K-A." Mooney carefully spelled out the first part of the name. "Injun word. I don't know what it stand for."

"So what makes this guy such a bastard?"

"He shot my coon dog Harley in the leg, and

he killed Porter Hayes's Plott hound. He keeps orphans over at that camp of his. Somebody told me he sends 'em out at night to kill strays."

"Why?"

"Pure cussedness. I told him I'd kill him if I ever caught him on my land again." The old man hitched up his coveralls as his pale eyes sparked with righteous indignation. "You ask me, any man who'd hurt a dog ought to be horsewhipped in the square."

Safer nodded in agreement as he closed the notepad. "Thanks, Mooney. I'll check this guy out."

Safer left Mooney at his still and drove west on the county road. Walkingstick with the woodsy eyes was the man he needed now. With the big Dodge pickup cruising easily up the potholed road, he shut his window tight against the cold mountain air and scanned the trees for Mary Crow, wondering how she could have disappeared as completely as her friend the judge.

Twenty minutes later, he pulled into the only store he could find along the Little Tennessee River. A beat-up yellow truck sat in the parking lot, computer boxes on the porch. It was the same store he'd driven Mary to when they came up from Atlanta.

"Son of a bitch!" he cried softly as he turned

off his ignition. "Walkingstick must be the old boyfriend."

Shaking his head, he hurried onto the porch. He'd sent Tuttle to check this joint three days ago. Tuttle had reported three fishermen, a woman sacking groceries, and two young men trying to find the Appalachian Trail. "Sorry, Big Dan," he'd said. "Our little civilian helper wasn't there."

Well, maybe she wasn't *here,* Safer thought. *But maybe this Walkingstick knows where she is.* Opening the door, he stepped inside. A slender, dark-haired woman stood with her back toward him. His heart leaped. Mary! She'd sneaked back up here! Of course she would come back to her old boyfriend, back to the place she felt at home.

"Hello," he said tersely, trying to tamp down his elation. "Long time no see."

"Excuse me?" The woman turned. His soaring heart plummetted. This woman was not Mary Crow. Her eyes were brown where Mary's were hazel; her skin, cinnamon to Mary's golden olive. She wore her hair in front in an Indian style, with small beads and a single white feather. Though she was pretty, her smile did not rearrange his insides the way Mary Crow's smile did.

"I'm sorry," he said awkwardly, his cheeks

growing warm. "I thought you were someone else."

"Who are you looking for?" The woman's dark glance intensified, and he felt as if she could see every female in his life crowding behind him—his daughter Leah taking her first steps; his ex-wife smiling at him under their wedding canopy, then beyond that, the girls he'd dated in high school, his mother kissing his scraped knee.

"A guy named Walkingstick," he replied, careful that the name Mary Crow didn't accidentally spill from his lips.

"Sorry." The woman's mouth curled down. "Jonathan's not here. He took a group out fishing yesterday."

"Will he be back any time soon?" Safer stepped forward.

"I'm not sure." The woman folded her arms under her breasts and looked at him warily.

"I see." Safer stood there, trying to decide what to do. As the woman hopped up on a stool behind the cash register, he looked around the store. Curved bows hung from the ceiling, while old slop jars were stashed high on one shelf. He strolled to the magazine racks in the front corner of the store. According to all the pages he'd read about Mary Crow, she'd come home from school to find her mother raped and strangled, probably lying very close to where he now stood. What would such a thing do to a girl just eighteen? How would horror that unthinkable twist her young soul? He thought of his Leah, and had to close his eyes. He turned back to the counter. A big poster caught his attention.

"What's REPIC?"

"Red People In Congress," the woman explained, not bothering to conceal her pride. "We're working to amend the Constitution and get all Native American tribes a seat in the House of Representatives."

REPIC. Mentally he ran through the file of fringe political groups Krebbs had pulled off the computer. He'd never heard of them; but nobody had heard of them all. He looked at this pretty Indian woman more carefully. Could she be involved in the killing of federal judges?

She seemed to sense his quickening interest. "Did you know that the Eastern Band of the Cherokees have served in the Army since 1860 and have paid federal income taxes from their inception, but were only granted the right to vote in 1946?"

"No," he said. "I didn't know that." He studied her face, noted her quick, curious eyes. "Do you and Walkingstick work for this group?"

"Actually, I'm the REPIC organizer here," she answered proudly. "I'm Ruth Moon. From Tahlequah, Oklahoma."

"Mark Danielson," he told her, covering this lie with a disarming grin. "Did you come east just to drum up support for REPIC?"

She shook her head. "No. I'm a Legend Teller. I came here to collect stories of the Eastern Tribe."

Safer frowned. The stories of his people would be the same to a Jew in Toledo, Ohio, as they would to a Jew in Toledo, Spain. "I don't understand. Why are they different?"

"Oral histories change. After we settled out west, our stories altered," Ruth explained. "We come back east to learn the oldest, purest forms of our legends."

"I see." Safer did not take his eyes from her. Curious, he thought. A political activist freely admitting the making up of stories.

Ruth held out a clipboard. "Would you like to sign our REPIC petition and make a donation?"

"Sure." Safer stepped up to the counter. Up close, as she handed him a blue Bic pen, he noticed she had muscular hands with short-cut nails. A small tattoo of some Indian symbol dotted the inside of her left wrist and he could smell a sage-like aroma on her skin. MARK DANIELSON, he printed on the sheet, listing his address as Charlotte, North Carolina.

"Thanks, Mark," she said, reading his name as

he dropped a five-dollar bill into her mayonnaise jar.

"My pleasure." Smiling, he looked around the store once more. "Well, I guess since Walkingstick isn't here, I'll be on my way."

"You wanted to book him for a fishing trip, didn't you?" Ruth Moon spoke as if she already knew his answer.

"Yes."

"Isn't that kind of an odd way to spend New Year's Eve?"

Safer let his shoulders sag and looked at the floor. In a way he hated to do this, but he had a hunch this Ruth Moon might be useful, somewhere down the line. "My wife left me a couple of weeks ago," he lied, keeping his voice low, trying to sound sad. "I needed to get out of town."

"Oh," Ruth murmured, instantly sympathetic. "I'm sorry to hear that. Did you two fish together? Your wife and you, I mean."

"No." Safer gave her a pained smile. "Terry liked to shop, I like the outdoors. The more I thought about spending New Year's alone in Charlotte, the better going fishing sounded. Get away from everything, you know?"

"Right." Ruth nodded knowingly. "Gosh, I wish I could tell you exactly when Jonathan will be back, but I just don't know. He said he'd be here for New Year's, though."

Safer reached in his pocket and jingled his keys. "Don't worry about it. I might try my luck at the little river across the road, and stop back later in the afternoon. Maybe I can book him for tomorrow."

"That sounds good," she replied warmly. "Start out the New Year with some fun."

"Right." He smiled at her, then turned toward the door. "I may see you a little later, then."

"Okay. We're open till seven."

With a final glance at the corner where Martha Crow died, he let himself outside and hurried down the steps to his truck, not bothering to look back, not seeing the wistful shake of Ruth Moon's head as she thought how sad and hopeless love is, whatever side of it you're on.

CHAPTER 35

At that same moment, love was the farthest thing from Mary Crow's mind. Several hours earlier, Sergeant Wurth had ordered her freed in the amphitheater. A number of boys had then tied her arms behind her back and held her head still while a husky blond youth had come at her with a scalpel. At first he'd waved the sharp little blade at her eyes, then her left breast. Finally he'd settled for her hair. Though she'd screamed and tried to squirm away, in very short order her long black locks lay scattered on the floor.

"There, Pocahontas," he'd said, raking his knuckles along her raw, tender scalp. "We take topknots, too."

She spit at him then, aiming for his eye but having to settle for a near miss on his upper lip. He jumped backward, then aimed his fist at her so fast she didn't see it coming. He hit her jaw hard, and for an instant she was sure he'd broken her neck. He hit her once more, for good measure, then as her eyes watched the overhead light spin with a thousand blurred colors, he strapped her ankles together with tape. As an afterthought, he also wrapped the tape around her head, ruthlessly covering her mouth. When he was satisfied, he nodded.

"Take her down to that last room in AR and give her another shot," he'd ordered. "She won't be able to go anywhere and we won't have to check on her every ten minutes."

"That wasn't what Sarge wanted," protested another boy.

"Sarge is busy with other things. For now, I'm in charge of this."

With that, one massive-shouldered boy lifted her like a sack of meal and carried her down flight after flight of creaky stairs, finally dumping her on a cold, gritty floor. Woozy from her beating, she heard his key turn in the lock, then his footsteps fading away. After that she heard nothing other than her own pulse throbbing in her jaw, beaming quasar-like waves of pain through her skull.

For a time she slept. When she woke up she was still bound hand and foot and clad in the cotton pajamas they'd dressed her in. She raised her head to look around. She lay in a square, dank room with beadboard walls. A rectangle of pale light, from high up on one wall, shone down on her. If she flopped over on her left side, she could see a tiny patch of sky. *This is better,* she thought, trying to take comfort in something. At least here she could sense the time of day.

As she lay gazing up at the distant sliver of sky, she felt something hard digging into her side. She wriggled back up and examined it. Hard, but with smoothed edges, the small object looked like several black rocks fused together. *A clinker,* she thought, recalling when she'd picked one up years ago behind Comer's Drugstore, convinced it was a meteorite from outer space. Finally her mother had explained that clinkers were pieces of coal that had melted together. She realized then that she lay in what had once been a coal bin, no doubt attached to a coal-burning furnace. She shook her head at the incongruity of it. In the middle of a whole forest of cheap timber, the old German aristocrat had chosen to heat his castle with costly coal.

She studied her prison more closely. The ancient furnace had long since been removed, but a huge hole gaped in the wall where the main vent pipe had joined it. Mary wondered if the ductwork had been removed. If not, might she be able to squeeze in that pipe and worm her way out? Of course, she would have to free her arms and legs first, and then manage to crawl in there before Wurth's boys returned. But anything was better than waiting for another session in the amphitheater.

Deciding quickly, she turned her attention first to her legs. The same kind of gummy tape that bound her mouth and arms also fettered her ankles tight together, making all movement difficult to impossible. Now she rolled herself up in a tight ball and wriggled to a sitting position. Using her bound feet, she pushed herself across the room, until her back rested against the door. She was trying to push herself up to stand when, suddenly, she felt something give a little on the door frame. A tiny movement of something other than her backbone. She twisted around to look. She'd managed to bump up against one of the hinges—two crude plates of rusty iron joined in the middle. The original pin must have broken years ago, and someone had repaired it with a long nail. That was what jostled against her spine. Clumsily she turned, and pushed her wrists against the hinge. She fumbled until she felt the nail jiggle again, then she wiggled her wrists beneath the sharp little point. Though it bit into her skin and made her fingers sticky with blood, she kept experimenting. If she pressed too hard, the nail jerked upward, out of the way; too gently and it wouldn't score the tape. After a number of attempts, she developed an awkward flicking motion where pressed hard against the nail before it lifted it in its cradle. Then it would, for an instant, bite into the fabric of the tape. If she knocked the nail loose, the game would be over, but as long as she could work it just right, she could conceivably get her arms free.

With a cold, nervous sweat stinging her eyes, she began to work, at first hearing nothing but her own shallow breathing and the *chink* of the nail as it lifted in its cradle. Then, after she'd counted 113 flicks of her wrists, her ears pricked as she heard a tiny, infinitesimally small tear in the tape.

After that she worked in a fury. Ten, twenty, fifty-six more strokes. Soon every flick of her wrists sent a jolt of agony all the way to her shoulder blades, but she persisted. She could wiggle her wrists, now. Just a little longer and she would be able to start working the tape with her thumbs.

Then she heard something. A single creak beyond her door, then another. It sounded as if someone were trying to walk quietly through fine, crackly gravel. She listened as they crept closer. Had all her thumping and bumping brought those boys back? Hastily she scooted over and flattened herself against the wall, willing her heart to stop its frantic romp as she sat and listened. The creaking came closer. Then it stopped. She watched the doorknob above her head, knowing it would turn at any moment. Her armpits grew clammy when she heard someone breathing on the other side of the door.

She pressed against the wall, determined to offer the smallest possible view of herself to anyone peeking in the keyhole. But then whoever stood outside retreated. The footsteps whispered away into silence. Flopping over, she pressed her face against the bottom of the door, straining to see who had sniffed at her prison. All she saw was a single fat roach, which waved its antennae at her, before it disappeared into the sooty darkness.

I've got to get out of here, she thought, struggling back upright. Any minute they are going to come back for real.

Ignoring the warm, sticky blood on her fingers, she flicked her wrists against the nail again, this time keeping a quick, stubborn rhythm. Once she pressed too hard, and for an awful moment she thought she'd knocked the nail out of the hinge, but it settled back into place with a soft *chink* and she continued.

After an eternity, she stopped again, fighting an insane urge to laugh, remembering how duct tape had been Jonathan's first choice for mending everything from leaky pipes to his broken sandals. Taking a deep breath, she closed her eyes and with her thumb felt the tear she'd made with the nail. She was nearly through the binding that held her wrists together. Just a few more strokes, and her hands would be free. *Yes!*

She scooted back and began to work harder than ever. The pain in her arms was gone, replaced by a prickly numbness. Still, she did not give up. One stroke, two strokes, three, then three hundred and she lost count; then without warning, her hands fell apart, flopping to the floor like dead fish. She looked at them in wonder, tears flooding her eyes. They were covered in blood, cold and numb from the strangling duct tape, but her fingers still worked. Wiping them on her pajama coat, she twisted around to pry the nail loose from its hinge. Now able to rip with its sharp point, she made quick work of the tape that bound her ankles, then pulled the final strands from her mouth. Though she tore the top layer of skin from her lips when she did so, she didn't care. For the first time in what seemed like decades, she could work her jaws. She spat up a lump of coagulated blood, then wobbled to her feet. Crossing the room, she stretched up beneath the high window, greedily sucking draughts of chill air deep into her starved lungs. Outside, the pewter sky was tinged with purple. *Dusk,* she thought with a sigh. It had taken her hours to remove that duct tape from her wrists. What day was it? If she could just get out of here and find Irene, everything might still turn out okay.

She hobbled across the room to where the old pipe had once joined the furnace. The opening was enormous by modern standards—roughly two feet across, with a corrugated iron pipe leading into a thick, palpable darkness. Though the idea of worming her way into that black void made her sick inside, she knew it was her only way out.

With a silent prayer to whatever saint might be in charge of those held at Camp Unakawaya, she ducked down into the waist-high opening and pulled herself into the darkness.

CHAPTER 36

"Ruth Moon," Safer said to the mechanical voice that answered his call. "M-o-o-n. Native American female from Tahlequah, Oklahoma, age about thirty. Suspected group is REPIC, acronym for Red People In Congress. Nothing further known." After the answering two beeps, he started to switch the phone off, then a page of the notepad he'd stuck under the sun visor caught his eye.

He pulled it out and studied the words he'd scribbled. "Worth," "Camp U-n-a-k-a- something or other," Mooney Garvin had told him. He ran his thumb along the thin wire spiral, then thought, *What the hell.* He'd just put Jonathan Walkingstick and Ruth Moon in the hopper. Why not add the man Mooney regarded as the biggest bastard in six counties? He had absolutely nothing else to go on.

"Robert Worth," he said to the same mechanical voice to which he'd just given Ruth Moon's name. "Male, U.S. Army retired, Hartsville, North Carolina, age unknown." *Now,* he thought grimly as he steered the truck out of the Little Jump Off parking lot and back onto the highway, *somebody come up with something.*

"Dammit, Mary, where did you go?" he muttered. He'd hoped beyond reason that he would walk inside that little store and find her there, holed up with Walkingstick. He had even pictured the expression on her face when she saw him—those hazel eyes would darken and her mouth would curl in defiance. Although irked to have been discovered, she would have gone with him willingly, and they could have joined forces to find Judge Hannah. But no. Ruth Moon had been the woman he'd found at Little Jump Off.

As hard little seeds of snow peppered his windshield, Safer sped east along Highway 441 back to Upsy Daisy Farm, turning over in his mind the scant information he'd gathered in the past five days. Tuttle and the guys in Hartsville had turned up every rock between here and Tennessee, and Krebbs hadn't looked up from his computer in over seventy-two hours. All of them together had only gleaned two names from an old moonshiner, along with Krebbs's conviction that something was going to happen on New Year's Eve. *But what?* wondered Safer. *And where?*

Usually the answer is right in front of you, one of his instructors at Quantico used to say. *Sometimes it's too plain to see.* Okay, Daniel. What's so obvious that you're overlooking it?

His phone beeped. He grabbed it. A mechanical voice informed him: "No records retrieved on subject Ruth Moon. Access 9746 for other information requested."

Okay, Safer thought. *Nothing on her, but everything else had made the charts.* He pulled over and punched another number in his phone. In a few moments, three messages appeared on the tiny screen.

The information on REPIC was only five lines long, listing a duly registered nonprofit political action group headquartered in Spokane, Washington, with another chapter in Tahlequah, Oklahoma. For the past five years REPIC's membership had held steady at 736 people, with an annual budget of less than ten thousand dollars. Safer shook his head. These Indians were going to need a lot more wampum to crack the hallowed halls of Congress.

He stored that message and began to read the one about Walkingstick. It was not any more suspect than the one about REPIC—Walking-

stick had joined the Army in 1988, served as a
medic in the Eighty-second Airborne for six
years, then been honorably discharged. Beyond
that, he'd done nothing to interest anybody in
Washington at all.

"Okay," said Safer as he stored that message.
"This time the Indians are the good guys. Now
let's see about this Worth."

The message about Worth scrolled down far
longer than the other two. By the time it ended,
Safer learned the Sergeant Robert Erwin
Wurth—not Worth—had been drafted into the
Army in 1967. After one tour in Vietnam, he'd
re-upped and gone through Ranger training,
ultimately rising to the rank of master sergeant.
Though his jacket listed a glittering array of dec-
orations, halfway through his nineteenth year of
service he'd abruptly left the Army. After that,
he dropped off the screen as fully as Walkingstick. Since leaving the service, the man had not
gotten as much as a parking ticket.

Safer frowned as he carefully reread the information. Why would a decorated veteran who'd
spent his life in the Army ditch his career one
year shy of his full twenty? It would have cost
Wurth a lot in pensions and benefits, not to
mention his pride. Absently taking a bite of the
granola bar he'd opened sometime before dawn,
Safer dialed a second number. This time he

spoke to the very female Susan Davis instead of electronic voice mail.

"Susan? This is Daniel Safer."

"Hi, Dan. How's it going up in them thar hills? You-all planning some fun for New Year's?"

"It's going okay," Safer lied, trying hard to remember the last time he'd had anything vaguely resembling fun on New Year's Eve. "Listen, I need you to pull up everything you can on one Sergeant Robert Erwin Wurth, U.S.A., retired. That's Wurth, W-U-R-T-H. I need to know why this guy quit the Army."

"Maybe he got tired of all those pushups," Susan quipped.

"Yeah, maybe." Safer chuckled. "Susan, I don't know what's on your plate right now, but could you get that for me ASAP?"

"Sure thing."

"And Susan—"

"Yeah?"

"See if you can find anything on a little non-profit called REPIC."

"R-E-P-I-C?"

"Yeah. Red People In Congress."

"You got it."

"Thanks, Sue. I owe you."

Safer switched off his phone and watched the snow falling. At this elevation it no longer pelted his truck, but floated down softly from the sky, melting the instant it hit the warm metal of his hood. Moments before, he had nothing. Now he had a Ranger whose career had abruptly ended just months away from retirement. Wurth might have good reason to be pissed at the federal government. And a Ranger would certainly have the skills to kidnap and kill anybody he pleased. By the same token, this Wurth could be just another gung-ho vet running a summer camp for kids.

"I'll put Tuttle on it," Safer decided as he started the truck and headed back to Hannah's farm. He'd have a look at everything they'd come up with one more time, then he was going to have to call Washington and tell them that after five days, the only trace of the judge was a single black bird feather, left on a bathroom floor.

CHAPTER 37

As the clock in Irene Hannah's living room struck three P.M., Daniel Safer had laid his head down on the kitchen table and closed his eyes. Over the past two hours he had reexamined every piece of paper strewn out on the table. Lab reports, evidence files, interviews with the locals—he reviewed everything his men had gathered since Irene Hannah vanished five days earlier. Every trace of a lead had come to nothing. The ultraconservative states' rights attorney Tuttle questioned had an airtight, corroborated alibi, and the two men they'd picked up in Asheville urinating on the windows of a Planned Parenthood building had blubbered like babies, but had come up clean. With high hopes Safer had dispatched Tuttle to check out this Robert Wurth's camp, but Mike had come back looking smugly superior, reporting that though the place looked creepy as hell, it was nothing more than a hyperpatriotic camp for kids. As Safer watched the colors dance on the backside of his eyes, he knew that in a few moments he'd have to call Washington and report his failure. After that, if he and his men were very lucky, his boss would make them school-crossing guards somewhere up near the Arctic Circle.

He sighed. He hadn't been able to save Judge Hannah. Worse, he'd inveigled a smart and spirited young attorney to come here to help and he'd lost her, too. A school-crossing job in Alaska would be too good for him.

As he sat thinking of Mary Crow, he felt someone touch his shoulder. He opened his eyes. Krebbs towered over him, grinning, his teeth looking slightly orange from pork-rind dye.

"I might have something," he said, his voice surprisingly high for a man so tall. "Take a look at this."

This was a printout of a message posted on an Internet bulletin board. Its URL was not one of the usual paramilitary sites the FBI tracked, but a porn site in France that dealt in everything from kiddy sex to snuff films. It had been posted just an hour earlier, from somewhere in the United States. The one-line message was in English. *Patriots be watching: Heads will fall in the mountains tonight.*

"Where did this come from?" Safer looked up into Krebbs's coarse-featured face.

"We're tracing it right now."

Safer looked at the message again. Shit, if this was for real, it could mean that Irene Hannah was still alive. Heads will fall tonight, just like the ball in Times Square. *Fuck,* he thought. *Krebbs had it right. She's still alive! "Heads will fall in the mountains tonight."* . . . And she's here, in the Smokies.

"You need someone with woodsy eyes." Mooney Garvin's advice rang in his head. The old buzzard had called that right, too, he decided as he gazed blearily at all the papers and electronic equipment spread around him. Up in these mountains the best FBI science would never beat the sharp eyes of a native.

He scooped up his keys and hurried to the door.

"Tuttle," he called over his shoulder. "I'm going out. Get everyone locked and loaded and ready to go."

"Where are you going?"

"To get me some woodsy eyes."

★   ★   ★

Forty-two minutes later he pulled up in front of Little Jump Off Store. Smoke curled from the chimney as the little cabin looked buttoned down tight against the cold. He parked his truck and hurried up the steps. Through the glass-paned door, he could see Ruth Moon and a dark-haired man behind the counter, cooing at each other like teenagers while they shared a small, old-fashioned bottle of Coke. Ruth Moon threw back her head and laughed, exposing a long, slender throat. The man laughed with her. His long hair hung in a ponytail, and with his high cheekbones and hooded eyes, he could have been the poster boy for her REPIC group. Safer was no great judge of male beauty, but he knew most women would consider this guy handsome. He opened the door.

Ruth Moon looked up, startled. "It's the fisherman! Jonathan, this is the man I was telling you about."

"Hi," said Safer, smiling. He walked over to the counter and extended his hand. "I'm Mark Danielson. I came here earlier about hiring you as a guide."

"Jonathan Walkingstick." The man who once loved Mary Crow reached to shake Safer's hand. His palm felt warm, his fingers strong. "Ruth told me you'd come by. What are you after?"

"Trout," Safer replied, noting the long Bowie knife sheathed just beneath the Cherokee's left arm.

Walkingstick nodded. "I know a few places they bite this time of year. When were you wanting to go?"

"How about right now?"

"Now?" Ruth Moon snuggled up against Walkingstick as if she'd taken a sudden chill. "It's freezing outside. And nearly dark."

Safer shrugged. "Where I come from, they bite pretty good at dusk."

Walkingstick peered at Safer. "I don't know. I just got back from fishing a few minutes ago." He cast a cautious glance at Ruth. "I think I might need to stay home tonight."

"I'll pay twice the going rate."

Walkingstick shook his head.

"I'll have you back in two hours," Safer promised and winked at Ruth. "I know you were probably counting on him for New Year's."

Walkingstick looked again at Ruth. She nestled against him, then nodded. "It's okay," she told him softly. "Mr. Danielson's had some bad luck lately. Catching a fish might make him feel better."

"Are you sure?" Jonathan frowned.

"Just get back before the ball drops in Times Square, okay? I love to watch that on TV."

"Okay." He caressed Ruth's cheek, then turned to Safer. "Let me change my socks."

Ruth Moon smiled at Safer as Jonathan thumped up the stairs. "How long did you say your wife has been gone, Mr. Danielson?"

"Three weeks," Safer lied, thinking that this woman had a way of asking the damnedest questions.

"It's an odd time of year for a woman to walk away from a marriage." Once again she looked at him as if she could see all the way back to the moment he was born.

Safer met her gaze evenly. "Yeah. Tell me about it."

"You really think trout fishing on New Year's Eve is going to help?"

No, he wanted to answer. But finding Mary Crow or Judge Hannah or even the person who sliced that one woman's head off sure would. But before he could come up with an acceptable reply, Walkingstick came down the stairs.

"Your truck or mine?" he asked.

"Let's take mine," Safer replied. "My gear's already in the back."

"Okay by me." Walkingstick turned to Ruth. "We'll be back in an hour or so. They feed late in those warm shallows on Pantherflat Creek."

"You be careful, Jonathan." Ruth Moon's words seemed to carry the weight of the ages as she looked up at him with anxious eyes.

"We're just going fishing." He bent forward

and kissed her. "You act like we're out to hunt bear."

"Just be careful," Ruth repeated softly, holding him until he pulled away. Safer lowered his eyes, remembering how it felt when his ex-wife had clung to him like that. Ruth Moon *and* Mary Crow. Jonathan Walkingstick was indeed a fortunate man.

Ruth walked them to the door, then stood watching as they stowed Jonathan's gear in Safer's truck. When they opened the doors to get inside, she called out something in a language Safer couldn't identify.

"I will," Walkingstick replied. "Don't worry."

"What did she say?" Safer asked as he started the engine.

Jonathan cast a sideways glance at him. "She told me to watch out for wolves."

Good advice, Safer thought as they rolled out of the Little Jump Off parking lot, watching Ruth Moon's pretty face disappear in his rearview mirror.

★ ★ ★

At first Safer drove in the direction Walkingstick pointed him, then a half a mile down the road he steered to a clearing edged with tall pine trees and killed the engine. Without a word, he pulled his IDs from behind the visor.

"Okay." He flashed the leather wallet at Walkingstick. "This is who I really am. And this is what I really do."

"I was wondering why you were going fishing with a sidearm." Jonathan's eyes were on Safer, flinty and hard. "Then I figured you must be the FBI agent who's chasing Mary Crow."

For an instant Safer was caught off guard. He'd underestimated Walkingstick; he hadn't figured on his being that observant. "When did you last see Ms. Crow?"

"Four nights ago. After she gave you the slip."

"Do you know where she is now?"

"I haven't seen her since early Friday morning. I figured she joined back up with you."

Safer shook his head. "I haven't seen her since I left her at the airport."

"Then where the fuck did she go?" Jonathan's voice grew alarmed.

"I've got an idea she might be wherever Judge Hannah is."

"Jesus Christ!" Jonathan cried. "First you drop her in the middle of all this shit, now you think she's with a woman who's been kidnapped? What the hell kind of G-man are you?"

Safer started to reply, but his cell phone bleated. Keeping one eye on Walkingstick, he pulled the thing from his pocket.

"Safer here."

"Dan, this is Susan. I'm about to make you a *very* happy man." Her voice bubbled with excitement.

"What have you got?"

"First off, forget REPIC. They're such non-players, everybody laughs at them. But Wurth might be your boy."

"How? He wasn't anywhere on our charts."

"Our charts don't access Army records. There, Wurth's got a trail of coincidences that look like bread crumbs through the forest."

Safer smiled. Every time Susan found something he'd asked for, her voice took on the teasing quality of female spies on the TV shows he'd loved as a kid. "Okay," he told her. "Shoot."

"In sixty-seven he did his first tour in Vietnam, showed a lot of talent for language and viciousness, so the Army turned him into a special kind of assassin the VC called a 'Feather Man.' Everything was peachy between him and the brass until seventy-two, when he caused a flap between the U.S. government and the Republic of South Vietnam. Seems that Wurth tortured and killed a woman who turned out to be a double agent, and an extremely well connected double agent, at that. Some ambassador's niece."

"And?"

"And South Vietnam wanted his hide, but the Army had held him up as such a wonderful example of American can-do, the Vietnamese couldn't get him court-martialed. They finally accepted a deal where Wurth got sent to Japan, with a promise that we would never return such a man to their shores, regardless of who overran their northern borders."

"Jeez, they preferred Ho Chi Minh to Sergeant Wurth?"

"Looks like it." Susan rattled some pages. "Then Wurth spent several years in Japan. At one time he went on a very deep assignment in Indonesia."

"I didn't know we had a presence in Indonesia," said Safer.

"We don't. Like I said, this was deep. He was also in Borneo, where they have some amazing ways of killing people."

"I'll take your word for it."

"Anyway, Wurth finally returned stateside to serve honorably at Fort Benning until 1980, when he was brought up on charges not only of sexual harassment, but of putting one particular female recruit under such pressure that she opened both her veins in the shower."

"She died?"

"She survived to testify against him, saying that he threatened to cut off her breasts if she brought his platoon down any further."

"Well, that could have been DI bullshit." Safer glanced at Walkingstick, who was staring out the window.

"Wait, there's more. That girl got reassigned to another platoon, but the next year her boyfriend found her dead in the shower, her throat slit. And get this: there was a feather on the bathroom floor."

"A black feather? Did they pin her murder on Wurth?"

"Nope. A pizza delivery guy took that rap. A *Vietnamese* guy. And yes, the feather was black."

More pages rattled, then Susan continued. "The capper is that a female lieutenant ended Wurth's career—years later by bringing him up on charges of harassment and brutality. This time the Army'd had enough. They offered Wurth choice of early retirement or a court-martial. He opted for early retirement, but the lieutenant who instigated the charges wound up—"

"Dead," Safer interrupted grimly. "Her throat cut and a feather on the floor."

"That would have been nice. No, this girl got the upgrade. Her partner found her dead in her bed, decapitated. No feathers, but her head was neatly severed by a single blow."

"Holy shit," said Safer. "Any links to Wurth?"

"Not enough," Susan replied. "They couldn't pin a thing on anybody. It's still an open case."

Safer gave a low whistle.

"That enough?" said Susan, her tone triumphant.

"More than enough, sweetheart. When I get back to D.C., I'm taking you dancing."

"Promise?"

"Absolutely."

Safer switched off his phone and turned to his passenger. "Okay, Walkingstick. Tell me everything that happened that night with Mary."

Jonathan frowned. "She drove down here in a rental car from Asheville. She told us about you and asked if I knew of anybody who might want to kill Judge Hannah. I didn't, but Ruth remembered some files she'd pulled off a computer that this guy had donated to REPIC."

"What guy was that?"

Jonathan looked at him. "The guy you were just talking about—Sergeant Robert Wurth."

Safer could barely breathe. Wurth's name had come up three times this afternoon. "And?"

"I had to drive to Asheville to pick up some computers. By the time I got back, Mary was gone. Ruth said she took a shower and ate some toast and said she'd be back in touch. We haven't heard from her since."

"Can you get me to Wurth's camp? Do you know the way?"

"I do."

"Okay, Walkingstick," Safer said as he shoved the truck into gear. "Tonight you get to be my woodsy eyes."

CHAPTER 38

Mary crawled for what seemed like hours, trying to be quiet, trying not to scream in the suffocating darkness. No light reached the pipe; even when she held her hands in front of her nose, all she saw was blackness. With the ductwork only an inch wider than her shoulders, turning back was impossible.

This must be what death is like, she thought, stopping to quell a hot, trembling panic inside her. *This must be a sneak preview of hell.*

She kept moving forward. In the darkness she had to feel her way with her fingers, groping in front of her like a blind person. Though she'd wiped the blood from her hands, wisps of cobwebs and fine soot stuck in between her fingers.

The air inside the pipe carried a dank mélange of smells—sour mildew, the sharp aroma of alcohol, a sickly-sweet odor that reminded her of rotting meat. Along one section, the ridges in the pipe grew rusty and cut into her palms; at another, she felt a pile of smooth, raisin-sized lumps. *Rat turds,* she thought, revulsion backing her up so fast she hit her head. She had to stop then, and breathe in huge gulps of air. As she drew the coal dust into her lungs, she could have sworn she heard a woman speaking, somewhere just a foot above her head.

"Irene?" Mary turned her face upward. "Irene, is that you?"

The woman's voice came again, but muffled and so soft that Mary couldn't make out her words.

"What?" she asked, straining to hear. "What did you say?"

"To hiju?" The Cherokee floated through the pipe in a singsong whisper.

Mary stared, openmouthed, at the pipe above her, then suddenly the words melted into all the other noises that were roaring inside her head. She realized then that she had imagined it. Irene wasn't here, talking to her in Cherokee. What she'd heard was her own internal library of sounds, mentally played at random. She shuddered, as a chill frosted her down to the marrow of her bones.

So she crawled on, knowing that it would not be long before Wurth's Troopers would be chasing her. In the darkness she could gauge neither time nor distance, though she thought she must be nearing the center of the huge old house. She kept feeling for other ducts to branch off the main one, but so far her fingers had not brushed against any openings that led in other directions. Finally, as her shins and forearms began to throb, she sensed something different ahead. Although she still couldn't see anything, the brilliant blackness seemed to lighten to a chalky gray.

Here the air felt slightly warmer, and carried scents that made her mouth water. Roast beef. Potatoes frying. She couldn't remember when she'd last eaten. An array of sounds filtered down from above—something metal clattered overhead through the thudding, primal beat of rock music. Somewhere a toilet flushed; somewhere else a young male voice cried "No!"

Dinnertime, Mary decided, putting the sounds and the smells together. They were either about to eat or were in the process of cleaning up after their evening meal.

She groped forward. All of a sudden two other pipes joined the main one at right angles. She'd reached the main junction. From here, the furnace had diverted all its warm air to the various rooms overhead. She remembered a long-ago case Irene had presided over in Asheville, a drug dealer who'd murdered his wife, but who'd also

kept a sizable portion of his stash in the ductwork of his central air. The DA had presented a
chart of the system, showing pipes branching off
wide, then narrowing to tiny vents. In that old
house the return—the place where cooled air
was drawn back into the furnace—had been big
enough to crawl out of. If this one was similar,
she might be in luck.

She stuck her head in the pipe that joined
from the right. The air here looked no lighter,
but smelled slightly fresher. Then, as she gazed
at the black nothingness around her, she caught
a whiff of a new odor. It came from the pipe on
the left. Rank and foul, it smelled like nothing
she'd ever known before. The hairs lifted on the
back of her neck. She knew *that* direction was
the last place she wanted to go.

Wiggling her shoulders into the right-facing
pipe, she crawled on.

Although the second pipe was just as dark as the
first, her instinct told her that she was creeping
deeper into the core of the house. Pipes too small
to crawl through branched off of this one at regular intervals. Bedrooms, Mary decided. Two
stories above them, Wurth and his Troopers
must dream about *muchis* every night. Could
Irene be lying in some room up there, too?

She continued on, her shoulders cramping in
pain. Almost imperceptibly, the tunnel grew

lighter. As she looked down to see the shadow of her own hand against the ridges of the pipe, the rock music abruptly stopped, replaced by what sounded like a herd of animals thundering overhead. She crouched, pressing herself against the corrugated surface as the footsteps echoed inches above her. For an instant she worried that the floor was going to collapse, then, like the passage of a great wave, the torrent of noise faded into silence.

She kept still and listened, wondering why all those boys had started to run. Where had they been going? Had the alarm gone out that she had escaped?

Come on, she scolded herself. *You've got to get out of here. You don't have much time.*

Another series of smaller pipes branched off the main one, then she saw a dim square of light in the distance. *Okay,* she thought as she slithered forward. *Here goes nothing.*

Slowly the dim square resolved into a large oblong grate, crisscrossed with metal strips. She crawled until she could press her face against the gridwork. The grate seemed to open into a long, narrow room. A back hall, she thought. The logical place for a furnace return. Now if she could just open the grate. . . . She started to jiggle the thing, then froze. Were all those boys who had just thundered by now lined up along the hall, waiting for her to stick her head out of this thing?

Without moving a muscle, she tuned her ears to the outside and listened. Nothing. Not a sniffle or a creak or the squeak of someone's weight shifting on the floor. Still, they could very well be out there, waiting.

She lay motionless, trying to think of what to do. She couldn't stay here, but neither could she go back and crawl through that maze again. If they hadn't yet discovered her gone, they soon would, and God only knew what they would do then. As much as she hated it, her best chance of escaping was right here, right now.

Holding her breath, she listened for one final moment, then she shoved the old gridwork. Nothing moved. She tried again. *Oh, no,* she thought, despair nibbling at her with icy teeth. *It can't be screwed in.* Mustering all her strength, she grabbed the grate with both hands and pushed as hard as she could. The thing gave a loud crack, as if she'd broken a seal of ancient paint, then it creaked forward. With her heart beating like a drum, she held the grate open and peered out into the room beyond. The hall stood empty. The only eyes upon her were from the portraits on the wall; the only noise that reached her ears was from the old house itself, its sad breath soughing through the dusty corridor like a sigh.

CHAPTER 39

"Do you know any alternate routes to Camp Unakawaya?" Daniel Safer took the twisting mountain roads fast, his back tires squealing around the curves. A full moon rose, huge and yellow, casting the woods in an amber light.

"Not to the old castle," replied Jonathan. "But I know a pretty good place to reconnoiter from."

"Tell me."

"A service road leads in about a quarter mile before the main entrance. It's blocked off most of the year, but I noticed it was open last week."

"Who uses it?"

"Beats me. Anybody making deliveries up here, I guess."

Safer followed Jonathan's directions. He called Tuttle, ordering him to get a warrant for the building and grounds of Camp Unakawaya.

"That's just a camp for kids, Big Dan. I checked it out already." Tuttle's voice was patchy, through the mountain static.

"I called in this Wurth character to the Bureau. He fits the profile of someone who might do this. And he's also got the property to cover his tracks."

"Safer, I'm telling you there's nothing up there but a bunch of underaged kids. You're gonna order up another Waco."

"Just get the warrant, Tuttle." Safer scowled. If Wurth was planning to drop Irene Hannah's head for New Year's Eve, they were going to stop him. Somehow they would have to work around the kids. "Sit tight until you hear from me."

Safer switched off his cell phone and turned where Jonathan directed, up a bumpy, overgrown trail where a startled possum shuffled quickly into the weeds. The road ended halfway up a mountain in a large grassy turnaround with "No Hunting" and "No Trespassing" signs posted around it.

Safer parked the truck, then pulled a new .40-caliber Glock from under the driver's seat. "You fire a pistol?" he asked Walkingstick.

"I can."

"Then take this." Safer handed him the gun and its holster.

Reluctantly Jonathan took off his jacket and strapped on the pistol. "I know why you're so concerned about the judge. But what is it with you and Mary Crow?"

"Like you said before, if it hadn't been for me, she wouldn't have come up here. I don't want her to get hurt."

"And that's it?" In the dim light Safer felt Walkingstick's eyes boring into him.

"For the most part."

A long, silent look passed between the two men, then Jonathan nodded. "Come on. We'll have to go this way."

Safer allowed Walkingstick to lead. The Eric Rudolph case had taught him that the mountain folk, be they white or Cherokee, had their own quaint ways. If you respected them, they might help you. If you didn't, you might as well try to squeeze water from a rock.

They fought their way through waist-high brambles that thrust up through a crusty layer of frozen snow, then left the thick scrub and entered a growth of evergreens. Pine needles pricked against Safer's forehead, and an icy breeze blew from the valley below, carrying a soft popping noise that sounded like distant hammers pounding. Unconsciously he touched the grip of his gun.

"How far are we from the castle?" he asked, his breath frosty.

"About a quarter mile that way." Jonathan pointed straight ahead.

"Do you know exactly what's on this property?"

"When I picked up those computers, I saw a pretty typical camp—cabins, a lake, a baseball diamond. An old cave resort abuts the west edge of the property, but it's been boarded up for years."

"Anything not your standard camp?"

"Nothing beyond the orphans and that oddball castle."

They walked on in silence, Walkingstick slipping through the woods, as casual as if he were on a Sunday stroll. Safer followed him more warily, watching for anyone who might be posted as a lookout.

Twenty minutes later, they crested the ridge. The moon was higher and whiter in the sky. Jonathan took cover behind a huge oak tree and beckoned Safer forward.

"There. Camp Unakawaya."

From their vantage point, they could see the castle rising from the cove below like a huge mother ship, with smaller cabins dotting the earth behind it. To one side of the great castle stood an oblong, ivy-covered building glowing with bright lights.

"That's the gym," Jonathan told Safer. "I picked up the computers there."

"How do they get all this electricity up here? That place looks like Madison Square Garden."

"Some rich old German built this place. Wurth told me he put in some kind of underground electrical system."

"Way before his time, huh?"

Jonathan nodded. "Out of his time. Out of his mind, too, if everything I've heard about this place is true."

The men watched as boys hurried in and out of the ivy-covered building like worker bees in a hive. Some hauled sheets of white cloth in, while others carried scrap lumber out. Others worked from a flatbed truck, unloading long spools of electrical wire and a gasoline-powered generator. They all wore dark green camouflage suits, and they worked not as boys in happy camaraderie, but as humorless men determined to complete a task. Safer recalled the flickering old newsreels he'd seen of Hitler Youth.

"What the fuck are they doing?" whispered Walkingstick, his eyes locked on the frenetic activity.

"I don't think they're planning a rockin' New

Year's Eve," Safer replied. "Come on. Let's see if we can get closer."

They waited until most of the boys had gone inside, then slipped through the trees to the far side of the gym. Keeping to the shadows, they crept up to the building itself. A shoulder-high window permitted an unobstructed view of the interior. At one end of the highly polished floor, Wurth's boys had built a platform. In the middle of the platform rose a T-shaped stand constructed of two-by-fours. Around the platform clustered an array of klieg lights and video cameras, all hooked up into one massive electrical panel. A strange eagle-and-cross version of the American flag hung from the ceiling at the back of the platform, and on each side of the structure, two boys stood guard over a pile of M–16 rifles.

Safer groaned softly. Suddenly it all fell into place. Heads were going to roll in the mountains. By the looks of it, from right here, and very shortly.

"What are they doing?" asked Walkingstick in a whisper.

"I think that sometime between now and midnight Wurth is going to strap Irene Hannah to that stand and whack her head off. Judging by the lights and cameras, I'd say he's going to broadcast it on the Internet."

"Why?"

"That's what we don't know yet," said Safer brusquely.

"So what are we going to do?" Walkingstick's voice grew urgent.

Safer checked his watch. "It's eight-thirty. Until Tuttle gets here, we wait. If Wurth starts the party early, we need to take out anybody who tries to walk Judge Hannah up those steps, I don't care how old they are. We've got clear shots at the door from here."

"What about Mary?"

Safer looked at him with troubled eyes. "Walkingstick, I don't have a clue what this all means. All I know is that it's big, and we've got to stop it."

"So Mary's just an acceptable loss?"

Safer glared at him. "Of course not. I intend to get both these women out, if in fact Mary Crow's here."

"How about we make a deal, Safer? You take care of Judge Hannah, and I'll worry about Mary Crow."

"Fine," said Safer. "However you want to cut it is fine with me."

"Actually, Big Dan, you guys won't have to worry about either one."

Safer froze as chill metal pressed against the back of his skull. The cocking of a gun's hammer snapped through the air. He reached for his Glock, but it was useless. Rough hands pried it from his grasp, as even rougher hands yanked him and Walkingstick up and spun them around. Mike Tuttle, the agent he had given his last orders to, stood grinning at him, dressed in the uniform of Wurth's army. Four brawny young teenagers stood behind him, pointing Uzis directly at them.

CHAPTER 40

The hall seemed to stretch for miles as Mary stood breathing hard, trying to clear her lungs of the ductwork's sooty air. With its twelve-foot ceilings and polished floors, the corridor would have made the ideal spot for fencers to parry and thrust up one side and down the other. Walnut-paneled doors opened along one wall, and between them hung old portraits of handsome young men in World War I Army uniforms— the German youths looking rakish and cocky, the British boys aristocratic and sad. Mary wondered if the subjects had been painted from memory, before their long, aquiline features had been blown off and their dreamy, blue-gray eyes opened to the brutal realities of war.

She wiped a fine film of grit from her face. Her crawl through the furnace pipe had left her disoriented. The castle walls seemed to tilt at odd angles, while the gleaming oak floor felt corrugated instead of smooth.

She tiptoed down the hall, all the while listening for the return of the thundering herd. Where had Wurth's foul little army gone? Two of them were supposedly guarding her in the basement. The rest must be patrolling this house. But where? And when would they return?

She crept on, passing one of the burled walnut doors. She was tempted to open it, in hope that it might lead outside, but as she neared it she kept on moving. She'd learned that the doors at Camp Unakawaya often revealed unpleasant surprises. She didn't know if she could stomach another one.

She saw an open doorway, down the hall to the left. Maybe it would lead her to the flag-draped foyer and front entrance beyond.

She picked up her pace, instinctively trying to hurry away from the feeling that something was following her. *Just a few more steps,* she thought. Just a few more steps and she would be there . . . .

Then she heard a tiny click. She whirled. Behind her, the walnut door swung open. She clenched her fist, ready to fight. She would die before she would let anybody strap her down to a table again.

A tall, thin figure peeked from behind the door. A boy. But not one of the older ones who'd tormented her and sliced off her hair. This boy had poorly mended glasses that magnified his blue eyes and his dark brown hair curled in unruly cowlicks on the top of his head. Without thinking she leaped forward and grabbed him by the neck, shoving him against the wall so hard, the back of his head bounced against the paneling.

"Not one word, you little bastard! I'm headed for the front door. Don't fuck with me and you'll be fine."

The boy opened his mouth to speak, but nothing came out. Sweat beaded on his upper lip. Up close, Mary realized that he truly was different from the other boys. Where they were thick-necked and had shoulders like football players, this one seemed barely strung together with nerves and thin wire. Suddenly she recognized him—this was the bookish sweeper who had first welcomed her to Camp Unakawaya. She loosened her grip on his throat. He began to sputter.

"Y-you came here after that old w-woman, didn't you?" His voice covered several octaves in one sentence.

"What if I did?"

"N-nothing." The boy's eyes had an edgy, haunted look. "I just thought I recognized you."

"Do you know anything about her? Is she still alive?"

"She was about fifteen minutes ago."

"Where?"

The boy pointed upward. "Third floor. I can take you to her."

Mary frowned at the boy. Did they know she had escaped? Were they using him as bait for some trap? Maybe he'd been sent to lead her to the third floor—and back into the arms of those thugs from the amphitheater. "Why should I trust you?"

The boy shrugged, his Adam's apple bobbing. "Because I want to get out of here just as bad as you do."

He spoke the trusting mountain speech of her childhood, but she drilled him as if she had him squirming on the witness stand. "And why is that?"

"Because I'm not like these others." He glanced over his shoulder as if invisible hands might grab him at any moment.

"Why should I believe you?"

"Because I've got the same marks on my backside that are all over your face," he confessed, now blushing a furious crimson. "Tallent and them jerk my britches down every night. Sometimes they beat me with that whip thing. Sometimes they do worse."

Mary considered his words. She did not have much experience with teenaged boys, but she knew that macho stoicism was the code they lived by. Telling a female that you had your ass whipped every night had to be an act of true desperation.

"That Wurth ain't fit to live," the boy added flatly, as if clarifying some basic principle of physics. "Someday I'm going to kill him."

Knock yourself out, kid, she thought. *The sooner the better.*

"So if I take you to her, will you help me get out of here, for good?"

Yew. Mary had to smile. Years ago she had sounded exactly like him. Though she had no reason to believe anything this boy said, she did. Anyway, her options were growing fewer with each passing second. "What's your name?"

"T–Tommy Cabe," he answered, his voice full of quiet pride. "From Harlan, Kentucky. And someday I *am* going to kill Sergeant Wurth."

"Okay, Tommy Cabe. For now let's just work on getting Judge Hannah out of here. We can worry about killing Wurth later."

"Come on, then." The boy held the door

open. Mary stepped forward, trusting Tommy Cabe with her life.

"Where did you say Irene was?"

"Up on the third floor."

"Then where are we now? Near the front door?"

"Pretty close, but you'd never have walked through it alive."

"Why not?"

"Tallent's posted there. He would kill you before you could stick a toe outside."

Tallent. That was the grinning blond ape who'd cut her hair. "Okay. Then get me to the third floor."

"Right this way."

She followed him as he opened another door and led her into an old storage room. Shelves rose to the ceiling, all filled with industrial-sized cans of food, cases of paper towels, and countless rolls of toilet paper.

"A friend and I used to spend a lot of time in here." He gave her a sly grin. "You'd be surprised what you can find out working in a kitchen."

He walked over to the shelves of toilet paper and reached high, behind the top shelf, and worked a small hinge. Suddenly the whole structure swung forward, revealing a minuscule elevator, set deep inside the wall.

Mary looked at the boy, delighted. "That's an old dumbwaiter."

"I don't know what it is, but it runs on pulleys and ropes. If you get in it it'll carry you up to a closet on the third floor."

Mary eyed the box dubiously, again wondering what surprises might be awaiting her on the third floor. "Who gets to go first?"

"I will. Then I'll send it down to you."

"Won't somebody hear us?"

"They've only got a few patrols in the house right now. Wurth and most of the Troopers are working in the gym."

"Working on what?"

Tommy Cabe looked at her in amazement. "Don't you know? They're fixing to chop your friend's head off. At midnight tonight."

Mary's knees wobbled as a wave of urgency swept through her. "Come on. Let's go."

Tommy hopped up on the edge of the dumbwaiter and folded his long legs inside. "When I get there, I'll send it back for you."

"How long will it take?"

"Not long. You'll see."

She watched as the box rose, squeaking, carrying Tommy upward. For far too long she watched the old ropes that ran the contraption, then, just as she was about to decide the boy had set her up to be found by Wurth's Troopers, the box creaked back down to her.

She hopped inside the crate, crouching like an animal inside a cage. At first nothing happened, then she felt a shudder as she began to rise. The box slowly rose past the old floor joists and she thought of Irene, trapped in some room above her. *Hang on, Irene,* she prayed silently. *I'm coming as fast as I can.* Another moment and the crate stopped with a bump. She crouched there, eye to eye with Tommy Cabe.

"See?" Tommy grinned proudly. "I told you it would work."

Mary clambered out of the cramped space and into the linen closet, a small room with empty shelves that smelled of camphor and dust. "Where is she?"

"Come on," he murmured. "I'll show you."

She followed close behind as he walked to the closet door and cracked it open. He peered into the darkness beyond, then quickly reclosed the door.

"Honeycutt's still out there." He mouthed the words. "We'll have to wait till he takes a break."

She wanted to ask Cabe how many boys guarded this castle, but she didn't dare make a sound. Beyond the door she heard the sound of young male laughter. She shrank back as it seemed to move closer, then suddenly, she heard footsteps, as if someone were walking away. Her breath snagged in her throat. Cabe put his finger to his lips.

"Come on," he whispered, cracking the door open again. "Honeycutt's taking his break. We've got about four minutes to get her out of there."

They crept into the hall. Here, old linoleum covered the floors, and the walls glowed with a sickly shade of white paint. Even now, almost a century after Baron von Loessing's damaged young soldiers, the scent of suffering hung in the air.

"Hurry, Tommy," Mary whispered, feeling like a lizard was crawling up her spine.

They whisked on, passing door after door, silent as nurses on night duty. Finally, at the door with an empty chair beside it, Tommy stopped.

"In there," he told her. "You'll find what you're looking for."

CHAPTER 41

An old-fashioned examination table stood in the middle of the room. On that table lay Irene.

At first Mary thought she was dead, then, she noticed the slight rise and fall of her breathing. Straps of thick leather bound her arms and legs, and she wore the same kind of black pajamas that Mary did. Though her silvery hair still curled softly around her face and her flesh did not bear the marks of the *muchi,* two thick wads of surgical gauze covered the stumps where both her little fingers had been, and angry red cuts covered her hands and wrists.

Wurth's been instructing his Troopers, Mary realized, a wave of nausea rising. *They've been practicing on Irene.* She rushed to the table and bent low over her old friend.

"Irene?" She brushed her lips against Irene's forehead. "Can you hear me?"

The pale eyelids fluttered. "Hi, baby," she whispered. "Did you feed the horses?"

Mary pressed her cheek against her old friend's hair. Her body gave off a sour, dry smell. She wondered if Wurth had allowed her as much as a glass of water after he'd sliced off her fingers.

"Irene? It's Mary. Can you hear me? Can you talk?"

Irene opened her eyes. They looked blood-shot, but returned her gaze with recognition.

"Mary? What are you doing here?"

Mary could barely speak. "Bodyguarding you."

"What happened to your face? Your gorgeous hair?"

Mary shook her head. She could not recount all that had been done to her.

"All that pain for my judicial principles," Irene said softly. "I'm so sorry, Mary."

"Don't think about it now." Mary kissed her cheek. "Don't think about it, ever. We both did what we had to." For a moment she simply rel-ished the warmth of Irene's cheek against hers, then she asked a question.

"Can you walk?"

"I haven't walked in days, but they haven't smashed my kneecaps or anything. I think they're saving me for some greater purpose."

If you only knew, Mary thought grimly as she looked over at Tommy, who stood near the door. "Help me get her up. Unbuckle her straps on the other side of the table."

Tommy hurried over and began to pick at one unyielding buckle. "We need to move fast. Honeycutt'll be back any second."

The old leather was thick and stiff from years of disuse. Tommy and Mary frantically pulled at the straps, then at last the stiff leather worked loose. As the straps fell away from Irene's arms, they helped her upright.

"Thank God!" Irene rubbed her wrists. "Do you realize what a blessing it is to be able to move?"

"Actually, I do." Mary glanced warily over her shoulder at the door. "Particularly away from here. How are we doing, Tommy?"

"I figure he'll be back in about two minutes."

"Help me, then." Together, Mary and Tommy supported Irene by her arms as she rose from the table. For an instant her knees wobbled as if she'd been at sea. Slowly Irene limped across the room, stopping when she nosed up against an old German anatomy poster entitled *"Die Hand und Der Fuss."* She walked stiffly, but her steps were steady and sure.

Thank God, thought Mary. *Now if we can just get past Honeycutt!* She looked at Tommy. "Ready?"

"Let's go."

Half carrying Irene between them, Tommy

opened the door and they inched back the way they'd come, Mary just waiting for a loud male voice to shout "Stop!" Though their steps seemed thunderous, they kept moving, not stopping until they came to a door that was different from the others—rather than having a knob and lock, it swung freely. Tommy pushed it open; the trio stepped inside.

Years ago it had been a communal shower. Hexagonal tiles covered the floor and a line of old-fashioned fixtures sprouted from one wall. A large drain was sunk in the middle of the room, and a tall, narrow window at the far end of the room.

"Here." Tommy hurried to the window. "We can get out this way."

He unlocked the window, pushed it up, and stepped seemingly into midair. Mary gasped, expecting him to plummet to the ground, but then she realized that Tommy wasn't falling anywhere. He was standing on some kind of ledge.

They hurried over. The boy stood on the top deck of an ancient fire escape. A tall hemlock clustered around the old structure, hiding it from all but the keenest of eyes.

Mary studied the rusted scaffolding. "Are you sure this will hold us?"

"It's pulled away from the wall in a couple of places," Tommy replied. "But it holds me okay."

Mary frowned at him. "There's one of you. How about all three of us?"

"It's the best way I know. That waiter thing'll only get us to the main floor, and we'd never get past Tallent."

Mary sighed. Tommy Cabe's escape plan must seem reasonable to someone young in body and mind. Her arms and legs felt like lead. She could only imagine what Irene must feel like. She looked over at her friend. "What do you say, Irene?"

Irene shrugged. "I've got nothing else to do but wait for Wurth to come up and chop off some other parts of me."

Mary smiled. Of course, Irene would vote for action. "Okay, Tommy. Lead the way."

Tommy helped Irene onto the ledge, then Mary followed. Outside, the hemlock-scented air instantly cooled the clammy sweat from their bodies. Mary felt the stairway give an ominous shudder as Tommy and Irene began their descent.

"Tommy, you hang on tight!" Mary called in a whisper, then realized with chagrin that she must sound just like his mother.

"I will," he assured her, his voice floating up from the shadows, buoyant with youth, calm as if he did this every night.

Cautiously they made their way down. The

tree had grown through the bars of the scaffolding, making it necessary for them to climb over branches as well as negotiate the loose, rusty stairs. Once Mary heard Irene yelp in pain; another time a rusty piece of railing came off in Mary's hand. The noise they made seemed deafening; with every step she expected Wurth to turn on some spotlight and cry, "Prisoners on the fire escape! Get 'em, boys!" That would end it for them. Then all they could do would be bid each other good-bye.

They passed a boarded-up window on the second floor, then, after an eternity, they finally reached the bottom. As Tommy dropped the remaining six feet to the ground, they heard footsteps, passing close by. Without a word, they shrank into the shadows. Mary and Irene huddled together, peering through the branches of the tree. Two boys came into view—both wearing Trooper uniforms.

"Are they really going to chop off that old lady's head?" one asked.

"Yeah. At midnight."

"Are they going to let us watch?"

"I don't figure we have much choice."

"What are they going to do with the other one?"

"Wurth said she would be treated like a captured female."

The first boy snickered. "Does that mean what I think it does?"

"Yep. Injun pussy for us tonight."

"Awwrriiight! Heat up the skillet, Pocahontas. Big meat's coming in."

The boys walked on, giggling, their footsteps fading into the night. Mary felt a hot revulsion boil up her throat. Irene reached over and put a comforting arm around her shoulders.

They huddled a moment longer, then Tommy called, "Come on. We have to hurry. Those two'll make a round of the castle every ten minutes."

"Okay," Mary called. "I'm going to lower Irene down. You catch her."

She helped Irene scoot to the edge of the platform. Tommy eased her down to the frozen earth below. Next Mary dropped from the railing. Finally all three of them stood hidden beneath the tree, breathing in the cold, sweet air.

"Where to now?" Mary peered through the thick green branches.

"I know a place they'll never find us," Tommy replied. "If we can just cross the lawn and get into the cover of the trees."

Irene shuddered, then nodded. "Lead on, Tommy. We're right behind you."

CHAPTER 42

The high winter moon cast a puddle of bright light on the floor of Robert Wurth's study. Wurth sat at his desk, savoring the one cigar he allowed himself each evening, watching as a single line of red type pulsed in the darkness.

What the hell do you think you're doing?

He watched as the thirty-one letters seemed to throb, just like the apoplectic vein that bisected Dunbar's forehead. The little webwatchers at FaithAmerica had duly reported the message he'd relayed to that French porn site, and now Dunbar was right this minute sitting in front of his own computer in California, waiting for Wurth to type in a reply. No doubt furious, thought Wurth, taking a long, relaxed drag of his smoke. No doubt cursing the moment he'd let me take that vote. Chuckling, he leaned forward and typed in three words.

Proving my reliability.

He clicked the "send" button and sat back. In a few moments another line of bright red letters came on the screen.

You're a dead man if you do this.

Wurth laughed out loud, for once amazed at Dunbar's naiveté. Did he take him for an utter fool? He'd been a dead man since the first day he'd signed on this job. That's why he'd taken steps to protect himself. That's why he could sit here calmly in North Carolina while Richard Dunbar was panicking in California. Another line of red type appeared on the screen.

I'm warning you!

Wurth laughed harder. How silly Dunbar's words seemed at this distance! Nothing more than verbal spitwads falling laughably short of their intended target. Though these little messages were funnier than anything he'd seen lately on TV, he knew it was time to end this. He put his cigar down and typed two sentences.

Visit the website at midnight. Watch your prophecy be fulfilled.

He punched the send button, then logged off the computer. He would not be talking to Richard Dunbar ever again. Taking up his cigar for a few final puffs, he considered everything that had happened. All in all, it had been an amazing week. The whole operation had gone far more smoothly than he'd expected. Mary Crow had alarmed him at first, but even she had blossomed into a flower more beautiful than his wildest imaginings. His boys had gotten a chance to learn female anatomy along with his physical interrogation strategies. Right now, with those two interlopers Tuttle had caught, they were learning how to deal with prisoners of war. Wurth chuckled. By this time tomorrow, he would have no more virgins in his Army. The last class of Camp Unakawaya would graduate well seasoned in the ways of both sex and death.

Smiling, he puffed his cigar down to the nub and ground it out in his ashtray. It was time to go. He had things to do, places to get to. He got up from his desk, dropped his keys in his pocket, then picked up a black leather briefcase. With a final, lingering look around his office, he walked to the door, the briefcase hanging heavy in his hand.

Seven of his best Troopers lounged in the flag-draped foyer. The moment they saw him, they snapped to attention. He looked at them and smiled.

"How goes it, Tallent? Any problems with our prisoners?"

"None, sir." Tallent reported. "Both are present and accounted for."

"Good." Wurth stashed his briefcase in a small closet beneath the stairs. "In half an hour I want you and Metzger to have all the other boys assembled in the gym. Have Earlington bring my sword case. When we get the Honorable Irene Hannah over there, we'll begin."

"Yessir."

With a brisk salute, Tallent left his post by the door and strode down the long hall. Wurth faced the boys in front of him.

"All right, gentlemen. Let's form an honor guard to move Judge Hannah out of her cell. A new phase in American history will begin tonight, and I want you all to conduct yourselves with as much courage as the patriots at Bunker Hill. Is that clear?"

"Yessir," the boys answered together.

"Okay. Quick march in formation, third floor."

With that, the boys turned and jogged up the old walnut staircase. Their jack-booted feet thundering in unison up the stairs sounded like fifty, and the flags that hung from the gallery swayed with their ascent. Wurth followed them. As they climbed, he could hear excited voices echoing from other parts of the building. He smiled. Though he'd told no one of his plan, his troops had whispered all week about what was going to happen. Secrets were always hard to keep in armies, be they the Troopers at Camp Unakawaya or the beaches of Normandy.

When they reached the third floor, he called them to a halt.

"I'll lead the way, gentlemen," he said as he moved to the front of the column. "We're soldiers here, not hooligans."

He looked at the six Troopers who faced him, then he turned and led them down the hall. *She must know by now,* he thought, his pulse rising in anticipation. *By now she must have heard us coming.*

They marched to the room, then he halted his troops as her guard, Honeycutt, snapped to attention and saluted him.

"Is everything in order, Honeycutt?"

"Yes, sir."

"Very well." With those words, he stepped forward and grasped the doorknob in his hand. *Soon,* he thought, *I will show these boys the power of a Feather Man. Soon I will teach Richard Dunbar all about reliability. Soon I will be far away from here, too far for anyone to find me.*

"Judge Hannah," he began, turning the doorknob as he spoke. "I'm happy to inform you that your period of incarceration is over. In just a few moments, we will escort you out of this building and over to a place where you'll be able to meet many of your old friends." He took a breath to explain away any objections the old woman might have, but when his gaze fell upon Irene Hannah's table, he felt a great sinking in his chest. Though the lightbulb still glowed from the ceiling and the table was still nailed to the floor, the straps that had bound the old woman hung limp and empty. Judge Irene Hannah was gone.

CHAPTER 43

The siren began screaming just as they crossed into the darkness of the woods. A shrill, incessant wail, it sounded like the alarm raised when convicts break out of prison.

"Uh-oh." Tommy Cabe looked over his shoulder at the now brightly lit castle. "I think they just found out we're gone."

"What will they do?" asked Irene.

"Hunt us down," Tommy said matter-of-factly.

"How much time have we got?" asked Mary.

"Maybe ten, maybe fifteen minutes." Tommy wiped his glasses. "They practice this stuff all the time."

"So what should we do?" Irene shivered as she spoke.

Tommy pointed to the mountain that loomed above them. "There's an old cave just beyond that ridge. My friend Willett had a hideaway inside. If we can make it there, they'll never find us."

Mary studied the hillside. As high, thin clouds raced across the full moon, she could see that it was a steep, tangled growth of laurel and pine. It would be a hard climb for someone in perfect condition. She couldn't remember when she'd last eaten, and she knew Wurth had not provided room service for Irene, either. "Is there anyplace else we could go?" she asked Tommy.

"Not that they wouldn't find."

Mary looked at Irene. "What do you think?"

"It doesn't sound like we have much of a choice."

Without another word, they hurried up the mountainside. Before they'd climbed fifty feet Mary heard Irene gasping for breath. She stopped and put her arm around her old friend's shoulders.

"Are you okay?"

"Just winded," Irene wheezed. "But you've got to promise me one thing."

"What?"

"If I ever tell you that I'm not fine, you and Tommy must go on without me. Otherwise, I'm not moving another step." Irene's voice brooked no argument.

"I'm not leaving you in these woods, Irene."

Mary's teeth began to chatter with the cold. "We've come too far—"

"You've already come too far, Mary. Far beyond what I deserve. I should have sent you back to Atlanta on Christmas Eve."

"I wouldn't have gone." Mary smiled at the face she loved so well. "Now you're stuck with me."

"Mary, I . . ."

"Come on, Your Honor." She grabbed Irene's arm. "We can argue the point on our way up this hill."

They scrambled upward. Tommy bounded up the steep hillside like a young goat, but Irene and Mary had to pull themselves up by the small maple seedlings that crowded the forest floor. Mary kept glancing over her shoulder, alert for any sign of Wurth's boys. So far, no shadowy figures were running up the hill after them.

Suddenly Irene groaned and fell.

"Irene?" Mary knelt beside her. "What's wrong?"

"My knee gave out. Give me a second to catch my breath."

Mary turned toward Camp Unakawaya while Irene rested. Every light in the old castle was glowing brightly. Through the trees Mary could see uniformed boys running toward the tennis court. A few had already formed ranks. She

knew it would now be only minutes until
Wurth sent them up into the hills, to hunt the
three of them down.

"We need to hurry, Irene," she said urgently.

"Okay. I'm ready."

Mary helped her up, then, together, they began to climb forward. After two more steps,
Irene cried out in pain.

"Damn!" she cried, collapsing again.

"What's the matter?" Mary asked as Tommy
hurried down the hill to see what was wrong.

"Oh, I hurt my knee years ago playing tennis.
It's real cantankerous when I run." She gave a
bitter smile. "This may be it for me, kids. Like
Hugh says, no foot, no horse." Her gaze turned
serious. "I'm not fine now, Mary. You need to
go on without me."

Mary turned to Tommy. "How much further
is the cave?"

"Not much. A couple hundred feet after the
top of the ridge."

"If you know the king's carry, we can get her
up the hill."

When Tommy shook his head, mystified,
Mary showed him how to intertwine his arms
with hers and make a seat for Irene between
them.

"Come on, Irene," said Mary. "Jump aboard."

Irene sighed, but she gripped Mary's shoulder

and rose to her feet, lowering herself onto their outstretched arms. "I don't think this is going to work. I'm too heavy."

"Not at all, sweetheart." Mary winked. "Just relax and enjoy being carried up a mountain by this handsome young man and me, your humble servant."

Tommy snorted, but Mary could tell her remark pleased him. Suddenly she felt as if she could run up the mountain with Irene slung over her shoulder, if she needed to. She had not been able to save her mother. She was going to do better by Irene. "Ready, Tommy?"

"Sure."

"Then let's go."

Irene was not a heavy woman, but neither was she light, particularly climbing uphill. After only a few steps Mary's arms began to tremble as her breath came in ragged gasps.

"You want to stop a minute?" Tommy asked.

"Not till we get to that cave."

Doggedly she sidled up the mountain like a crab. Though the temperature was well below freezing, sweat began to drip from her forehead. A gust of icy wind carried the distant howl of a dog. Mary felt a new terror rising inside her.

"Wurth doesn't keep dogs, does he?" Mary asked, wondering if Wurth might keep a whole kennel of rottweilers hidden away, always at the ready to track his escapees. If he let dogs loose on them, they wouldn't have a prayer.

"Nah. He hates dogs. Says they're just C rations with tails."

"Thank God for small mercies," Mary whispered, the taste of her own fear receding in the back of her throat.

They inched their way up the mountainside, Irene clutching her shoulders, Tommy's fingers digging into her arm. Finally they crested the ridge. After struggling through a thicket of witch hazel, they broke into a cleared area. An old, weedy parking lot lay in front of them; ahead, another mountain loomed in the darkness.

"Straight ahead," panted Tommy. "Not much farther at all."

"Good." Mary's arms tingled, almost numb. "Let's hurry."

With Irene holding on, Mary and Tommy tried to find a common, ground-covering gait between them. Tommy galloped like a racehorse, and Mary had to pump hard to keep up with the boy. Though they were both gasping as they crossed the treeless expanse of grass, they did not slacken their pace until they reached the shadowy growth of rhododendron that clustered around the cave itself. Forcing the last bit of strength from their legs, they set Irene down at the mouth of the cave, leaning her against the ancient, fading sign: "It's always coooool inside!" Only then did they sit down and give their racing hearts a chance to slow.

Far away, another dog howled as a truck ground its gears, lumbering up a mountain road. As always, night sounds up here were deceptive. Sometimes you could hear things miles away; sometimes you could miss a twig breaking right beside you.

"How far is the highway from here?" Mary asked Tommy.

"This cave road joins the county road about half a mile that way." He pointed to his left. "It hits 441 about two miles away."

"You seem to know a lot about it." Mary raised an eyebrow at the boy.

"My friend Willett told me. He was gonna run away."

"And did he?" asked Mary.

Tommy Cabe swallowed hard. "I'm pretty sure Willett's dead. I think Wurth killed him." For a moment his voice sounded thick with tears, then he nodded decisively. "But he could have run away. All you have to do is sneak over to 441 and hitch a ride with someone."

"Where are you from, Tommy?" Irene asked gently.

"My mom and I were renting a trailer in

Cherokee. But I grew up in Harlan, Kentucky. My grandfather has a farm there. That's where I'd like to hitch a ride to."

"Sounds nice." Irene smiled.

"Willett told me about a bridge and an overlook where those trucks pull off the road to let their brakes cool down. I bet at night they'd pick most anybody up, just for the company."

"I'm sure they would," said Mary. "Right now, though, we need to get ourselves hidden inside your cave."

"Okay." Tommy darted over to the tall iron grate that apparently sealed off the cave from the outside world. He worked one of the iron bars enough to budge it slightly, then he said, "Come on. I'll show you Willett's Den—the best hiding place ever."

Mary helped Irene to her feet. With a final glance at the moon that glowed like a spotlight in the sky, she helped her old friend through the bars of the cave and into the utter darkness beyond.

CHAPTER 44

Robert Wurth sat on an old picnic table, rolling a quarter across his knuckles. The moon shone from a brilliant, black-diamond sky, and he'd had his boys set up a makeshift command post just beyond the tennis court. Now he sat trying to control his rage by manipulating the coin with his fingers. It was bad enough that Judge Hannah had gotten loose, but the situation had grown grimmer when Honeycutt reported that Mary Crow had disappeared as well. When Rogers accounted for all the Grunts except Tommy Cabe, he'd put it together. Somehow that little faggot had found both prisoners and turned them loose. He couldn't imagine how, but he'd done it. Now he must be helping them escape.

"That little bastard!" Wurth muttered as he scowled into the darkness. Everything was turning to shit. Unless he found Irene Hannah in the next hour, his plan would fail. Once again he was being brought down by women. This time by two of them abetted by a skinny, stuttering boy.

"Damn!" he cursed. Who would have thought that they would be so clever? And who would have guessed that the Troopers he'd drilled for the past five years would be such dolts? Hell, they'd scoured the entire compound and had come up with nothing. An hour ago, he would have bet his life that they would have had all three hog-tied on the tennis court within fifteen minutes. He'd trained them so well, he thought. He hadn't forgotten anything.

His field radio squawked. He dropped the coin back in his pocket and lifted the radio to his ear. Static assailed his eardrum, then Tuttle's voice came through, sounding distant and tinny.

"Tuttle here."

"I copy."

"We've reached the end of the creek by the highway. No sign of them."

"Did you sweep both sides of the creek? Did you search all level ground?"

"We checked any place they could hide. They didn't go in this direction." More static, then Tuttle said, "Shall we sweep back to the house?"

"Yes. And if you find Tommy Cabe, shoot to kill."

"That stuttering kid?"

"Right. The two women I want alive. You can use Cabe for target practice."

The radio went dead. As Wurth clipped it back on his belt, it bleated again. This time the boys in Badger Company reported from the other end of the creek.

Wayne Tallent's voice came over more clearly, but his report was identical to Tuttle's. Badger's sweep of the creek had likewise revealed no sign of the three.

Wurth repeated his orders concerning Tommy Cabe, then told Tallent to sweep back to head-quarters. He switched off the radio. Logic told him that two beaten and demoralized women would stay on level ground, close to a creek that would provide them with cover and possibly lead them somewhere. Yet neither Tuttle nor Badger Company had found a trace of them. That left Anaconda, the squad he'd sent back to the castle, in case the trio had been canny enough to dou-ble back and try to commandeer some kind of vehicle. That would take more cleverness than most women possessed, plus a lot of luck. With all the cameras and Troopers running around tonight, he didn't think it possible, but that Crow woman was resourceful. Suddenly he heard someone cough behind him. He jumped and looked over his shoulder.

The Anacondas had not bothered with the radio. They came slipping through the shadows, their shoulders drooping.

"Anaconda Company reporting, sir." Frank Upchurch gave a dispirited salute.

"And?" Wurth looked past Upchurch and noticed Stump Logan huffing over toward him. Christ, he thought, for once he's early. He wasn't supposed to pick him up until one A.M.

"We didn't find anybody within the compound."

"You searched everywhere? The castle? The cabins? The lake?" He couldn't believe this. Anaconda was his best squad.

"Yes, sir." Upchurch kept his eyes straight ahead. The other members of the patrol stood behind him at attention, grim-faced and mute.

"Take five, then, Anaconda. Over there and out of my way." Wurth nodded at the tennis court.

Upchurch saluted, then Anaconda broke rank.

"You having some night exercises?" Stump Logan's voice rumbled over Wurth, who bent to relace his boots without replying. When he looked up again, Logan stood there, his Stetson pulled low, rolling a toothpick around one corner of his mouth like some dime-store cowboy.

"You might say that," Wurth replied through gritted teeth, rankled, as always, with Logan's silly Western affectations. "How come you're here so early? I'm not supposed to meet McClary at the plane until two."

"I thought I'd help you ring in the New Year." Logan looked over at the bonfire burning next to the tennis court. "What's going on here, no kidding?"

Wurth sighed. "Just a little nighttime escapee drill."

Logan's eyebrows lifted. "It's Mary Crow, isn't it?"

"Her and the judge, along with that kid Cabe. My boys have searched the house and grounds. They can't find them anywhere."

"Fuck it, Clipper. Can't all your boys find one old woman and a beat-up girl?"

"They haven't yet," Wurth snapped. "I'm going to take Tuttle and ten of my best and go up the mountain." He stared into the darkness a moment, then turned to Logan and smiled. "If you're so nervous about Mary Crow, why don't you come with us?"

Logan flicked the toothpick to the other corner of his mouth and studied the height of the mountain ridge that loomed above them. In the dark it seemed a gargantuan escarpment, thrusting up into a brilliant sky.

"Come on, Stump." Wurth's eyes glittered as he pulled on a black knit cap. "It'll get your sap running, just like the old days. They aren't gooks, but two women and a boy can be pretty good fun." He gave a sour laugh. "Or does going after Mary Crow scare you?"

"Not particularly," Logan replied evenly.

"Then come on, Feather Man. We'll take a patrol up the mountain, just like we used to. It'll be fun."

"You're the one who got such a kick out of Vietnam, not me."

"Oh, you know you loved it. Remember how alive we felt? Remember what it was like to have all those little yellow monkeys pissing in their pants at the very sight of you?" Wurth stepped forward, stopping inches from the sheriff's face. "Don't you miss the feathers?"

Logan looked at him. "You're insane."

"Why? Just 'cause I've got me a little army and a few guns? I'm no worse than you, with that pistol on your hip and your jail in town. We've taken different routes, buddy, but we're still the same bad boys." He clapped Logan on the back. "How about it? You in? Or have you grown soft in your old age?"

Logan spat the toothpick out of his mouth and

smiled at Wurth in the moonlight. "I might walk a little ways with you, Clipper. I'd like to see you go one-on-one with Mary Crow."

"Good boy, Stump. I knew I could depend on you."

CHAPTER 45

Mary's heart sank. Though the cave was considerably warmer than the outside air, it smelled like a sewer and gave her a slimy feeling in the pit of her stomach. She turned to the thin, myopic boy who had led them there.

"How do you stand this smell?"

"You get used to it," Tommy replied. "Anything's better than hanging around the castle, waiting for Tallent to get you."

Mary had to agree with that. Though she hated the idea of leaving the comforting little puddle of moonlight they stood in, she knew it was terribly foolish to stand here in the open, with Tallent and the others gathering on the tennis court below. "I guess we'd better go hide, then."

"Willett's Den is down that way. Just follow me."

"Will we have to crawl?" asked Irene.

"Not till the last few feet."

Mary turned, listening for any sound of Wurth's troops coming up the mountain. She heard nothing. "You go first, Irene. I'll bring up the rear."

Irene stepped forward and grabbed onto Tommy's jacket. "I'll walk behind you, like this."

Tommy smiled down at her. "Keep one hand against the wall. Sometimes the darkness makes you dizzy."

Irene looked at Mary. "Are you coming?"

"I'm right behind you," Mary promised. She pressed her palm against the cave wall. It felt cool and damp. She squelched an absurd wish for a mine-shaft canary. Though the air stank, it couldn't be lethal. After all, it hadn't seemed to hurt Tommy or his friend Willett.

"Everybody ready?" Tommy called.

"Go ahead," said Mary.

Tommy slid into the darkness, with Irene at his heels. To Mary, it looked as if they had stepped off the world itself, never to return. Ignoring a tight fear that coiled inside her, she followed.

After three steps, the blackness swallowed her. She tried squinting, then opening her eyes as wide as she could, but soon she gave up. The rods and cones of human vision required light. Light did not exist here.

Keeping her left hand on the wall, she inched deeper into the passage, feeling nothing but the cool, malodorous breath of the cave. The only thing that riveted her to the earth at all was the slightly clammy stone against her palm and the hard rock floor under her feet.

"Everybody okay up there?" she called a little too loudly, suddenly needing to hear a fellow human.

"Honey, we're doing fine." Irene's firm reply rang like a bell.

Tommy led them on, creeping through the darkness. Somehow it felt wrong to speak, to interrupt the millennia-old dialogue between Mother Earth and the Old Men. *Disgagistiyi. Dakwai. Ahaluna. Now I am inside you. Now I will find out why you hate me so.* She took a deep breath of the dank air, then suddenly she gasped. Her mother was looking at her, not five feet away! Martha wore a loose white blouse that was buttoned to just above her breasts. Her husband's Saint Andrew medal dangled from her neck. Her raven hair hung long, and she looked at Mary in silence.

"Mama?" Mary whispered. In all the years since her death, Martha Crow had entered her daughter's dreams only twice, in nocturnal dramas where she'd played a walk-on part, then vanished. Never had Mary seen her for this long, in such detail!

"Mama?" she cried.

Her mother tossed her long black hair and beckoned her deeper into the cave, but another voice protested, "Wait. I need you!" The second voice was deep and tender. *Jonathan,* Mary thought. She turned, wondering how he could be here, but what shimmered before her was not Jonathan but a young, sandy-haired man dressed in green Army camouflage. Grinning, he waved at her, then leaped to catch a football. As he bobbled the ball in his arms he turned, and she saw that the lower half of his body—his legs, his spine, everything below his waist—was just trailing ribbons of blood. Then without warning, both specters vanished.

Mary began to tremble. The darkness was suffocating; it was all she could do not to turn and run headlong out of the cave, shrieking. The world started spinning, and all around she heard the mean, high-pitched laughter of children as they pelted rocks at a dead crow. *You no nummah one! You nummah ten thou!* She opened her mouth to cry out, and the cave floor disintegrated beneath her feet. She was falling. Falling forever down a bottomless hole, tumbling endlessly into nothing. No one could catch her. No one could save her. . . .

"Mary!" Irene's voice sliced through the darkness like a bolt of lightning. "Calm down, honey! You're hallucinating!"

Mary felt strong arms wrap around her waist as another, younger voice sailed through the shadows. The sound was green, like a clarinet. "Don't be scared, Mary. We're almost there."

Tommy. Suddenly she stood upright again, braced against firm ground. She was not falling anywhere. Irene's arms held her. There was no mother, no disfigured soldier, no monstrous, taunting children. She became aware of the warmth of her own body, of the blood flowing through her veins.

"Did I just do something weird?" Her voice and legs trembled as if she'd stepped off a roller coaster.

"Kind of." Tommy sounded worried. "You kept calling Mama and Jack."

Irene squeezed her hand. "Don't worry about it. Let's just get to our hiding place."

Tommy led them further into the darkness as Mary kept her hand on Irene's shoulder and her mind on the task at hand. Limestone, she recalled, forcing her brain into the discipline of a geology course she'd taken in college. Water dripping over limestone, over time, will make a cave. The temperature in most caves is a constant 56 degrees. Stalagmites grow up, stalactites hang down. She had just started to repeat what she could remember of the periodic table of the elements when Tommy's voice rang out.

"Okay. Hang a right here."

"And then what?" Irene asked.

"Then you need to kneel down and crawl forward about four steps. We're almost there."

Mary turned sharply to the right and dropped to her knees. A few moments later, Tommy stopped and Irene and Mary collided.

"All right. Everybody sit still and I'll get the flashlight."

"You've got a flashlight?" Mary cried. What she would give for just a drop of light! A flashlight would seem like the sun! She waited, listening. She heard something bump against a rock, then a bright white light pierced her vision so sharply, she had to look away. When she could focus again, she saw that they sat in a small enclosure. Dense shadows hid the ceiling from view, but the smooth, topaz-colored walls glistened with moisture. On a ledge about five feet above the floor were two cans of Coca-Cola and an old Polaroid shot of a scruffy little terrier.

"Welcome to Willett's Den." Tommy beamed with pride. "Want some Coke?"

He popped one can open and handed it to Mary, who passed it first to Irene. She drank as if she were dying of thirst.

"It tastes as good as champagne," she said, handing the can to Mary. "It's been so long since I've had anything in my mouth."

Mary took several swallows of the Coke. Though it was warm and much too sweet, it felt wonderful sliding down her throat. For a second she was absolutely content, sitting beside the small flashlight, drinking Coca-Cola with Irene and this young stranger who'd helped them escape Sergeant Wurth's domain.

"Thanks," she said to Tommy as she wiped her mouth with her sleeve. "That tasted awfully good." She stared at him in the glow of the flashlight, pondering their situation, wondering. How far away had he said that road was?

Tommy returned her gaze without speaking, the light reflected in the lenses of his glasses. "I bet I know what you're thinking."

"What?"

"That I should try and get to the highway."

Mary looked at him. This boy grew odder by the minute. That was precisely what she was thinking. "You know, if you could get over to 441, you could flag down the first thing you see. Semi, pickup, it wouldn't matter. Just get in and ask the driver to take you to a phone."

"But who could I call?" asked Tommy. "Sheriff Logan's real tight with Sergeant Wurth."

Somehow Tommy's words did not surprise her. Stump Logan had been in the PR photo with Wurth and Gerald LeClaire; he would almost have to be involved in Camp Unakawaya on some level. Wurth couldn't run an operation this big without the consent of the local law.

"Tell the driver to take you to Upsy Daisy Farm, on Lick Log Road. The FBI is camped there. Tell them that Robert Wurth is holding Judge Irene Hannah at Camp Unakawaya. When they hear that, they'll know what to do."

Tommy frowned uncertainly. "What will you do while I'm gone?"

Mary looked around at the darkness that pressed down upon their heads. "We'll stay here. With any luck at all, you should be back with the Feds in three or four hours."

"That's a pretty heavy load for Tommy," Irene objected softly. "Do you have a Plan B?"

Mary shook her head as she fought a sudden, numbing fatigue. "We'll have to make up Plan B as we go along. What do you say, Tommy? Think you can do it?"

The boy grinned. "With one hand tied behind my back." He scrambled to his feet and stuffed the photo of the dog in his pocket, then he stepped over to the wall and reached into the shadows. A moment later he pulled out a small object wrapped in plastic. "This computer disk belonged to Willett. He told me to take it if I ever got the chance to escape," he explained. "He said it would get Wurth in a shit pot of trouble."

"All right," said Mary. "Then go and give it to the FBI!"

"And be careful!" added Irene.

"Okay." He hesitated. "I guess I'll see y'all in a couple of hours, then. . . .

"Hurry, Tommy." Mary wanted to kiss him, for luck, but she knew it would embarrass him. Instead, she reached out and squeezed his hand. The boy's fingers felt like ice. "Do you want to take the flashlight?"

"Y'all keep it. I can find my way without it."

"If Wurth comes up here, is there any place else we can hide?" asked Mary as he ducked down to crawl into the outer passage.

"Crawl out here and turn left. About ten yards away, there's a room with a bunch of old furniture. You can find lots of places to hide in there."

"Okay. Hurry now. And be careful!"

With a sly smile, Tommy Cabe crawled back into the murky darkness beyond. Mary and Irene listened until the soft *shrush* of his footsteps faded away, then Mary scooted next to Irene and put her arm around her shoulders. As she turned off the flashlight to save the batteries, it occurred to her that a cave might be the best torture chamber of all. All you had to do was lock somebody in one and let the demons inside their own head gnaw their way out.

CHAPTER 46

Jonathan Walkingstick opened his eyes. An inch from his nose, irregular spots of knotty-pine paneling wavered before him. One spot looked like the profile of Abraham Lincoln; another reminded him of a small birthmark on Ruth's arm. For an instant he smiled at the memory, then a wave of sick, hot pain dissolved the spots into darkness. *Christ,* he thought, squeezing his eyes shut. *What have they done to me?*

He lay motionless, hardly breathing. Gradually the pain ebbed away, like poisonous floodwater receding into some sick river. When his pulse slowed, he lifted his head. He lay on his side, curled into the same fetal position that he'd seen coma victims assume. He inched his hand down between his legs and held his breath. Gently he touched his penis, then, spreading his legs just a little, his balls. They were shriveled hard and

tight against him, but everything still felt attached to his body, where it ought to be. Thank
God. Whatever those bastards had done to him,
at least he was still whole.

Gingerly he straightened his legs, then rolled
over on his back. His head bumped against
something. He looked up. More knotty-pine
planks disappeared into the gloom overhead. If
he extended his left hand, he touched a wall. If
he stretched his legs, he touched another. He
seemed to be lying in a tiny room. The air hung
cold and rank around him, and a sour, sweet
smell like something rotting made him want to
recoil from the very air that kept him alive.

Easing forward with infinite care, he sat up.
For an instant the room spun so crazily, he
thought he might vomit, then images began to
resolve around him. Instinctively he felt for
Ribtickler, his knife. It was gone, as was the gun
Safer had given him. Curiously, his wallet remained in the back pocket of his jeans. He
opened it and thumbed through its contents.
His lips curled in a faint smile. Tucked behind
his driver's license and insurance card was a tattered picture of Mary Crow.

As he checked the rest of his pockets, his feet
banged against a rough-hewn door, where a
thin ribbon of light seeped in. Along the back

wall of the room stood two wooden boxes with dingy, cracked toilet seats; beyond them lay Agent Daniel Safer, hunched in the same fetal position from which Walkingstick had just arisen.

"Safer?" he called. His voice rasped like a dry corn husk. "Are you okay?"

The agent did not respond. Jonathan stared at his motionless body and struggled to piece together what had happened. He remembered Safer's turning around and saying *Tuttle?* And then the other man's insane grin as he said *Hello, Big Dan;* then teenagers taking his gun, their eyes shiny with rage. Then his balls felt as if a dozen mules had kicked him all at once and his knees buckled as he slid into a mindless oblivion.

"Safer!" Jonathan called again. "Wake up, buddy."

Safer's eyes flickered open. They looked at Jonathan, unseeing. His mouth moved, but no words came out.

"You're okay," Jonathan reassured him. "You've still got all your parts."

Safer blinked.

Jonathan struggled to his feet and hobbled over to the door. Pressing his face against the slit of light that shone from outside, he tried to pinpoint where they were, but all he could see were pine trees melding into an endless forest of darkness. In a fit of mad hope, he tried the door. It wobbled in its frame, but did not open.

"Christ, it stinks in here. Where are we?" Safer wheezed from the floor.

"In a latrine," Jonathan replied. "They've locked us in."

"It feels like somebody's done a war dance on my balls."

"I think they must have used some kind of phaser on us. Nothing else would hurt this long, and this bad."

"Bastards." Safer's voice was as rusty as an old man's. He struggled to his feet and checked his own pockets, pulling out a set of keys, a wallet, two quarters, and a penny. "They took my gun and my phone."

"And my knife," said Walkingstick. "But they left everything else. Have you got anything we could make some kind of tool from?"

"I don't think so." Safer blinked at the array of items in his hand.

"Then we'll have to try something else." Jonathan ran his hands over the surface of the door. Constructed of four wide boards nailed together, it was hung from the outside, a curious arrangement for a simple latrine. The hinges were on the exterior of the structure, and when he pushed against the door it didn't budge.

Someone had shoved a bar into place to wedge it firmly shut.

"We could get out easy if we had something to lift up the bar on the other side."

Jonathan studied the door for a moment, then he unbuckled his belt and slid off the empty knife sheath. The leather was worn, but long and stiff. If he could squeeze it through the gap in the door, they might have a shot. "Let's give this a try."

At first the sheath seemed too thick to squeeze through the gap, but Jonathan manipulated it until finally half of it emerged on the other side of the door. Working upwards, he felt it nudge against the bar.

"Okay," he said softly. "I'm there. If the leather is strong enough to raise the bar, we're out."

"Hold it tight against the door." Safer moved closer. "And lift real slow."

With sweat beading his forehead, Jonathan wriggled the sheath upwards. The bar felt heavy, but moved freely in its cradle. Centimeter by slow centimeter, he inched the sheath higher, knowing he risked getting the bar almost up and having it flop back down, locking them in again.

"When I say push," he murmured to Safer without taking his eyes off his task, "push this door hard."

"You got it."

The seconds dripped by. Up the bar came, inch by inch. Finally he felt it jiggle, free of its frame.

"Push!" he cried.

Safer slammed against the door. As it flapped open, a rush of cold, sweet air filled the rank latrine. Both men dropped to the ground in case a guard stood lurking outside, but the woods remained silent except for a screech owl shrilling far off in the shadows.

They crept out of their prison and back toward the castle. When they reached the tree line they saw that the lights that had once glowed so brightly from the gym had spread; now every window in the castle blazed like a beacon in the dark.

"Jesus, what the hell's going on?" murmured Safer.

The two men watched as the boys who had been laboring in the gym now gathered around a bonfire built at the edge of the old tennis court. Its leaping flames illuminated their serious young faces, and as the blaze grew higher more boys came from the castle, all dressed in black camouflage suits, carrying rifles slung over their shoulders. The young Troopers ignored the cheery warmth of the fire and paced up and down the tennis court, focusing their attention on the broad mountain ridge that thrust into the darkness beyond them.

"I'll be damned!" whispered Jonathan. "They must have escaped!"

"Oh, come on," Safer scoffed. "Mary and Judge Hannah? They're probably beaten and hungry. They couldn't break out of that castle and get past those armed boys."

Jonathan chuckled. "If Mary Crow went in there to rescue Irene Hannah, it would take more than armed boys and a big castle to stop her."

"But where would she go?" asked Safer. "There's nothing around here but forest."

"Russell Cave." Jonathan pointed in the same direction that Wurth's Troopers were gazing. "At the top of that ridge. Best place in the world to hide."

"Can we get up there before they do?" Safer nodded at the boys around the fire.

"We can sure as hell try," said Jonathan as he slipped silently into a growth of shadowy pines.

CHAPTER 47

Tommy ran through the forest, keeping the ancient, barely visible road on his left, praying that Willett hadn't been kidding when he'd said it joined a paved highway just a couple of miles to the east.

"Two miles," he said out loud, mostly for the comfort of hearing his own voice. In the summer, when he and Willett had ventured out at night, the woods had roared with noise—crickets chirping, night birds calling, unseen predators shuffling through fallen leaves, on the track of some hidden prey. Now the forest stood hushed and silent, as if the wintertime trees themselves resented his intrusion into their brittle, leafless world.

He zipped his jacket up closer around his neck and ran on, pushing branches away from his face, falling into a ground-covering stride that allowed him to plow on through the night. He wondered if Willett's ghost might not pop out from behind the trees, his face stretched in a grin. *Tommy-boy,* it would say. *What took you so long?*

Finally, when his legs began to feel rubbery from fatigue, he glimpsed something. The dark gray of the cave road seemed to dissolve into a wide expanse of lighter gray. Slowing, he crept behind a tree and peered through the branches ahead. His heart flopped in his chest. He saw the intersection, just as he expected. But what he hadn't expected to see was one of Wurth's Jeeps parked in the middle of it.

He blinked at the eeriness of the scene. Five young men sat in the vehicle, all armed but doing nothing except looking straight ahead. It was if all five had known exactly where to find him; now they were just waiting for him to come walking down that road.

Damn, he thought. Wurth must have known about the cave all along. Grice and Rogers and the other three were sentries Wurth had posted at the mouth of the cave road.

Why hadn't they heard him? He had been tromping through the woods like an elephant, yet they all sat in the Jeep as if they were in some kind of trance. Suddenly the driver bent his head and raised his arm. He was looking at his watch.

"Okay." Cabe heard Rogers's voice so clearly, he could have been standing right beside him. "Let's get going."

He held his breath as everyone but Spooner leaped out of the Jeep. They divided up into two-man teams, each taking one side of the cave road. With their rifles pointed at the ground, each boy pulled a flashlight from his pack and held it at shoulder level, just like cops on a raid. At Rogers's single command of "Go!" they slid into the forest, their flashlights flickering through the trees. It would be only moments, Cabe knew, before those lights fell on him.

Hastily he pressed his body against the chill forest floor. He would have to crawl now, and crawl fast, staying under the beams of flashlight. He started snaking through the underbrush, inching forward on his belly. Twenty yards away he could hear Grice and Armbruster, rattling through the leaves, moving remorselessly toward him.

With his heart beating wildly, Tommy crawled, trying to be quiet, using his toes to push himself along the frozen earth. Close to the ground the air smelled like iron, and his fingers touched icy little pockets of snow. For an instant he feared he might sneeze. Flattening himself behind a rotting log, he grabbed both nostrils tight and breathed through his mouth. When the tickle in his nose finally passed, he raised his head. The flashlights were flickering on the tree he'd hidden behind only minutes before. Step by step, Grice and Armbruster were coming straight toward him.

Crawling was not getting him out fast enough. He was going to have to try something else. Swiftly he rolled over the log, burying himself along its mossy underside. If Grice and Armbruster's lights fell on nothing but empty forest, they might move on somewhere else.

He heard a twig snap, then a male voice whispered "Ouch!" His muscles were rigid with apprehension as he lay motionless while the Troopers neared. Beams crossed above his head, one light catching the rough branches of a shagbark hickory. *Just play dead,* he told himself, trembling so hard his teeth chattered. *Play dead now, or be dead in a few minutes.*

The footsteps neared; the lights played a kind of tag inches above his head. He could hear Armbruster's thick breathing, almost smelled his cigarette-tainted breath. Suddenly both lights converged just inches above his head.

"What the fuck's that?" Armbruster said incredulously.

"Don't know." Grice took a step forward. "I've never seen nothing like it."

Cabe heard leaves rustling, then a cry, then something scuttled through the underbrush, not a foot away from him.

"Don't shoot!" Armbruster cried. "It's not them."

"What the fuck was it?"

"Bobcat, maybe. Or a skunk. It wasn't either of those women or Cabe." Armbruster giggled. "You look like you just shit your britches, Grice."

"Shut up," Grice snapped. "Let's get the fuck out of here. They couldn't have gotten this far, anyway."

Cabe held his breath as they lingered a moment longer, then he heard their footsteps moving away. When the flashlight beams disappeared, he looked up. All he could see were shadows now, slipping through trees, flicks of light issuing from them like dying stars. He knew he didn't have much time left. Soon they would figure out that Mary and Irene weren't in the woods at all. Soon they would find out that those two were in the cave, cornered and helpless.

Tommy counted backward from fifty, then got to his feet. The search party moved on, and the hushed emptiness returned to the forest like snow sifting down from heaven. Without a glance back, he turned and ran, forgetting about Grice and Armbruster, forgetting about everything except the minutes ticking away for the ladies in the cave.

He threw himself up a hill, slipping on pine needles that had less traction than black ice. Something yowled and skittered through the bushes ahead of him; a thorny vine nearly pulled off his glasses. Finally he struggled to the top of the ridge, his lungs heaving. He blinked, astonished. There, just as Willett had told him, stood the bridge that spanned Highway 441. He ran.

Across the highway was a parking lot and a sign that read "Scenic Overlook." To his left, the road twisted up the dark mountain like a coiled piece of grapevine. To his right, it curved less precipitously down into the valley below. At night, a semi driver might well pull into the overlook parking lot to cool off his brakes.

He crossed over to the parking lot, rubbing his arms, listening for the growl of an engine decelerating down the mountain. A screech owl cried in the darkness, near enough to make him jump, but he heard nothing that sounded remotely like a truck.

"Come on," he urged. "Somebody drive down this damn road right now!"

He paced up and down, his footsteps echoing

as a raw wind stung his cheeks. Suddenly he stopped. Had he heard the distant rumble of a motor? The sound came again—sketchy, but crisp enough to convince him that he wasn't imagining it. In the dark, a truck was barreling down the mountain. Now he just had to figure out how to stop it.

He studied the road. If he stood in the middle of the pavement a hundred feet before the parking lot, he might be able to flag a semi down in time for it to stop. Provided, of course, that the truck wasn't going over twenty-five miles an hour and the driver was alert enough not to flatten him like a possum. Two big if's, but what the hell. Time was running out. He had no choice.

He pulled off his jacket and shirt as he ran, running past the overlook and stationing himself on the center line of the highway. Already he could hear some big engine downshifting, the low diesel whine of speed tamped down by gears. Suddenly he wanted to laugh. This was crazy. Insane. Willett would have loved it. *You're flyin', Tommy boy,* he would say.

Cabe jumped up and down to keep warm, his clothes in his hands, his bare chest puckering from the icy air. When the beam of two headlights flashed across the treetops above him, he started waving his shirt like crazy. Before he could draw another breath, lights brighter than the sun blinded him. White ones, yellow ones, red. An airhorn screamed. Although his arms were flapping like bird wings, his legs seemed frozen to the road. All he could do was wait for the truck to smack him far out into the overlook, where he would soar over a million trees before falling, like Icarus, dead to the ground. *Flyin'*, he thought, grinning as Willett's voice echoed in his head. *You'll be flyin', Tommy-boy. Flyin' for real!*

CHAPTER 48

Stump Logan followed Wurth as he spread his boys out in a sweep, just as he and Wurth had led other boys, so many years ago. Most of those boys were dead now. Though this terrain was mountainous instead of flat, the air cold rather than hot, the trees and the damp and the inscrutable darkness were the same. A hard, tight knot tingled in Logan's gut just as it had back then, when he'd slithered along on his belly, listening for the enemy that made no noise until the last sound you ever heard: the single, sick *criiick* of the trip wire you just stumbled over or the *chuuuunk* of a grenade dropping at your feet. What he remembered about the war were the tiny little noises. They still had the power to drench him in a cold sweat and send his pulse skyrocketing.

Logan frowned. Where most guys had hated

every second they spent in that miserable swamp of a country, he and Wurth had relished it. Each patrol turned them into hunters like they'd never dreamed of, and after a week or two in the bush they always came back to camp honed like the straight razors in his uncle's barbershop. He and Wurth always made their body count, sometimes bringing back an occasional ear as a souvenir. Jack Bennefield said they were sickos, but then Bennefield never had been a Feather Man. An operative, yes, but Jack had never had the balls to be a Feather Man. Bennefield just did his job and strummed his damn guitar, mooning over the pretty wife he'd left at home. The Feather Men drank whiskey and played more lethal instruments. Women, beyond a ready one to fuck, held little interest for them. Stump spat as he remembered Bennefield crawling back from one particularly bad patrol, holding on to his sanity by singing broken bits of "Sweet Dream Baby" under his breath. Poor Jack Bennefield. Everybody was so sorry about him.

Now, as they crested the mountain ridge, he felt his old rage at Bennefield consuming him all over again, even though the bastard was long dead and he was now helping Wurth hunt two beat-up women and a boy whose voice still cracked.

But one of those women is Bennefield's daughter. The words rattled through his brain like wind through bamboo. *One of those women is Mary Crow.*

The whole thing had fallen into his lap so perfectly, he couldn't believe it. Wurth decided to undertake this insane execution of Irene Hannah, and the next thing Stump knew, Bennefield's girl came waltzing into his office with that Fed, on some equally insane mission to protect the old broad. At that point, Logan thought he'd let it go. The Fed looked formidable, and he wasn't willing to put himself at that much risk to get rid of one troublesome girl. But when Wurth had called four days later and said that Mary Crow was snooping around his camp with some fake story about a nephew, he couldn't pass it up. It was as if fate were giving him the final nail for Jack Bennefield's coffin, and all he had to do was drive it in. Though he knew giving Wurth the go-ahead would leave him vulnerable, he didn't care. Wurth didn't scare him. Mary Crow did. *How much like her mother she looks,* he thought. *But how much like her father she acts. Real straight arrows, those two.*

He jumped as a twig snapped behind him. With every nerve quivering, he peered into the darkness. It looked as if two shadows were slipping through the trees behind him. He reached for his gun, but as he watched, the shadows changed from men into mere bushes. *Damn,* he thought, grinning as he pulled his hand away from his gun. *This is just like the old days.*

He looked up the mountain and watched Wurth creep forward as point. He had to admit, for a man of fifty-five, Wurth still moved like a drop of liquid darkness. What a shame his intellect never matched his military skills. After Vietnam he'd been an honorable, though hotheaded, soldier, unable to leave the Featherhood behind. When the Army had kicked him out he'd nosedived so badly that Stump had called his FaithAmerica pals, asking if they had any work for an old Army buddy. In the years since, Wurth had become their puppet, his strings regularly and viciously tugged by Richard Dunbar. *And me, scamming the state with those orphans.* Logan shook his head. Everybody had made a lot of money off Wurth, and the poor stupid bastard still hasn't caught on.

At the edge of the trees, Wurth halted. He signaled to his boys to spread out, then he motioned for Logan to join him.

"You gotta keep up, Stump." Wurth frowned at the gray cast of Logan's face. "I'm working on a deadline here."

"You know, Clipper, if either of those women makes it to a phone, they'll skin you alive. And neither me nor Tuttle will be able to do a thing to stop it."

"Nobody knows that better than me." Wurth looked at him with glittering eyes, then, without another word, he turned and slipped back to the middle of the picket line. He lifted his left hand once, and ten boys began to move toward the old cave. When they'd reached the entrance, Wurth motioned one forward. The boy withdrew something from his pack that looked like a bolt cutter, and a moment later the chain that secured the cave's iron gates fell to the ground. With a single wild screech, the gate opened, and the boys marched inside. Stump Logan chuckled as he hurried forward to rejoin his old platoon leader and the combat neither of them had truly left behind.

CHAPTER 49

"You know, this cave is quite mephitic." Irene's thoughtful voice sounded like warm velvet in the dark.

"What does that mean?" asked Mary.

"It means it stinks," Irene replied. "But so probably do I."

Mary switched on the flashlight and smiled. "Are you okay otherwise?"

"Just tired. Sometimes my hands throb." She frowned, as if willing some bad thing away, then looked at Mary. "Did they take you to that amphitheater?"

Mary nodded. The table, the *muchi,* the knives, and ultimately her hair lying in a pile on the floor. She felt a cold fury at the memory. "Yes," she answered softly. "I put in some time there."

Irene reached out and touched her hand. After

a moment, Irene spoke. "I wonder if Lady Jane's foaled yet. I wonder how Hugh likes being a father."

"I'm sure they're fine." Mary bit her lip, wondering if they'd ever see Hugh or Upsy Daisy or the long-awaited offspring of Lady Jane. She changed the subject quickly. "Can I ask you a question?"

"Of course."

"Remember that file of my mother's you told me about?"

Irene nodded. "I'm sorry I didn't give it to you the moment we started talking about it."

"I took it."

"You took it?"

"I sneaked into your closet and found it. Please forgive me."

"Nothing to forgive," Irene said placidly. "The file belonged to you. Considering the circumstances, I would have done the same thing." She stared down at her hand. Blood had started to seep through the bandage. "Was it like I told you?"

"Yes, although I haven't been able to figure out those letters from the Army."

"Letters from the Army?" Irene frowned. "I don't remember any letters from the Army. Your mother had a will and a deed of sale. That's all that was in the file."

"You didn't know that the Army was investigating some allegations about my father's death? That there were letters about that in the file?"

"No." Irene's eyes grew wide. "Your mother must have just given them to me to keep, no action required, so I never looked at them."

"A Sergeant Green had suspicions about the way my father died. Mom had given the Army some letters from my dad that she thought proved something."

"What did they say?"

"He seemed to be having some trouble with two guys named Clete and Bobby. He and Clete had gotten into a fistfight, and Clete seemed to know my mother."

Irene leaned closer, as if she hadn't heard correctly. "What did you say their names were?"

"Clete and Bobby."

For a moment she looked as if the blood in her veins had turned to poison. "Oh, my God," she whispered.

"What?" Mary demanded. "Irene, what is it?"

"Clete . . . Cletus Logan is Stump Logan. He was a star quarterback for the Hartsville Rebels. He got the nickname Stump when he was shot in the foot, in Vietnam."

Mary couldn't speak. Irene's words floated down into her consciousness like ash from a volcano. Stump Logan. She thought back to the pictures she'd seen in his office. Logan in a football uniform. Logan in an Army uniform, standing with those other young men, a python draped like a malevolent stole over their shoulders.

Irene leaned forward, alert as if she were listening to testimony. "Mary, tell me every detail you can remember about those letters."

Mary told her about how her father played football with these two men, about how one checked the fields for mines before they played in them, about how Clete always insisted on playing quarterback. "The Army told my mother that my dad stepped on a land mine in combat," she concluded. "Now I'm beginning to wonder."

"If he was set up?" asked Irene.

Mary nodded. "At first I thought I was thinking too much like a DA, but if this Sergeant Green had suspicions, maybe those two men had some kind of grudge against him." She frowned. "But what would Stump Logan have to do with my father?"

Irene opened her mouth to answer when both women froze. Did something infinitesimal just squeak somewhere in the darkness? Was it even a noise at all, or just another thing their brains had manufactured for their own amusement? Putting her finger to her lips, Mary turned toward the passage and listened, every nerve in her body taut as a bowstring. She switched off the flashlight and peered into the blackness, listening with her eyes. There! She heard it again. A muffled but measured squeak.

"Irene?" she whispered. "Did you hear that?"

"Yes. What do you think it could be?"

"Maybe Tommy and the FBI. Maybe not."

"What should we do?"

Mary knew that if Tommy had returned with Safer, everything would be all right. She also knew that if Wurth was the one making the noise, she and Irene were in desperate trouble. Wurth had boys and weapons. She and Irene had nothing but one flashlight and a can of warm Coke.

"I'll crawl toward the front and see what I can find out," she told Irene. "You stay here."

"What if it's Wurth?" Irene's question crackled with fear.

"Then we'll have to hide," replied Mary. "Right now, let's try to find out who's there."

Leaving Irene in the darkness, she crawled out into the passage. Though the cave air felt cool against her cheek, it also carried the gagging stink of sulfur. Ignoring the foulness, she pushed forward. With her ears open to everything, she listened to the dark. Beyond the sounds of her own breathing, she heard nothing. Had the squeak been something they'd both collectively imagined in their dark cocoon? She'd almost decided that it was when she heard it again. Only this time it was no squeak. This time it was the single word "here," spoken deep and far away, like someone murmuring from the bottom of a well. Mary shivered. Someone was out there. But was it Safer? Or Wurth?

Pressing herself flat against the cave floor, she listened. For eons, she heard nothing but the blood rushing through her veins. Then a single small light flickered high along one wall. It darted around the rocks, then a second light joined it. Flitting around like bright moths in some crazed mating dance, the lights dashed around the ceiling, drawing closer by the second. Someone had entered the cave. Someone was looking for them. She lay still, not daring to move or breathe, listening with every cell of her body. She strained her ears until she felt as if she could hear atoms crashing against each other, then it came. High and boyish, it uttered the single word that told her everything—"sir."

Instantly she started to scramble back to Willett's Den. Groping, she crept until her fingers brushed the notch in the stone wall. She turned right, then banged her head against Irene's knee.

"It's Wurth!" she whispered. "We need to get out of here!"

"Where can we go?"

"To that storage room Tommy told us about. Quick, I'll help you."

Swiftly she scooped up the flashlight, and then on an afterthought, the can of Coke. She helped Irene to her feet and began to light their way deeper into the cave. Finally the light found a wide, keyhole-like opening, and they hurried inside. The room was huge, and filled with old furniture—bentwood chairs, an ancient upright piano, a horsehair love seat furry with mold. Apparently, it had been used for storage when the cave had been a dance hall.

"Come on," Mary urged. "Over here."

She hurried Irene over to the piano, which was wedged at an angle, far back in the room. If Wurth's boys searched every inch of this place, they would surely find them. If they didn't, she and Irene might have a chance. As Irene curled behind the dusty old upright, Mary hunkered down beside her and switched off the light.

"What shall we do if they find us?" Irene asked softly.

"Fight," Mary whispered, thinking how dimensional words became in an absolute darkness. Like Chinese kites, they swooped and swirled against each other, bloodred and awesome. "We fight them as long as we can and give Tommy a chance to bring Safer here."

"We don't have anything to fight with," said Irene.

"Sure we do." Mary handed Irene the can of Coke. "Hide that in your pocket. Then come up with some kind of plan."

"To kill Robert Wurth?"

"He would be my first choice," answered Mary, making herself small as she and her old friend hid behind the piano, each praying that the searchers would pass the piano room by.

CHAPTER 50

They lay in absolute darkness, the silence hanging thick as a curtain around them. Mary lay close to Irene, straining every nerve to hear. Wurth's boys should have gotten back here by now. Had she been wrong? Had Tommy brought back Safer and the FBI? Maybe the Feds were looking for them right now, maybe their flashlights were flickering and probing. She battled the desire to tiptoe out into the passage and look around when Irene touched her arm.

"Mary," she said, her voice the barest whisper. "I just figured it out."

"What?"

"What happened to your father. And maybe to your mother, too."

Before she could say another word they heard scuffling, like someone trying to keep their balance on a gritty floor. Mary felt Irene's shoulders tighten. She wondered if she had time to crawl to the entrance of the room. That way, if one of Wurth's boys did poke his head in, she could possibly grab his gun and use it to her own purpose. Then she could dart back behind the piano and pick the others off as they came into the storage room. Eventually she would run out of bullets, but it would buy her precious time. She had just leaned over to whisper her plan to Irene when she saw a streak of light against one wall.

Soft white, it moved erratically, back and forth, the way UFOs are reputed to. It flashed over her head, then along the wall in front of her. Another joined it, then a third.

"What the fuck's in here?" a male voice called, so close that her heart seemed to stop.

"Smells like a great big fart." A second boy laughed.

"Look," said a third with delight. "An old pi-ano. Wonder if it still plays?"

No, Mary thought. *It doesn't play at all. It's just a heap of old ivory and broken strings.*

"Come on," said the first. "We've got to search this cave. Sarge'll kill you if you stop to play the piano."

That's right, kid. Sarge will kill you. Deader than the proverbial doornail.

"Oh, come on. Just a couple of notes won't hurt—"

Shit, she raged. The lights bobbed closer, scattering around the room, briefly illuminating something that looked like copper wire high against one wall. Footsteps crunched along the floor; she reached over and in the darkness rested her palm against Irene's cheek.

"Here," said the piano player. "Hold my flashlight."

For a moment Mary heard nothing, then the sound of ancient hammers striking long-dead strings reached her ears. One high note tinkled like shattering glass. *It's broken, you idiot,* she screamed inside her head. *Get the fuck out of here before Sarge finds out!*

"See? I told you," the first boy jeered. "Come on. Let's go. This place smells worse than the latrine where we dumped those cops."

He's right, he's right, he's oh, so right. Go quick, go now!

"Okay." The pianist sounded disappointed, but the footsteps faded toward the door.

They're leaving, thought Mary. *Dear sweet God, they're leaving.*

"Hey," the piano player said. "Look at this."

"What now?" The third boy sounded petulant.

"Over here. On the floor."

Mary held her breath. What could those boys have found? An odd silence fell over the space, as if the same idea struck everybody at exactly the same instant. With a sinking feeling, she suddenly realized her mistake. She and Irene hadn't crawled behind the piano. They had walked. Wurth's boys had found their footprints.

Before she could draw another breath, three bright lights were shining into her face.

"Sergeant Wurth!" cried one. "We found 'em!"

Mary leaped at him, all fists and flailing arms. She got in a solid blow to his mouth, sending one front tooth chipping across the piano keys. Infuriated, the boy shoved her to the floor, pummeling her face and breasts with his flashlight. She tried to protect her head with her arms, but by the time the other two pulled him off, her skull was ringing as if she'd stuck it inside a bell.

"Come on, Upchurch, save a little of her for the rest of us," one grumbled as he shoved his pal onto the tottery horsehair sofa.

"She hit my mouf!" Upchurch protested, blood spurting. "She knocked out one of my teef!"

"Yeah, yeah." The first boy remained unsympathetic. "Too bad she didn't knock out a few more."

He turned away from Upchurch and yanked

Mary to her feet. Another boy already held Irene's arms behind her back.

"You guys take the old lady," the first boy ordered, grinning as he beamed his flashlight in Mary's face. "I'll take care of this one myself."

Moments later, they stood in the main passage of the cave, blinking as flashlights beamed into their eyes, wincing as the hooded boys shoved them brutally against the wall. It seemed to Mary that they were going to play some kind of human pinball with them; then, without warning, they all snapped to attention.

Irene gasped as Robert Wurth strode down the passageway, Stump Logan close behind. Both men's eyes glinted like chips of ice. For an instant Mary's heart leaped; maybe the sheriff had come to save them. . . . But then she saw that Logan's gaze held no mercy; like Tommy had suspected, Logan and Wurth were partners in this madness.

"Where do you want them, sir?" asked the boy who was wrenching Mary's arms behind her back.

"Take them up to the front room. We'll have to move them back down to the gym, but we can get them ready up here. Time's running short."

Marching as a single unit, the boys escorted them back to the first huge chamber of the cave.

Irene stuck close to Mary, whispering as they moved forward.

"What now?"

"Try to hold them off as long as we can," Mary replied.

Irene looked at her. Her eyes had regained their old, feisty brightness. "Let me see if I can still get a confession like I used to."

"You want to put somebody on the stand?"

"Trust me, darling girl." Irene smiled. "And pay attention. You might find this interesting."

When they reached the big cavern, their captors forced Irene and Mary to stand back-to-back. Each young man carried a big flashlight, so when the Troopers stationed themselves in a loose circle around the two women, they lit the old cavern with an eerie glow. As Mary glanced over at Upchurch, who was still dabbing at his mouth, her gaze fell on an old metallic box just behind his shoulder. It was the terminal for the copper wires she'd glimpsed in the piano room! The switch still looked intact, and a thick wire that led somewhere outside the cave was still connected to it. Though she was foggy on most of her general science, she knew what would happen if any kind of electrical spark jumped in a cave filled with methane. If any juice at all still ran through those old wires, flipping that switch might blow them all to kingdom come. But what did she care? She and Irene had nothing to lose.

Irene cleared her throat. Mary watched in amazement as she squared her shoulders and took two steps toward Wurth, falling into the stance of a prosecutor at summation, her face quizzical, but her arms relaxed at her side.

"Sergeant Wurth, Ms. Crow and I have truly enjoyed your hospitality for the past several days. In consideration of our rather extraordinary experience, I wonder if I might ask you a few questions."

"I don't think so, Judge Hannah," Wurth growled. "You've cost us enough time."

"But you're a decorated veteran. The bravest of the brave. Surely you aren't afraid of the questions of an old woman?" Irene held out her maimed hands beseechingly. Mary smiled. Her years on the bench hadn't dulled her prosecutorial skills one iota. What a pleasure to watch the old tigress stalk her prey once again.

Wurth's eyes narrowed. "I'm not afraid of any question. I just don't have the time to answer."

"It won't take more than a minute or two, I promise."

Wurth glanced at his watch before replying. "What do you want to know?"

"Your first name is Robert, isn't it?"

Wurth nodded.

"And you served in Vietnam?"

"From sixty-seven until the fucking country fell down around our ears."

"Did you serve there with Clete Logan?"

Mary watched as Stump Logan gave a little choking cough. Wurth looked at him and smiled. "Why do you want to know that?"

"Because I believe you must have been there when a man named Jack Bennefield went up for a forward pass and came down on a land mine."

"What the hell are you talking about?" Logan roared.

"I'm talking about you, Stump. About how you and your chum Bobby here conspired to murder Jack Bennefield."

"You don't know . . ."

Mary's head began to whirl. Here she stood, at the very end of her life, with yet another mystery beginning to unfold. She leaned forward, straining to catch every syllable of every word.

"Let me tell you about Sergeant Wurth and Sheriff Logan, boys." Irene's words rang like a silver chime as she turned to the Troopers clustered around them. "These two men went to Vietnam together, along with Jack Bennefield, this young woman's father. They offered friendship, but in reality Sheriff Logan here was gunning for Bennefield. Logan was too big a coward to confront Bennefield alone, so he cooked up a plan. He got your Sergeant Wurth to clear most, but not all, of the mines from one field, then the two of them asked Bennefield to join them in a game of football. Jack agreed, happy to be asked to play, believing that the field had been cleared."

Irene turned and looked at Mary, her eyes sharp, but infinitely sad. "Guess who always had to throw the ball in those games?" She snapped her eyes at Logan. "And guess who told Jack Bennefield to go long for a pass?"

Logan swallowed as if his tongue had suddenly grown too thick for his mouth.

"Is that pretty close, Sergeant Wurth? Is that the way you remember it?" Irene asked.

"Personally, I had nothing against Bennefield," Wurth replied easily. "Logan just asked me to help him settle a personal score."

Personal score? Mary's brain spun. Between her father and Stump Logan?

"Years later, Stump, when you found out that an Army investigator was talking to Martha Crow, you got real scared that Martha had figured it out. So you shut her up. Oh, you had a little fun with her first, but you made damn sure she wasn't going to talk to more Army investigators."

With her heart beating madly, Mary realized that the secret that had tormented her for most of her life had been revealed. No drifter had killed her mother that day at Little Jump Off. It had been Logan, all along.

"You can't prove that," Logan said smugly.

"I don't have to," Irene shot back. "It's oozing from your pores, Stump. You stink with the smell of it!"

"You shut up!" he snarled, lunging forward. "Crazy old bitch!"

He moved to strike her, to bury his fist in her face when suddenly Irene pulled a bright red can from inside her pajamas. She smashed it into his nose, striking him again and again.

The whole cave erupted then, boys yelling, Wurth bellowing orders. Running as fast as she could, Mary leaped over Irene and Logan, heading straight for Upchurch. The boy gaped at her, stunned, his bloody mouth flapping in some approximation of speech. She heard Irene yell, then footsteps, and more shouting.

She longed to look back, but she kept her eyes focused on the electrical box behind Upchurch. She would only get one shot at this. She had to make it work.

Furious yells bounced off the stone walls as if fifty men were fighting within the bowels of the cave. Boys cursed. As someone yelled her name, she flung herself against Upchurch. He reeled backward. She crawled up and over him, struggling, stretching her arm to reach the switch on that box. Her fingers brushed it, then Upchurch shifted and they slid off. She aimed a vicious kick somewhere in his direction. When she felt her foot connect with something soft, she reached forward again. This time her fingers curled around the switch. *Pull,* she told herself. *Pull* NOW!

She pulled. The switch creaked into place. For an instant nothing happened, then a brilliant flash of blue stung her eyes as a freight train seemed to roar down upon them. Her eardrums popped against a deafening crash and the sharp smell of ozone crackled through the dark air. Upchurch's arms flailed at her, but the whole earth lifted up beneath them both. For an instant she left the ground, then rocks and earth started crashing all around her. She tried to open her eyes but she couldn't; she tried to speak, but her lips would not move. Then she relaxed, knowing that she was dead, hoping that she would soon join her parents and they could explain her whole entire history, from its earliest beginning to her last final gasp of life.

CHAPTER 51

Mary groaned. She lay on the ground, covered with a blanket, an awkward splint on her left arm. When she lifted her head she saw a rocky lunar landscape, churning with blue-jacketed men with flashlights. She wondered whether she was lying in heaven or hell, then she saw flesh-and-blood people she recognized. Jonathan, and Tommy Cabe. Safer. Hugh Kavanagh. They huddled together twenty feet away, staring at something on the ground. Slowly, ignoring the pain that throbbed through her body, she got up and walked toward them.

As she drew closer, she saw that Jonathan was attending someone like the medic he'd once been, holding someone's wrist to find a pulse. Suddenly she realized that the wrist was a woman's, and a head of soft silver hair protruded from the blanket.

"Irene?" she cried, her voice thunderous in the strange silence around her.

Everyone swung around to stare at her. Mary pushed her way forward and knelt beside her old friend. Although the left side of Irene's skull looked as if it had been shattered with a sledge-hammer, her brown eyes were open.

"Mary?" Irene's breath was a whisper. "Did you see our Cushla McCree?"

Mary looked at the photo in Hugh Kavanagh's hand. A spindly-legged little foal pondered the camera bright-eyed, with an impish expression exactly like Lady Jane's. One corner of the picture was a blur of white where Lucy, the goose, had managed to insert herself in the picture.

"She's beautiful," Mary replied, at first not trusting her voice to speak as she cupped Irene's chill fingers against her cheek.

"Hugh did a great job." Irene was breathing as if she'd been running too hard.

"Yes, he did. You did a wonderful job, too, Irene. You figured it out."

"Not bad for an old bench warmer, huh?" The right side of her mouth curled in a smile.

Mary leaned closer and spoke softly. "How did you know it was Logan?"

"Something your mother told me," Irene whispered. She spoke further, but Mary couldn't catch her words, and her wispy voice faded into nothing. For an instant she pinned Mary with eyes as sharp as they'd ever been, then her focus softened as she began to stare at something above Mary and Hugh. With some effort, she brought her gaze back to them and spoke one more time. "You two . . . take care of things."

"Aye, girl." Hugh bent down and pressed his lips against her cheek. "That we will."

She smiled at Mary, then, as if she were just falling asleep, Irene Hannah closed her eyes. Her rapid gasps eased, and at the end of one labored respiration, her chest did not rise again.

"Irene?" Mary cried, stroking her friend's cheek. "Irene! We've still got so much to do! There's Cushla McCree and Lady Jane and Hugh and Lucy. They all need to be taken care of. They all need you!" She stroked her cheek more firmly. "Irene, talk to me! I don't know enough yet. I don't know nearly enough!"

"It's no good, girl." Hugh said it softly. "She's gone." He reached over and held Mary in his arms.

The two of them knelt, clinging to one another. "I'm so sorry," Mary sobbed. "I shouldn't have let this happen."

"Hush, girl." Hugh kissed the top of her stubbly head. "I know how hard you tried to save her."

This is the last one, Mary thought as hot tears streamed down her cheeks. *My mother, my grandmother, now Irene—all gone.* From now on she would truly be an orphan; the sole measure of herself.

For a long time she wept against Hugh's solid warmth, crying for herself, crying for Irene, then she wiped her eyes and leaned close to her old friend and mentor.

"*Dona dago huhi, elisi,*" she whispered. "Be at peace." She picked up a small piece of mica that had exploded from one of the cave rocks and pressed it against Irene's lips, then she kissed the rock and clutched it in her hand.

Jonathan covered the judge's face with the blanket. Tommy Cabe helped Mary to her feet. They stood there for a while, stunned and silent, then others began to arrive. Farmers whose land abutted Camp Unakawaya rattled up in pickups, more Feds roared up in vans. Although the area had been cordoned off with yellow tape, mountain folk continued to gather and gape at the mounds of rubble and scattered boulders. After all, it wasn't every New Year's Eve that Russell Cave got blown to bits.

"Mary?" She heard a voice behind her. She turned. Safer was standing there.

"I'm so sorry." He wrapped his arms around

her without hesitation, as if it were something they both knew he would do. "I know how much you loved her."

She held him tight, battling her tears. She would not cry anymore. She had tried her best to save Irene, and she had failed. Now there was nothing to do but bury the dead and carry on with their memory. "What in the world was this all about?" she asked Safer.

"Wurth was going to decapitate Judge Hannah at midnight. By the looks of it, he'd planned to broadcast it on the Internet."

"But why?"

"Wurth was an operative for a secret political group connected with the FaithAmerica movement. The plan was to skew the off-year elections this November and elect Gerald LeClaire President two years from now."

"LeClaire?" Mary frowned, unbelieving. "The TV preacher?"

"Wurth had been training political assassins for LeClaire's man, Richard Dunbar, for years. Dunbar had Wurth offing the federal judges to fulfill a prophecy that was supposed to jolt the faithful into action."

"How did you find this out?"

"According to Krebbs, that kid who showed up at the farm had this amazing computer disk that spelled out everything, chapter and verse."

"Willett's secret weapon," Mary said softly.

"Anyway, everybody on that disk should be getting a knock on their door right about now. Some pals of mine are going to see that they celebrate New Year's in ways they've never dreamed of. Gerald LeClaire's already in custody, though it looks like the poor bastard didn't have a clue about any of this. He thought God just wanted him to be President."

"So you stopped it?"

"You stopped it, Mary. You and that kid. It's over."

The trees and the rocks and even the hard, bright moon overhead swirled around Mary like a carousel out of control. She would have to sort this out later, sometime when she could be quiet and alone. Her gaze fell on Jonathan, who was wrapping another blanket around Hugh Kavanagh, talking to the old man, who now looked a decade older than when she'd first met him seven days ago.

"How did Jonathan get here?"

"I asked him to come with me," Safer answered. "But he wouldn't have had it any other way. He's a brave man. He was a big help."

Mary smiled at Jonathan. *How like him,* she thought, *trying to save me all over again.*

Safer cleared his throat. "Do you feel up to identifying some of Wurth's boys?"

"Tommy Cabe is the one you need to ask about that. He knew everybody at this camp far better than me."

"What's his story?"

"He's a DHS boy. We couldn't have done any of this without him. He's one terrific kid."

They walked over to what had been the mouth of the cave, now just a jumble of rocks and boulders. Mary motioned to Tommy. He left Hugh and Jonathan and hurried toward them.

"Hi, Tommy." Safer smiled. "I'm Agent Daniel Safer, FBI. Ms. Crow here says you were a resident at this camp."

"Yessir."

"Do you think looking at a dead body would bother you?"

"Not any of these dead bodies," replied Tommy flatly.

Mary watched as Safer began lifting up the blankets covering those who had not survived the explosion she'd triggered. Robert Wurth lay stretched out like a dead fish, his neck at an extreme angle to the rest of his body. Tommy's old nemesis Tallent's chest was crushed, while Upchurch had had his already misshapen face permanently rearranged by a rock. Grice looked as if he'd died from massive head trauma. The rest of Wurth's bitter army sat dazed but alive, some with broken arms and legs, some weeping like children. Mary thought of Irene and felt no pity for them at all. She turned away and noticed two other bodies covered by blankets, a little distance away from the others.

"Who are they?" she asked Safer.

"One's my old pal Tuttle," he replied tersely. "The other's Logan."

"Can I see him?" Mary asked.

Safer studied her face for a moment. Then he walked over and lifted one corner of the blanket.

Mary braced herself, waiting to see Stump Logan's face contorted in his final agony. Instead, when Safer pulled the blanket back, all they found was a jumbled pile of rocks.

"He's gone!" Tommy cried.

Safer looked down at the rocks that had been arranged to look like a body. "What the fuck? I laid him here not fifteen minutes ago. The whole back of his skull was mush."

Mary felt suddenly as if she were the only person in the universe who understood what a huge obscene joke life could be.

"Happy New Year," she told Safer bitterly, and turned away.

CHAPTER 52

By dawn the first search parties came back from the mountain, empty-handed. There was no trace of Logan. As they turned to the cleanup and began to load the corpses into a panel van, the crowd finally dispersed. Despite the fact that it was now New Year's Day and the FBI was hauling bodies away like firewood, the mountain folk returned to their trucks and drove home. They had cows to milk and fences to mend. All the fun now would be in the endless retelling of what they'd been doing the night Mary Crow blew up Russell Cave. Hunched under a blanket, Mary watched as they sauntered along the old road, still looking over their shoulders to catch a glimpse of the heap of rocks that had once been North Carolina's premier dance cave. Then she noticed Tommy Cabe. He sat on one of the boulders, his head buried in his arms.

She hurried over to him. "Tommy? What's wrong?"

He raised his head and looked at her, his tears making crooked tracks through the grime on his face. "That Agent Safer's fixin' to fly me to my grandpa's. And I still don't know for sure what happened to Willett."

She put her arm around him and murmured his name.

"It's hard," she whispered, squeezing his shoulder. "But you have to go on. You have to live your life in the best way you can. Willett would want that for you."

"I know, but I can't leave here not knowing. I just can't."

She of all people knew how hard it was to leave a place where something terrible had happened and not know the why of it. Tonight she had come closer to finding the why of her mother's death, but she still hadn't been able to grab it and hold it in her hand.

Mary saw that the big FBI chopper's rotor had started to turn. "Did you tell Agent Safer about Willett?"

"Yes," Tommy said miserably.

"Then I'll make sure they investigate. I promise I'll find out what happened to Willett."

Tommy blinked. "You can do that?"

"I'm the assistant DA of Deckard County,

Georgia." Mary smiled and wiped the tears from his face with her fingertips. "What I say, goes."

"Will you let me know?"

"Give Agent Safer your grandfather's phone number. I'll call you first thing. I'll call you anyway, just to say hi." She kissed his cheek. "Now go get on that chopper. The DHS caseworkers will be up here pretty soon. You don't want to wind up with them again, do you?"

"No." He stood and looked down at her awkwardly, as if he couldn't decide whether to hug her or shake her hand. "Thank you," he began.

"Go, Tommy!" She stood and hugged him. "Go tell your grandfather what a brave young man he's got!"

He started to say something else, but turned and ran to the helicopter instead. Safer spoke to him a moment, then shook his hand, then Tommy Cabe ducked under the rotor and boarded the aircraft. Moments later the chopper lifted off, flying him north, out of the mountains and into the green hills of Kentucky.

"*A siyu!*" Mary whispered, wondering if Tommy would leave his mystery behind any better than she had. For his sake, she hoped so.

They loaded Irene's body into a special ambulance that would carry her to Hartsville. An FBI agent helped Hugh Kavanagh into the back of the car, and she waved sadly as she watched the scarlet taillights bouncing down the old road. She would meet Hugh at the county hospital later, after she'd cleaned up a little. She felt someone touch her shoulder. She turned. Jonathan stood beside her.

"Hey," was all she could say before she put her arms around him and held him tight, listening to the drubbing of his heart, breathing in the scent of his skin. What had happened to them? She had to get them back on track, somehow. She had to make it right between them.

"Jonathan, we need to talk," she said. She looked up into the face she knew as well as her own, and saw the kindness hidden in the hawkish eyes, the whimsical curve of his mouth. "I was wrong in Atlanta. I didn't listen to you like I should have . . ."

"Don't worry about it, Mary," he said softly. "We were two people headed in different directions."

"Yes, but we don't have to be." The words tumbled out of her. "We could try again. We could do it differently this time. I could take the North Carolina bar exam and start a practice up here. Civil stuff, not crime. We could live at Little Jump Off. I could work in Hartsville . . ."

He stepped back, recoiling from her torrent of words. He looked stricken, his face a dark eddy of emotions she could not identify. When at last he spoke his voice was gentle, but his words cut her like a knife.

"Mary, we're having a baby."

For an insane instant she thought he meant *them,* but that was impossible; she had not taken him inside her in over a year. Then she realized that he was speaking of Ruth Moon. *He and Ruth Moon are having a child.*

"A baby?"

He nodded, his eyes mirroring the pain in hers. "She told me yesterday."

She stood there, frozen. A week ago she'd come up here hoping to talk Irene into federal protection and perhaps renew her relationship with Jonathan. Now those options were gone forever. Irene was dead and Jonathan was starting a family with someone else.

"I don't know what to say . . ." he began. He reached out to hold her again, but she took a step back.

"Then don't say anything," she told him, shaking her head. "It would be better if you didn't. You and Ruth Moon go and have a fine, strong child." She looked up at him and smiled. "You and Ruth Moon go and have a fine, strong life."

"But—"

"Go!" she whispered. "I can't stand here and say it any better than that, Jonathan."

He looked at her as if he were bidding good-bye to something he would never see again. Then, with a sad, lingering smile, he turned and began to walk down the old mountain road, alone.

She watched him until she could see him no longer, then she looked up at the mountains. They looked like hazy humps of blue in the thin light of early morning. Dakwai, Ahaluna, Disgagistiyi. Usually she loved to watch the dawn break around them. Today it was hard to see them and not scream her outrage at all she'd just lost.

She felt someone walk up behind her. She turned. Daniel Safer stood there, his eyes dark and unreadable.

"Found Logan yet?" she asked.

He shook his head.

"You won't, you know." She nodded toward the mountains. "They'll hide him from you. Just like they did Rudolph."

"Just like they do you?"

She looked at him curiously. "What do you mean?"

"Nothing," he said, his odd expression melting away. "I guess a rock must have hit me on the head." He stood beside her and watched the sky, then he spoke again.

"You going anywhere in particular?"

No, she thought. *Five minutes ago I had plans to*

go someplace very particular. Now I'm going nowhere at all. "Back to town. I need to see about Irene's arrangements."

"Well, I've got some errands to run, but I could give you a lift."

"Errands?" She shook her head. Safer had just stopped a nationwide conspiracy in its tracks and sounded as if he had to run out and grab a loaf of bread. "What kind of errands?"

"Oh, get some gas for the truck. Eat some breakfast. Search for that bastard Logan and some runaway kid named Willett." He held out a blue baseball cap. "Want to ride along?"

She looked at the gold FBI embroidered on the cap, then up at him. She saw the smile in his dark eyes and she realized that she was seeing him for the first time, all over again. All at once she realized she had a number of places to go. She had to look in on Hugh, she had work piling up on her desk in Atlanta, and she had Irene's precious, precious foal to care for.

"Yes," she answered, smiling as she tugged the cap down on the stubble of her shorn hair. "I absolutely do."

ABOUT THE AUTHOR

Sallie Bissell is a native of Nashville, Tennessee. She currently divides her time between her hometown and Asheville, North Carolina. She has three children and is at work on her third novel, *Call the Devil by His Oldest Name*.